THE HALIFAX CONNECTION

THE
HALIFAX
CONNECTION

MARIE JAKOBER

VINTAGE CANADA

Published in Canada by Vintage Canada, a division of Random House of Canada Limited, Toronto, in 2008. Originally published in hardcover in Canada by Random House Canada, a division of Random House of Canada Limited, Toronto, in 2007. Distributed by Random House of Canada Limited, Toronto.

Vintage Canada and colophon are registered trademarks of Random House of Canada Limited.

www.randomhouse.ca

Library and Archives Canada Cataloguing in Publication

Jakober, Marie
The Halifax connection / Marie Jakober.

ISBN 978-0-679-31492-9

1. United States—History—Civil War, 1861–1865—Fiction.
2. Canada—History—1841–1867—Fiction. I. Title.

PS8569.A42H34 2008   C813'.54   C2007-906933-9

Text design by CS Richardson

Printed and bound in the United States of America

4 6 8 9 7 5 3

To the memory of my father, who could never understand why his teenaged daughter kept bringing home all those books about dead generals from another country. He would be intrigued now, I think, to see where it all led.

CAST OF CHARACTERS

◆━◆━◆

Historical Persons Mentioned or Appearing in the Text

Canadian and British

John Bright, British manufacturer, member of Parliament for Birmingham

George Brown, editor of the Toronto *Globe*; Liberal politician and subsequently a Father of Confederation

William Gladstone, British Chancellor of the Exchequer

Joseph Howe, popular Nova Scotia politician, leader of the movement for responsible government

Lord Lyons (Richard Bickerton Pemell), British ambassador to Washington

John A. Macdonald, Conservative politician, subsequently a Father of Confederation and first prime minister of the Dominion of Canada

Vice-Admiral Sir Alexander Milne, commander of the British fleet in North America

Lord Monck (Charles Stanley, Fourth Viscount Monck), governor general of British North America and subsequently of the Dominion of Canada, 1861–68

Lord Palmerston (Henry John Temple), prime minister of England

George Wade, a Nova Scotian recruited by the Confederates under John Braine

Sir Fenwick Williams, commander of all British military forces in North America

American (Union and Confederate)

John Braine, British-born Kentuckian adventurer and petty criminal, hijacker of the ship *Chesapeake*

Clement Clay, Confederate commissioner to Canada

Jefferson Davis, president of the Confederate States of America

Mortimer Jackson, United States consul in Halifax

George Kane, former police marshal of Baltimore; Confederate agent in Canada

Robert E. Lee, Confederate general

Abraham Lincoln, president of the United States

General John Hunt Morgan, Confederate cavalry commander and leader of raid into northwestern states in 1863

Captain Raphael Semmes, captain of the Confederate raiding ship *Alabama*

Jacob Thompson, Confederate commissioner to Canada

Captain John Wilkinson, Confederate naval officer

Important Fictional Characters Appearing in the Novel

Bryce Amberson, English naval officer, related by marriage to Erryn Shaw

Sylvie Bowen, English mill worker and immigrant to Canada

Aggie Breault, housemaid at Den, a Halifax boarding house

Jonathan Bryce, Montreal police constable and spymaster

Matt Calverley, Halifax police constable

Daniel Carroll, Montreal businessman, Confederate supporter

Susan Danner, mistress of the Den

Harry Dobbs, manservant at the Den

François Dufours, Halifax police constable

Jackson Follett, chief Confederate agent in Montreal

Nathaniel Foxe, captain of the U.S. merchant ship *Osprey*

Frances Harris, aunt of Sylvie Bowen

James Fitzroy Hawkins, commander of the Halifax militia

Maury Janes, Confederate agent

Latour, Canadian undercover agent in Montreal

Annie MacKay, scullion at the Den

Alexander MacNab, Halifax businessman, Confederate
   supporter

Louise Mallette ("Madame"), Halifax widow

Edmund Morrison, Montreal businessman, Confederate
   supporter

Jack Murray, friend of Erryn Shaw

Isabel Orton, daughter of James Orton

James Orton, Halifax lawyer, Confederate supporter

Jabin Romney, chief Union agent in Halifax

"Captain William Ross," alias of blockade-running English
   naval officer Bryce Amberson

Emma Sanders, cook at the Den

Erryn Shaw, exiled English aristocrat

David Strange, friend of James Orton, Confederate supporter

Brad Taylor, Confederate courier killed in Halifax

Zeb Taylor, Brad Taylor's brother

Gideon Winslow, Erryn Shaw's landlord

A Historical Note to the Reader

———⊱⋆⊰———

IN 1860, ABRAHAM LINCOLN was elected president of the United States on a platform that would have prohibited the further expansion of slavery into the nation's western territories. Within months of this election, seven Southern states had seceded from the Union and formed the Confederate States of America. Civil war broke out between the sections in April 1861, and four more border states joined the Confederacy. Its capital was established in Richmond, Virginia.

From the very beginning, the main objective of Confederate foreign policy was to obtain European support, especially from England. Considerable hostility already existed between Britain and the United States, carried over from the American Revolution and the War of 1812. A new war between the two powers would have thrown the full weight of the British Empire into the camp of the Confederates.

The best place to provoke such a war was Canada. It had a long, unwatched border with the United States, allowing for the possibility of Confederate raids—raids that might be followed by American retaliation and the outbreak of war. Although England was officially neutral, many Englishmen, mostly of the wealthier classes, sympathized with and aided the Confederates, both in Britain and in Canada.

Since the Confederacy was not recognized as a nation, it did not have official diplomatic status in any country. However, many Southerners came to Canada to further the interests of the Confederacy in various ways, and the Union sent a number of intelligence operatives north to try to keep track of their activities.

At the time, Canada was not yet a nation state. In official documents and usage, all of the British territories on the continent were collectively known as British North America. The region that was actually called Canada comprised only small parts of what today are Ontario and Quebec. Colloquially, however, on both sides of the border, the terms "Canada" and "Canadians" were used more indiscriminately, to refer to the entire region and its inhabitants. I have chosen to follow this usage much of the time, partly in the interests of clarity and simplicity, and partly because I believe we were a nationality before we were a nation state; this was one of the reasons Confederation was possible.

Each of the North American provinces had its own elected parliament and a measure of self-rule, but all were under the authority of the British crown, administered by the governor general, whose capital was maintained at Spencer Hall in Quebec. In late 1861, this office was taken over by Charles Stanley, Lord Monck. The governor general bore the ultimate responsibility for British North America's security and defence. When the Civil War began, his most critical task was to prevent the use of colonial territory as a base for acts of war, and thereby to preserve its neutrality and peace.

A Note on the Terminology of the Period

A variety of terms were used to refer to the two sides in the American Civil War. Here are the most common:

United States of America: the Union, the North, Northerners, Yankees, Unionist, Federal
Confederate States of America: the Confederacy, the South, Southerners, Rebels, Rebs, Johnny Rebs, Confederate
    The term "Grey Tories" is an invention of the author, referring to those Canadians who actively supported the Confederate cause.

    Just as today, the meanings of the words "east" and "west" varied in Canada depending on one's location. In Nova Scotia, "the West" generally referred to the settled areas west of the Maritime provinces, i.e., Quebec and Ontario. In Montreal, "the West" generally meant Ontario, not the Prairies.

. . . The Confederacy has its hand on the mane of the British lion, and that beast, so formidable to all the rest of the world, must crouch at her bidding.
—*The Whig* (Richmond), December 1861

———◆◆———

The people of Canada . . . are not prepared to support any Government in a wanton interference in matters with which it has no concern, and more especially they have no desire to fight on behalf of the Southern slave power.
—*The Globe* (Toronto), November 1862

———◆◆———

Of all things, at once the most unjustifiable and the most impolitic is an unsuccessful Intervention.
—*The Times* (London), November 1862

PROLOGUE

＊━◆━＊

Halifax, July 7, 1864

We shall do such deeds within the next three months
as shall make European civilization shudder.
—*Unidentified Confederate agent,*
quoted by John Cordner, Montreal, 1864

"ANOTHER TOAST, MY FRIEND," the Carolinian suggested,
pouring generously. His name—or at least the name he chose to
use here—was Maury Janes. "To the Vessel of Retribution!"

Erryn Shaw smiled, clinked glass to glass, and drank. The vessel in
question, the English *Dover*, was sitting down at Taylor's Wharf at
the moment, grubby and tired-looking in the late evening sun.
She was, as far as he could judge, the most ordinary ship imaginable, laden as usual with ordinary goods. All day she had rested at
anchor, yielding up blankets and cast iron cookstoves and second-rate
rum, while blockade-runners were slipping into Southern ports with
desperately needed weapons and supplies, and Confederate commerce raiders prowled the seas, burning Yankee ships from Newfoundland to India. It was remarkable, to say the least, that anyone
would call such a scruffy English freighter the Vessel of Retribution.

Erryn knew his companion was given to strong statements, even to exaggeration sometimes, but he had no reason to believe the man was mad. And Janes was happy tonight, triumphant, a fact all the more remarkable because he rarely showed feelings of any sort; indeed, there were times when Erryn wondered if he had any. Janes had never mentioned his age, but Erryn guessed him as close to forty, a man of average height and build, with indifferent features and straight, dull brown hair—the sort of man who looked like everyone's fourth cousin. The fine waistcoat and trousers he had bought for tonight's celebration were appropriately expensive, but they did not give him any kind of style. They seemed, instead, an elaborate costume on an actor unsuited for his role. Janes was never going to be gentry, however hard he tried.

Erryn regarded him thoughtfully, remembering the first time they met, back in October, the first time Janes had spoken of his unlikely mission: *If this comes off like it should, it's going to end the war.* At the time Erryn considered it a reckless promise, and nothing had passed since to make him change his mind. Even as they sat together, superbly wined and dined in the mahogany-panelled confines of the Halifax Club, the war in the States went on relentlessly. The armies of Grant and Lee were dug in at Petersburg, in a brutal standoff that was likely to last for months. More Union and Confederate forces were going at it in the west. Abroad, the leaders of Europe watched and sniffed the wind, less willing than ever to intervene. Try as he might, Erryn could imagine nothing that would end the war any time soon, save a massive victory by one side or the other, or the defeat of Lincoln's government in the fall elections. What could a nondescript North Carolina adventurer possibly ship in that might accomplish either of those things?

Unfortunately, it was not the sort of question one agent could ask another. Nor did it help that he disliked Maury Janes, and longed to dismiss him as a self-important ass. *Oh, certainly you'll end the war, Mr. Janes . . . right around the time I turn into an orange salamander.*

"Mr. Shaw!"

Erryn rose smoothly, smiling at the man who approached his table with two companions—a mountain of a man, well over six feet, and red-haired as a highland chieftain: James Dougal Orton, lawyer, businessman, philanthropist; and also, as it happened, one of the most eminent and respected Confederate supporters in Halifax.

"I have some guests who want to meet you, Shaw," he said. "I mentioned you were here, and nothing would do but they must come over and shake your hand."

There were introductions and greetings all round. One of Orton's guests clasped Erryn's hand warmly in both of his. "Honoured, Mr. Shaw. I've been hearing so much about you."

"I worry when people say that sort of thing," Erryn replied, smiling. "I fear they may have heard the truth."

"Oh, I expect it's all true. For instance, I've heard you smuggled a certain countryman of mine to safety, with the whole Yankee nation howling for his head on a plate. They say the law was closing from three sides, and the man just up and disappeared."

The law was closing from three sides? Bloody hell; it gets better every time I hear it.

Erryn gave a small, self-dismissive shrug. "He must have found himself a conjuror. Do you know, I saw that sort of thing at a circus once, when I was a boy. A big skinny sod in a silk robe, lighting candles everywhere and chanting the most horrid pile of gibberish. And then, presto, he simply folded his hands and went up in smoke—and came round from the other side of the tent after, asking for money."

"God love you, Erryn Shaw," Orton said, "but you do tell stories."

"Will you join us for a drink or two?"

"Why, that's good of you, lad, but no. We're on our way out."

Orton clapped his shoulder lightly and wished him luck, and the trio moved on its way. Janes settled back in his chair.

"Is it true what they're saying?" he asked. "You were the one who got Captain Braine out?"

Erryn's gaze drifted briefly over the dining room. It was bright with linen and candles, quietly a-murmur with the talk and laughter of men—lawyers, doctors, businessmen, members of the government, here and there a distinguished visitor from the West or from abroad. He turned his wineglass between his fingers, wondering if he was the only man present who thought a gentlemen's club, by definition, was altogether too much of the same thing.

"Aiding and abetting a fugitive is against the law, Janes," he murmured. "You wouldn't suggest that there were felons in a place like this, would you?"

Janes stared at him a moment, and then he laughed. "No, I suppose not. The captain found himself a . . . what the devil did you call it?"

"Conjuror. You know, a magician. Abracadabra and all that." Erryn reached for the wine bottle and calmly changed the subject. "So. You're sure there isn't something I can do for you, now that your shipment is here? I'd be happy to help if I can."

"Well, I'm much obliged, Shaw, but like I said, everything's took care of. With all the damn delays, God knows there was time enough. Since we're celebrating, though, I wonder . . . that house you told me about, before? There wouldn't be a chance we could drop by, would there? What with you knowing those fine ladies and all?"

"Oh, I think I could be persuaded. But it's still early. Let's have another drink, shall we?"

❖

Be a robber's moon tonight, it will . . .

That was what the stableman used to say sometimes, back at the manor house in Surrey. He would smile down at Erryn like an old gnome and tell him stories of the moors where he grew up. He would certainly call this one a robber's moon, racing as it did out of fast-moving clouds and vanishing again in moments, like a thief. It was high above the Point, and almost full; its pale light glinted off the church spires and danced wanton on the harbour. Most nights Erryn would have taken genuine pleasure from the beauty of it; tonight it only made the streets seem darker and the hours ahead of him more uncertain.

He heard a shout somewhere nearby and pulled his attention sharply back to the moment. The corner of Prince and Argyle was not a safe place at midnight. He and Janes were both armed, and reasonably sober. Still, in this part of town a wise man kept his wits sharp and his eyes on the street, especially if his companion seemed to be thinking of other things.

"They're all young and pretty, right, these ladies?" Janes asked.

"Young I'll not swear to," Erryn said. "I never ask a lass her age. But I'll wager there isn't one you won't find pretty."

It was a fine summer night, and many people were still abroad even at this hour. A carriage passed behind them, rattling along Argyle; men stumbled out of taverns with drunken laughter following them; a couple quarrelled bitterly somewhere behind a dim-lit upper window. They were moving into what were called the upper streets, those nearest to the fortress and the barracks. It was here—not along the waterfront, but here, in the military heart of the city—that one found the roughest part of town. Here were most, and the worst, of the brothels; the wildest bars; the dirtiest broken-down tenements. Here too, always, was violence.

There were, so Erryn had been told, more than four hundred liquor vendors in the city. He doubted that anyone ever counted the places used for prostitution. By day they were ordinary shops and taverns, boarding houses, even homes. Some were clean and well kept; others were collapsing hovels, reeking of dirt and disease. Officially they were illegal, but nobody bothered with them much. Halifax was an imperial outpost, and empires routinely courted the loyalty of their men with bread and circuses. Rum and brothels were merely a variation.

To the men's left now, its door wide open to attract passersby, was a tavern called the Grange. A tinny piano hammered out a tune Erryn could barely recognize, lost as it was in raucous talk and laughter. Janes paused on the street for a moment. Perhaps a dozen men were visible inside, most of them in uniform. Among them, in various states of undress, were several young black women.

Erryn knew what Janes would say before he said it.

"Well, there you have it, Shaw. Abolition in all its glory."

Erryn said nothing. He had been opposed to slavery all his life, as most Englishmen were. He had not reversed his public stand when he began to work for the Confederates, but he had moderated it, showing himself ready to listen to a slave owner's point of view; allowing that the future of the institution was, in the final analysis, their business and not his. Usually he found it easy. The Southerners who came here understood local opinion; most of them trod softly on the subject, whatever their personal opinions happened to be.

Maury Janes was not the sort of man to tread softly on anything.

"Back home," he went on, "where they're looked after, niggers live useful and productive lives. Set 'em loose, and they just turn into thieves and whores. And nobody can see it. Even your friend Orton can't see it. Last week he give me a big lecture about how we could have the whole world behind us in our fight if we'd only stop dallying and free the slaves. Might as well tell a man how much fine new land he can get for himself by burning down his crops."

"Did you tell him so?" *Christ, I would have paid a shilling to see Jamie Orton's face.*

"Nah. I was going to say something, but MacNab jumps right in and starts talking about the poor *Alabama* going down, and that was the end of it."

They had reached Grafton. It was the first of the disreputable streets, and therefore the least disreputable. The Grafton Street Theatre had been here for years, before it burned in '61. A soap factory rose now on the land, a squat, foul-smelling place that saddened Erryn every time he passed it. Some distance beyond it was their destination, the fine frame home owned by Louise and Robert Flynn. Erryn knew them well; for years they had been among his theatre's most devoted patrons. As it happened, they also ran a discreet and elegant bordello. Erryn had mentioned it to Janes a few days earlier, just in passing. It was the house most favoured by the city's wealthier young gentlemen and by the ranking officers.

But, Janes suggested, they'd welcome anyone who had plenty of money, right?

"If they don't know you, mate, you don't get in the door."

"They know you?"

Erryn had shrugged. "Most everybody knows me."

"You wouldn't consider an introduction sometime, would you?"

"Oh, certainly. Why not?"

Why not, indeed? Janes's ship was in at last, his mission ready to move into its final, triumphant stage. It was time to celebrate, and what would please Janes more than a splendid dinner at the club and a visit to the most prestigious sporting house in town?

So it was that they came to be walking late on Grafton Street, on the night of the robber's moon.

———◆———

Afterwards, of course, the events of that night would be discussed all over town. Everyone knew how the trouble ended; less clear to them was how it actually began, whether the peace officers made an honest mistake, or whether, as some said, Constable Calverley purely hated the Johnny Rebs and would turn on them for any shabby reason he could find.

There were witnesses of a sort. A tipsy carter remembered passing the men at Prince and Grafton—two young chaps obviously out on the town, one of them tall and skinny, just like

Mr. Shaw who ran the theatre here before it burned. The men were talking and laughing, the carter said, and seemed on the best of terms. Up ahead, McKenna's Tavern was noisy as a street brawl, but the honest shops were dark and still. The soap factory lay all along the street like a fortress wall.

There, everyone agreed, was where the footpads must have hidden: right across from the tailor shop, in the shadows of the factory gate. There was nowhere else they could have hidden, to come out behind the two men so silent and so quick. No one saw them attack, but one of the villains, it was supposed, took down Mr. Shaw with a blow to the head, and a dreadful blow it must have been, for he fell like a stone and did not stir again. Both then turned their attention to Mr. Janes, and obviously found him a handful. He was still on his feet when a door some yards away was suddenly flung wide. Lantern light bounced off the factory wall, and a single commanding voice roared into the night:

"Ho, you there, what the devil are you at?"

That was when tailor Robert Hillier, wakened by the ruckus, leaned out through the bedroom window above his shop. The ruckus stopped dead, he told people afterwards, and he heard a man growling right below him, "Bloody hell, Joss! It's the guard!" He saw, just barely in the light from the constable's lantern, two shadowed figures dashing away. Whether the peace officers saw them or not, well, that was anybody's guess.

The man the robbers had not downed, the one who was later identified as Maury Janes, scrambled for something in the dirt—a pistol, maybe, Hillier thought—and then crouched by his companion's side.

"Shaw, are you all right?"

There was no answer. The lantern was closer now, and Hillier could see the downed man lying limp as a rag. Janes rolled him clumsily onto his back.

"Shaw! Chrissake, what's the matter, are you dead?" He groped at his companion's face and chest. By then the policemen were on him. Hillier recognized them both: young Connor, who was a two- or three-year man, and Matthew Calverley, the senior constable in the ward. Most everyone considered Calverley an honest man, as far as crime and criminals and such things went. But no one believed he was neutral in the matter of the American war. He favoured the Northerners, and now that the fighting had gone on for three long years, he did not trouble much to hide the fact.

"Here, you!" he said harshly, bending over the two men on the ground. "Well, damn me, anyway. If it isn't Erryn Shaw." He hauled the other man to his feet, and Connor shone the lantern close into his face. "Ah, yes. And another of his darling Johnny Rebs. What's the matter, Jones? Your friends aren't putting enough pennies in your war chest anymore, so now you have to rob them?"

"I wasn't robbing him, for Christ's sake! I was trying to see if he was hurt! And the name is Janes."

"Right, mate. You can tell it to the judge."

"Judge? What the hell do you mean, judge? We were attacked! What's the matter with you idiots? You saw them yourself!"

"I know exactly what I saw. You were fighting with this man and now I find you digging for his purse—"

"You're crazy! Somebody jumped us! Two of them come at us from behind! They ran away when they saw your lantern. Ask Shaw, for Christ's sake! He can tell you!"

Matt Calverley took the lantern. "Watch the bugger, Connor." He dropped to one knee beside the fallen man, shook him lightly by the shoulder. When there was no response, he bent to look more closely, and then cursed.

"Is he conscious?" Connor asked.

"No." Calverley wiped his hand on his pant leg. "The son of a bitch smashed his head open."

"Smashed his head open?" Janes wailed. "You dumb Brit bastard, I never touched him!"

By this point a handful of people had gathered in the shadows, scarcely more than shadows themselves. Several others stood framed in the light of the open tavern door. The tailor Robert Hillier stepped back a little from his window. He thought about shouting down to the policemen, to tell them what he had seen . . . or what he thought he had seen. But he was not absolutely sure. It was dark, after all, and he had just waked up. Maybe it was footpads he saw. Or maybe it was just a pair of street toughs, waiting to see what they could scavenge when the fight was over, and then running away when the constables appeared. Maybe that man Janes really had bashed poor Mr. Shaw's head in, meaning to rob him, and then where would he be, helping the scoundrel to get away? No, he told himself, he would hold his peace. He could always speak at the trial later, if it came to one.

Calverley got to his feet again and turned to Maury Janes. "All right, let's go."

"Go? I ain't going anywhere with you. Take your dirty hands off me!" He punched the constable hard in the stomach. A Halifax man would have known better, Hillier said afterwards. You never took Matt Calverley on when he had you two to one. You took him on—maybe—when it was the other way around.

Calverley buckled, but only a little. Then he struck back, once, twice. "You won't come peaceable? Fine, you'll come on your bloody arse!" A third blow followed, the bone-crunching sort that made everyone who heard it flinch. Janes sank to the ground like a sack of meal, and Connor promptly manacled his hands behind his back.

The constable wiped his arm across his face. "You lads," he shouted at the gathered watchers. "I've tuppence for anyone who'll run to the station and send us the paddy wagon. The rest of you find something else to do. It's over—go on home."

"Shouldn't we take Mr. Shaw inside?" Connor asked.

"Into that rum-hole? He's better off here. At least nobody's going to puke on him. Keep an eye on things, will you? I want to have a look at this ruffian's pockets. Could be Shaw wasn't the first he robbed tonight."

Calverley took the lantern and knelt beside the prisoner. Hillier could not see clearly what he did, but he took his time about it, even troubling to remove the prisoner's boots. Just then a small private carriage rattled down the street from the north, stopping almost beside them. The passenger jumped out before the driver had secured the reins.

"Lord help us, constable," he said, "what's happened here? No one's been killed, I trust?"

"Colonel Hawkins. Good to see you, sir. No, no one's dead, but I fear Mr. Shaw's been battered rather badly."

Hillier had not recognized the man from the carriage, but he recognized the name. James Fitzroy Hawkins was practically an institution in the city. He was retired from one of Britain's famous lancer regiments—Hillier could never remember which—and was now commander of the Halifax militia.

"Can I be of help, perchance?" he offered.

"Actually . . ." Calverley, back on his feet, looked down at the injured man, still unmoving on the ground. "It's a lot to ask, sir, but if you could take Mr. Shaw here to a doctor, then Connor and I could deal with this ruffian—to say nothing of the others who might be out tonight."

"Why, certainly I could. Glad to be of help. I'll wait till your wagon comes, though. In case that one's got friends."

By this point most of the strangers attracted by the fracas were losing interest. The passersby moved on; the tavern's patrons drifted back inside or left for home. For a time it was almost quiet on Grafton Street. In his bedroom above the tailor shop, Robert Hillier rubbed his neck and poured a small shot of rum to help him sleep. When he heard hoofbeats and creaking wheels, he looked out one last time. It was the police wagon come at last, a lumbering hack whose worn-out horses must have shuddered every time they passed the soap factory. The officers loaded the prisoner first,

and young Connor climbed inside with him. Then Calverley and
Colonel Hawkins picked up Erryn Shaw's shoulders and feet, and
eased him into the colonel's carriage. The two men bid each other
a weary good night and drove away in opposite directions.

Hope the poor bugger doesn't die, Hillier thought, and sank back
into his bed.

———✦———

The carriage pulled away at a steady, dignified pace. Erryn Shaw
lay limp across the seat, his long arms and legs splayed out in all
directions. Once the carriage had gone a few hundred yards, he
opened his eyelids just enough to see through the lashes, to note
who was in the carriage with him and whether the curtains were
well and properly closed. Then he sat up with a groan of relief,
wiping his face and hair with a linen handkerchief. Hawkins, sitting opposite, watched impassively. He was considerably shorter
than Erryn, but built like a standing stone; his thinning grey hair
was the only hint of his sixty-odd years.

"Good evening, colonel."

"Mr. Shaw. I trust you're all right?"

"Oh, quite, thank you. Did Matt get anything?"

"Get anything?"

"On the cargo, sir."

It was difficult for Erryn to keep impatience from his voice. He'd
had far too much time to worry, lying limp in the dirt, wondering
what might be hidden in the *Dover*, wondering also if they would
have to discover it at the cost of his life. He had been able, just
barely, to see Matt hunched over the prisoner, systematically going
through his clothing. It seemed to take forever, and the longer it
took, the more he grew afraid. What if there was nothing to find?
They could not let the vessel sail. They would have to impound it,
search it from stem to stern, looking for something whose very
existence should be unknown to them. Only a handful of men in

Canada had known of the *Dover's* secret cargo, quite possibly as few as three: Janes himself, Alexander MacNab, and Erryn Shaw. To the Confederates, MacNab was above suspicion. That left Erryn.

My brother had you figured from the start, Shaw. Said you was too perfect by half, and yet you was always around when things went to pieces. Just like now . . .

It was always with him, that voice like Arctic ice, and the words colder still, always sitting in some dark, quiet place in the back of his mind, waiting to come at him like a ghost. The man was dead now, but the threat would stay with him forever. He might die at this. After twenty years of choices leading him farther and farther away from his glittering genealogy of knights and captains-general and admirals of the fleet, he might nonetheless die in some damned foreign war.

"For Christ's sake, sir, did Matt learn anything about the cargo?"

Hawkins pulled an envelope from an inside pocket and withdrew a narrow piece of printed paper, like a page from a book torn in half down the middle. "He had this."

"What is it?"

"Dickens. *Great Ex* something or other."

"*Great Expectations*, no doubt. How fitting."

Hawkins unfolded a letter. "He also had this. Quite harmless if a chap didn't know what to make of it, just family news and such. Except for a bit. 'Your trunks will arrive Dover early July. You will need this.'" Hawkins waggled the torn book page. "'This,' I expect, is *this*. And the captain of the *Dover* likely has the other half, and will only surrender the cargo to the man who has its mate." He paused and added wryly, "Or, of course, to an officer of the port authority with a lawful warrant."

It was not much, Erryn thought, but perhaps it was enough.

"Thank God for lawful warrants, eh, colonel?"

"Do I detect a small note of cynicism?"

"Cynicism? From me? Never in a thousand years." Carefully Erryn shook out the handkerchief he had used to wipe his head.

Bits of sand and other rubbish, best not examined, scattered onto the floor. The cloth itself was sticky and red.

"What the devil is that, anyway?" Hawkins asked.

"Theatre blood. You don't want to know how we make it." He glanced down at himself, brushing briefly and uselessly at his fouled vest and sleeves. He had looked altogether elegant when he left his room. "I fear the governor shall have to pay handsomely to have me scrubbed and mended."

"Knowing you, I'm sure the governor will."

"Cynicism would appear to be contagious."

Hawkins merely smiled. Erryn had never asked him, but he often wondered if the colonel had a history in this sort of work; if somewhere, in one of the empire's innumerable conflicts—or perhaps in many—he had done it all before.

"I wonder what we're going to find," the colonel murmured after a bit. "In the *Dover*. How did Janes put it to you, back in Montreal? He'd have the whole Red Sea coming down on Pharaoh's army? Something like that, wasn't it? Do you suppose the man is sane?"

"Yes, actually. And all the more dangerous for it."

"Aye." Hawkins edged his curtain back just a whisper. "We're almost there."

"I don't suppose an empty shed in Her Majesty's Ordnance Yard would contain anything so civilized as a bed, would it?"

"A bed?"

"Whatever Janes has in that ship, you're not likely to get it over here before lunch. And my head's smashed in, remember? A bed would be bloody nice."

Hawkins considered him for a small time, the way men considered strangers in a tavern or the morning sky at sea. "You're all right, Shaw," he said.

"Why, thank you, sir."

"I wondered about you, you know," the colonel continued. "When Calverley took you on. I knew you had the skills, of course.

But I wondered how you'd wear." A ghost of a pause. "I mean no offence."

"None taken, sir. If I'd had any sense back then, I would have wondered too."

If I'd had any sense back then, I wouldn't have signed on at all.

But no, that was quite untrue. He had done some good work, and he could never wish it undone. Still less could he wish that he had never gone to Montreal in the fall, or walked by the Irish Stone, or met a woman there, a woman with midnight hair and heartbreaking, melancholy eyes . . .

But this much was true: when Matt Calverley took him on, he had not wondered in the least how he would wear. He had been . . . well, he thought, the kindest word would be "innocent." He had looked upon it all as a passing adventure. He would be generously paid; he would be of service to his country in a time of crisis; he would not be bored. All of these things proved true. The trouble was, two and a half years ago he had little notion of what else might be riding on the same train.

Two and a half years ago. February of '62 it had been, winter as only the North Atlantic knew it. The whole of Halifax was gone grey as a stone, and the life he had fashioned there seemed over.

BOOK ONE

———◆———

Halifax, February 1862

CHAPTER 1

———✦———

The Review

Our feet on the torrent's brink,
our eyes on the clouds afar,
We fear the things we think
instead of the things that are.
—*John Boyce O'Reilly*

THE WILD, PROUD MUSIC of pipes and drums soared out from the Grand Parade, echoing against the ironstone warehouses and wooden sheds of the waterfront, sweeping up through narrow streets to the stone casements of the Citadel and beyond. Four blocks away, amid the ruins of the Grafton Street Theatre, Erryn Shaw raised his head a little at the sound, but made no move to get up. Instead, he let his eyes travel one more time across the burnt-out lot; every detail of it tore at his heart. A gaunt stray cat sat shivering in the broken chimney. Indifferent citizens had dumped off piles of trash that tumbled about now in the bitter February wind. There was no snow. The ground was blackened and horrid, the charred beams lying strewn across each other like battlefield dead. Everything felt unbearably empty and abandoned; everything stank of old, wet ashes and decay.

Seven weeks ago he had sailed for Bermuda, hoping to escape his sadness for a time, imagining that when he returned the rubble would be cleared away, and plans for rebuilding would be in the air. Instead, he found the owner had no money to rebuild; he had sold the land to a soap maker. As for those in the city with plenty of money, a theatre was not considered a good investment. It was unlikely to earn impressive profits, and it was, in any case, a thing of dubious respectability, the best of a long line of tainted livings, running down through the music hall, the tavern, the Barrack Street dive, and finally the whorehouse.

Or so it seemed to Erryn Shaw, sitting on a few broken bricks in the rubble, wondering why his life kept going up in smoke. For eight and a half years the Grafton Street Theatre had been his work and his joy, his hope of mattering a little in the world. Now it was gone, and he had no idea how he might replace it. He felt devalued and defeated, and everywhere he looked he saw grey skies, grey water, and grey mud.

It did not help that the entire Halifax garrison was on parade just a few blocks away, the drum rolls soaring to make a young man's blood race, and the bagpipes keening to bring tears to his eyes—all of it so bright and glorious, the men proud as peacocks in their fine red coats and their furry black hats, with the whole city waving and cheering them on.

Maybe I should have joined the bloody army after all, back in England, before any of this happened . . .

Then he laughed, bitterly, shoved his hair out of his eyes, and got slowly to his feet. When he started thinking in those terms, even in self-mockery, it was time to go. The military life, God almighty, how he had dreamt of it when he was a boy. He knew every English warrior hero back to Boudicca; he had paintings of Nelson and Wellington hanging on his bedroom walls; and the fact that he loved books and plays and poetry just as much, and learned to play the flute before he was ten—none of this ever made any difference. He saw no contradiction in his dreams, though he was smart enough to wonder, even as a boy, how he would manage to have it all, the pipes and the drums and the waving banners, and the quiet charm of a study, and the glittering magic of a lighted stage, all of it in one lifetime, in one body. But he believed it was possible. When you were twelve and clever and the son of an earl, anything was possible. When you were past thirty and no longer the son of an earl, except by the irrevocable fact of blood, it was all very different.

Erryn tucked his hands into the warmth of his pockets and started walking. He knew exactly where he would have found himself if he had joined the army with his peers—in the bloody Crimea, and more than likely dead, along with twenty-one thousand others, one out of every five who marched for queen and country, their young lives flung away in a war so bungled its stupidity was already legendary, so pointless it was rare to find an ordinary Englishman who understood what it was about, except that it had something to do with stopping the Russians.

Now the drums were beating again. Now the same damn fools were screaming about stopping the Americans.

⊰•⊱

The reviewing stand was packed to its edges with important people. In the very centre, in the place of honour, sat Sir Fenwick Williams, supreme commander of all the military forces in British North America. Immediately beside him were Vice-Admiral Alexander Milne, chief of England's Atlantic squadron, and the Earl of Mulgrave, lieutenant-governor of Nova Scotia. Ranged about were a veritable flock of dignitaries. Casually Matt Calverley picked out the mayor of Halifax; the captains of several English warships currently in harbour; Nova Scotia's leading politician and beloved favourite son, Joseph Howe; the Roman Catholic archbishop, Thomas Devin, dressed to the episcopal nines and wearing enough gold to ransom a ship; a dozen or so members of the Halifax Club, who between them accounted for most of the best names and even more of the best money in the colony; and the United States consul, Mortimer Jackson, who was undoubtedly watching this display of British military pride with something more than casual interest.

At Matt's side, quite distant from the official ranks, was Colonel James Fitzroy Hawkins, commander of the Halifax militia. At breakfast, or possibly last night at supper, poor Hawkins had eaten something unidentified and nasty. Having no wish to embarrass himself by dashing away from the reviewing stand to throw up, or worse, he had respectfully declined his appointed place, and sat instead among the crowd, at the end of a bench, where a trim line of marines guarded a narrow passageway between the parade ground and the street.

Matt Calverley was a sergeant in the colonel's militia unit, and also served from time to time as his unofficial ADC. All afternoon he had kept a discreet eye on the officer's welfare. Somewhat less discreetly, he also watched the crowd. He was not on police duty at the moment, but ten years in the Halifax constabulary had made him a peace officer down to his bones. He knew just how many grog shops lined the upper streets, and what an excellent business they did on festive days like this. He knew how volatile crowds could be, even at the best of times—and this was not the best of times.

Three months ago a Yankee naval captain had waylaid the British mail packet *Trent* on the open sea and seized two envoys from the Southern Confederacy who were bound for postings in Europe. The whole British Empire howled at this slight to imperial dignity, and some members of the British government spoke openly of war. The Prince Consort, wiser than most of the world in the face of his own advancing death, dragged himself from his sickbed to defuse the crisis, ably helped by the U.S. president, Abraham Lincoln, who thought one war at a time was quite enough. The envoys were released, the naval captain was censured, and the world went on just as before . . . only now vast numbers of Yankees were mad as hell at England and all her minions, and vast numbers of English, including many colonials in British North America, were mad as hell at the United States. War talk still heated up the taverns and the editorial pages, and drifted here and there through the crowd at the Grand Parade.

"Aren't they magnificent? Just absolutely *magnificent?* Why, they could whip absolutely *anybody*—especially those miserable Yankees!"

Matt Calverley turned his head a little so as to identify the owner of this breathy feminine voice: Isabel Grace Orton. He had never met the woman personally, but he knew exactly who she was: the spoiled daughter of one of the richest men in town, the queen of the winter social whirl, and the dream of every lonely officer in the colony, all of whom were magnificent in her eyes merely because they wore a uniform.

Ah, yes. Dizzy Izzy. I might have guessed. Matt did not like the Ortons. Undoubtedly, the Ortons would not have liked him, either, if any of them had noticed his existence.

Beside him, Colonel Hawkins smiled. "I dare say she's right, constable. We still have the finest-looking army in the world. Wouldn't you agree?"

Below them, the Seventy-eighth Highlanders were marching onto the Grand Parade, while the pipe band soared into "Scotland the Brave." The crowd was frantic with delight. The Highlanders were everybody's favourites, with their splendid kilts and tall black hats, marching with absolute precision and yet always with grace.

"Yes indeed, sir," Matt said. "They do look grand. And they make the bloody best targets I've ever seen, too."

The old man glowered at him. "What the devil do you mean?"

"Well, sir, when you go hunting, wouldn't you just love it if all the deer had nice red fur like that, and great big ostrich feathers on their heads?"

"You have no soul, Calverley."

Matt shrugged. Soul, in the sense that Hawkins meant it, was not something he felt in need of; his friend Erryn Shaw had quite enough for both of them.

He forgot Hawkins, however, as an argument erupted nearby between a young dockworker, a woman who was probably his wife, and big Jack Fisher, who kept the Owl's Rook Tavern on Albemarle. Fisher thought it was time for England to recognize the Southern Confederacy, send a few battalions to Boston, and teach the bloody Yankees a lesson.

"And then what happens to us?" the dockworker demanded.

"What do you mean, 'what happens to us'?"

"Ah, for Christ's sake, look at a map. There ain't nothing between us and the Yankees for a couple of thousand miles except a few broken-down forts and some trees—"

"There's fourteen thousand British regulars who just shipped through here a month ago!"

"Sure," said the woman, "and what did the Yankee president call up with his very first muster? Seventy thousand, wasn't it, just with a snap of his fingers?"

"They're all busy with the Southerners—"

"There's more where they came from," said the dockworker. "And they won't take kindly to us teaching them no lessons."

"Poppycock. They'll just bolt, like they did at Bull Run."

"Maybe. And maybe not. Myself, I'm not for finding out."

"Oh, come now!" A fourth person entered the argument, leaning over his companions to speak. This was another man whom Matt knew by face and reputation: Edmund Milroy, a midshipman from the vice-admiral's flagship; one of those cocky, natural-born hotheads, the very sort who should have been prohibited by law from ever wearing a uniform. "You don't think there's any way we can *avoid* a fight with the Yankees, do you? It's coming no matter what we do, so I say strike first!"

"Midshipman."

This new voice was soft, cultured, yet it carried even over the music and the cheering, the way the voices of actors carried in a theatre. Standing at the end of the bench, beside Colonel Hawkins, was Erryn Shaw.

"Sorry to butt in, mates, madam," he went on, with a small nod to the dockworker's wife, "but I knew this chap in India, you see, who was always trying to stop trouble by starting it first. One day we had to trek through some jungle and he cut both his feet off so he wouldn't get them snake-bit. Of course, he wasn't the brightest candle God ever lit, but do you want to know the strangest sorry thing about it? A few months later a cobra crawled up on him in his wheelchair and bit him dead. Colonel Hawkins, Constable Calverley, good afternoon. I trust you saved me a place?"

Then, without waiting for an answer or taking the hand Colonel Hawkins extended, Erryn Shaw swung himself up into the grandstand, stepped carefully past both men, and sat down. He was a long, thin beanpole of a man, who looked as though a quick snap might break him into pieces, but Matt knew him to be far more sturdy than he looked. Beautiful he was not, however, by anyone's measure. He had ragged blond hair and a large hooked nose, and today an aura of melancholy heavy enough to carry around in buckets.

Matt grinned him an affectionate hello. Midshipman Milroy glared at him.

"Your story is idiotic and utterly beside the point," he said. "The British Empire is not some dumb nitwit you tramped about with in India."

"It ain't beside the point," the dockworker flung back. "A man's a plain fool who goes looking for trouble, don't matter where. There's only one bunch needs a war here, far's I can see, and that's those Southern Rebels, and why the devil should we get ourselves shot to pieces for them?"

Two or three voices answered him with approval: "Hear, hear!"

"You have no idea what's going on, do you?" Milroy said scornfully. "None of you." He did not say, "None of you *colonials*," but he might as well have done so. Colonials by definition could understand nothing, not even the colonies they lived in, quite as well as a genuine Englishman could. "The situation here is a powder keg waiting to go off. And who do you think is going to prevent it? Monck? That Anglo-Irish nobody who ended up in the governor general's office because no sensible man in London would take the job? God almighty! The governorship of British North America is one of the prize postings in the empire, and they were turning it down like a plate of spoiled meat. They knew whichever sorry fool took it, he was going to be blamed for getting in a war God himself couldn't stop. He was going to be drawn, quartered, and hung out to dry—"

"Sure makes a man admire politics, don't it?" Matt said cheerfully.

"Do you think Monck's going to stop what half a dozen of the best men in London *knew* they couldn't stop?"

This was entirely the wrong sort of thing to say in front of Colonel Hawkins. He towered to his feet.

"That will be *Lord* Monck to you, midshipman. And you would do well to remember, sir, that important offices are not always offered first to men who have ability, but to those who are owed favours. It's to Lord Monck's credit that he would take on so difficult a responsibility. As for your best men in London, midshipman, do you think it's to their credit that they refused?"

Hawkins was only a colonel of militia now, but he was tall, stately, and impeccably dressed; he looked every inch the retired military gentleman he was. Young Milroy backed off fast.

"I meant no offence, sir. I merely suggested that even Lord Monck cannot do the impossible."

"And you, I presume, know for certain what is possible and what is not? You must have a very close relationship with God."

"Ohhh," murmured Erryn Shaw. The dockworker smiled so broadly Matt could see it through the back of his head. Milroy returned his attention to the parade ground.

"A powder keg waiting to go off," the colonel muttered bitterly, settling back on his bench, "and they send us idiots like that one, running around with torches."

Matt refrained from pointing out that imperial ambitions and idiots with torches had a tendency to turn up together. After all, he liked the old man. Hawkins was a decent sort, as imperialists went. He was also one of those rare and necessary contradictions, a military man who genuinely loved and preferred peace.

So Matt said nothing, but turned instead to talk to Erryn Shaw. He noticed in passing that Milroy's bout of torch waving had made a grand impression on Isabel Orton. This was in no way surprising, since her father, James Orton, belonged to a group that had come to be called the Grey Tories: Canadians who actively supported the Southern cause; or, in plainer words, Confederate agents. Unofficial Confederate agents, of course. Officially, all British subjects were neutral—rather, Matt thought, the way all judges were impartial, all sheriffs honest, and all clergymen pure.

"So, Mr. Shaw," Matt said amiably. "What happened to you? Was your landlord moving the furniture again?"

"No," Erryn said. "I went by to have a look at the theatre."

"Now that was not a good idea."

"No. It wasn't."

Matt placed a brief, comforting hand on his shoulder. "Things'll get better again, mate."

Things would, of course. This was a simple, banal fact of life. But it was not, Matt suspected, a fact Erryn Shaw was likely to acknowledge. When Erryn soared, he was an eagle, brilliant, tireless, almost out of reach. When he faltered, he was a shot crow, crashing straight down and landing in a sorry black huddle.

"By the way," Matt murmured to him very softly, "when were you last in India?"

Erryn cocked an eyebrow at him but did not reply. Both of them knew perfectly well he had never been to India in his life.

"You aren't going to be marching?" Erryn asked. "The militia, I mean?"

"The awkward squad? In front of Fenwick Williams himself? Not likely."

Lord in heaven, Matt thought, wouldn't that put a crimp in the day. Except for Governor Monck himself, nearly every ranking Englishman in British North America was down on that reviewing stand, trying his damnedest not to notice that, for all the pomp and pageantry, for all the war talk and blustering, ordinary Nova Scotians did not seem particularly interested in fighting this supposedly inevitable war with the United States. The legislature refused to vote more than a pittance toward equipping a militia, and the citizens came out to drill without noticeable enthusiasm. Every senior officer was somebody's great-grandfather, and most of the junior officers were young bloods from rich families, valuing their commissions mostly as marks of social status. Matt's sergeant's uniform was a merchant seaman's discard with some chevrons tacked carelessly onto the sleeves. His men had no uniforms at all. They drilled with wooden sticks, and although he did his best to drill them well, after the high-stepping Highlanders they would look . . . well, there was no other word for it: they would look embarrassing.

No, very definitely no. The Halifax militia was not going to be part of this parade.

───◆───

CHAPTER 2

The Old Man is Looking for Some Spies

There is a great war raging in the South, and it would
undoubtedly suit the interest of some if the fires of war could
be lighted up here . . .
—*John Cordner*

ALL IN ALL, the review went off very well, ending with speeches
and a salute from the Royal Artillery. Only two fights broke out in
the crowd, both of them handled tidily by the marines. The brass
and their guests were piped away to a great rousing cheer. By then
the sun was low, lost in the clouds behind Citadel Hill. In the harbour, the water was slate grey; the far shore had blurred to a long
line of dark ridges, and the near one to clustered silhouettes of
ships and black masts spearing an ashen sky. Several small fishing
schooners were drifting home for the night, and the Dartmouth
ferry chugged manfully to Queen's Pier.

Erryn Shaw sighed faintly, watching it all. He had lived with
exile so long that he scarcely noticed anymore, except sometimes
at nightfall, when the whole world scurried to its dens, and he
remembered that his was a rented room in a colonial garrison

29

town, in a small frame house where no one else lived except an old man and a cat.

"Are you on duty tonight, Matt?" he asked, hoping very much the answer would be no.

"'Fraid so. I'm taking a certain out-of-work stage manager I know down to Corey's and stuffing him full of good cod and plum pudding and such."

"That's a duty, then, is it?"

"Erryn, you're so damn blue they could dip you in a laundry vat and use you for dye. What's a good mate good for, if he don't think he ought to do something about it?"

Erryn grinned and salaamed. "The stage manager is at your disposal. Stuff away."

Corey's was a fine place to eat. Tucked into a narrow lot on Hollis Street, with a harness maker on one side and an upscale whorehouse on the other, it was not favoured by the better people of Halifax; and since it had no barroom, it was not favoured by the worst. This arrangement suited the respectable working class very nicely. As in most eateries, except for the best hotels, meals were served only between certain hours, and the choice was limited to whatever was cheap and plentiful in the markets at the time. Tonight it was haddock, beautifully fried and served with great scoops of golden chips and a bottle of excellent white wine. Erryn dug in with a will.

"When did you eat last?" Matt murmured.

"Don't remember," Erryn said. Then, realizing he was being absurdly melodramatic, he added, "Breakfast."

The food was simple, but very tasty and satisfying. In spite of himself, he started feeling better. A good meal—and most especially a good meal with friends—could lift the gloom from almost anything.

"So," Matt asked after a bit, "have you seen the posters for Mr. Rutherford Sanstrom's lecture tomorrow night? On the Just and Legitimate Claims of the Confederate States to their Freedom and Independence, amen?"

"Oh, quite. And the editorial in the *Recorder* too, telling us how all our natural allies in America are in the South, because we all have better table manners than the Yankees."

"Well, they *did* mention one or two other reasons."

"All of them equally to the point."

"Agreed." Matt slid his empty plate away and pulled his wine-glass closer. Erryn never understood how the man could eat so fast; perhaps a childhood of near starvation was the likeliest explanation. He thought Matt would drain the glass in one go, just like his supper, but instead he only wrapped his hands around it and said, very quietly:

"You know, mate, the old man is looking for some spies."

Erryn regarded him, puzzled, wondering what he had missed in the conversation.

"Which spies?" he asked. He knew there might be quite a few in town. Halifax was a colonial outpost and the summer base of the entire Atlantic Squadron. It was a major trading port as well, a rough garrison town filled with seamen and soldiers, with strangers from every palace and gutter in the world. Even in quiet times there would be a spy or two among them; with a war ablaze next door, there were likely to be many.

"His own spies," Matt said.

"He's looking for . . .? Sorry, Matt. Start over."

Matt leaned forward a little, glancing at the nearest table. They were loud and boisterous there, paying no attention to their neighbours. Nonetheless, he lowered his voice even further. "Nova Scotia's crawling with these bleeding Southerners, Erryn, as I'm sure you've noticed. Oh, there was some here before you left, but nothing like now. They're starting newspapers, making speeches, cuddling up cozy with the shipowners and the politicians and even the Church. Rutherford Sanstrom's staying at Arch-bishop Devin's house, did you know that?"

"No."

"Now, nobody past the age of three believes they only want to tell their own side of the story and buy a little coal for their blockade-runners. There's way too many of them for that. So what do they want?"

"Well, that's easy. They want us in the war. We're their natural allies, remember?"

Matt raised his glass. "One for you, mate." He drank briefly. "Now, I have another question. Would an out-of-work stage man-ager be interested in a job? Five pounds a month plus expenses, guaranteed by the Crown."

"When did you start speaking for the Crown?"

Matt tapped lightly at the sleeve of his makeshift militia jacket. "This speaks for the Crown." Then, perhaps realizing that *he* was being absurdly melodramatic, he added: "Now and then."

Erryn said nothing for a time. Matt Calverley was his best friend, a friend who knew exactly how much he lost when the Grafton Street Theatre went down, and how desperately he wanted to replace the loss. Matt was not joking. The offer was genuine, and Erryn was not at all sure he liked it.

"Doing what?" he asked finally. Cautiously.

"Making friends with that bleeding pack of Southerners. Nodding and smiling when they talk about the just and . . . what the hell did they call it? . . . claims of the Confederate States—"

"Legitimate."

"Right. Legitimate. Well, we all can dream. Anyway, you snug-gle up with them, and drink with them, and find out what the hell they're up to, and then you tell me, and I tell the old man, and he tells the GG, and then maybe, just maybe, we get to keep our necks out of their God damn war."

The old man is looking for some spies . . . SPIES? ME?

"You fell out of bed and hit your head on something, Matt."

"Think about it. The Confederates are crawling all over us. In the West, Niagara's just as bad, and Montreal's even worse. The lieutenant-governor is practically in bed with them, right along with Jamie Orton and the rest of his miserable lot. As for Fenwick Williams, he's pure soldier. He's not thinking political. All he's thinking is how many men he's got and which way to point the cannons when the shit's in his face. So the plain truth is, nobody's watching our backs here. And Monck knows it, up in Quebec—"

"That will be *Lord* Monck to you, constable," Erryn quipped.

"Two," Matt said amiably, and raised his glass again. "Anyhow, he and Colonel Hawkins go back twenty years. He's sharp as a headsman's axe, the colonel says, but real quiet about it. Real careful. He doesn't want any cannons going off anywhere. But the only way he's going to manage it is by staying one step ahead of the Confederates—"

"Matt, for Christ's sake, stop. You're not saying a damn thing I don't already know. The answer is no. I'm not a . . . This isn't . . . I'm sorry, but it's just no."

Matt filled Erryn's glass and then his own.

"All right," he said. "Just thought I'd ask."

"Aren't the Americans doing anything? About the Rebels up here?"

"Sure. Following them around like burrs on a bear's ass. Trouble is, when they learn something, they don't talk to us. They talk to Abe Lincoln."

He leaned back in his chair. He was only four years older than Erryn, and they had much in common, but in appearance they were very different. Matt was a man of barely medium height, elegantly made and darkly attractive, with a short beard and moustache he always kept immaculately trimmed. When he was quiet, as he was now, draped lazily over the arms of a chair, he looked nothing like a policeman, much less a drill sergeant; he looked like someone's friendly pet kitty. Through the years, a number of angry sailors and lumberjacks had reached the same unfortunate conclusion, and made to toss him over a bar or down a set of stairs, only to discover they had laid rude hands on a bobcat—a creature created entirely of bone and sinew, with lightning reflexes, four compact limbs too fast for a human eye to follow, and mean, mean teeth. Moreover, Matt Calverley knew every dirty trick ever tried in the stinking dens of Barrack Street. He had, after all, grown up there.

"What'll you do, then?" he asked. "For work?"

"I'll find another theatre."

"Until then?"

"I don't know. Live on my father's money, I suppose."

"Man said to me once—I was fourteen, fifteen maybe—he said, 'What are you really good at? Find that out,' he said, 'and then do it, come hell or damnation.' After I thought about it awhile, I decided I was good at figuring other people."

"So you joined the constabulary. A reasonable decision."

"Well, I didn't join right off," Matt said wryly. "Those were the days when they were still trying to lock me away." He had chosen a table tucked right into a back corner, where they had relative privacy. He watched now as the noisy guests nearby picked up their hats and jackets and started to leave. "And what about you, my friend? Have you ever thought about it? What might be your most remarkable talent?"

"Putting plays together."

"What else?"

"Bloody hell, Matt. You've known me long enough to know what I can do. And what I can't."

"Sure I know. Just wondering how you see it yourself, that's all. What else, besides plays?"

Erryn shrugged. "I can act well enough for an amateur production. I play a fair to middling flute."

Matt watched him with patient expectation, as he might have watched a small boy figuring out a puzzle. And it occurred to Erryn that his friend was not asking about artistic talents at all.

Matt was, after all, a city constable, a member of the militia, and now, apparently, some vague sort of colonial spymaster.

"I'm a crack shot. And I can run very fast. But then," Erryn added, "maybe to the people you spend your time with, running very fast isn't counted as a talent."

"What else?"

"What else? God, I don't know. All things considered, I suppose I have a talent for survival, or I wouldn't be here at all. Oh, and I'm very literate. I can speak French, read Latin and Greek, name all the kings of England, and do figures in my head. Now, will that do?"

"You've left out your most exceptional talent of all."

"Which is?" Erryn asked, genuinely curious.

"You can fit anywhere. Handle yourself anywhere. You're a fish to whom the whole world is water. You could dine with the bloody House of Lords or piss in a trough by the Water Street livery, and there wouldn't be a soul, neither one place nor the other, would think for one minute you didn't belong there."

Erryn opened his mouth and closed it again, silent. He was not sure if he had been complimented or royally insulted.

"And that, Erryn Shaw, makes you the best God damn natural spy I've ever seen, or ever hope to see. And I can't think of one reason why you shouldn't put such a fine talent to use."

"Well, I can think of some reasons. Lots of people here know me, and they know exactly what I think of the Southern Confederacy. God knows I've said so often enough."

Matt shrugged. "Early on, people said all sorts of things. There's four states in the Confederacy that voted for the Union, first time around. There's a fellow I know down at Logan's Wharf, solid man, with a damn fine head on his shoulders. He was expecting Abe Lincoln to declare a crusade against slavery, and he was all for it. Instead, Lincoln overruled some general who tried to free the slaves in his own bailiwick, and the lad snaps around, just like that. He's all for the South now, says the Yankees are just bullies kicking some smaller chap's ass. People change their minds,

Erryn—that's the first thing. And the second thing is, far as I ever noticed, you did most of your talking to me. You're way too well bred to get in political battles at other people's dinner tables. What with you running the theatre and then going to Bermuda, and being so damn polite, I don't think the Grey Tories know what you think, really."

"Maybe," Erryn said. "As to the war itself, maybe. But it doesn't matter. A man's politics are of a piece. I don't care for oligarchies, remember? For people being shoved into boxes because of who their fathers were, or weren't. I don't see how a man can call himself civilized and keep slaves. And frankly, on a bad day I don't have much use for the British Empire. I'm not a Tory, Matt, Grey or otherwise. And that's something most of Halifax *does* know."

"What of it?" Matt asked very calmly.

Erryn shook his head in exasperation. "*What of it?* Matt, for Christ's sake—!"

"Jack Murray blew back into town while you were gone. He's as strong for the South as Jamie Orton now. Stronger, maybe. All he's missing is some little Rebel flags growing out of his ears."

Erryn stared at him. Jack Murray was his friend—not as dear and close a friend as Matt, but nonetheless a friend. Jack Murray was a liberal and a freethinker, a supporter of change-minded English Radicals such as Cobden and Bright. Politically, Jack Murray was a great deal like himself.

He's as strong for the South as Jamie Orton now?

"It doesn't split clean, Erryn," Matt said softly. "Men's politics aren't of a piece. Or maybe they are, but the pieces fit damned peculiar sometimes."

Which was something Erryn knew, of course. He knew it as a principle of history, as a recurring theme in drama, even as a fact of this war: the Liberal Gladstone in England, making speeches in praise of the South; the fossilized Conservative he had met in Bermuda, condemning secession as the very essence of anarchy. It did not matter what one used for a marker—rank, race, religion, party; wealth or privilege or power or the lack of them—men from the same group still came down on both sides of every fight. More of them on one side than the other, usually, but always on both. He knew that. He had simply never thought of it as applicable to himself.

Matt leaned forward again, resting his elbows on the table and linking his hands. "Jack Murray is supporting the Confederates for the purest of liberal reasons. They're fighting for national independence, just like the Greeks and the Poles. Why shouldn't he support them? Why shouldn't you? You don't have to like slavery—hell, James Orton doesn't, either. The war isn't *about* slavery—"

"The hell it isn't."

"Oh, not once the Confederates cross their own borders. Soon as they cross a border, they turn it into a whole different war, all noble and proper like a cutpurse dressed for church. Your views on slavery won't matter if you don't make a fuss about it. And it won't matter if you had doubts at first, either; lots of people did. But the more you saw and read, the more you understood the truth. The Yankees are only after power, the Southerners are honourable and civilized, and so on and so forth as you please. The Rebels love converts, Erryn. They're like religious folk that way: they're so sure they're right, it's just natural if you come around to their way of thinking."

"Matt . . ."

Of course, he protested further, but for all his protests Matt Calverley had an answer, and bit by bit he found himself yielding. It was obvious Matt desperately wanted help. Five pounds a month plus expenses was a tempting offer, and whatever else, he would at least have something interesting to do. Finally, and most importantly, there was the political question itself. The prospect of a war here, between his own people and the Americans—a war that might kill him or his dearest friends, a war that might smash this small and promising world to ruins, smash it for no good reason at all—Lord, it made him cold to his bones. So, in a different way, did the prospect of a triumphant Confederacy. He had been raised an aristocrat himself, after all. He recognized the qualities of his own kind when he saw them—their arrogance, their astonishing audacity, their faith in the use of force. The cold smell of authoritarian empire lay all over the Southern Confederacy's supposed fight for freedom.

Against all of these things his natural common sense, such as it was, grew less and less persuasive, even to himself. The evening passed. The fish bones on their plates grew dry and sorry-looking, the wine bottles empty, the dining room more and more deserted. Spent, Erryn struck his colours for good—*All right, all right, I'll do it*—and wondered just how quickly and how badly he would come to regret it.

There was, however, one last matter to be settled. As they rose to leave, he put his arm around his friend's shoulder and asked wearily: "Matt, you don't really think I'd piss in the troughs by the Water Street livery, do you?"

"No," Matt said, with his wicked street arab's grin. "But if you ever start, I'll damn well toss you in jail."

BOOK TWO

———◆———

*The North Atlantic,
Summer 1863*

CHAPTER 3

The Osprey

We are going to burn, sink, and destroy the
commerce of the United States.
—*Captain Raphael Semmes, Confederate Navy*

THE TALL SHIP passed them miles to the east, under full sail in
the last of the afternoon light. A dozen or so of the mail packet's
passengers clustered by the starboard rail to admire it. Such a fine
ship, they kept saying, so stately and graceful. Sylvie Bowen stood
alone, apart from the others, and said nothing; but when the
strange vessel moved off into the distance, and the other passengers lost interest, she remained by the rail until the last trace of it
was gone. The *Osprey* had been a ship much like it, the beautiful
Osprey she and Fran had boarded at Liverpool in May . . . nine
weeks ago if you reckoned by the calendar, a lifetime otherwise.

She brushed away tears with the back of her hand. Sometimes
she could think of Fran without this rush of grief. She could look
out across the grey water and acknowledge quietly that Fran was
dead. Fran would never have the promising new life in Nova

Scotia they had dreamt of. She would never be courted by Captain Foxe—or, if he changed his mind, by anyone else. She was gone forever, lying in a churchyard in a wild Caribbean town, where drunken blockade-runners brawled in the streets until daybreak, and sand barely hid the bones of pirates.

Nassau. Back in England, Sylvie had only heard of the place because of the American war, through a few small items in the newspapers Fran borrowed from her friends. Nassau was coming to matter in the world: a friendly port for Confederate raiders, a transfer point for commerce running the blockade. This much Sylvie had learned from the papers, but she never imagined she would go there. That last wonderful day on the *Osprey*, they were speeding northward from Bermuda, and Nassau was a thousand miles away . . .

⟫━•◆•━⟪

When they first sailed from England it had been late in May, the sun hot as summer and a fair wind blowing. Such days, Captain Foxe said, were God's gift to good ships, and his *Osprey* flew like the lean bird she was. From Liverpool she made Bermuda in twelve days, where she unloaded bales of English textiles, cases of tools and copperware, and carefully packed china; sundry stocks of medicines and books; and three pianos. Into the partially emptied hold went crates of oranges; barrels of sugar, molasses, and rum; and last of all, a shimmering, squalling parrot in a cage, purchased, apparently, by a gentleman in Halifax, though no one could imagine why. By then June had come, and the *Osprey* was winging for Nova Scotia under a full spread of sail.

Sylvie had been on deck for much of the day, with Fran and the others. She was still twenty-six back in June, thin to the point of frailty, and dressed in a plain cotton frock without lace or trim or hoops—a frock that clearly marked her as a member of the working poor. People noticed this, of course, on a ship like the *Osprey*.

They also noticed her hair, beautiful hair as dark as midnight, always hanging long and loose about her face. It gave her a certain aura of wildness that caught everyone's eye, and that men and women judged as it pleased them. She could do nothing about their judgments, and had long ago stopped trying.

Her aunt, Frances Harris, sat on the bench behind her, peeling and partitioning an orange, one of the tiny luxuries they had bought for themselves in Bermuda. She did it slowly and carefully, keeping the sections in a bowl on her lap, and eating them with voluptuous pleasure, one by one.

"Here, Sylvie," she said, "have a piece or two, before I gobble it all."

Sylvie smiled, and went to sit beside her. Fran looked so content, she thought, and every day more so. It was beautiful to see.

"Thanks," Sylvie said. She had never tasted oranges in England. Once, in Darwen, a peddler had brought some in his wagon, and she had stood nearby like a beggar, staring, aching for them. They looked so glorious, like handfuls of heaven in a basket. Then Johnnie Morris came up behind her and said, "I'll buy you one, if you do it with me," and she walked away. She did not want to look at them anymore, or at him either, the mean little sod. He always had a bit of money; he could have bought one for himself, and given her a piece, just one tiny piece, so she could know what they were like . . .

The orange was heavenly indeed. She accepted a second offering, and then, when it was all gone, she sucked a small gob of juice from her finger and looked wryly at her aunt.

"A lady like Miss Caroline would never do that, I suppose?"

Fran smiled. "Miss Caroline? How could she? She'd be wearing gloves."

Miss Caroline never came on deck without gloves. She always wore a great floppy bonnet too, and carried a parasol, as if all this glorious, soul-warming sunshine were rain. The rich were peculiar, and there was no denying it.

"Well, at least she's friendly, and willing to talk a bit," Sylvie said. "There's one or two among the others who still be wondering how we got on board."

"We bought our passage the same as everyone," Fran said coolly. And that, for Fran, was the end of it. They were here; their fellow passengers and the whole rest of the world could deal with it, or not, as they chose.

"I should tell you," Fran went on, in the most casual manner possible, "Captain Foxe has invited us to supper in his cabin tonight."

"Us?" Sylvie whispered. Then she laughed softly. "Go on. You're teasing me."

"Not a bit. Master Schofield will be there too, of course. The captain says it be his birthday, and he's serving up a fine chicken and a bottle or two of his best port. So of course I told him yes."

Sylvie did not know what to say, so for a time she said nothing. Early in the voyage, almost as soon as the women recovered from their seasickness and emerged from their cabin to eat and take the air, Captain Foxe had shown a remarkable degree of interest in Frances Harris. This did not surprise Sylvie nearly as much as it surprised everyone else; all her life she had watched Frances attract the interest of men.

But Nathaniel Foxe was a ship's captain, wealthy enough to own this splendid vessel—not the usual sort of man to invite a pair of Lancashire ragpickers to a birthday supper in his cabin. No wonder Fran was so light of heart today, so quick to smile.

"You like him awfully, don't you?" Sylvie said.

"Rather more than is good for me, I suppose. You're not a bad judge of people, Sylvie. What do you think of him?"

"I think . . ." She paused, searching for the right words. "Well, he got all that authority, but I never seen him throw his weight around. And he always treats us same as the others, as if being poor don't matter. Is that what Americans be like?"

Fran laughed softly. "I haven't met a lot of them, love. But unless they all died and turned into angels, I doubt it."

"Well then, I'd say he's a good man."

"Yes. That's rather what I think, too."

Sylvie leaned back against the bench. She felt impossibly content, warm and well fed as a sunning cat. She would have purred if she had known how. This, she thought, must be how slaves felt when they escaped from their masters, or prisoners when they fled from their dungeons—when they had actually made it. When the past was too far away to ever catch up with them, and everything ahead was only possibility.

She wondered what Halifax would be like. A well-ordered, prosperous city, Miss Susan's letter had promised them, with plenty of work for anyone who wanted it. A sailor town, Frances had added wryly, garrison to half an empire, and sitting right next door to that nasty American war. Prosperous it might well be, Fran said, but she was taking "well-ordered" with a grain of salt.

For her part, Sylvie did not care; whatever it was like, she would have a future there. Sylvie Bowen, clerk. Or chambermaid, or scullion, or God knew what. Something. Something that would not kill her, as the mill would have done. As the mill had begun to do, fibre by deadly cotton fibre. She had watched it kill others, a few of them every year—six or seven, maybe; not enough for anyone to notice, down there in London where they made the laws. It was only a matter of time until she became another. And she had known as much, the days she looked into Fran's little mirror and saw her face as dead as lime, only the eyes alive, red and always watering, half blind with pain; the nights she had choked in her bed, coughing and coughing into the blankets, trying to muffle it, trying not to keep Fran awake . . .

Now she was free. The great rattle of the spindles was silent, and the sea air was as wild and as clean as the sky.

——◆◆——

Until the morning she climbed aboard the *Osprey*, Sylvie Bowen had never been among what they called "the better people." Oh, she had seen them from time to time, when some owner came to the mill to give orders, or when the church ladies came to their tenements with bits of food and old clothing, and endless talk of cleanliness and God. Now, on the *Osprey*, the fine folk were in sudden, disturbing closeness, elbow to elbow at the dining table, and out on the deck, walking past her almost close enough to touch, smiling, perhaps—even bowing a little, if they were men. *Good morning, ladies. A fine day for sailing, ladies* . . . They were polite, of course. Even the horrid Draytons were polite now, but she knew what they thought of her.

The ship had been three days out of Liverpool when she and Fran first came out of their cabin for a proper meal. She walked into the grand saloon and saw the whole pack of them gathered as at a king's feasting table: the captain in his trim uniform looking for all the world like a hero out of a book, the others practically shimmering in the lamplight, dressed to the very nines.

She had not expected this. She had expected . . . oh, she was not sure what, a room like the eateries in Rochdale, perhaps, through whose windows she had seen scattered tables with small groups of men. She thought she and Fran would sit off by themselves in a corner—not here, at this long, sparkling table. Not with all the others. She could feel their eyes on her, taking due note of the unbound hair, the pathetically cheap dress. But there was no possibility of flight; Captain Foxe himself stepped toward her and pulled out her chair: "Good evening, Miss Bowen, please be seated."

She sat obediently, and found herself face to face with the most insufferable snobs on the vessel, quite possibly the most insufferable snobs in the whole British Empire: a certain Mrs. Drayton, made entirely of silk and lace and baubles; and beside her, her husband, who stared at the mill-town women as if they were livestock who had wandered up from the hold.

At first, all Sylvie wanted was to flee, yet by the evening's end she was glad they had come. Divine odours drifted out from the galley, and her humiliation gave way to a sheer longing for food. It came at last, enticing beyond all her expectations, a roast of beef with turnips and yams and thick slabs of bread. She watched in wonderment as the steward loaded her plate. Surely this couldn't all be for her? But it was, and it was achingly good. Bit by bit she felt better. Bit by bit the company mellowed too. Captain Foxe was friendly and polite, treating them as if they were perfect ladies, and in his presence no one seemed ready to do otherwise.

But when the passengers were alone among themselves, it was different. The very next day, Sylvie came upon a gathering in the saloon, the proud English couple in their midst. None of them noticed her come in, engrossed as they were in their own conversation. She caught only the last of Mrs. Drayton's words:

"—never allow my *servants* to wear clothes like that."

"It's appalling, really," her husband said. "We understood the *Osprey* to be a fine, respectable vessel. I for one did not expect to be sitting at the table with factory women, or whatever the deuce they are. I can't imagine how it was allowed."

"Well, it is an *American* ship."

"Quite beside the point." This was Mr. Paige, who was from the States himself. "I know hundreds of Americans who'd never lower their standards like this. I fear the war has made our captain desperate. He'll take anyone who can pay."

"Yes, and how were they able to pay, I wonder? A decent servant girl is doing well if she's got a shilling to spare for a pair of shoes."

Well, Sylvie thought bitterly, *m'appen you should pay them better, then!*

She stood irresolute, curious to hear what else they might say, yet desperate to escape unseen. She looked at each in turn: the English Draytons, Mr. Paige, Miss Caroline, the other young American, Mr. Canfrey. Rich, every blighting one of them. Well-tended bodies that never dreamt of hunger. Hair fashioned just so. Nails all trimmed and clean. Rings that sparkled even in the lamplight. Clothing so fine and precious you could stroke it like a cat.

And they were wondering where *she* got her money?

"Maybe an inheritance?" Miss Caroline suggested hopefully.

"Good heavens, no. People like that don't know anyone with money to leave them."

"Well, however they came by it," Mr. Drayton said, "I'll wager it wasn't honest labour, or they'd value it more. Really, I ask you: creatures like that, travelling first class? A pair of honest immigrants would stay with their own kind, and hang on to their money so they don't end up in the workhouse!"

It wasn't honest labour? Day after day, she and Fran had tramped to the cotton mill before the sun rose, and stumbled home again in the dark. They worked in air no human could safely breathe, in noise to shatter the nerves of a stone. They did it from the year she turned eleven until the day the mill shut down, and they had not earned their passage out?

She stared at Drayton, unable to find words to answer an accusation so monstrously unjust. While she floundered, Miss Caroline stepped into the breach.

"Really, Mr. Drayton, I dare say you've gone too far. I'm sure these women worked and saved for their passage, as most of the immigrants do. We do the lower orders a great injustice, you know, if we assume that just because they are poor they are also criminals."

"Oh, come now, I didn't say that—"

"With respect, sir, I fear you did." This was Mr. Canfrey, the youngest of the group, who until now had said nothing. He got to his feet; perhaps he had had enough of the conversation. "I'm going topside, Paige. Are you coming?"

Mr. Paige lifted a glass still half filled with wine. "When I've finished."

"I'll see you later, then. Ladies. Mr. Drayton." He turned and saw Sylvie. He had the decency to seem embarrassed, but before he could say anything, she shook her head faintly. They both retreated, very quietly, in opposite directions.

———◆———

She cried over it for most of an hour. It had seemed a miracle, getting onto this ship. They did not choose it so they could travel first class. They chose it because the war had made it cheap, because her lungs were bad, because they wanted to get to America alive. So she cried, bitterly, but in time she cried herself out, and there was nothing she could do in the cabin except sit on her bed and read a battered dime novel she had already read twice. After another hour she found herself both hungry and bored. It would be lunchtime soon. Her mouth watered, remembering yesterday's dinner. She would go and see the steward, she decided, and ask him to bring her plate to the cabin. Then the bloody Draytons could eat and strut in peace.

But there was Fran. She knew what Fran would say to this: "Then they've won, Sylvie." That was exactly what Fran would say, with a little brush of Sylvie's hair across her forehead. "You can't do it, love. Because then they've won."

No, she had to face the buggers down, so she might as well just do it. Besides, she had not been on deck since they left the Mersey and everyone got seasick; she wanted desperately to get out in the sun, to walk, to look at the sea.

And there Mr. Canfrey found her and apologized for his companions. The English upper classes, he said, were such intolerable snobs. He did not mention that his countryman Paige had been cheerfully agreeing with them. Nor did he ever look directly at her face. But he did apologize, and day by day things got better. It was a long voyage and a small group of passengers; simply getting through the days required a measure of civility. But more than anything, it was Captain Foxe who set the standards of their social world. His passengers were his guests, and he treated them all with unfailing courtesy; it was hard for them to do less. Moreover, he *liked* these Lancashire ragpickers, and whatever the others may have thought of his taste, or of his morals, Sylvie doubted that any of them were willing to make him mad.

Now he had invited the ragpickers to dine in his cabin.

Oh my, Sylvie thought, this was going to cause a stir. Mr. Drayton would say democracy had corrupted the whole American race and here was the proof of it. Mrs. Drayton would fan herself and ask for smelling salts. And tomorrow, when Fran and Sylvie turned up on deck, everyone would look at them and wonder what they had been up to, besides devouring chicken and port.

I suppose if we were terribly proper and respectable ladies, we'd have to think twice about going. This way . . . well, there be advantages to everything, even to being factory trash.

She was licking the last bit of orange juice from her fingers when a shout of "Sail ho!" brought everyone to the railing. The sea in all directions seemed clear and empty. Sylvie glanced up, where a lookout clung to the rigging with one hand, holding a glass to his eye with the other.

Between one breath and another the deck had gone silent. Conversations died in mid-sentence; even the work sounds stopped. A sailor stood with a bucket in his hand, the water from his mop draining over his feet. In the sudden quiet they could hear every slap of the sea, and every squawk and cluck of the chickens. Any strange ship could be a Confederate raider. According to Mr. Canfrey, the *Alabama* under Captain Raphael Semmes had burned and sunk seventeen American ships—merchants, whalers, fishing vessels, anything that crossed her path. Seventeen already, he told them, as of the day they left Liverpool.

On the quarterdeck Captain Foxe, silent like the others, scanned the horizon with his own glass, and then shouted to the lookout:

"Can you make her out, Watson?"

"No, sir, not yet. But she looks like a merchant brig."

"D'you see any smoke?"

"Not yet, sir."

Sylvie and Fran exchanged uneasy glances, but said nothing. They had passed seven or eight ships since leaving England, and every time it was the same. Every time, the deck of the *Osprey* went tense and still. Every time, she remembered the tenement in Rochdale, and the night Frances came home with a newspaper and showed her a small notice under the shipping head. *The* Osprey *out of Baltimore, Captain Foxe, accepting cabin passengers to sail May 15, or shortly thereafter, for Bermuda £8.6s. For Halifax and Baltimore £10. Inquire Drake & Sons, Liverpool.*

She had stared at Fran in astonishment. "Ten pounds for cabin passage to America? It must be a mistake."

Maybe it was, Fran said. And maybe it wasn't. She had been talking to people from the mill. They had friends in Liverpool, she said, and they told her that on the ships coming in from the States there was talk of pirates, Southerners who were burning and sinking Yankee merchantmen. There was near panic in the ports; insurance rates were going so high there was scarcely any profit in carrying a cargo. Fewer and fewer merchants were willing to risk their goods, so the Yankees were slashing their rates to the bone to fill their holds, or selling their ships off altogether; and the agents were telling passengers straight out not to sail with them, it was too dangerous.

The women made a pot of tea for their supper and talked about it. Supper was over quickly. The tea they made from used leaves they had begged from the church women the day before; supper was two wrinkled carrots and a piece of dry bread. There was nothing else in the house. Even the mice who used to live in the corner behind the stove had left.

Under the floor, in a cracked vase, were twenty-two pounds and six shillings. There were many things they would endure before they would spend it, but hunger could break anyone's courage. Sylvie knew that one day soon they would take the vase from its hiding and bit by bit the money would go.

And then it would all be for nothing: all the years, all the bitter labour, all the going without—sometimes without coal or medicine or clothing, always without pleasure, without pretties, without even an apple from the market or a ribbon from the fair. All of it would be for nothing—the astonishing gift from a dying comrade, a small dirty bag with coins in it, thrust into Sylvie's hands: *Take it. My brother will only drink it up. Take it, and get away from this place.* The foreman, Demerey, tossing names from the roll like rubbish from a wagon, smiling at her, opening his trousers: *You can stay, wickerface, if you're nice to me.* And Fran, dear God, what had Fran done through the years, what had she sacrificed, salvaged, stolen? To whom had she sold herself, one way or another, for a cracked jar of coins and a dream? To lose it now was a prospect utterly beyond enduring.

Many others would have left years before, taken cheap passage on an emigrant ship, the kind that carried hundreds of the desperate to America in a single run, packed between decks like cattle. On this matter, too, Fran had talked with people, and she had read about it as well. Passengers in steerage lived in a nightmare of crowding and filth. They slept on rotting mattresses on floors soaked with vomit. If it stormed, the hatches were battened down and they were locked in, breathing the same rotten air for days, perhaps for weeks. The rolling of the sea flung their meagre belongings about, smashed their food, drenched their clothing in bilge and excrement. Now and then a tumbling trunk tore open someone's leg or crushed the hand of a child. Typhus took them, cholera, dysentery, and they were slid from a plank into the grey Atlantic, one out of every fifteen or twenty; on the really bad ships, one out of eight.

No, Fran said. Not steerage; never. She was a worldly woman. She had six years of good schooling, acquired before the family sank into total poverty. If she had not taken on the care of an orphaned child, she might well have moved to Liverpool, or even to London, and made a little something of her life. She was smart, and hard as iron when she had to be; she could probably have crossed the Atlantic on a raft and survived it. But on this point she would not yield. They would not travel steerage. Every time it was mentioned, her answer was the same:

"We didn't go through all this so I could bury you at sea."

They would save for something better, she said, something safer; they would get to America alive. But almost as fast as they could save their money, others took it away. Fran had two sisters still living. Both of them had children, and husbands who drank. One time it might be an accident, the next time an illness, and then a woman would come haggard and desperate, with tears in her eyes, *Oh please, Fran, do you have anything, anything at all?* Every time, almost till the end, Fran yielded. And so the years went by, bitter and exhausting years, two of them, seven, twelve, slipping their coins into that wretched piece of pottery. Sylvie never really accepted it. She hated the mill so badly sometimes, she would have risked anything to get away. She even considered taking half the coins and simply running off. She could find her own way to a ship, thank you very much.

But she loved Fran. That held her when she was younger and willing to be reckless. As she grew older, she began to understand that she had become the meaning of Fran's life. Everything else, Fran's hope of maybe leaving Lancashire, her hope of love or children of her own, even the small, simple pleasures of her working life—a glass of ale now and then, a pretty scarf, a Sunday trip across the county—everything had been surrendered for this damaged child, this child to whom she would give a decent life, no matter what the odds. She could not risk losing Sylvie. There was the beginning and the end of it: she simply could not. They would work longer and harder than anyone else, they would save more desperately, and they would book a decent berth on a good ship, and go to Canada, and life would begin again. Certainly it was possible; she even made it seem reasonable sometimes. Then Sylvie's lungs began to go, and getting out of the mill was no longer a dream; it was her only hope of living past her twenties. By that point a transatlantic voyage in the fouled guts of a steamer would have been truly hazardous. It had all turned into a trap, as perilous now to go as to stay. A war began in America, choking off the cotton. Finally the mill closed, and even the work that was killing her disappeared. There was nothing now, only a few shillings of relief money each week and the cold charity of strangers.

So they sat, their elbows on the rough wooden table, and read the newspaper Fran had cadged from one of her friends, mostly news about the Queen and Lord Palmerston and all the big shots in London. But there was a bit about the American war, even about the Southerners who burned American ships. The paper called them privateers, and seemed to think they were bold and daring and much to be admired. Sylvie and Fran read everything, and looked again at the small notice, at the magical numbers, ten pounds each for a cabin to Halifax. Not even a second-class berth, God help us, but a *cabin*.

"Let's go, Fran! Oh, please, let's take it! We'll never have a better chance."

"No, probably we won't. You're not worried about the pirates?"

"Compared to what?" Sylvie said softly. Darkly.

Fran said nothing. She rubbed at a scar on her hand.

"Anyway, it's a big ocean, ain't it?" Sylvie went on. "They can't possibly find every ship."

"We'll have to buy a few things, you know. And there be fare to Liverpool, too. We'll be dead broke when we land."

"We'll be *there*! And your friend Miss Susan said it's easy to get work."

Fran rarely smiled anymore, not real smiles, the kind that used to sparkle in her eyes and brighten up the world. But she smiled now.

"We should get a decent night's sleep. The coach to Liverpool goes by at six."

"You want to do it, then?"

"More than anything in the world. I just wanted to be certain you did."

They did not get a good night's sleep; they hardly slept at all. Having made the decision, they were terrified of everything that might possibly go wrong, terrified especially of arriving in Liverpool and discovering that half the world had been there ahead of them, and all the precious cabins were taken.

As it happened, the *Osprey* sailed from England with three places still open, and from Bermuda with five. The destitute could still not afford her, and the sensible chose to pay more and go elsewhere.

Still, as Sylvie had said, it was a big ocean. All the ships they had passed so far were honest travellers like themselves.

And so it proved again, that last wonderful day. The *Osprey* changed course, giving the strange vessel a wide berth. The latter paid no attention, but swept on her way in grand, majestic indifference. Sylvie watched her for a time, wondering idly where she might be bound. The sea was full of ships—hundreds of them, one of the sailors had told her, just on the North Atlantic alone. Hundreds. And only one of them was the deadly *Alabama*.

"We'll be all right, Fran?" she murmured. "We'll make it, won't we?"

"Last time I checked, love, nobody ever promised us anything. But if I were making wagers, I'd say yes, likely as not we'll make it."

Sylvie smiled. "Likely as not" was fine. "Likely as not" was the best odds they had ever had.

———◆———

Unlike the heroines in the storybooks they read, Frances Harris and Sylvie Bowen did not trouble themselves over what they might wear to Captain Foxe's birthday supper. They owned but a single decent dress apiece. Nonetheless, Fran took her time getting ready, brushing her hair until it shone, wrapping it into an elegant pompadour with nothing more elaborate than a scarf and a pair of street vendor's combs. She had always been a striking woman; not beautiful, perhaps, not like the splendid creatures in the magazines, with the pale, perfect faces of angels, but nonetheless striking. She had a full, sensual body and dark, alluring eyes. Even the mill town had not robbed her of those gifts; it had merely altered them, wearing away every trace of youth and lightness, laying bare a depth of quiet, worldly intensity.

She looked especially splendid tonight, and she glided into the captain's small cabin with astonishing grace. Watching her, Sylvie understood completely why her aunt could always attract men, why she never needed silks or jewels to do it. It was all in the body, in the way a woman moved, the way she listened, the way she laughed. Whatever came of Fran's magnetic power in the end, whether it gained her something she wanted or something she did not want—or, most often, nothing much at all—it was part of her, as easy and as natural as breath.

Captain Foxe greeted them with a warm, almost boyish smile. "Miss Harris, Miss Bowen. How good to see you both. Please come in."

Foxe was by no means the biggest man Sylvie had ever seen, but he seemed easily the most solid; if he ever collided with a brick wall, she thought, the wall would probably take the worse of it. He was gallant, however, bowing a little and kissing their hands, the way men did in books. Master Schofield, the first mate, did the same, but not with the same obvious delight. He was very young, probably younger than Sylvie herself, and he seemed ill at ease.

He's only here because the captain wants him here, to be company for me, and to make it all proper. He'd rather be in the saloon, talking about the war.

For a while Sylvie almost felt the same way herself. Nathaniel Foxe's birthday supper got off to a slow, clumsy start. The cabin was small; the steward could scarcely serve them without elbowing someone's face. The table was tiny, and when a lurch of the ship and a slip of the knife combined to send a piece of chicken flying off Sylvie's plate, it landed splat in the captain's glass of port.

That sort of thing happened in the saloon too; it was a hazard of dining on a rocking boat. But here, at this special birthday supper, it was painfully embarrassing, and she blushed scarlet to her toes. He simply stabbed the offending bit of fowl with his fork, smiled, and said, "Drunken chicken. There's a fine place in Baltimore serves that. I always liked it." And he popped it into his mouth.

The man certainly had style.

Master Schofield did not. He was terribly well bred and terribly shy, a lethal combination from Sylvie's perspective. Shy herself, she had no idea what to say to him, and he seemed to have no idea what to say to her.

"Do you have relatives in Nova Scotia?" he asked at one point.

"No. Aunt Frances has a friend there."

"Oh. That's good." After a moment of silence he asked, "Is that why you're going? To see her friends?"

To see her friends? It took a few seconds to understand. *God bleeding almighty, he thinks we're just . . . travelling.*

"No. We're going to live there. To work."

He looked quickly at his plate. Obviously he came from the sort whose women never had to work; the sort who looked on it, not as sinful perhaps, but as a sign of general, collective decay: *If your men were any damn good, you wouldn't have to.*

"What trade is your father in?" he asked.

"My father is dead," she said. She didn't add "Hanged," although for the briefest moment she considered it, simply to put the nail in the coffin. "My mother too."

"I'm very sorry," he said.

She could see that he meant it. He was not cruel, and he probably was not stupid. If he had met her in a tavern, God knows he might have known how to talk to her. But here, at his captain's courting party, he was completely at a loss. After a time, by gradual and probably mutual agreement, they gave up trying to converse, and chose instead to enjoy the splendid food and listen to Nathaniel Foxe, who could talk enough for four people all by himself.

He had seen most of the world, it seemed, and many kinds of men. He had opinions about nearly everything, not least the American war. In the saloon, when he was asked, he had made it quite clear that, slave state or not, Maryland had thousands of committed Unionists, and he was one of them. But he wanted to maintain courtesy and amity among the passengers, so he rarely said more.

Here, in the privacy of his cabin, among people he ranked as friends, he was considerably more blunt. Rebellion was treason, sea raiding was piracy, and the men responsible—the leaders— deserved to be hanged.

"And would you hang them?" Fran asked him. "Yourself, personally?"

He did not say anything for a time. He was, Sylvie thought, somewhat annoyed that she had asked so probing a question, and also somewhat pleased.

"You mean, if it was my decision, would I put my signature on the paper? No, probably not. More likely I'd dump them off on a rock-face island with a box of matches and herd of goats, and tell them: 'Here. You all want to be little princelings? Be my guest.'"

Dinner was well eaten and the second bottle of port was almost gone before the talk grew more personal, before he told them how he had run away from home at the age of twelve, from a factory tenement and a father who had beaten him once too often, and how he had sneaked aboard a brigantine bound for India.

"We were two days at sea before they discovered me. The captain called me a worthless little rat. He would've liked nothing better than to throw me overboard and let me swim back to Baltimore. But he was afraid it might bring him bad luck. So I could stay, he said, but I'd darn well earn my keep. I did a grown man's work on that ship, and the scoundrel paid me nothing but my food."

Thus he learned about sailing the hard way, he told them, through storm and hunger and curses and blows. He learned well nonetheless, changed ships, changed masters, but never changed his dream.

"A ship of my own—that's what I wanted. One of those beautiful square-riggers I used to watch when I was a boy. God, how I loved them! And I don't know how many times I swore it, swore it way deep down, like an oath on the Bible, that I'd have myself one of those ships before I was fifty."

"And you did," Frances said, smiling.

"With five years to spare."

He was showing off a bit, of course he was, trying to make a grand impression on a woman who attracted him. But as she listened, Sylvie thought perhaps he was sending a different kind of message as well. *I was nobody once, too. I owned nothing; I was kicked about and taken advantage of—and, yes, I got out, I have a place in the world, I even have this ship, but I remember how it was. So it doesn't matter if you come from a mill town, Frances Harris . . . or maybe it does matter. Maybe it matters terribly, because it means we are alike, and there are things I can tell you I can never tell my peers, because they wouldn't understand. They can't even* imagine *half the things that I remember . . .*

Eventually the supper ended. It was night by then, a glorious summer night, with the moon rising almost full. Not surprisingly, Captain Foxe invited Fran to walk with him on the deck.

"Would you care for a bit of a stroll as well, Miss Sylvie?" Master Schofield asked.

For the smallest moment she met his gaze, knowing well what she would see there: the careful yet uneasy courtesy of a man trying to be kind, doing what he knew was expected of him.

"Thank you, Mr. Schofield, but I'm quite tired."

He saw her to the cabin she shared with her aunt, where he bid her a gracious good night, lingering a little—not long, but enough to make her wonder if she might have misjudged him. Perhaps he would have liked to stroll with her. Perhaps on a ship, where women were few, and where young, unmarried women were fewer still, perhaps men were easier to please.

Perhaps.

Ten years ago she would have walked with him. She would have walked with anyone, anyone who was not abusive or howling drunk or escaped from a madhouse, rather than be alone. Ten years ago she still believed there was someone who might love her. In theory she still believed it. She always smiled and was heartened when Frances said, "For God's sake, Sylvie, you have the body of a nymph. You've hair most women would kill for. Forget the scar. You're pretty, love. Damn it all, you're *pretty!*"

They were words to grow strong with in the full light of day, words to hold and carry out into the street, proud-eyed and smiling. But when the night came down, they were only empty words.

She thought of Frances, arm in arm in the moonlight with Nathaniel Foxe. Frances was forty-three. She had crow's feet around her eyes, and bits of grey in her hair, and yet the captain was falling in love with her.

Sylvie understood then, quite suddenly, why she could not have borne to go walking with Master Schofield. She would have cried every time she passed them on the deck. Not out of envy, but out of the simple recognition of her loss. No man had ever looked at her in such a fashion, treasured her company so much, tucked her arm against his side with such protective tenderness. And the odds were high that no man ever would.

She dug Fran's mirror from their trunk. She turned her face into the light, drew her loose-hanging hair back behind her ears, and regarded herself. Sometimes she could do it with absolute detachment, as if she were looking at a picture in a book. Sometimes she could not bear to do it at all.

From just above her left eyebrow a tangle of scars spread down her face, reaching almost to the centre of her cheek; the longest and cruellest of them twisted to the line of her jaw. The tropic sun, darkening her face a little every day, had made the marks a small bit less distinct. Here, in the cabin, the lamplight softened their awfulness.

Yet here they were nonetheless. She would carry them forever. Even in old age, when she grew tired and forgetful, when even the worst of her memories might fade if they were left alone, the marks would still be here, reminding her.

You can run, Sylvie Bowen, from everything but this . . .

<hr />

It was very late when Frances returned to the cabin—so late that Sylvie wondered, quietly, if they had retired to the captain's cabin first. Fran looked extraordinarily happy.

"Well," Sylvie said, "I take it you enjoyed yourself?"

"I did." Frances sat on her bed and took her shoes off. "He asked if he might call on me, when we're settled in Halifax."

"And you said yes, then, did you?"

"Oh, certainly. But I warned him that a woman on her own for the whole of her life were likely to be set in her ways. And he said a man who'd been at sea since he were twelve would be much the same. If I weren't scared of it in him, he said, he weren't scared of it in me."

"I don't think there's much that man be scared of."

"No." Bit by bit, Frances began to undress. "He's such an interesting man. A good man, I think—certainly he's been good to us. But so *interesting*. I think I could sit for the next ten years just listening to him talk about his travels."

"Well, with a bit of luck you will."

"Luck?" Without a flicker of warning, a shadow passed across Fran's face. "It be a very long time now, Sylvie, since I believed in luck."

CHAPTER 4

—◆◆◆—

The Raiders

Whenever we heard a Yankee howl go up over a burned ship, we
knew there were fewer dollars left with which to hire the *canaille*
of Europe to throttle liberty on the American continent.
—*Captain Raphael Semmes, Confederate Navy*

SYLVIE WOKE to storm the next morning, to bits of pale dawn
light and the realization that the cabin was tipped like a hillside
and she had just been tumbled against the wall. Grey water came
at her in waves, smashing into the tiny window. She ducked her
head, terrified. For a small moment she believed they were sinking and about to die. But the water fell away; she saw light again,
and steadied herself. It was a bit of high wind, that was all. Last
night at supper, Captain Foxe had promised as much. He could tell
by the sky, he said.

They dressed and groped their way to the saloon. The steward
was nowhere to be seen, but four other passengers were there: the
Draytons and the two Americans, Canfrey and Paige. No lamps
had been lit, but the windows were generous here, and the grey
dawn was turning into day. She could see the tension in Canfrey's

smile as he rose to greet them, the dark anger in Mr. Drayton's eyes.

"All hands are on deck except the cook," Canfrey told them. "We're on our own down here."

"Is the storm that bad, then?" Fran asked.

Canfrey tried to answer, but Drayton did not give him a chance. "Bad?" he cried bitterly. "It's a bloody howling gale out there and that lunatic is flying every piece of canvas we've got! Everything! Even the topgallants! He's going to kill us all!"

"He's an experienced seaman," Canfrey flung back. "He knows what he's doing."

"No, he doesn't. He hates the Southerners so bad he can't think straight!"

"Southerners?" Fran said very softly.

"We're being chased." Canfrey did not quite meet her eyes as he spoke. "The lookouts spotted her at first light, on our port bow, no more'n a few miles off. Just miserable bad luck, that she got so close in the dark. By then the wind was high. He told the men to raise sail, we were running for our lives. He sent me below, and they battened down the hatches." Canfrey was still on his feet, holding on to the table with one hand. "I expect it will be a long day."

They were locked below for hours. Later, one of the younger officers told them what it had been like on the deck—every hand on the ropes, even the poor steward, and the ship listing till the lower sails were trailing in the water. There wasn't a soul could hear himself think, he said, with the waves crashing over the deck, high enough to drown a man where he stood, and the wind howling like a banshee, and every beam and spar crying out from the strain. Some feared they would lose their mainmast, or go over, but the *Osprey* was built to take the worst of weather; she could take all of this and more. Captain Foxe meant to run, and if the Rebels meant to catch him, they'd have to learn to fly.

So they tacked, he said, they tacked like very devils, with the captain tied to the foremast, roaring out his commands. And yes, he was good, and they all knew it, but that day he was something more than good, he was one of those sea gods they painted in books. He knew the ship as though it were part of him; he knew the wind as though he had called it up himself. Sometimes, when it got bad enough, he would reef the sails a bit. Then he would raise them again in a breath, bleeding the gale for all it could give him of its power. And the *Osprey* flew.

Hour after grey morning hour she flew, and every time they looked behind them, the pirate ship was a little bit farther away.

———◆———

In the saloon, the cook brought the passengers sandwiches filled with slabs of cold meat, sweet cakes, and all the hot coffee they could drink. The second mate made a brief, drenched appearance, bringing them Captain Foxe's reassurances—and, for what they were worth, his own: "Just a bit of rough weather, nothing whatever to worry about, sailed through a score of these myself, I have . . ."

Whether this comforted Fran, Sylvie could not judge. It certainly did not comfort Mr. Drayton. He simply grew angrier than ever at Captain Foxe.

"If we survive this," he promised, "I will see him in the courts, by God! I'll have him pilloried for risking our lives like this!"

"Oh, shut up," Sylvie said.

The effect was magical, like dropping a piece of ice into boiling water. Everything went quiet. Everyone stared at her. She was young and unassuming; she never said much. For her to speak out now, in this blunt fashion, was decidedly shocking.

"You are impudent, miss," Mrs. Drayton snapped.

Sylvie glanced about the room. The tables and benches, bolted to the floor, were still in their places, but everything movable was scattered and sliding about the saloon. Out there . . . ? How much ocean was out there, she wondered, cold and deadly and uncaring? How many ships had it snapped like a matchstick already? And who was in the ship that chased them, and what did they mean to do?

In the face of such questions, what was a little bit of impudence?

"Why did you book your passage on the *Osprey*, Mrs. Drayton?" she asked. "Mr. Drayton?"

"That most certainly is none of your concern!" Mr. Drayton said coldly.

"Well, it were your concern why *we* did," she replied. "Any fool can see you got heaps of money, and you don't like the Yankees. If you took yourself a good English ship, you wouldn't have to worry about no bleeding lunatics, now, would you? Or did you just help yourself to a bargain, the same as us factory trash?"

There was no telling what Mr. Drayton might have said next, but the ship lurched suddenly to port and he lost his balance. He fell like a great tottering piece of furniture, landing with his face on a silver plate. Mr. Canfrey helped him to his feet, which only seemed to make him angrier. There was nothing for it then but to gather up his wife and what little remained of his dignity and retire to his cabin.

Sylvie settled on the floor and wrapped her arms around her knees. "Come and sit, Fran," she said lightly. "The floor be the only safe place around."

She reached, drawing Fran close beside her. Her aunt was rigid, and Sylvie could guess why. *We didn't go through all of this so I could bury you at sea.*

"We'll be fine, Fran," she said. "We'll outrun the villains and sail into Halifax tomorrow with all flags flying."

"You're not scared of much, Miss Sylvie, are you?" Mr. Canfrey observed.

Not scared of much? He was an innocent sod, that one. It would take her an hour to tell him all the things she was scared of. Dying in Rochdale, for starters. Looking down a long grey tunnel and seeing a dirt mound at the end of it, coughing her life out with winter coming on, the damp going into her bones and hardly any coal in the house, hardly any food. She would be scared of that forever, even when Rochdale was only a memory. She would be scared of drunken quarrels too, of men with raised fists, or broken glass in their hands—oh, yes, broken glass most of all. There was a world of things to be scared of, a thousand hard ways to die, or to live so broken there was no more point in living at all. Going down in a ship like the *Osprey*, in a daring flight from pirates— well, if you had to go, it was a better way than most.

⟡

All day the Rebel raider chased them, and bit by bit the storm began to lessen. Sylvie grew more hopeful from the change, so innocent was she of seafaring and war. "Look," she said to no one in particular, "the storm be lifting, I think."

"Yes," Mr. Canfrey said. "We're losing the wind."

His choice of words undid all her hope in a breath. They were *losing* the wind . . .

They still might make it, the American went on. They could escape in the dark, if they could stay out of the raider's reach until then.

But it was near to summer solstice; there still were hours of daylight left.

The passengers were allowed back on deck late in the afternoon, and there they could see the peril for themselves. It was a race now, sail against steam, skill against mechanical power, fortune against time. With a wind so small it barely ruffled Sylvie's hair, the *Osprey* was still running—spent as a dying bird, but still running. The strange ship came on, riding low in the water and painted a dark, deceptive grey. She needed no wind. Smoke poured from her funnel, billowing over the few sails she still carried, rolling like black clouds across the water. From his high post on the *Osprey* a lookout kept scanning the sea, hoping perhaps to spot a Yankee warship or even the signs of a rising storm.

Neither came. The horizons lay empty except for their pursuer. The frail wind fell away to almost nothing. The sun was low when Captain Foxe summoned everyone on deck and spoke to them.

He was very calm, but his eyes were like those of a man condemned to die, and sometimes, under his quiet words, Sylvie heard a knife edge of anger in his voice, all the more bitter for being so well contained.

"Ladies," he said, "gentlemen, men of the *Osprey*, who have served me so well, some of you for many years . . . unless a miracle takes place in the next half hour, we will be taken. The Rebels will help themselves to everything on this vessel they can use, and then they will burn it. We will be brought aboard their own ship as prisoners.

"To the best of my knowledge, all of these raiders are commanded by officers of the Confederate navy. That means we will be treated as civilians according to the normal usages of war. None of you, especially the foreign nationals among you, and most especially the ladies—none of you should have anything to fear. We may be with them longer than we like, but we won't be killed or badly mistreated, and eventually they'll drop us off at a neutral port, or onto a neutral ship, as it suits them.

"One thing I want to make very clear. These are fighting men, and while their officers may be gentlemen, they are all dangerous, and some may be little more than bandits. Which means, my friends, that once we strike our colours, we are surrendered, and we act accordingly, however much it hurts.

"To my crew, I want to say thank you for your hard work and faithful service. To my passengers, I can only say how sorry I am that I can't take you safely into harbour as I promised. Nothing will change when we leave this ship. I won't consider my responsibilities ended until every one of you is home. And every member of this crew will be paid in full.

"That is all. Good luck, and may God protect us all."

After so many hours of waiting, it ended with a suddenness that astonished her. She saw a small puff of smoke on the *Alabama's* deck, and had a brief second to wonder about it before a sound like an explosion shattered the afternoon calm. Someone shouted, "Oh, my God! Oh, my God!" but she still did not understand until the shell hit, screaming into the sea right alongside. Sheets of water lashed across the deck, drenching them. She spun about to look for Fran, and saw only chaos: Mr. Drayton was on his knees and Mrs. Drayton stood with her arms in the air, screaming as though she had been knifed. The chickens were plunging and squawking and the ship's cat was a small streak of black and grey, bounding for the hatch.

"Sylvie! Are you all right?" Fran appeared suddenly beside her, wiping tangles of wet hair from her eyes. "The bloody bastards are shooting at us!"

"Well, they missed," Sylvie said.

"No, they didn't."

She turned sharply at Canfrey's words.

"It was a warning shot, Miss Bowen," he went on. "I reckon it landed just about where they wanted."

There was a rush of activity near the quarterdeck, followed by a calm so icy she could hear the captain's voice even where she stood.

"Mr. Schofield, run up the colours and heave to."

"What's he doing?" Sylvie whispered.

"Surrendering. Once they're in firing range, we have no choice."

So easy it was, after all. A steam engine and a few guns, and all the splendour of the *Osprey* was undone. The magnificent creature, who could fly like the wind when the wind was true, folded her splendid sails like broken wings and turned against the last of the dying breeze to wait for her enemy.

The enemy came on fast now, her black funnel puffing, her sharp prow slicing water like the fin of a shark. Even the passengers, without the benefit of spyglasses, could count the eight heavy cannon mounted on her sides, and see the men who clustered on her deck in small, eager packs.

The deck grew very still. Even Mr. Drayton stood voiceless, staring. They had no weapons and no way to run. They could only hope the captain's promise would prove true: *We will be treated as civilians according to the normal usages of war . . .*

——✦——

Beyond Sylvie's cabin window there was only darkness now; within, only the steady churning of the mail packet's engines to tell her they were moving. It was a fine little ship, this mail packet, tireless and fast. It was an honest ship, too. It should not have made her think of the *Alabama*, and yet it did, simply for the sound of its engines, for its unrelenting speed.

It be a very long time now since I believed in luck . . .

Fran's words, she thought, would stay with her forever. They would sit quietly in all the corners of her life, as they sat now in the shadows of her cabin, the cabin Captain Foxe had booked for her when she left Nassau, and paid for with his own money. Some people would call it luck, no doubt, this fine lodging on a fine, fast vessel. Luck also, the envelope he pressed into her hand before he said goodbye, in which, when she opened it, she found twenty-five pounds. She was grateful. Life was too hard for her ever to be ungrateful. But it was not luck. It was simply something that happened, like she and Fran finding the *Osprey*, and the *Alabama* finding them.

Everything the captain told them had proved to be correct; they were treated as civilians according to the normal usages of war. Sylvie had feared all sorts of violence, not least a battle on the high seas, the *Alabama* going down and all her captives with her. She had never feared Nassau; she all but wept with thankfulness when they docked. She had not thought to fear the yellow fever, or the long line of quarantine cabins she could only stare at through a fence, or the windswept hillside where they took the dead . . .

It was impossible to sleep. More than anything, just now, she wished she had something of Fran's—anything, a scarf, a comb, or best of all the little book of Mrs. Browning's sonnets Sylvie bought for her years before. It was the one fine gift she had ever been able to buy, and she could afford it only because the spine of the book was wrecked and the pages stained with wine. The damage mattered to neither of them. Only the words mattered, and the words were astonishing, divine. Many a night in Rochdale they would sit and read together, awed by the beauty of the poetry, awed also by the poet's story. Elizabeth Barrett had been almost as old as Fran when she encountered Robert Browning. She had not been poor, admittedly, but she had been frail, living a constrained and lonely life with very little future. Love, for her, changed everything.

For Fran it changed half a dozen days.

Steps approached Sylvie's door, passed by quietly, faded into silence. Of course they would pass by: it was the middle of the night. Nonetheless they reminded her that she knew no one on this vessel, and no one in Halifax; she was altogether alone in the world. She bit her lip, bending to rest her chin on her knees. She could have gone with Captain Foxe to Baltimore. He had offered to take her, to introduce her to friends who might help her find a place. She could even have stayed in Nassau—God knew there was work enough. Only they had shared a dream, she and Fran. They had believed in it so desperately, and worked for it so long. Nothing seemed right except to go on. Tomorrow she would step out onto the pier at Halifax, find Miss Susan's inn, and begin her life again.

That was all she could do. Just go on.

BOOK THREE

Montreal, October 1863

CHAPTER 5

———◆———

Little Richmond

Some extremely nice Southern families had taken refuge in
Montreal, and added much to its social amusements.
—*Field Marshal Viscount Wolseley, British Army*

THEY CALLED THE PLACE Little Richmond, and Erryn Shaw
could certainly understand why. St. Lawrence Hall took up most
of a city block on St. James Street, and day after day its parlours
and smoking rooms were filled with the mellow, drawling voices
of American Southerners. Its dinner menu offered such marvels as
lobster crepes, gumbo filé, and Georgia-style country ham. Its
beautiful mahogany-panelled barroom was the only watering
hole in the entire length and breadth of British North America
where a man could buy himself a mint julep.

Why a man would ever *want* to buy a mint julep, well, that was
an altogether different question. To drink bourbon mixed with
stomach herbs and sugar, when the world was full of delicate
wines, divine Madeira, and even better port? *Sweet God in heaven,*
Erryn reflected silently, *only in America.*

He smiled across the table at his companion, Jackson Follett. Follett was a slender, very personable man in his thirties, a wealthy planter and former member of the South Carolina State Assembly. He was also, since early in the year, the Confederacy's senior operative in Montreal.

"Your health, Jack," Erryn said.

"And yours." Follett raised his glass, returning the salute, then paused with the glass held close to his face, savouring the bouquet of fresh crushed mint. "They *do* do it well here," he sighed.

"Almost as well as the best Charleston butler, I suppose," Erryn replied with a smile.

"Almost."

It was three in the afternoon, but the bar of St. Lawrence Hall was full, as most always. There were, by Erryn's estimate, at least two thousand Southerners in the city of Montreal—political exiles, refugees, escaped prisoners, and agents of the Confederate government. They found lodgings where they could—among sympathetic citizens, in boarding houses, in hotels. The poor and the frugal stayed at the scruffy Donegana, down on Notre-Dame; those who could afford it stayed here. Jackson Follett had a fine, balconied room on the first floor.

"Do you remember the last time you came?" Follett murmured. "It was like a wake."

"Christ, yes," Erryn said. "Worse than a wake." August, it had been; early August, and the expatriate community was reeling with bewildered shock. For several months the war had gone impressively in favour of the Confederates. In December they defeated the Union's eastern army at Fredericksburg; in the spring they all but destroyed it at Chancellorsville. Even in the States, Erryn suspected, a majority of Southerners believed the war was almost won. In Canada, they were sure of it. Buffered by distance, fed a steady diet of optimistic exaggerations by pro-Southern newspapers, distrustful of anything pro-Yankee, even a fact, they allowed themselves to be confident to the point of making plans for going home.

Then the news came, stark headlines they could scarcely bring themselves to believe. Vicksburg, their strategic fortress on the Mississippi, had surrendered. The great continental river was gone up, and the whole Confederacy was cut in two. Then, before all of this could be properly absorbed, came the slow-breaking story out of Pennsylvania: General Lee's bold invasion running into trouble, a costly battle outside a small country town, a withdrawal. Not a defeat, dear God, no; even as they sat and stared at their comrades, or at their knotted hands, they would not call it a defeat. Nonetheless, the invasion had failed. They were not going home anytime soon.

These were the military losses, the ones the whole world knew about, and talked about. But Confederate policy had non-military objectives as well: to garner foreign support, especially from England and her North American colonies, and to foster disaffection within the Northern states. To many of the exiles, this part of the war was almost as important as the battlefield. Every time Erryn came west, he was told about the growing numbers of Copperheads in the Northern states: angry men who met by night with false names and deadly oaths of secrecy, preparing for a great uprising against Lincoln and the Black Republicans. He was told of meetings held all across the region, of arms purchased, of numbers reaching thousands, tens of thousands, finally hundreds of thousands. Southerners poured into Canada, especially in the West, hoping to make contact with these future rebels. They spoke boldly of opening a second front against the Yankees, right in their own backyard.

At first, Erryn took it all very seriously, passing on to his superiors every scrap of information he could find about this extraordinary conspiracy, and spending many a troubled hour wondering what impact it would have on the British colonies. But as the months came and passed, and nothing seemed to happen—or even to change very much, except for those fascinating numbers— he began to wonder how much of it was actually conspiracy and how much of it was chimera. He was an outsider, granted, but just the same it was damned hard to see anything in Wisconsin that looked like the second American Revolution.

Then, on July 9, 1863, Confederate general John Hunt Morgan led a brigade of tough, battle-hardened cavalry into Indiana, on a raid that was to sweep through the entire Northwest, gathering the disaffected to its banners as it went. In Canada, the spirits of the Southerners soared again. Now, finally, all the work and struggle would bear fruit. Young men would thunder through the night like Paul Revere, calling their countrymen to arms. Long-hidden weapons would be snatched from cellars and haylofts, and the thousands who had bided their time would storm the Yankee garrisons, the supply depots, the jails. They would climb on their lean country horses and race to Morgan's side. And then the fall of Vicksburg would not matter. Gettysburg would not matter either, even if it had been a defeat. With enemies all around it, Lincoln's government could not hope to stand.

So ran the talk in the crowded rooms of exiles, in the bars where they gathered, in the parlours of their wealthy Canadian friends. Back in Halifax, big James Orton had thrown a comradely arm around Erryn's shoulders—even he had to reach up to do it— and said, "Och, and won't it be a great shock for the buggers to see Rebels coming at 'em from the North?"

It would have been a great shock, no doubt, had it ever come to be. But there was no rising in the North. No legions flocked to Morgan's banners, only the barest handfuls. Such men as thundered through the night with messages were mostly racing to the army posts for help, or calling out the militias. As for the Northern Copperheads, they seemed to think there was a difference between opposing their government and overthrowing it by force. And most everyone, Copperhead or not, seemed to think John Morgan's men were horse thieves; raiders who strayed from their comrades in search of food or fresh mounts rarely came back. Within a week, the raid was plainly in trouble; within three, it was over. The entire brigade was scattered, captured, or dead, and Morgan himself was in an Ohio penitentiary.

Such was the state of affairs in August, the last time Erryn sat in the bar of St. Lawrence Hall. Morgan's defeat and capture had been confirmed for more than a week, long enough for even the most optimistic Southerners to have no choice except to believe it. Terrible as the losses at Vicksburg and Gettysburg had been, for many in the colonies the failure of the Northwest rising was even harder to bear. That had been *their* fight. They had believed in it; they had worked and schemed and gone hungry for it, utterly convinced it would change the course of the war.

And then it had simply faded into smoke.

Now it was October, and everything was promising again. St. Lawrence Hall sparkled with triumph and excitement. At a table near their own, a young soldier was rising to his feet. He was thin and ragged, no doubt one of the many escaped Confederate prisoners in the city.

"Gentlemen!" he shouted. "A toast!" He raised his own glass, somewhat unsteadily. "To General Braxton Bragg!"

Scores around him rose as one, and drank to the victor of Chickamauga.

"A damned necessary victory, that one," Follett said, sitting down again. "Some of our friends were getting a tad skittish, after what happened in July. Even Morrison, you know. Sat me down one night and asked me if the Confederacy might possibly be coming apart at the seams. Not saying it, you understand, just asking."

"I trust you reminded him that July was the first time the Yankees won anything decisive since the war began?"

"I did," Follett said. "And he agreed with me, of course. Said we couldn't expect it to be all fair sailing. But still, he said, it gave a man a bad scare. And I asked him, if it scared him, being a Canadian, how the devil did he think we felt?"

You felt somewhat the way I feel now, I suppose. In July, I was the damn fool who thought it was almost over. Now it looks as if it could go

on for years. I might be chasing your bloody Rebels around the colonies
until my teeth start falling out.

Or until you kill me . . .

This was not a good subject for meditation. Erryn leaned back
in his chair and allowed himself to be drawn into a discussion of
the Confederacy's military prospects. At the moment, one of the
Union's western armies was surrounded in Chattanooga. A
smaller one was stranded at Nashville, and rumoured to be running out of food. The army in the east, the one that clawed up
General Lee at Gettysburg, had been inactive now for more than
three months. It was clawed up just as bad, Follett said, or else its
new general was yet another military mouse; the Union seemed
to have no end of them. Either way, the prospects looked good for
turning back the disasters of the summer.

"All the more need, then, for our work here to prosper." He
leaned forward earnestly. "Morrison's having a gathering at his
house on Saturday. A celebration, of course, now that we have
such promising things to celebrate, but also a chance to build support. I trust you'll come?"

"I would be honoured."

"Good. There's some people coming that I want you to meet,
one in particular, a man named Janes. Maury Janes. A very bold
fellow, from what I've seen. He'll be heading to Halifax later if his
plans come together. He'd like nothing better than to share a glass
of wine with you."

"Not a mint julep?"

"No. I understand he hates them."

"Ah. A man after my own heart."

"There's one other thing, Erryn. I hesitate to ask—you've done
so much for us already. But is it possible I might impose on you
one more time, for a small favour?"

Erryn nodded. "Yes, of course," he said, "but there is one condition." He paused just long enough to make Follett look uneasy.
"I'm not searching for any more kidnap victims."

Follett's laugh was relieved and slightly embarrassed, as well it should have been. Early in the war, almost a year ago, he had persuaded Erryn to find a Georgian who had disembarked at the railroad depot in Montreal and promptly disappeared. According to the lad's companion, the Reverend Andrew Boyle, the young man was part of a vital secret mission, and had undoubtedly fallen into the hands of Yankee agents. Erryn had his doubts about the Yankee agents—desertion seemed a likelier explanation—but he wanted very much to discover what this vital secret mission might prove to be. Boyle, the leader, was a man of mature years, with excellent credentials from Richmond. He would say nothing whatever about his plans, only that he must absolutely have his comrade back. So Erryn went on the hunt.

Seventeen days and many good English pounds later, with a case of grippe mean enough to die of and an almost broken wrist, he found the missing agent on a country farm, cheerfully picking apples, shovelling manure, and courting the farmer's pretty daughter. As for the mission, according to the Georgian, the Reverend Boyle meant to go secretly about the wilds of Canada—most secretly, lest the Yankees got wind of it—and persuade all the runaway Negroes to come home. Africans as they were, used to the heat, and innocents as they were, barely able to survive as free men in the North—how they must be suffering here, poor creatures, in a world of snow and rocks, with no white men looking after them, and nothing to live on but pine scrub and beaver meat. All it would take would be a word or two of encouragement, and someone to pay their passage, and they would follow him home like boys behind a piper.

Erryn Shaw sat in the farmer's snug little house, wrapped in a blanket, drinking all the hot apple juice spiked with lemon he could force down his throat, and let the young man tell his tale. He was, as far as Erryn could judge, not a day past seventeen.

"Y'all got to understand, see, when I was at home, I thought it was a good enough idea. We never had but one slave ourselves, and we never whopped him or anything, and I figured he'd rather be with us than off in the wilderness somewheres. So I went along with the Reverend, to help him out, and to see a bit of the world. He wanted me to stay with him, once we got to Canada. But I'd been talking to Miss Lucy on the train, and she told me there was some runaways living right nearby, and I was awful fond of her, so's I figured I could just start here instead. But them niggers got themselves little farms—" Here Miss Lucy's eyes turned on him, troubled. "Negroes, I mean—the both of them got farms. They ain't well off, but they's eating okay, and when I asked one of 'em how they got through the winters up here, he just looked at me bold as brass and says, 'Same as you get through the summers down in Georgia, I reckon.' And I started wondering if maybe the Reverend got it a bit wrong. Someone wanting to be rescued cain't afford to be so mouthy. So I asked him right out, would he ever think of coming home, was we to pay his way and such? And he went and got me a drink of whiskey, and says, 'Here, you rest easy for a bit, young feller. Someone's whopped you good on the haid.'"

In a way, Erryn thought, it was fortunate he was so sick and miserable. Had he been healthy, his hard-earned victory would have had him doubled over in his chair.

He smiled faintly now, remembering. He had come west twice before, following through on matters that began at the coast, and each time he had gone home muttering to himself: *Bunch of bleeding nitwits . . . Confederate intelligence is a contradiction in terms . . . we don't need spies here, all we need to do is stay conscious . . .* And each time he had pulled himself up short. There were some bleeding nitwits in the expatriate community, certainly. There were others who were simply young and inexperienced, with way too much time on their hands. Both groups were given to sitting up nights, fashioning hare-brained master plans for winning the war. And some concerned Canadians, alas, found themselves sitting up as well, worrying themselves silly, and ultimately discovering they had used a broadside of cannon to exterminate a beetle.

All of this was true. But it was also true that the Confederates had good men here—Jackson Follett was one of them—and that even a foolish plot, left unwatched, could turn deadly, could succeed even as it failed, simply by creating chaos.

No, he reminded himself, it would not do at all to get cocky, to underestimate his enemies. There was, after all, a young man in a family vault in London, a young man of considerable ability and excellent bloodlines, who had once made the understandable but decidedly foolish mistake of underestimating *him*.

"No kidnap victims this time," Follett said amiably. "I guarantee it. And by the way, just so you know, Richmond has severed its connections with the Reverend Boyle. He has no more claim on our funds or on our people."

What a pity. They clinked glasses, smiled.

"Well then," Erryn said, "how can I be of service?"

It rained that night, ferociously. Erryn did not mind the rain; a chap could hardly go on living in Halifax if he minded rain. Besides, a good downpour shielded a man's movements, and helped to keep the idle and the curious indoors. He dressed himself with an actor's care: black wig, lumberjack's boots, a great heavy jacket and baggy working man's trousers that disguised his height a trifle by making him bulky; over all of it, an old shapeless slicker. Eyebrows darkened with makeup, lean cheeks puffed out with cotton, a peculiar twist to his mouth . . . Yes, he observed to his mirror—perhaps for the thousandth time—a life in the theatre was very useful to a spy, quite apart from anything he might have learned about acting.

His rendezvous point was a quiet house near the Champ-de-Mars. Whoever owned it, or lived in it by day, it was always empty when he came there, except for one or two men. Both were there tonight, dressed in dark, nondescript clothing and wearing a familiar air of boredom and exhaustion. One was Jonathan Bryce, a detective from the Montreal constabulary; the other a civilian who used but a single name, Latour. Erryn himself was known to them as James Todd.

They began with little ceremony, a brief handshake and a greeting, and then on to the matters at hand.

"What have you got for us, Todd?" Bryce asked.

"Follett wants me to buy ten good Colt pistols, sixty rounds of ammunition for each, and ten good knives—the sort that might have the authority of a cutlass, as he put it."

"How interesting," Latour murmured. "Did he say what he wanted them for?"

"No. But I come from a long line of naval officers. When anyone mentions a cutlass, I think of sailors boarding an enemy ship."

"Ah, yes," Bryce said. "And twenty-two sailors in particular, I suppose?"

Bryce's tone was ever so slightly patronizing. It annoyed Erryn a little, but he gave no sign. "It did cross my mind, Jon."

Bryce wiped his forehead, where rainwater still trickled from his hair. He was forty or thereabouts, a quiet, experienced policeman, the man in charge of intelligence operations in Montreal insofar as anyone seemed to be in charge at all. Spying on the Confederates was a slapdash affair everywhere, even in Halifax, and this man did not have Matt Calverley's talent for organizing the work or reading the evidence. Still less did he have Matt's killer instinct.

It was Matt who had smelled trouble when the blockade-runner *Robert E. Lee* steamed into Halifax harbour with twenty-two Confederate naval officers and men, among them the already well-known and well-respected Captain John Wilkinson. They were all supposedly bound for England, perhaps to take charge of a newly purchased vessel. Matt was having none of it; the scuttlebutt, he said, was way too loud. Moreover, the *Lee*'s valuable cargo had been sold by Alexander MacNab, who was the Confederacy's chief supply agent in Halifax, and who was, in Matt's opinion, a conspirator of the first order. Matt put every informer he had onto watching the waterfront, the hotels, the boarding houses, and the stagecoach depot. He had good descriptions of several of the men, and Erryn had personally encountered one. Also, as with most Southerners, their accents were difficult to hide.

As far as anyone could discover, none of the twenty-two Rebels boarded an outgoing ship. Indeed, none of them were spotted on the waterfront again. Two were discovered waiting for the stage-coach to Windsor—almost certainly the first leg of an overland journey west. As for the others, in a matter of days it became impossible for any of Matt's men to find a trace of them. Even among the Grey Tories it was quietly and casually assumed that the men had sailed.

All of this Erryn had explained in detail to Bryce and Latour when he first arrived in Montreal, along with Matt's conviction that the sailors had come west to do some mischief on the Lakes. The Montrealers had listened politely, and Latour had promised to watch for any sign of Wilkinson's men. But now, sitting in the house in the Champ-de-Mars, Erryn wondered if their efforts would all prove too little and too late, if the Rebels would slip away and do whatever harm they intended, long before the Canadians learned enough to stop them.

He shifted restlessly in his chair. His great sodden boots were by the door, but every time he moved, more water slithered down his trouser legs.

"Do either of you have anything for me?" he asked.

"Yes, actually," Latour replied. "It seems you're not the only chap who's been sent out shopping. Do you know Daniel Carroll?"

"Only by reputation." Second-generation Irish. Importer/exporter. Rich. Pro-Confederate. Very low-key, however; not the sort to sit in the bar of St Lawrence Hall drinking toasts to Dixie.

"About eight days back," Latour went on, "Carroll paid a long visit to George Kane's house, accompanied by Jackson Follett. On

Monday he placed an order at Frères Desmarais for fifty dumbbells. Of course"—this with a quick, almost apologetic glance at
Jonathan Bryce—"Carroll's a wholesale merchant, with a half-
dozen country stores up the Ottawa Valley buying stock from him,
so . . ." He shrugged. "So it probably doesn't mean very much."

Erryn thought it might mean quite a lot. Kane was the former
police marshal of Baltimore. He had spent several months in a
Federal jail for suspected disloyalty. Immediately on his release, he
bolted for Richmond, and soon afterwards turned up in Canada.
He was now the second most important Confederate agent in
Montreal. According to Latour, there were four men staying at his
house, four quiet young men who almost never went outside. It
was no great stretch to wonder if Daniel Carroll's visit—and his
purchase—was in some way linked to them.

"What the devil would a country store in the Ottawa Valley
want with fifty dumbbells?" Erryn asked.

"I don't know," Bryce said. "What would the Confederates
want with them?"

"Cannon shot."

"Well, that's what Latour said too. Maybe cannon shot. But
where are the cannon? You can't go out and buy them the way you
buy pistols."

"Any kind of weapon can be bought," Erryn said wearily. "If
you can pay for it, you can buy a cruiser, armed and manned and
ready for action. The Confederates have already done it twice."

Neither man could argue with him. After all, the *Alabama* and
the *Florida* were already abroad, every beam and ratline and brass
cannon built in England, paid for in Rebel gold.

"The *Robert E. Lee*," he reminded them, "sold a raft of blockade-
run cotton in Halifax—about seventy-five thousand dollars'
worth. That would buy a nine-pounder or two. To say nothing of
some pistols and knives."

He was right, of course, and they knew it. He was also spinning,
and they knew that too. He was fashioning a fabulous, intricate

web, just like one of Matt's pet spiders, building himself a marvel of airy geometry—but come a single swat from the landlady's mop and nothing would be left of it, just a flutter or two on the ceiling, and a little grey blob on the floor.

He sighed, and they talked on of other things—what he had heard and seen in St. Lawrence Hall; who might attend Edmund Morrison's party; word of Southerners arriving or departing; all the gossip, the quarrels, the rumours of ill-doing or desertion. This Bryce and Latour truly valued, for neither of them could get as close to the expatriate community as he could. For this, if for nothing else, they were willing to accept his outsider's involvement, and listen to his opinions with respect, if not always with conviction. When he had told them all he could, he asked for one thing from them.

"Is anyone watching this Carroll chap? I mean, watching him personally, all the time?"

"All the time? No. We haven't the people. It's enough keeping track of Follett and Kane."

"Could you find one from somewhere? Just for a few days?"

Bryce began to object, but Latour was faster.

"I can," he said cheerfully. "But it'll cost you a beer."

"How much beer do I owe you now?"

"Oh, barrels. I mean to collect, too."

Erryn laughed and shook hands with them. "I always pay my debts," he said. "Eventually." He pulled on his slicker and went back into the rain.

❖

All the way back to his hotel he mulled it over in his mind. Matt's suspicions were reasonable enough on the surface. Wilkinson and his men did not appear to have left Halifax by sea. They were no longer there, so they had probably gone west. They were an elite group, with a disproportionate number of officers. Therefore, if they had gone west, perhaps they were on a mission. If so, it followed that, being naval men, they would likely target something on the St. Lawrence or the Lakes.

It was all perfectly reasonable, with just enough snatches and snippets of evidence to provide an illusion of substance. Yes, Erryn was certain he had spotted one of the men in Montreal, the same man he had met in Halifax. Yes, there were four exceptionally quiet Southerners staying with George Kane, and there was a large amount of traffic between his home and a nearby boarding house where, it turned out, some other very quiet guests were staying. Yes, Erryn had been asked to buy a small amount of weapons, and it was Follett's practice to spread such tasks around among a number of his friends, so no one attracted much attention. Yes, dumbbells could be used as cannon shot, and Dan Carroll ordered fifty after visiting George Kane's house. And yes, oh yes, there was a Federal prisoner-of-war camp on Johnson's Island, just outside Sandusky, holding some fifteen hundred Confederate officers, as tempting a target as any band of naval commandos could ever hope for.

It was all perfectly reasonable . . . and all spider silk, every frail thread depending for its existence on another just as frail. Maybe a handful of those twenty-two naval men were here. The rest of them could just as well be anywhere, scattered across the length of the colonies, doing nothing of interest whatever; indeed, they might be halfway home by now. As for the four men in Kane's house, they might be the leaders of a mission—or they might just be his friends; they might be sick; they might be deserters, or fugitives from ordinary justice. And what could a handful of weapons possibly prove? Jackson Follett had been buying them since forever, mostly for Southerners heading home through the western states.

Most importantly of all, the United States had a gunboat stationed on Lake Erie, mounted with eighteen-pound cannon. No cross-border raid would take Johnson's Island, or any other target on the lake, without taking the *Michigan* first.

No, he told himself, he had nothing of substance. He was merely giving in to his natural flair for the dramatic, and to his desire for a grand coup, something to hold up and wave the next time Lord Monck sighed and wondered what that man Shaw *did* with all his money.

Back in his hotel room, he shucked off his drenched clothing piece by piece, hung it carefully to dry, and crawled naked into bed. He was heading home soon, he decided, and be damned to it. And when he got there, he was going to drown Matt Calverley. That was a promise. He was taking the sorry bugger out behind some barren rock face and damn well *drowning him.*

CHAPTER 6

———◆———

Brownie

If Mr. Thornton was a fool in the morning, as he assured
himself at least twenty times he was, he did not grow
much wiser in the afternoon.
—*Elizabeth Gaskell*

EDMUND MORRISON was to Montreal what James Orton was
to Halifax: a prince of business, a pillar of the Church, and a
powerful leader of the pro-Confederate faction in the city.
Erryn did not especially look forward to his grand dinner and
ball. Still, he knew he had no choice except to go, and go in
style, which was a dubious proposition at the moment. His
frock coat was gone, loaned to a destitute Confederate for a
wedding, along with his best white linen shirt. For whatever reason, neither item had been returned. His boots had mucked
through far more mud and horse dung than ever was good for
them. Then, a few days back, his hat had been run over by a carriage. So it was that Friday afternoon found him in the heart of
the old town, with a good supply of cash and a melancholy incli-
nation to indulge himself.

It was a perfect Indian summer day, lazy and hot, yet with a hint of autumn greyness in the sky. He made his way without haste toward the Bonsecours Market, through small, winding streets and narrow stone buildings rising side by side, Continental-style, each with a small shop opening to the street and dwellings directly above. From these latter came the smells of chicken and beef and cinnamon and onions, along with the clamour of voices and the laughter of children. Carts and drays rumbled over the cobble-stones, dogs barked, wooden signs creaked on their chains above the doors, offering the goods and services of the tenants: shoes, millinery, gentlemen's apparel, apothecary, tailor.

He bought an apple from a street vendor and ate it as he walked, grateful to be far away—at least in spirit—from anything connected with the American war. He had been nineteen solid months on duty, talking the Confederacy, eating, drinking, dreaming the Confederacy; he was sick to death of the Confederacy. More than anything in the world he wanted a furlough. A few hours spent alone, buying himself fresh fruit, and books, and some fine new clothes, was as near to the thing as he was likely to get.

So he poked about the shops, bought a few trifles that pleased him, stopped in a tiny café for a glass of wine, and walked on, wistfully admiring all the young women he passed. One in particular he admired—a sylph stepping down from a carriage, barely touching the hand the coachman offered her, a sylph with astonishing black hair, all of it hanging loose about her shoulders and shimmering in the mid-October sun.

Ah, he thought, now that was pure, perfect grace . . . A second woman followed her out of the carriage, an aging woman, bent and heavy, moving with such care that he wondered if she might be blind. Was she the younger woman's mother? No, he decided. She was dressed conservatively, as befitted her age, but in garments of the finest quality. The other, the black-haired one, was dressed like a servant, in a plain, dark blue frock. He slowed his pace, hoping for a clear glance at her face, but she was bent toward her companion, helping her over the cobblestones to a tiny shop that offered rosaries and religious books.

The street was narrow, crowded, and he was in the way. He stepped backward hastily, his eyes still following the woman, and crashed into an old man dragging a wheelbarrow.

"*Pardonnez-moi,*" Erryn said quickly, reaching to steady him. "*Je ne vous ai pas vu. Je suis désolé. Êtes-vous blessé?*"

The old man glared at him and spat. "Why don't you look where you're going, you bloody frog?"

"Oh." He considered answering this question in the fashion it deserved, but turned instead to steal a last, parting glance at the woman. Such divine hair, he thought, well worth a second look, even for an insult or two. And so, watching her go, he caught sight of a man in a slouch hat and brown flannel shirt slipping quickly through the doorway of a shop perhaps a hundred feet away.

Some minutes earlier, when he had glanced about before crossing a street, he had seen a similar hat and shirt, a similar distance behind him. Which might mean nothing, of course; slouch hats and brown flannel shirts were hardly rare, and the streets were filled with people.

He went on as if he had noticed nothing. In an hour or so, after impressively replenishing his wardrobe, and depleting his purse in a comparable fashion, he finished off with a visit to Chez Maurice. Perhaps the good monsieur could do something clever with his hair?

The good monsieur smiled, draped a white cape around Erryn's shoulders, and examined him with the air of a salvage expert studying a shipwreck. Like so many Frenchmen, the barber himself had splendid dark locks, thick and wavy and shimmering like fur. He lifted Erryn's meagre offerings sorrowfully, as though he wondered what he could do for this *pauvre anglais*, with such thin, straight, straggly hair, the dreary colour of watered-down beer.

"What is your pleasure, *m'sieu?*"

"Just do your best," Erryn said. Then, after a moment, he added: "*Il y a un grand bal, demain. Très important.*"

"Ah, oui." The barber smiled. *"Un grand bal, et peut-être une jolie demoiselle?"*

A great ball, and perhaps a pretty young woman?

"Peut-être," Erryn said, although he doubted it, at least as far as he might be concerned. It would be splendid, though, if it were to happen. He was hungry for a woman—very hungry, when he thought about it, so he tried not to think about it very much.

The barber took his time, chatting pleasantly, sometimes in French, sometimes in English. When he finished and held up the mirror, it was clear he had indeed done his best. Erryn paid him, adding a generous tip, and went back out into the afternoon sun. A small distance down the street he glanced back. Sure enough, there was Brownie in the slouch hat, or someone exactly like him, slithering out of a small café.

Nothing about this surprised him. The Federal agents watched the Rebels here as faithfully as the Canadians did. More than once Erryn had found one of them lounging outside his boarding house in Halifax. When he left town, they sometimes turned up on the same trains and steamers. It was a tribute to his credibility as a Grey Tory, he supposed, but he did get tired of it.

He walked on, turning twice onto adjoining streets. Brownie followed. The man was obviously inexperienced; the really good agents could follow a man for days before he noticed—and there were probably some he never noticed at all.

Well, bugger you anyway, Erryn thought, and settled down on a shaded bench in the gardens of Place Viger with his new French novel. It was his favourite spot in the whole city, this garden, laid out English-style, with radiating pathways and a grand fountain in the centre. The Royal Artillery band gave splendid concerts on Wednesday evenings, complete with fireworks. He stretched his long legs out carefully, making sure not to trip any innocent strangers, and began to read.

Very soon he discovered that he could not concentrate. Perhaps he was tired, or simply restless, or perhaps it was Brownie in the slouch hat, sitting just opposite, hiding ineptly behind a patch of shrubs. The silly sod was impossible to ignore; all Erryn had to do was lift his head from his book and cast his eyes a little to the left. *Well, really. I'm not to have a moment's peace, I see. If it isn't the damn Rebels in my face, it's some damn fool Yankee.*

The sun was low now. Off to his left he heard a church bell, the sailors' church down on the waterfront, calling the faithful to evening Mass and reminding him that his small self-appointed furlough was almost over. It was time to get rid of Brownie. As he contemplated the task, the prospect of a bit of chaff at the man's expense grew irresistible. *Yes, indeed,* he thought, *a fair return for being such an unconscionable pest.* He dug a pen and paper from his pocket, scribbled briefly, folded the note, looked about, and slipped it into a crack in the bench, every motion at once theatrically furtive and absurdly obvious. The message was brief and to the point:

> Little Robin Redbreast sat upon a tree;
> Up went pussycat, down came he.
> Down came pussycat, away Robin ran,
> Said little Robin Redbreast: *Catch me if you can!*

He was smiling a trifle as he hurried away, imagining Brownie's quandary: should he continue the chase, or fetch the note, or wait to see who claimed it? (Oh, and a sweet wait that would be!) The American leapt to his feet, standing irresolute for a moment, staring one way and then the other. But Erryn had a mighty stride, and considerable experience in losing his watchers when he seriously wanted to. Before Brownie could decide what to do about him, he had jumped into a carriage and was gone.

CHAPTER 7

The Irish Stone

A heavy heart, Belovèd, have I borne
From year to year until I saw thy face . . .
—*Elizabeth Barrett Browning*

IT WAS SURELY the most melancholy spot in the world: a small cluster of burial mounds, a fence of weathered palings, a great granite boulder on a slab—only these, and scrub grass long gone to seed, and white gulls, and the river. Wilted flowers lay scattered here and there, and the grass was trampled down, proof that others came to mourn from time to time. But now there was no one. Sylvie walked softly to the fence and placed her offering. It was a foolish thing, of course, coming down here alone; any sensible person would say so. Madame herself had refused to come. Far too dangerous, she said, not a decent soul about, and the docks with all their ruffians just a small distance off. Madame would be horrified to think she had come anyway . . . but then, Madame need never know.

The wind tugged at her hair, pressed her thin cotton dress

against her thighs. It was different here, not like Nassau at all, no sand, no tropic sun; the river was grey and cold. And yet it was the same. These dead were strangers too, strangers who had come by sea. Few remembered them, and fewer cared. No one in Nassau would remember Frances Harris . . . except perhaps another stranger, a passerby, seeing a lonely grave all untended: *Ah, poor thing, she has no one, so I will give her a flower, and say her a prayer . . .*

Perhaps it would be so. Things went around sometimes, and came back; she believed this sincerely, not in any traditional religious sense, not as bread cast upon the waters, but in an older sense, older and purer and harder. Perhaps there was justice in the afterworld. Perhaps God was up there in some great counting house of deeds, keeping records and paying men back; this she did not know. But there were cycles of good and evil in the common world. They were strange and unpredictable; she knew she could not count on them for justice, or indeed for anything at all, but sometimes things came back.

So she bowed her head and said a prayer for the Irish exiles, the ones Madame Louise had spoken of, the ones who lay all along the riverbank in unmarked graves, half forgotten until the Grand Trunk Railway began laying piers for the Victoria Bridge. Right here the work began, beyond the tag end of the waterfront, and the soft earth yielded bodies at every turn: men and women in their immigrants' rags; small broken children, their skinny limbs shattering like eggshells, so many of them that tough, brawling workmen who could smash a tavern in two minutes flat wept like boys in the mud, and never cared who saw them do it.

For here was where the city had placed the quarantine station back in '47, when the Irish exiles started coming in—the second quarantine station, after the hospital on Grosse-Île could no longer handle the numbers. Devastated by famine before they ever left home, packed into steerage like so many cattle, with many a captain never caring if he took sickness on board as long as he was paid, they came by the shipload; and here, by the shipload, they died. The nuns came to care for them, Madame said, and so did some other brave souls, but they were too many, arriving too fast. Even the wooden sheds that shielded them from sun and rain were thrown together in reckless haste. No one could spare time or strength for the dead; they were buried with a blessing and a spadeful of earth. Their only monument was this one, raised twelve years later, raised neither by the city nor by the Church, but by the ordinary men who had disturbed their graves. Carefully they reburied all they found, and fenced the ground, and inscribed one of the massive granite stones they had taken from the riverbank:

> TO PRESERVE FROM DESECRATION THE
> REMAINS OF 6000 IMMIGRANTS WHO
> DIED OF SHIP FEVER A.D. 1847–48 THIS
> STONE IS ERECTED BY THE WORKMEN
> OF MESSRS. PETO, BRASSY AND BETTS
> EMPLOYED IN THE CONSTRUCTION OF
> THE VICTORIA BRIDGE
>
> A.D. 1859

Six thousand . . . It was hard to imagine so much death, so many betrayed hopes, for even the weakest and most desperate must have dared to hope a little. They were going to a New World, and life would be better there. It had to be better, for nothing could be as bad as starving Ireland—nothing, not even the Lancashire mills, where those who found a place, working from dawn to dusk in mind-numbing noise, and sickening of the cotton dust, nonetheless told Sylvie they were blessed compared with their families at home.

And after all of it, ship fever. No New World waiting, just a cramped hold ankle deep in bilge, and the sickness running through it like fire through September grass, and neither man nor God caring in the least what they dreamt of, or how bravely they had once believed in the future.

We didn't go through all this so I could bury you at sea . . .

She wept then, thinking of them, and of Frances. And so, lost in her grief, she forgot to watch the path that led back to the docks, and did not hear the approaching steps until they were much too close.

She looked up sharply, a spasm of pure, hard fear knotting her belly and her throat. All she could tell about the man at first, framed as he was against the lowering sun, was that he was big, or at least very tall, and he was carrying a parcel under his arm. He had left the path and was picking his way through the scrub, not to where she was standing by the stone but well to the side—the way the decent sort might do, not wanting to frighten her, or to bother her in her grief.

Her fear had been instinctive, an old fear, born of too many years spent far too close to violence. It eased a little now as the stranger moved yet farther from her, and stood like any quiet mourner by the paling. She turned away, wiping her face discreetly on her sleeve, and glanced along the riverbank. It was utterly empty, just the railway yards and the long, splendid span of bridge veering out from them, low and straight as an arrow across the water. The stranger was alone, and so was she.

It was time to go.

Oh, Fran, Fran, if there is another world, I hope you're happy there, I hope they make it up to you, because I can't. I wanted to so much, and now I can't.

She bit back tears as she turned to go, and froze at the sound of his voice.

"Forgive me," he said. It was a very gentle voice. Almost anywhere else, she would have trusted it. "I happened to be passing, and I noticed you were alone. In all decency I could not go on and leave you so. It's not very safe here for a lady."

"Thank you," she said. "But there were no need." She kept her voice—and her brief, polite glance in his direction—as cool and indifferent as possible. Modest, the way the church ladies taught her. "And I be going back now anyways. Madame is waiting."

"Let me accompany you, then," he offered.

Oh, Christ, I suppose I'm for it now. She were right; I never should have come.

He made a small, apologetic gesture with his hand. "Just to where there's people, if you like. I meant nothing more."

Sylvie Bowen was a brave woman—some might well have called her reckless—but she was not naive. She knew she was unsafe here. She knew also that pleasant manners in a man were proof of absolutely nothing, least of all for a servant girl prowling a deserted riverbank where everyone from Madame to the Lord Chief Justice would tell her she had asked for anything she got. Yet she had grown up in a rough mill town, and rubbed shoulders with many kinds of men, the decent and the dangerous alike. Her instincts read nothing predatory in the stranger. They read something quite different.

He was not at all good-looking. If she had needed to describe him to a friend, she might have said: "A great scrawny beanpole sort of chap, but graceful, and dressed real nice, with a voice like a pot of honey . . ." She liked what she saw, and she knew perfectly well that he liked what he had seen. Men often liked her, until they saw her face.

So she turned full toward him, directly into the lowering sun, and then, casually, as if she were brushing away a fly, she flicked her hair back.

There, kind sir, it ain't what you thought at all, is it? Not some pretty damsel in distress, just me, just a nobody with a face like a wicker basket. Feel free to go now; they all do . . .

He stood utterly still, as though she had clubbed him with a hatchet. Ah well, she thought, no reaction at all was better than most, better than disgust or pity, better than Oh-my-God-in-heaven-where-did-you-get-that-*face*?

"Good day to you, sir."

"Wait!" He swept past her with a couple of long strides and turned. "Please. My name is Erryn Shaw. I don't know if I look it at the moment, but I'm quite respectable. I'll see you safe into town regardless. But it would please me very much to walk with you."

He seemed quite unchanged by what he had seen. It was courtesy, she supposed, the kind of perfect manners some people had. They would never let anything improper show, not if it killed them. On the other hand, she had been approached once by a man who ran a brothel for the weird sort, and polite as hell he was, too. He thought she would make a smashing addition to his stable. In this world, anything was possible.

It was even possible that Erryn Shaw still liked her, that he was striding backward in the scrub with one hand clutching his parcel and the other held out appealingly, like a boy with an angry parent, because he really did fancy her company.

"Besides," he was saying, "if you won't walk with me, then I'll have to walk with myself, and that gets to be a frightful boring business after a while."

She smiled in spite of herself, just a little. He was charming, she thought, whatever sort of chap he might turn out to be. She felt an uncommonly strong temptation to think well of him, to be pleased that he had wandered so unexpectedly into her day. Later she would reflect on this temptation, and wonder how much of it was born of good judgment and how much of loneliness. A dangerous emotion, loneliness, especially for a woman—for what was there, really, to judge him by? A certain delicacy of manner, a touch of humour, decent clothing, and a parcel obviously wrapped in one of the better shops . . . Dear God in heaven, half the villains in the world could boast as much, and more.

But loneliness won out—loneliness and her own reluctance to snub a friendly stranger who so far had done nothing to deserve it.

"All right," she said. "But I have to go straight back to the church."

"Anywhere at all," he agreed, falling in step beside her. "Would you think me too forward if I asked to know your name?"

"It's Sylvie. Sylvie Bowen."

"A pleasure to meet you, Miss Bowen. I'm Erryn Shaw."

"Yes. I remember." This, she realized, might show altogether too much interest. She changed the subject quickly. "You got people there, do you? By the stone?"

"No. I was just passing. I like to walk by the river sometimes, when I'm out of sorts and need to think." He hesitated a moment, and then went on, cautiously: "And yourself? Someone in your family, I suppose?"

"No. My aunt died in Nassau, of the yellow jack. She were the only real family I had since I were twelve. I'll never get to put a flower on her grave. So's I thought, you know, I'd put one here, and m'appen someone there would do the same for her. I suppose that sounds awful silly."

"Not in the least. I think it's a fine thing to do, and I am sorry for your loss."

"She would have loved it here, every bit of it. I just came back from St. Catharines last week, with Madame. It's where her sister lives. We come on the riverboat, and all that long way I kept thinking of nothing but how Fran would have loved it. Especially the Thousand Islands. Have you ever seen them?"

"Yes."

So they talked for a while about sailing through the Thousand Islands, and running the rapids at Galouse and the Cedars and Lachine, the boat plunging from smooth water into frothing cataracts, as if over a cliff, speeds of twenty-five knots and better, rocks and islands looming dead ahead, evaded at the last possible moment, or so it seemed to the passengers. Some of them were falling to their knees in the saloon, heads bent and prayer books clutched to their hearts, waiting for the end, while others were on the deck, laughing with the pure, wild pleasure of it.

"And you were one of them?" she asked.

"Oh, quite! And you?"

"I wouldn't have missed it for the world. I thought Madame might be cross, for my getting all drenched, but she only smiled, and said if she could see better, she'd've been there with me."

"And Madame is?"

"Madame Louise. I work for one of her relatives in the boarding house. Madame wanted to go see her sister, and her own lady's maid were begging to be left behind because her son were sick. So she asked Miss Susan for one of her girls, and I were the newest and could be easiest spared. It's been grand. If Fran'd been with me, it would've been the best four weeks of my life. Madame's an odd sort, really. I've never met anyone like her. She's got piles of money, but she don't top it over people, if you know what I mean. She can be so kind, so un . . . unpretentious, she seems like ordinary folks. And then some little thing will happen and she'll turn *frightfully* proper."

She wondered what Madame would think of Erryn Shaw. Probably she would approve of him, since he was acting every inch the gentleman. But she would not approve of Sylvie's meeting him this way, not in the least. Decent young women, even those of the servant class, did not strike up acquaintances with strange men in public places. Of course, Sylvie knew perfectly well that decent young women did it all the time—perhaps Madame Louise as well, a long time ago. How else had the sheltered daughter of the richest man in town come to marry a seaman?

They had reached the boardwalk. Ahead was the Bonsecours Docks, where a paddlewheeler lay at anchor: the steamboat for Quebec, Erryn told her, travelling always by night so the businessmen who scurried back and forth need never lose a day of work. Beyond, along the waterfront proper, great ships lay in a curving row, snuggled by the jetties like weary beasts settling in for the night. The wharves were still abustle: men and horses, wheelbarrows and wagons, and once a long caravan of swiftly rolling barrels, with bent workmen slapping them along, their shirts sweaty and their hair in their eyes. With infinite tact Erryn Shaw tucked his arm around hers, and so they strolled past the harbour and up the long slope to rue de la Commune. She pointed to a church spire rising over a cluster of shops and markets—the Chapel of

Notre-Dame-de-Bonsecours, or the sailors' church, as it was called by most ordinary people.

"That's where Madame is," she told him. "She's doing a novena of Masses there."

"She's from a seafaring family, then?" Erryn asked.

"Her family? Heavens, no. They're merchants, the lot of them—and a great proper clan of rich Presbyterians to boot, except for the one who ran off and married a French-Canadian Papist from some Boston merchant brig. M'appen they'd've got over it, since the ship went down with all hands just two years later. But she turned Catholic herself when she married him, so now she got kin who still won't talk to her except at weddings and funerals, when they got no choice. I don't see the sense of it, their being so snotty. She's a good woman."

"People get frightfully snotty over religion. I don't see the sense of it either."

The sun was very low when they came to the church. The last trickle of departing worshippers had thinned down to nothing. Madame would have said her rosary by now, and a few other prayers as well. She was a patient woman, especially in church; she did not think a few extra Our Fathers ever hurt anyone. But by now her patience might well be running out.

Which was a pity, Sylvie thought. She would have liked more time with Erryn Shaw. She dug her thin scarf out of her pocket and wrapped it around her head.

"It were kind of you to walk with me, Mr. Shaw. I know it weren't the best idea, going down there by myself. But I didn't have no choice."

"Wasn't there anyone to come with you?"

"Only Madame, and she wouldn't. She said it were too dangerous."

Sylvie caught the irony of this only after she had spoken it. Her companion inclined his head faintly; she wondered if he did it to hide a smile.

"I've enjoyed your company so much, Miss Bowen. I'd be honoured if you'd join me for tea sometime soon? Or perhaps you'd enjoy the concert in Viger Park? The Royal Artillery band plays there every Wednesday night, very fine music, and fireworks, and vendors with all sorts of things to eat, and wonderful ices. I'd be delighted to take you. Would you come?"

"Oh . . ." How splendid that would be! Hours and hours to spend together, with lights, and sweets, and music. She adored music. She had stopped on the street just the other day, staring at a poster for the concerts, thinking, *Oh, if only we could go!*

She dropped her eyes quickly. It would never do. She would have to explain him to Madame, and ask her permission; God knew what might come of that. Besides, he probably only offered out of courtesy.

"You're very kind, but Madame expects me to stay with her."

"Surely not every minute?"

"Pretty much, except when she's in church. I'm not a Catholic, you see. She'd think it a great sin to go to someone else's services herself, so she don't make me come. But she's nearly blind, so"—Sylvie made a small, apologetic gesture—"I have to help her."

"Perhaps she'd enjoy an afternoon tea or a concert herself. I'd be happy to escort you both."

"She's doing a novena." He looked puzzled, and she went on: "Penance, fasting, that sort of thing. It's for her husband. She does it every October, ever since his ship went down thirty-seven years ago."

"That's admirable loyalty."

"Yes," Sylvie agreed, though she knew the woman's actions were rooted in something far more complicated than loyalty. Louise Mallette's brief, reckless marriage had not been a happy one.

They had reached the steps of the church. There was no help for it now; she had to go. She dropped a small curtsy. "Thank you, Mr. Shaw. It were real nice meeting you. Goodbye."

"How many days are left in the novena?"

"What?"

"Novenas go for nine days, don't they? How many are left?"

"Five, after today."

"Always here, at the sailors' church? The afternoon Mass?"

"Yes—"

"Then I'll be back. I promise." He bowed gracefully, as if he were at a fancy dress ball, taking her hand and raising it to his lips. "Good day, Miss Bowen, and thank *you*. You've brightened my whole day."

It was the loveliest thing any man had ever said to her. She walked astonished into the chapel, carrying the words in her thoughts as she would have carried loose diamonds in her hands. All evening she carried them, riding in the carriage with Madame, eating supper with her, sitting in their lonely hotel room and reading aloud from *The Imitation of Christ*—a very fine book, admittedly, but not the sort of book she could keep her mind on tonight. She stumbled over words she had read without difficulty many times before, until Madame grew tired of it and said they should go to bed.

She lay awake for a long time. She wondered if Madame slept or only brooded. She wondered about Erryn Shaw's life, who he really was, and where he came from. He had offered nothing personal about himself, and she had been far too polite to ask. He was obviously well bred, a man with means and some standing in the world. Surely he had a choice of women for companions, pretty merchants' daughters who would happily go for tea or to the concert in Viger Park. And yet he had asked *her*.

She lingered over every detail of the afternoon, every word he spoke, the pleasure she felt when he touched her, such fierce pleasure, out of all proportion to the occasion. And even though she knew he was probably just being kind—liking her a little bit, perhaps, but mostly just being kind, doing a gentleman's duty by a poor lass without friends—even while she knew this in her

sensible mind, in another part of herself she revelled in his interest, believed in it, imagined there would be more. Something
more, a walk through the streets, maybe tea while Madame was at
church. A tiny gift, perhaps, some trifle she would keep forever,
and show to old friends when she was old: *A gentleman gave me this
once, a long time ago . . . a very fine gentleman he were, too, so very
sweet. He could say things to make a beggar girl think she were a queen.*

All the good sense in the world could not stop her from thinking thus, or from finding the next day intolerably slow, breakfast,
forenoon, lunch, mid-afternoon, every part of it dragging worse
than the last, and the sun stuck rigid in the sky like a dog on the
end of a chain. Never had she been so happy to hear the summons
of a church bell. It rang and rang as they rode through the cobblestone streets. She had five days, five long Masses, five meditations
on death and Resurrection, five slowly counted rosaries, oh, a feast
of time, if he came as he had promised.

But he did not come. There was no sign of his tall bony figure
anywhere near the church when they arrived. She helped Madame
from the carriage, walked her to her pew, and sped back into the
afternoon sun. Then she waited, watching the slow trickle of
worshippers—not many, for it was a working day, just a few aged
women, a few cripples, a few sailors on liberty. When a coach and
four came tearing up, her heart bounded with hope. Of course he
would come in a carriage; he was a gentleman, after all. But it was
only the priest, sweating and weary, with his stole still draped
around his shoulders—rushing back, she supposed, from some
poor devil's deathbed.

The sun sped away now, heartless. Rue St-Paul was noisy as a
beehive, with a great coming and going of hacks, and wagons, and
people on foot. *I'll be back,* he had said, *I promise.* The church bell
rang for Communion; could it possibly be so late already? She
walked back and forth, back and forth, watching the traffic. Still
he did not come. People began drifting out of the church, just a
few at first, hurrying, then the great body of them, then a few

again, and finally no one. Madame was a humble shadow among the pews, entirely alone.

As I will be in my turn . . . This fact of course she knew, and had known for years. So she did not cry, except a tiny bit, too little for Madame to notice. She spoke cheerfully at supper, and took her mistress for a quiet evening walk. But she could not read aloud, not from these holy books with all their talk of love—God's love or any other kind—all of it just a great pack of bleeding lies. Madame asked her what the matter was and she lied. She said she had seen something very sad on the street, a crippled child being beaten, and Madame was kind as always and told her she did not have to read.

But late, very late, when the moon was a hanging sickle in the west, she went to the window and pulled the curtain open and watched it drifting there, with its dirty scarred face. They said it was made of rocks—she had read it in a magazine—just a small, earth-like thing made out of rocks, with no water and nothing left alive.

You didn't really think he'd come, Sylvie Bowen? Surely you didn't?

But she had. That was the sorry truth of it; she had.

CHAPTER 8

———◆———

Morrison's Party

No people ever had more at stake. In the maintenance, in all its
integrity, of the relation of master and slave between the white and
black races of the South, it is our universal sentiment that property,
liberty, honour, and civilization itself are involved.
—*James P. Holcombe*
Richmond, Virginia, 1860

IN THE WEST END of Montreal, between its commercial heart
along St. James Street and the lonely ribbon of Côte-des-Neiges
Road, lay a long swath of scattered, magnificent estates. These
were the homes of the city's richest and most powerful men,
Molsons, McTavishes, Ogilvies, and Dows, among others, their
spectacular mansions surrounded by acres of gardens, designed to
be works of art as well as marks of pride. Except for Hugh Allan's
Ravenscrag, rising in solitary splendour from the wooded slopes of
Mount Royal, none was more spectacular than Edmund
Morrison's Tilbury Hall. In truth, Erryn doubted there was much
to surpass it anywhere in North America, even among the moguls
of New York.

For Morrison had built himself a Gothic castle with flamboyant
gables and high, medieval turrets, an immense thing, yet fashioned

with so light a touch that, when snow was falling or when a bit of fog drifted up from the river, it appeared to an approaching visitor like something out of fairyland, magical and shimmering with lights. How Morrison fastened upon so poetic a construction Erryn could not imagine, for the man was one of the toughest, most unsentimental empire builders he had ever met.

Nonetheless, his party on Saturday afternoon was, as Jackson Follett had promised, fabulous. The tables were laden with a king's feast, and Erryn took full advantage; he could rarely afford to eat so well. A fine chamber orchestra played in the garden, among the elms by the Montmorency wall. The women wore the finest Paris silks; their laughter sparkled like their wine; their wrists were drenched in filigree. The men were the elite of Montreal—merchant princes and sons of the great colonial families, diplomats from abroad, officers from the British garrison . . . Oh, yes, it was all very splendid and very familiar.

Too familiar. Erryn felt disoriented, as if he had walked out onto a set of Hamlet and found himself in Elsinore Castle, the real Elsinore Castle, but looking exactly as he had staged it in the theatre, even to the spilled tankards and the smoke-blackened walls, even to the bodies lying in the hall, lying gracefully, the way dead heroes were supposed to lie on the stage, only this time it was absolutely real, this time they were really dead, they were never getting up again . . .

Well. He shook the punch around in his glass. Maybe he was not *quite* so disoriented. But he found it eerie, being here. It was not like consorting with Southern exiles in bars, or partying with the easygoing, provincial, garrison-town elite of Halifax, who could not afford to be too excessively exclusive or there would hardly be any of them left. This was like home; these were the lords of British North America. He could name every stone in their signet rings and judge the precise amount of disapproval in one of their flickered eyebrows. He could move among them, if he chose, like a minnow in a pool, seeming perfectly at ease. He would not even have to call upon his acting skills to do it. Yet there was, he thought, scarcely any ordinary, livable world where he belonged less.

"Erryn! There you are!" Jackson Follett was weaving his way through the gathering, accompanied by a thin stranger in obviously borrowed finery. Everything the man wore was appropriate; none of it fit particularly well. Follett introduced him: Mr. Maury Janes, from Wilmington, in North Carolina.

"Mr. Shaw. Delighted, I'm sure." He did not nod. He held out a hard, sweaty hand for Erryn to shake.

"I told Mr. Janes a bit about you," Follett said. "He was mighty keen to meet you."

"That's right!" Janes barely waited for his companion to finish. "Jack tells me you are one smooth operator."

"I trust that's a compliment?"

Janes was surprised. Then he laughed. "I suppose you Englishmen would say it different. What I mean is, you sound like a man who gets things done. Real quiet, without any loose ends hanging out. I could use a man like that, a ways down the road."

Oh, could you, indeed?

"Perhaps we should go and have a drink together, then," Erryn suggested.

<hr />

Edmund Morrison was an impeccable host, and he had made it quite clear to his servants that some of his guests, on this occasion as on many others, might wish to carry on certain conversations in absolute privacy. So it was that Erryn Shaw and Maury Janes were led to a small study, supplied with a decanter of superb wine, a plate of hors d'oeuvres sufficient for a large family, and a heavy, discreetly closed door.

"I don't believe this place," Janes said. Everything in the room was of the finest quality: Indian tapestries, panelling and furniture of mahogany and teak, crystal glassware that glittered in their hands. "I never seen anything like it," Janes went on. "Have you?"

"Once or twice."

"I was out at Sheldon Wade's plantation house a few times, and I thought that was awfully grand. It was nothing like this. Jack says your family's pretty high, back in England."

"Well, we're certainly respectable."

Janes laughed. "Oh, you Englishmen. You'd rather die than brag, wouldn't you? Not like Americans. Well, I can tell you straight, sir, when I get my independent fortune, I'm not going to be shy of a little bragging. I'll figure I earned it. My pa came down to Carolina with nothing but the clothes on his back and an old bowie knife with the point broke off. For three weeks he lived on clams, digging them out of the sand with that knife. Can't stand a clam to this day, he says. But he built us a fine plantation, over the years—not as big as Sheldon Wade's, but hell, Wade *married* his, he didn't work for it. War's over, I'll have myself a place like this."

"Where did your father come from?"

"Massachusetts. How about that, eh? He was a dad-blamed dyed-in-the-wool Yankee. Took to the South like a hound to a rabbit chase. Bought himself his first nigger on credit, before he had a house. Hell, he said, the damn nigger might as well build the house."

"Very practical," Erryn murmured.

It was the wrong thing to say, or perhaps the wrong tone in which to say it. Janes's dark eyes hardened slightly, took on a quiet, calculating watchfulness.

Your arrogance will be the death of you, Erryn Shaw . . .

This man, he reminded himself, might well be a fine example of the rough-edged, grasping, nouveaux-not-quite-riches on the climb, but he was nobody's fool. And he had probably had more than enough of well-born men looking down on him, his own fellow Southerners among them.

Erryn reached to pass him the tray of hors d'oeuvres. "Please," he offered. "They look quite irresistible." He bit into one himself, and went on: "Personally, I've always thought that being practical is one of the great lost virtues of the Western world. Consider the Romans. They were infinitely practical men, and think what they accomplished. Now, it seems to me, everyone's up on a soapbox, blathering about some new ism or another, and causing no end of trouble instead of getting on with the job."

"I'll be damned," said Janes. "You took the words right out of my old man's mouth. He thinks this war's about nothing but some damn fool ideas."

"And what do you think?"

"I think in a way it is and in a way it ain't. I mean, there's a lot of talk about fool ideas, both sides. But I figure if you look a little deeper, it's about power. Who's going to run things? Are we going to be our own masters, or are a handful of rich hypocrites with ramrods up their asses going to tell the whole damn country what to do? That's what it's *really* about."

This, Erryn thought, was by no means the worst summation of the matter he had ever heard.

He raised his glass. "To being our own masters, then. And confusion to the enemy!"

"Damn right, sir! I like that. Confusion to the enemy!"

"Now," Erryn went on, when the glasses had been manfully emptied and refilled, "Jack Follett said there might be some way I could be of service to you. In Halifax."

"I don't know when I'll get there. It depends on . . . well, let's just say it depends. But if you could set me up when I arrive, put me in touch with the right people, folks I can trust, you know. And I'll need someone to set up a job for me. I'll choose the man myself, you understand. I won't buy a pig in a poke, not from my best friend. But if you could point me to a few likely fellows, I'd be much obliged."

"What kind of job?"

"A delivery. Across the border."

"Halifax is a fine seaport. Deliveries shouldn't be a problem."

"I take problems for granted, Mr. Shaw, when I have to deal with Yankee revenue cutters and harbour police. I want the best man I can get." He leaned forward. Bit by bit, his voice dropped almost to a whisper. "This ain't no ordinary project, Mr. Shaw, like most I've heard about up here. I ain't trying to criticize anybody. What the boys are doing in Canada, planning raids and such, it all helps. But this project is . . . well, this is the work of a genius, and I can say so myself, because it wasn't my idea, not one bit of it. And if it goes off like it should, it's going to end the war."

"Well." Erryn saluted him with a lifted glass. "I wish you all possible success, Mr. Janes. But I fear I have to tell you that ending the war strikes me as somewhat"—he made a generous, apologetic gesture with his arms—"forgive me, somewhat . . . over-ambitious?"

"That's right," Janes agreed. "It's going to be the whole damned Red Sea coming down on Pharaoh's army. That was a bit over-ambitious too, wouldn't you say?"

God bleeding almighty, now we're in the Promised Land . . .

"Well," he said again. It was all he could think of for a considerable moment. Well. "Then I must say, Mr. Janes, I will be truly honoured to welcome you to Halifax."

———◈———

Erryn wondered sometimes about the nature of lying. He wondered if there was some kind of limit, some critical mass of lies a man might tell, after which he became a liar by nature. And he wondered, if there were such a limit, if he might be approaching it. His count for the day was well into the hundreds, and going up fast.

He was back in Morrison's astonishing garden with the host himself, Jackson Follett, and perhaps half a dozen Southern exiles. Sir Fenwick Williams, commander of the British garrison in Montreal, as well as commander-in-chief of all the British forces in North America, had just left the group, and was now some distance away, paying his compliments to the ladies.

Outwardly, the general's behaviour could not have seemed more neutral. He had offered the Southerners nothing more than the usual polite greetings, the blandest political observations: *Her Majesty's government is following events in the current conflict with great interest—God willing there will soon be a satisfactory resolution— et cetera, et cetera.* It was, however, widely understood that Williams's *personal* inclinations were pro-Southern. This led to a long and lively debate as to how soon and under what circumstances England would enter the war.

"All she wants is a good excuse."

The speaker was one of two military officers in the group, a lieutenant who had escaped from the Yankee prison camp at Johnson's Island. He was still thin, weary, and malnourished. With a cool pride that Erryn deeply admired, he had come to the party in the plainest of garb, covered over with a frock coat of Confederate grey, sufficiently decent and clean to pose as a dress uniform.

No one else could have got away with such *lèse-majesté*. But the Southern fighting men were heroes here, disadvantaged merely by the fortunes of war. Their poverty was almost a mark of pride.

The lieutenant had complete faith in England's support. All she needed to enter the war, he said, was a good excuse. "So the English people will accept it, and so the rest of the world can't accuse her of meddling."

Ah, Erryn thought, *and when was the last time England ever cared if the world accused her of meddling?*

"The *Trent* was a plenty good excuse," said another. "I still don't understand why she didn't pick up the gauntlet then."

"Because the Yankees backed down," Follett said. "Lincoln let the envoys go, and bowed and scraped all over the place, and said sorry, sorry, sorry. I suppose in all fairness England felt she had to return the gesture."

"Yes, but only because she never saw it as a threat, merely as an insult. She's lord of the sea and she knows it. Here it's different. In

North America the Yankees really are a threat. She might as well take them on now as later."

It went on. The Southerners discussed this question endlessly, but they did not, in Erryn Shaw's opinion, understand it very well. They assumed a deep and passionate commitment on the part of England to her North American colonies; and a natural alliance, based on blood, class, and cotton, between the Confederacy and England. Both of these assumptions were false.

The fact was, England did not care very much about North America at all. Her most lucrative commercial interests were in the Far East, and her great rivals for imperial wealth and power were in Europe. Of course, if her colonies here were openly attacked, she would defend them, simply because they were hers. Empires, by definition, could not afford to be attacked with impunity. But short of that, she was too busy elsewhere to want a war with the United States. When she lay awake at night brooding on the dark plots of her enemies, she did not worry about Yankees steaming across the Lakes to sack Toronto; she worried about the Portuguese in Africa, the Dutch in Southeast Asia, and the French just about everywhere.

As for the colonies themselves, they were not beloved in London, not anymore. They cost £200,000 a year merely to garrison, and thousands more for the salaries of imperial administrators. The glorious days of the fur trade were over, and nothing comparable had replaced it, just timber, fish, and the products of modest farms and factories—respectable exports, certainly, enough to make a good living for many, and small fortunes for some, but rarely the stuff of great fortunes. And the empire needed great fortunes—great coffers of money for her ships and her mushrooming industries, money for her pampered upper class, money for her wars. From Africa came diamonds and gold; from the Far East, spices, silks, and tea; from the west, mostly lumber and salt cod, alas. More and more, British North America was resembling an orphaned niece who ate too much and spun too little. London could scarcely wait for her to grow up and leave home.

But the Southerners—at least the ones who came north—never seemed to notice. Erryn Shaw might have found this fact amusing had he not found it so dangerous. The Anglo-American war they desired could still happen, not for any of the reasons they imagined but simply because, believing in those reasons, they might yet find a way to provoke it. Here was another of those troubling contradictions between reality and non-reality that, as a man of the theatre, he thought about rather often. Plays were only make-believe, yet what passed in them took on its own, quite substantial reality. Lies were purely lies, but when enough people believed in them, their belief was a fact—a fact that could change the whole world.

So he listened to the debate with attention, but avoided contributing anything of substance. When asked, as the only Englishman present in the group (Morrison himself was a native Canadian), he said of course the *better* people supported the Confederacy with all their hearts, and left it so.

"Well." This response came from a civilian of thirty or so, a man named Darius Gavin, whom Erryn had met for the first time that day. Gavin spoke softly, with an exceptionally heavy Deep South accent. "I wish you all could have a talk with young Zeb Taylor, then. He just about wore me out the other day, telling me we had no friends among the Brits, and even fewer among these damned colonials, as he called you—begging your pardon, gentlemen. He's grieving for his brother, and there wasn't much I could say to him made any difference."

"His brother?" Morrison asked sharply. "Good God, was his brother Brad Taylor? The poor lad who was killed in Halifax?"

"Yes. You knew him, I suppose?"

"I knew him well. He ate many a dinner here in my house, and a fine lad he was, too. A fine lad. It was a damn shame the way he died."

"What happened to him?" asked the Confederate lieutenant.

With a quick, discreet glance, Morrison left it to Jackson Follett to explain as much of it, or as little, as he saw fit.

"You never heard? No, I suppose not—you were still in that prison camp. Brad was a courier, one of the best we ever had. He came through from Richmond maybe three, four times, overland, when we were using that route a lot, carrying dispatches to the coast to go to Europe. Last May he was found knifed to death in a little back street off the Halifax waterfront. The police took it for a common robbery, apparently."

"And was it? Or did some Yankee agent get him?"

"Either is possible," Erryn said. "There's Yankees crawling all over Halifax. They're generally careful about not breaking the law—the last thing they want to do is step on the lion's tail. But in the dead of night on a dark street, who knows? On the other hand, Halifax is a sorry rough place betimes. He might well have run into a footpad."

"As anyone might, God knows," Follett added. "But Taylor's kid brother didn't know anything about it. He was with Morgan on the Northwest raid. He got separated from his unit, like a lot of them did, and escaped into Canada. The first he heard of it was in Toronto, talking to the boys there. I haven't met with him yet, but I understand he's pretty tore up."

"He's half crazy," Gavin said, "and that's meaning him no disrespect, since I don't figure it's his fault. He's wounded, same as if he'd been hit by a minié ball. But he's hunkered down in that little rooming house he's in, and he won't be comforted by anyone. I asked him to come with me today, said it would do him good to be with some of his countrymen. He told me Southerners who got into bed with the Brits were no countrymen of his. Said England was using everybody, playing both sides against the middle."

"Can't anything be done for him?" Erryn asked. "A visit from a clergyman, perhaps?"

"All he wants is to go home. I gave him enough money to get him to Halifax, and to feed him for a while, till a blockade-runner can pick him up. The only thing likely to help him now is time."

Time. The venerable cure for all mortal grief . . . or so men said. And in part it was true, Erryn thought. Time had healed his own terrible wound, or at least covered it over, slid it out of his immediate, daily line of sight, into some quiet place in the back of his soul. But a chance word, an unexpected familiar face—all sorts of things could draw it back, not least of them the thought of a nineteen-year-old boy gone half crazy for the killing of his brother.

He made his way thoughtfully toward the outdoor facilities, tucked behind an immense hedge well beyond the house. The estate and its gardens were huge; if a man took his time, the journey there and back could eat up a quarter of an hour. He felt the need of that quarter of an hour just now: time to think, to steel himself again. The Irishman Daniel Carroll had arrived at the party—the man who was buying dumbbells for Jackson Follett. The man who might or might not be involved in a plot with the missing naval officers who might or might not be staying at George Kane's house. The man who was next on Erryn Shaw's list of people to have a quiet drink with.

He barely heard the mingled voices of other guests, someone's sudden loud laugh, the fallen leaves crunching under his feet. He barely noticed how the sun had slipped away, how the reddened maples on the slopes of Mount Royal had gone dark and brooding as the sun abandoned them. But the church bell he heard, a great heavy bell, ringing slowly and muted with distance—the sailors' church, perhaps, down by the riverfront. He turned to look back over the curve of the city, at the tall spires still traced in gold, one of them just beyond the docks, by the dome of the Bonsecours Market.

I could be there with her instead of here. In a sane world I would be, laughing and telling stories, buying her ices.

God almighty, where would we all be if the world were sane? Brad Taylor would be back in Kentucky, I suppose, plowing his father's farm. I wonder who killed him? Maybe a Yankee, maybe a footpad. Maybe me. How far do you trace it back? Matt knew everything about him, and he knew because of me, and maybe the Yankees knew because of Matt. Maybe a lot of people knew. Even a thief might have gone for him then, thinking to get his hands on something secret and dangerous, something he could sell.

A very real possibility, for whoever had killed the Rebel courier, they had taken not merely his purse, if he had one, but his hat, coat, and boots; they had sliced open the cuffs of his shirt and his trouser legs—all of which had caused Matt Calverley to raise no more than one cool eyebrow. "Hell," he said, "on Barrack Street a man's lucky if they don't take his liver too."

But Erryn, being Erryn, wondered. It was not guilt he felt; it was something more diffuse and probably more permanent: a sense of loss, of dislocation, of irremediable, tragic absurdity. He had liked Brad Taylor, ate with him, drank with him, asked himself in quiet moments what the devil the man was doing on the other side . . . and finally, quite possibly, caused his death. And yes, one could blame it all on the treacherous life of the spy, but that was mere hypocrisy. A spy was much like an actor: he put on a mask and in doing it laid bare a truth. War *was* the killing of those who should have been one's friends, most of the time. Banners and uniforms were the real deception, the great We and They denying everyone's common humanity.

He stepped into the privy. As it was part of Tilbury Hall, it was not a privy of the ordinary sort, but a genuine outdoor dressing room, with three water closets, a table holding a marble basin and several pitchers of water, and a fine stuffed chair. On the wall hung a full-length mirror. He paused walking past it, studying the image there not with vanity but with quiet, professional approval. He knew the value of costume. He had spared no expense in the shops, buying the proper accoutrements for this party. He had dressed himself with the care of an actor giving a command performance. The effect was impressive. Not beautiful, but very impressive: a tall, slender gentleman in impeccable clothing, his every thread implying wealth, position, blood; his face thin, hawk-nosed, with an air of natural hauteur and eyes as icy grey as the North Atlantic. Yes, definitely, this was someone to reckon with. The playmaker and the spy in him were satisfied.

The man knew it was all illusion. Beneath the cambric and silk was title to nothing, no lands, no ships, no warehouses filled with cinnamon and cloves; only a paper that came every first week of January, drawn on Lloyds of London, worth seventy English pounds. Edmund Morrison could buy him with pocket money and serve him on a small plate of hors d'oeuvres.

Edmund Morrison rose when he walked into the room: *Mr. Shaw, how very good to see you back, sir!*

Not just illusion, he thought. Something more. Something Morrison saw, and Matt Calverley too—not blood or race or any of those genuine illusions, but irrevocable lived experience: tapes-tried ballrooms and liveried servants and coaches and six at the gates; dead heroes eternally staring down from their painted frames, live ones smiling briefly, passing on, Wellington himself once, proud and silent. So much silence in that house. His great-uncle the admiral erect as a pillar, one arm gone, one eye, scars all over him, Trafalgar, Sicily, Martinique, his body a map of Napoleon's wars. Never Uncle to anyone, or even John, always the "admiral," the undaunted hero: *How are you, sir? Capital, capital, couldn't be better!* And so the boy thought it little to be wounded, even horribly, if a man could be a hero. Then he found the old man in a hallway once, buckled to his knees and blubbering with pain, so wrecked that he was pissing himself, and mewling like a small, chewed-up animal.

Still he might have saved the moment—plucked victory, as they said, from the jaws of defeat—if he had laughed, however bitterly; if he had wrapped his one stiff arm around his great-nephew and told him everybody cried once or twice in his life, even Wellington. Instead, he cursed: *Get out of here, God damn you, what the devil are you staring at?*

That night there was a ball, and music and fireworks, the whole sky lit with glory and the admiral as capital as ever. The boy watched him from a quiet corner, still worshipful, but also hurt, bewildered, troubled less by his harshness than by the silence that lay beneath it, some unspoken thing hinting at more unspoken things, at a whole ciphered world they were not telling him about, a world he was simply to accept, as the old man accepted such appalling pain.

The following year he went to Eton. He went joyously, expecting to find a banquet of learning and friendship, and found instead that a pack of privileged young men at a boarding school were not much different from a pack of convicts, take away the chapel and the fine silver plate. Everyone had to make his own way among them, scrap for his own place, take what was dished him, and keep his mouth shut. Rank was not worth much; too many others had it. Nor did it help a boy to have gangly limbs too long for his body and a big, bony head with a hooked nose and a rag of pale hair, walking around among his peers with a name like Herron.

All of which he had explained to Matt Calverley, some five or six years back, during a long night of affectionate, melancholy drinking. His first years at Eton had been hell on earth, he said; he grew to hate the place right down into his bones, the way slaves hated their galley ships and prisoners their dungeons.

"I don't suppose they were any harder on me than they were on other new boys, although I didn't realize it at the time. Cruelty was a way of life there, a philosophy. Toughen the little sods up. Turn them into stern, hard-nosed agents of the empire. And anything was fair game. I'd barely arrived before some sixth-former told me I'd obviously been named Herron because I looked like one. Of course I objected. I'd been named for my mother's family, I told him—my mother was a Herron."

"Oh, dear," Matt said softly.

"I know. I was too innocent to be let out without a keeper. And the buggers never quit. Once, they gathered a pile of jagged stones, about the size of heron eggs, and made me sit on them all night. It was December, cold as bleeding hell. They took turns standing guard. Every time I tried to get up, they knocked me down and kicked me, told me to hatch my chicks. That sort of thing went on all the time. And worse things, some that hardly bear speaking of, even between friends. Once the doors were locked, there was no supervision; the sixth form chaps were supposed to keep order."

"Setting the wolves to watch the chickens?"

"Precisely."

"Didn't anybody fight back?"

"We never stopped fighting. The whole damn school looked like a sick bay sometimes—black eyes, broken hands, missing teeth. God knows I was never pretty, but my face has quite a few bumps and ruffles I wasn't born with."

He drained his wine, noting the long thin scar running from his thumb down the side of his wrist—one of dozens he had not thought about for years. He knew that many of his peers looked back on Eton with affection. They forgot the painful times, remembered the good ones, and valued what they had learned. Some of the teaching had been excellent; those with good minds flowered in it, as he had himself. And yet he knew that if he ever had a son, he would never send him near the place. Its gifts were like many others he had received in his life: fine gifts indeed, but at a price he judged intolerably high.

"You never went to a boarding school, did you, Matt?"

"No. I never had the misfortune to be born rich."

"Touché, my friend. Being rich isn't a misfortune, I admit. Rich means you have enough to eat. You have coal in the wintertime—"

"My point exactly."

"But being born an aristocrat—that, Constable Calverley, *is* a misfortune. From one point of view you might as well be born a puppet, with strings on your fingers and strings on your toes, and a whole tribe of puppet masters pulling on them, fathers and grandfathers and uncles and cousins, the lords of the realm and the lords of the Church, every last one of them telling you what to be, and what to do, and what to think. And from another point of view you might as well be born a bandit, because you can get away with anything as long as you pick your targets with a bit of care. When I got older, and stronger, and stopped being a target myself, that was when I really saw it—saw it as a pattern, not just something that was happening to me."

He leaned back in his chair and put his feet up on the window ledge. "It's all hollow, the aristocracy. Like an old iron temple in the woods, glittering and hard, with wind blowing through its cracks and a ton of rubbish inside . . ."

Silence. With Matt, it was always a comfortable silence. "Is that why you changed your name?" he asked after a bit.

"No. Changing my name was a condition of my departure from England. I killed one of my peers. Not at the school. Later, in London. There was no trial, of course. The scandal would have hurt my family, but it would have been a disaster for his—I would have made sure of it. I knew enough about him and the pack he ran with, I could have wrecked them all, socially and politically—hell, odds are even I could have brought down the government. So it was handled as such things often are among my peers: quietly, behind closed doors. I was told to go away somewhere and never come back. My family agreed to send me money for my support, but only if I changed my name and allowed nothing of the matter to be known, even among my relatives and friends."

"And what did they tell your relatives and friends? As to what became of you, I mean?"

"The usual sort of thing, I suppose. Touring the colonies, chasing the great auk in Timbuktu. I'm sure there were rumours—very quiet and discreet, of course . . . *Odd about milord's son, very odd. Daresay there was trouble there . . .* Anyway, I picked Shaw because it's a nice, ordinary name. And I picked Erryn because it sounds enough like Herron I can recognize it even when I'm drunk.

Besides, it suits me. If you asked my father, he'd tell you I've been errin' since the day I was born."

It was the first time he had spoken so frankly of his past. Matt did not seem particularly surprised. Perhaps he had seen violence often enough, and close enough, that nothing surprised him very much.

"The fellow you knocked on the head," he asked quietly, "did you mean it?"

"I don't know. He and his pack were responsible for the death of my dearest friend, a young actor who'd never hurt anyone in his life. It was an ugly business. They. . . . Oh, Christ, never mind. It was unforgivable, that's all. And I knew the villain would never be prosecuted, because his mates would all say he was somewhere else. He wouldn't fight me—couldn't, really. His sight was terrible; he wouldn't have known his mother at twenty paces. But the worst of it was, he didn't care, Matt. He said it wasn't his fault, who could have guessed the little libertine would die? He told me to sit down. He had some capital Madeira, fresh off the ship—or would I prefer a tincture of laudanum, I was looking a bit shaky? I put him through the fourth-storey window."

"Witnesses?"

"Two. Both of them his mates. It doesn't matter. They've as much reason as anyone to let the matter die—and they have, as far as I know."

"But they didn't try to stop you?"

"They didn't have time."

"God almighty. You're dangerous, for a scarecrow."

Chalk it up to an Eton education. "Have you ever heard of ber-serkers, Matt?"

"As in crazy people?"

"No. As in the old stories—the chaps who'd wear bear skins to be stronger and fiercer than ordinary men, and who'd keep fight-ing with an arm chopped off, or their guts hanging out, and never even notice . . . It was something like that . . . that kind of passion.

Not madness. I knew exactly what I was doing, and I remember it well enough. But I think his two friends would have needed knives to stop me. Afterwards, they just stood aside and let me walk out the door.

"So did I mean it? To tell you the truth, I really don't know. I don't even know how I feel about it now. Most times I regret it. I wish I hadn't taken any man's life. But once in a while . . . once in a while I think of what he did, and how he'll never do it again, not to anybody, ever . . . and then I'm not so sure.

"In any case . . ." He filled his wineglass and emptied it. "In any case, it's hardly the sort of thing I should be discussing with a police constable, now, is it?"

Matt shrugged. "Listen, mate, they judged you in England as they saw fit. Far as I'm concerned, that's the end of it. Besides, standing up for a wronged friend ain't the worst reason for breaking the law, not by a sorry sight."

"Well." Erryn raised his glass. "Thank you for that."

Matt's return salute was an unspoken promise. He would not judge Erryn Shaw—not on this. Maybe on something else one day, some other bad mistake. But not on this. He settled back in his chair, crossed his boots, picked briefly at a strand of torn upholstery.

"So," he mused. "You're a genuine aristocrat, then? A real one? The kind that stand around getting their portraits painted in fur coats and silly wigs?"

"The same."

"And what would you be if you still . . . if you still were what you was? If you don't mind my asking."

Erryn thought for a bit before he answered.

"Just between us, then? Word of honour? This is not something I want bandied around the taverns."

"Word of honour, mate. Your secret will die in my stomach."

"I'm the son of an earl, and an heir to the throne—very far down the line, but an heir nonetheless. Count back through all my great-greats and you'll eventually find William the Conqueror."

He took another long, meditative drink. "Just think of it, Matt. If enough people were to keel over and die on the same day, I could be king of England."

"Now there's a terrifying thought."

"Especially to me. Which is why I'm in the absurd position of having to pray often and earnestly for the good health of my kin . . . quite a few of whom I thoroughly detest."

"Very sad," Matt agreed. "And here I thought being born a bastard in a Halifax brothel was bloody hard luck. It's all relative, isn't it?"

In the silence that followed, Erryn could hear the rattle of a late night carriage fading down the hill, and the soft, maddening tick of a clock across the room.

"There must be times," he said finally, "when you'd like to empty a keg of beer on my head and throw me out in a snowbank."

"No," Matt said. The smile on his face was warm, affectionate, utterly genuine. "Why should I do that? I'd lose my best friend. And anyways, I was only partly joshing you. I think it really *is* relative, most of it. There's only so much a body can hurt without dying, doesn't matter who you are. Bottom is bottom. I've been hungrier and colder and scareder than you ever dreamt of, probably, but I'd be a sorry damn fool to say I'd been further down. There's a whole lot of different handbaskets a man can go to hell in."

"That's true. Wooden ones, iron ones, pretty purple paper ones—"

"Oh, Christ, forget I mentioned it."

They laughed and clinked their glasses, and decided that five-thirty in the morning was far too late to be going to bed and far too early to do anything that might require rational thought and attention; therefore the only sensible thing to do was open another bottle.

Erryn would always remember it as the warmest, most companionable drunk of his life.

CHAPTER 9

———✦———

At the Sailors' Church

O Belovèd, it is plain
I am not of thy worth nor for thy place!
—*Elizabeth Barrett Browning*

THE BELLS of Notre-Dame-de-Bonsecours had rung their long, melancholy summons and fallen still. Erryn sat on a rock a small distance away, his arms wrapped around his knees. Memories of Sylvie Bowen whispered across his mind: her rare bits of laughter, her North Country speech, the flash of hunger in her eyes when he offered to take her to the concert; the first shocking image of her face, turned full into the sun. So honest, that gesture, and so brutal, shredding all his fantasies like paper. The pretty sylph he had admired on the street two days ago was gone forever. In her place was a woman close to thirty, wounded and wary.

A woman who still fascinated him. This he reflected on as well: his own fascination, and her remarkable ability to kindle it merely by existing. He wanted to untangle all the contradictions he saw in her: the decorum of the house servant, the toughness that spoke

to him of something rather different—of waterfront taverns, perhaps, or Lancashire's dark, satanic mills—a toughness not unlike
Matt's, self-contained and unapologetic. He wanted to talk to her
for hours, to buy her exquisite dinners and take her to the theatre.
He wanted to see her laugh, really laugh, full-hearted and joyous,
for the sheer wild wonder of being alive.

He thought of these things, and all the while he thought of
them he remembered yesterday at the Morrisons', the two experiences reflecting off each other like light in mirrors—or, perhaps,
like ricocheting billiard balls, veering into unexpected corners as
they struck. He was not so naive as to imagine that Sylvie
Bowen's life was a haven of innocence and honesty, and yet,
remembering the party, he found himself waiting for her as for a
clean summer rain.

Certainly the party had been a success; he had accomplished
everything he intended, even a first meeting with the Irish
importer Daniel Carroll. Still, an air of unpleasantness remained
with him, a deep distaste for some of the men he had encountered
there, and equally, a measure of discomfort with his own manipu-
lations and lies. And then there was Edmund Morrison's collection. It had come just after suppertime, the host at the head of his
table, the whole long grace of it shimmering with candles, the
taste of superb food and wine still lingering in everyone's mouth,
and Morrison reminding them of the poor Southern refugees, the
escaped prisoners, the brave soldiers who longed to return to the
battlefield. Money poured into his silver tureen like wine.

English money. A fine fat wad of it from Erryn Shaw's hand.

This was, of course, a legitimate expenditure for a spy, and
indeed a familiar one. All such generosity bought Erryn status,
credibility, trust. He was always quick to offer boat tickets, rent
money, meals; gifts to ragged men from Johnson's Island shivering
in the cold. *Here, for God's sake, buy yourself a coat.* He begrudged
none of them food or shelter; they were not, after all, the men
who had started the war. But he begrudged the Confederacy

every man he helped to send back into its armies, and he begrudged in particular the good English money that paid for it. It was blood money, plain and simple, and more and more he disliked the smell of it on his hands.

So he waited for Sylvie Bowen with impatience—far too much impatience for a sensible, grown-up man. The clamorous rue St-Paul was quieter than usual. Most of its traffic was pedestrian, and most of its shouting came from street vendors selling food: meat pies, fruit, chips in little pockets of newspaper. He noticed a carriole swing by, driven rather too fast, he thought, for a narrow Sunday street, but he paid no particular attention until he heard the crash, and the great stream of shouts and yelps and curses that came after.

A hundred feet away an old cart lay tumbled on its side, its small, bony horse pulled down with it. The vehicle had obviously been overloaded, and its load was now rolling across the cobblestones: turnips and potatoes, hundreds of them, scattering willy-nilly like brown and yellow cricket balls. Dozens of strangers were stopping to gather them; others, equally numerous, stuffed as many as possible into their satchels or their clothing and fled. Curses flew in at least three languages and four directions, and dogs and running children chased after the tumbling vegetables as though it were all a game.

Erryn unwound himself from his rock and went to help, as much from boredom as from any belief that he would be of use. And indeed, all he managed to save was one small turnip and the cart driver's ruined hat, in return for getting his ribs elbowed and his left foot thoroughly tramped on.

But he did see a carriage some distance back, a very fine carriage, waiting for the street to clear, and he was swept by a sudden, astonishing rush of happiness.

What a fool I will feel if it is someone else.

But it was not. The carriage stopped beside the church and he watched Sylvie Bowen step down with the same easy grace as before, watched her take the old woman's arm and lead her slowly to the church steps. Her face was half hidden by her hair, and all her attention was fastened on her companion. She did not look for him. On the contrary, it seemed that she purposefully avoided looking for him. Nor did she come out of the church again for several eternal minutes, and then slowly, idly, as any servant might who had an hour to herself and was wondering how she might spend it.

"Miss Bowen."

"Oh, Mr. Shaw. How nice to see you again."

There was not a trace of warmth in her voice. She might as well have been speaking to the milkman, polite and matter-of-fact: *Three gallons today, thank you. Put it on our bill.* Only her eyes betrayed her for a small, perilous moment before she lowered them.

He said all the usual things—*The pleasure is all mine, I trust you're well, etc., etc.*—and offered to take her to see the clowns in Place Viger.

"Thank you, Mr. Shaw. But there's not enough time for anything like that."

"But it's Sunday. So it'll be High Mass, won't it? I thought a High Mass took more than an hour."

If she wondered how an English Protestant happened to know this, she gave no sign. "There's no Mass at all," she said. "Mass be in the morning Sunday. It's only Benediction."

But you said . . . ! He stifled his involuntary wail of protest. "And how long is Benediction?"

"Maybe twenty minutes."

"Oh." Time to walk to Place Viger and turn around and walk back again. He forced himself to smile. "Well, no clowns, then. Where would you like to go instead? We could have tea. Chez Robert has wonderful sweets and pastries. Or we could just walk about and eat ices, and try not to get hit by a turnip." He placed one arm over his breast and bowed elaborately, gracefully. "I am at your command, my lady."

Her mouth crinkled, just a tiny bit, such a tiny bit that he was not absolutely certain if he had seen it or if he merely wished to see it.

"I'm most always inside with Madame," she said. "It'd be nice to walk."

It was the briefest twenty minutes of his life. He bought them *tourtières*, and a pair of beautiful, mouth-watering apples. She ate hungrily, with obvious pleasure. They wandered up to the Champ-de-Mars, where there were benches and a vendor selling strawberry ice. They found a spot to sit. By this time the bell was ringing again at Bonsecours, and scarcely anything had been said between them except pleasantries.

Through it all she remained cool to him—altogether proper and polite, thanking him for the food, answering freely to everything he said, and yet cool, distant, a stranger—a stranger she had not been on the riverbank two days before.

He did not believe she was the sort to tease, to blow hot and cold merely to pique a man's interest. He had not offended her in any way, as far as he knew. Which left the gloomy probability that she had given it all some thought and decided he was not the sort of man she would invite into her life—too much the fine young gentleman, perhaps, the sort who seduced and abandoned servant girls for sport.

"Are you afraid of spiders, Miss Bowen?"

"Spiders?" She regarded him as though he were daft. "Scraggy little things no bigger than my fingernail? Course not."

"That's good," he said. "Because there's a big black one sitting"— he reached very slowly, very carefully—"right on your collar."

"Oh."

She did not react at all except to turn her head as he nudged the spider onto his finger. It panicked, of course, and dashed madly across his wrist and over his sleeve. Astonishing, he thought, how the little buggers could run.

"Don't kill it," she said quickly. "Please."

"Wouldn't dream of it. I rather like them, actually. Back home I had a friend who kept them for pets. The last time I saw him he had twenty-three." He smiled. "Now you really think I'm daft."

"No," she said. "I think you might be the sort what makes up stories."

"Me? I never told a fib in my life." He plucked the creature off him with a dead leaf and dropped it in the bushes.

"He really had twenty-three spiders?"

"He probably had more, but they kept moving around. We got bored trying to count them and gave up."

That glorious little crinkle was playing on her mouth again. He went on:

"They were his second hive, or swarm, or whatever it is you call a bunch of spiders. His landlady killed off the first ones. He had an arrangement with the maid, you see: he left her tuppence every week and she left his spiders alone. One day the maid was sick and the landlady came to do his room. Of course she saw all the spiderwebs hanging in the corners, and being one of those who look on cleanliness as next to godliness, she fetched herself a great godly broom and swept them all to perdition. When he came home, he found one poor spider scared half to death, hiding under his pillow. All the rest were gone."

"What did he do?"

"He told the landlady someone had been in his room and taken his personal property. She went all into a dither. First the maid had left his room a shameful mess, and now someone had robbed him—and him her favourite tenant, too, a fine young constable who always paid his rent on time and didn't steal the silverware . . . Well, the poor lady was practically beside herself, until he told her what it was he'd lost. Then, I understand, things got interesting. I wouldn't have minded being a spider on the wall myself. But he won the day when he called her a heretic."

"A *heretic?*"

"Quite. She put her foot down, you see. She told him no,

absolutely not, nobody could keep spiders for pets, she wouldn't stand for it, it was unnatural. So he asked her, wasn't she a Christian? 'Yes, of course,' she said. 'No, you're not,' he said. 'You're a heretic. You're saying God didn't make spiders.' 'I'm saying no such thing,' she said. 'Of course God made spiders.' 'Oh,' he said, 'then you're saying God went around making unnatural stuff. That makes you a worse heretic.'

"Well, he turned the thing upside down and inside out till the poor lady didn't know what she believed. Besides, it meant a lot to her, having him in the house, old as she was and living in a rough part of town. So she went back to her parlour and he went out for a beer, and that was the end of it. Nobody bothered his creatures again."

All the time he was telling the story Sylvie was watching him—cautious, he thought, unsure of him, but also intrigued. Bit by bit her coolness left her, falling away like a forgotten shawl. He was sure now she had never really felt it; she had only wrapped it around herself for safety.

"So why did he pick spiders? Instead of a cat or something? Did he ever tell you?"

"He said they were elegant, and they killed flies. Said he hated flies."

"I can understand that." She stood up—regretfully, it seemed. "I must go back, Mr. Shaw."

"Will Madame Louise be in a good mood, do you think? Being Sunday and all, and having been to church twice?"

"Why?"

He tucked her arm into his as they moved quietly onto the street. "Because I would like to meet her. Reassure her that you are in the hands of an honourable gentleman from a perfectly respectable family, and persuade her to let me take you to the concert."

"She'd be horrified."

"Dear heavens, am I as ugly as that?"

"Oh, no, you're not ugly at all, you look perfectly fine. I mean she'd be horrified at me. Going down to the river when she told me not to. And meeting you like this."

"Well, we don't have to tell her about the riverbank. You can say I helped you rescue a poor old man who got knocked over by a carriage on the street."

She regarded him very dubiously indeed.

"Well," he said cheerfully, "I did rescue a turnip."

"Mr. Shaw."

"Erryn. Please."

"Erryn. I'd like to walk out with you. I'd like it more than most anything. But Madame . . ." She paused, searching for words. "Madame has been so kind to me. I don't want to make her angry."

"But—"

"She's a good woman, please don't ever think different. But she told Miss Susan right out she didn't want someone who'd be flirting with the lads every time she turned around. I think she were frightfully unhappy with her husband, and she hasn't much use for it at all—young folks walking out, I mean, and courting and such. She told me once I were the only young woman she knew who had any sense. And she'd think I'd lost it all, taking up with a man on the street. Especially one so . . . so fine and well bred like yourself."

Especially? But of course. We should all keep to our own . . .

"But I thought you worked for someone else. A Miss Susan, you said, wasn't it? So even if Madame got annoyed at you, would it matter very much?"

"It might. She can't read anymore, and she used to love it. She has a house full of books. She says after I go back to Miss Susan, I should come on my half day to read to her. I read to her every day now, since we've been travelling together. When I don't know what a word means, she tells me, and tells me how to say them. She says I be learning fast, and if I take care of them I might have books to take home with me, to read by myself. She says even a poor lass can make something of her life here in Canada, if she has a bit of ambition."

She had stopped walking, and turned to him. "It be a chance for me, see, though I suppose it don't sound like much, with you having all the books you want. But I love reading more than anything. If I can go every week, I can learn all sorts of things, m'appen enough to get some other work. She has a piano, too, and I could hear her play—I'd die for that. But if she gets mad at me, and won't let me come, then I've lost it all. Then I just make beds and scrub dirty floors. Nobody'll ever hire me for anything else, not with this face. So . . ."

She looked at the cobblestones, and at a wheelbarrow going by, and then at him again. He knew her fear was exaggerated. Madame was old and almost blind, apparently at odds with many of her kin. Surely she would be glad to have someone come to read to her, and talk, and admire her Mozart sonatas. Surely she would not give it up simply because Sylvie had befriended a stranger in the street. Surely she would do no more than sniff, and offer up a proper wise-old-lady lecture, and then the world would go on as before.

Surely.

But maybe "surely" wasn't good enough. Maybe, when you had nothing, "surely" was only hope concealing terror. Nobody knew for certain what those who were stronger might do when they got angry. Madame could buy herself another Sylvie Bowen as fast as laying down a coin.

He opened his mouth to speak, to say it was all right, he understood, but she spoke first.

"If we lived here, it would be different. But it's just a visit. After she's finished her novena, we'll be going home. And I won't see you anymore, anyway. So . . ." She met his eyes, openly, honestly, the way she had on the riverbank. "So if you came to the church again, and spent an hour with me once or twice, I'd like it awfully. And I'll always remember it."

He was ready for most anything, but not for this.

"You're going home?" he said. "I thought you lived here, you and Madame. Where is home, then?"

Nassau, where her aunt was buried? No, it couldn't be; she said she would never put a flower on the grave. Quebec? No, Madame was not French; it was her husband who was French.

England? Oh, please, God, not England . . .

"A long way," she said. "In Nova Scotia. Halifax."

"*Halifax?*" He laughed, and took her hard by the shoulders. "Sylvie Bowen, you're a veritable sorceress! You can say a single word and make the whole world perfect!"

"I'm going a thousand miles away, and the whole world's perfect? Well." She drew his hands away and turned to walk again.

"I live there." He was grinning like a cat in a creamery, and he did not care.

"I don't believe you," she said.

"I ran the theatre on Grafton Street, before it burned in '61. I live on Morris, about a block from the Governor's Grounds. When I'm flush I eat dinner at Compain's, and when I'm poor I eat at Corey's. And I'll wager five bob the Miss Susan you work for is Susan Danner, Jack Danner's wife. They keep that fine four-storey boarding house on Barrington, the one they call the Den. Now do you believe me?"

She stopped again. "You never said a word."

"Neither did you." He brushed her hair back from her forehead, lightly. "I think we've talked about everything in the world except ourselves. How are you travelling home? By way of Portland, I suppose?"

"Yes, from Quebec. Madame has a sister-in-law there, in a convent, one of those dreadful strict ones where they let you see somebody once or twice a year, and you have to talk to them through a screen. We'll take the night boat, and go and see her, and catch the Portland train the same afternoon."

"Which boat? I mean, which day? I'm heading home myself. It would be grand if we could go together."

"Thursday."

"I'll move heaven and earth to be on it," he said, and was rewarded with a flash of sheer shameless pleasure in her eyes. Too late, she looked away and changed the subject.

"So you ran a theatre?" she said wistfully. "That must have been wonderful. Did many people come?"

"Most of our shows were packed. Though I must tell you, it wasn't much of a theatre—just a big bare room, really, the upper floor over Richey's Warehouse. We had a raised stage at one end, and wooden benches for the audience, and some pot-bellied stoves so they didn't all freeze to death. The actors had to dress in a little hole in the back of the warehouse, and come up the back stairs to the stage. But I brought in some fine touring companies from the States, and every year the lads from the garrison and I would put together a decent amateur production. It wasn't London, but it was all right. Have you ever been to the theatre?"

"No. Madame says her cousins and their friends do plays sometimes, at their parties, and even at the balls at Government House. But I've never seen a play. I'd love to, someday."

Madame's cousins at Government House? That brought him up short, until he recalled how Sylvie had first described the blind woman's family: *Merchants, the lot of them, and a great proper clan of rich Presbyterians to boot, except for the one who ran off and married a French-Canadian Papist from a Boston merchant brig.*

Oh, hell, he thought. *That's* who Madame Louise was. Bloody damned hell.

The connection had never crossed his mind. It should have, he supposed, but he had been thinking so much of other things, and he had simply assumed that Sylvie and Madame lived in Montreal, or at least somewhere in the West. And so none of those other people had ever crossed his mind—the other widow who was named Louise, the other clan of rich and proper Presbyterians— the clan of Halifax timber magnate David Scott, whose daughter had indeed, many years ago, eloped with a junior officer from a

Yankee merchant ship, to the universal horror of her kin. David Scott, whose sister married Douglas Orton, and who had himself wed a sister of the same house. Living in Halifax, there was but one person Madame Louise could be: Louise Doreen Mallette. David Scott's daughter.

James bloody Orton's first cousin.

This was a complication of the first order, but before he could begin to think seriously about it, they had reached the church. He lifted her hand to his lips, caressing it rather longer than was proper. If she minded, she gave no sign.

"Tomorrow, sweet Sylvie Bowen?"

"Yes," she said. And she did something then that quite amazed him. She reached, quietly, deliberately, and played the back of her hand across his cheek. He had never considered himself handsome—nor had anyone else, as far as he knew—yet there was a fierce admiration in her eyes, as though she found him astonishing and perfect.

Only after she had fled, wordless, into the church did he see the meaning of it—the possible meaning, at least: that to a woman who bore such cruel scars, perhaps he was.

CHAPTER 10

——◆——

The Grand Conspiracy

With the *Michigan* under our command . . . we would have had
the lake shore from Sandusky to Buffalo at our mercy, with all the
vast commerce of Lake Erie as our just and lawful prey.
—*Captain Robert D. Minor, Confederate Navy*
Report to Admiral Franklin Buchanan, February 2, 1864

AFTER ERRYN LEFT Sylvie at the sailors' church, he found a fallen
log in the grass near the river and sat for a time to collect his
thoughts. Five days back, in the quiet house in the Champ-de-Mars,
Agent Latour had told him of Daniel Carroll, the man who had
gone with Jackson Follett to George Kane's house and afterwards
ordered fifty dumbbells. Yesterday, at Morrison's party, Erryn had
drawn the Irishman quietly aside and offered him an enticing business proposition. Alexander MacNab in Halifax was looking for an
agent in the West, he said, a good, sharp man with contacts on the
Lakes who could buy Western goods at favourable prices and ship
them to the coast. The offer was genuine; MacNab had broached
it months ago, and Erryn had tucked it into his back pocket, to
offer to precisely the right man at precisely the right moment.
Carroll bit like a hungry fish, and invited him to Sunday supper.

Sunday supper was now an hour or so away. Erryn ran his hands across his face, and watched a small squirrel scamper past his feet and vanish in the scrub. Carroll was his only possible link to a conspiracy on the Lakes—if indeed such a conspiracy existed—and Erryn knew scarcely anything about him. Carroll was a good businessman, he was second-generation Irish, he liked music. That was all.

He liked music . . . Well, Erryn thought, it was something, and tonight it would have to serve, because it was all he had.

The first thing that struck him at Daniel Carroll's house was its air of unpretentious friendliness. He was thoroughly charmed by the man's family. Mrs. Carroll was a striking woman, fine-featured, gracious, and obviously with child. They had two daughters, whose ages Erryn guessed at ten and nine, and a boy of perhaps seven. Erryn had been to many suppers where children were fed separately and shooed away. Here they sat at the table, even the youngest, and they behaved adorably. Erryn told stories to make them laugh, many from the life of his boyhood idol, the admiral.

"He was a grand old chap, the admiral. My father was a close kinsman, you see, so we were often invited to his house. And I've no wish to speak ill of him, for he was a great hero, but sometimes he could be a grouch. Now, the admiral had a cat. Oh, he had dogs too, like any English gentleman, but to him a dog was nothing but a dog, something to chase after foxes and make a lot of noise. But cats . . . well, cats were lordly creatures, cats were the ancient companions of kings. One day he found this poor, bedraggled kitten on the road and brought it home with him. Nobody ever knew what was wrong with it, but it sneezed. All the time. Over and over. It would hunch its shoulders and go *uh-choo!* And wipe its paw across its face, and go *uh-choo!*" All of this Erryn demonstrated, very politely and delicately, to the vast amusement of the table. "So everyone in the house called the little thing Sniffles. No matter how hard the admiral tried to name it something grand, it remained Sniffles. Eventually he gave up.

"Now, as the tale was told to me, the older Sniffles got, the more he came to be like his master. He got grouchy. Only the admiral, being an officer and a gentleman, kept his grouchiness mostly to himself, but Sniffles, being only a cat, let the whole world know. And do you want to know what Sniffles did when he was mad about something?"

Erryn turned expectantly to the children, who quickly exchanged glances with their parents and with each other.

"He bit people?" the eldest suggested.

"Oh, heavens no. He was a *gentleman's* cat. He'd never bite anyone. No, he hid things. And always only one of them. One glove. One stocking. One cufflink. When Sniffles got his back up, one of everything in the house went missing. And it was a big house."

The children giggled. "He took only one?"

"Only one."

"And did anyone ever *find* it again?"

"Oh, most everything turned up eventually, in some corner or another. At first the servants were blamed, or the younger children, and they were all very indignant, as you can imagine. But the admiral never blamed anyone. I think he always knew it was the cat."

And I think it tickled him, too, the sorry old sea hound with his one arm and his one eye and his hard, hard memories. "There, the rest of you can get along with one for a while too, ha ha!" He'd never have admitted it, of course, not even to himself, but it tickled him.

Tickled me, too, if you want to know the truth of it.

"Sniffles got caught finally, when he tried to drag a boot up to the attic in the middle of the night. Of course, he couldn't lift it properly, so it thumped on every step. Some people thought the ghosts were out, and pulled their covers over their heads. But three of us went to investigate. And there he was, hauling away on that poor old boot like a sailor on a rope. We didn't try to stop him. We just stood there and laughed ourselves silly."

—◆—

It was much later when they rose from the table, admirably fed and contented. It might have seemed to Erryn that he had known this family for years. It might have seemed so, that is, if he had allowed himself, even for a moment, to forget why he had come.

"I'm told you have a liking for a ballad or two," he said, "so I took the liberty of bringing along my flute."

"Oh, and did you now? What a grand idea! Let us have some of that fine Madeira in the parlour, Annie, and I'll teach this young Englishman to sing!"

"Can we come too, Papa?" pleaded the elder daughter.

"Mr. Shaw and I have business to discuss, my love," Carroll said, "so you can't stay for very long. Just for a while."

The parlour of Daniel Carroll's house was large and finely furnished, yet it had a plainness about it too, an air of warmth and easy comfort rather than of show. For an hour and more it rang with song. Annie Carroll could play most anything on the piano, merely from hearing a verse sung or a few bars of the melody from Erryn's flute. And there was nothing Carroll loved better than an old song. He had a fine tenor voice, a prodigious memory for verses, and he sang everything with passion, as if the heroism of the ballads, and the love and the grief, were all of it his own.

Erryn was genuinely sorry when his hostess bade them a gracious good night and took the children off to bed.

"Don't be putting your flute away just yet," Carroll said after the door had closed. "Annie so loves to play, I can't deny her. But I'd fancy hearing that pipe of yours just all of itself, if you'd do me the honour."

"It would be a pleasure," Erryn said. "You have a beautiful family, Mr. Carroll. I dare say I envy you."

"Why, thank you for that. I love them dearly, and that's the truth of it. There's no luckier man alive."

They settled into their chairs, as comfortable together as old friends. If less had been at stake, Erryn would have been sorely troubled by his role here tonight. As it was, he was troubled nonetheless, but he was prepared to live with it.

He blew a few tentative bars and then asked for his host's preferences.

"Ah, play whatever you fancy. You could break a man's heart with that pipe, you could."

He played a bit of O'Carolan, and a bit of Mozart, and a bit of Southern Confederacy. Between the songs they talked of one thing and another, the cities they lived in, and the American war, and even, for a little while, Ireland. So the evening sped away, along with two more bottles of excellent Madeira, some of which Erryn regretfully consigned to a sodden handkerchief, tucked into a wineskin in his pocket. This was a simple manoeuvre at a crowded, noisy dinner party; it was far more difficult in a company of two. Fortunately, Carroll got up twice to tend the fire, and once again to fetch a book he admired. When he left the room altogether, probably to relieve himself, Erryn quickly emptied the wineskin and most of his glass into a potted plant.

By then the hallway clock was striking eleven. The rest of the house was quiet, the children long asleep, and the servants gone to their rooms. Carroll was cheerfully but thoroughly drunk.

A likeable man, Erryn reflected. An altogether decent man, as far as he could judge. Surely not the sort to be hatching plots with Jackson Follett? What reason could he possibly have? He had a future as promising as a gold brick road. He had a beautiful family. He had, as one might say, every damn thing a man could want.

You are chasing phantoms, Erryn Shaw. Give the man your hand, thank him for dinner, and go home.

No. Not yet. Men like this have been on the wrong side of wars since war began.

He took up the flute again and played softly, almost idly.

"That's a fine, melancholy piece," Carroll said when he paused. "I've not heard it before."

"It's called 'Sweet Lorena.' A favourite, I'm told, in the Southern camps." He leaned back into the pool of comfortable silence and stretched his long legs out over the carpet. For a considerable time he had been studying Carroll, wondering how to play him, hoping a turn in the conversation might lead to an opening. Nothing had. He would have to gamble, that was all—gamble on Carroll's friendliness, gamble on the wine. "I say, Carroll, have you ever been tempted . . . Oh, I suppose not. With a young family and all, a man wouldn't be. But sometimes I am, you know. Tempted. To get my hand in. I've done a few things for Jack Follett and the lads, but so often I think it's not enough, I ought to be doing more. At the same time"—here he paused with a small, self-conscious laugh—"at the same time, I don't fancy spending the next five years in a Yankee prison camp. Least of all that one on Johnson's Island."

Carroll tensed a little at the name; or perhaps he only shifted in his chair. In lamplight, it was hard to tell.

"No," he said. "You certainly wouldn't want that." He reached for the Madeira. "You'll have a wee drop more, won't you? And then, if you'll not mind me being forward, perhaps we might talk about your business? Be a sin to keep you out all night, it would, with my going on forever about Ireland."

"Ah, yes, thank you," Erryn said. He held out his glass and went on as though he had heard nothing except the offer of another drink. "The truth is, I've been tempted a great deal more of late, and I was hoping perhaps you could advise me."

"I don't see how, and that's a fact. A decision like that a man has to make for himself."

"Oh, the decision is made. I want in. The question is how and where. And I've heard rumours there's something grand afoot, a raid across the Lakes, and it seems pretty obvious where it's going.

I mean to ask Jack Follett if I can go along, but to tell you the truth, though he's as fine a man as I've been privileged to know, and bright too, his followers . . . well, his followers have planned more than one disaster.

"So I'm in a bit of a dilemma. And I was wondering—oh, it's damnably impertinent to ask, I know, but the hell of it is, there's no one else. I can't tell Jack I want to go along and then, if I find it's all some piece of folly, turn about and say to him: 'Ah, sorry, mate, I've changed my mind.' So will you tell me, Carroll, friend to friend: How the devil are we going to take that gunboat? Or have a hope in the world of capturing Johnson's Island if we don't take it?"

He waited for Carroll to laugh, to stare at him in astonishment, to ask the immediate, obvious, bewildered questions: What gunboat? Who's capturing Johnson's Island? God in heaven, man, what are you on about?

But Carroll's astonishment was of a very different kind. Even in the lamplight his pallor was remarkable, and his response was far too controlled and far too late: "I have no idea what you mean, sir."

So. Not a phantom at all, then.

"Of course you do. I know you've been meeting with Jack, and with George Kane. You brought in the dumbbells they want for cannon shot—at least I hope it's what they want them for. And don't look so panicked, for God's sake, we're on the same side. I'm just tired of standing by and watching, that's all." He waited for a breath and went on: "I swear it, Carroll, I'll never let on we ever spoke of this. And I'll get you that deal with Al MacNab, too."

Carroll got up and prodded distractedly at the fire. He spoke while still on one knee, with his back to his guest.

"Was it himself that said I bought him dumbbells, then?"

Erryn hesitated. No answer to this question was safe.

"He didn't mean to. He made a slip, that was all. But I've been buying arms for him too, so I just put two and two together."

Carroll walked back to his chair. He did not immediately sit. He stared down at Erryn Shaw as if he could not comprehend how their evening of camaraderie had come to this.

"I mean no unkindness, Mr. Shaw, but when a matter's told a man in confidence, he ought to be keeping his word. It isn't right, now, you asking me to break it."

"You're not breaking your word. You're sounding out a new recruit. How the devil do you suppose the others got to be part of this? Somebody told Jack Follett, didn't they? Somebody told you. Bloody hell, man, if nobody ever told anybody, there'd still be but twenty-two of them, sitting in Halifax twiddling their thumbs!"

Carroll sat heavily. He had had far too much to drink to untangle the web in which he found himself, much less to set one himself. Worse, he appeared to suspect nothing hostile. He was surprised, bewildered, perhaps even a little angry, but he did not imagine he was in the presence of an enemy.

"Sure, and what else is drifting around in the streets, then, that I don't know about?"

"Easy, mate," Erryn said. "It's not in the streets. But there's a few lads around Jack who . . . Hell, you know how it is. Between friends, things get said. Maybe they shouldn't, but they do. And there's no harm done. In fact I'm glad, because I've been hoping for some action, and this might be just the thing."

"Then it's Jack you should be asking, not myself."

"He's my friend. How the deuce can I tell him I don't always trust his judgment? Could you do that to a man like Jack?"

"No. I don't suppose I could." Carroll poured more Madeira and drank his portion at one go. "It sounds to me like you know most of it already."

Erryn laughed softly. "Enough to have a damnable itch, my friend, but not enough to scratch it."

Carroll did not smile. In truth, he looked miserably unhappy.

"For God's sake, Carroll, I want to help. And surely they can use another man."

"You'll swear it on your mother's grave, then? You'll not let on we spoke of it—not to Jack nor to anyone?"

"Never. And least of all to Jack. You have my word."

"Well, I can tell you this much. You won't regret it if you go along. The lads in charge are navy men—they know what they're about. And the Yankees won't suspect a thing. Our boys are going down as labourers, off to the waterworks in Chicago. They had it all planned out weeks ago, to get on a passenger steamer somewhere quiet, maybe off the canal, and take it over once 'twas in the middle of the lake—out of Canadian waters, you see. But the Yankee boats don't stop on our side, except once in a while, and they couldn't count on it. So they were all at sixes and sevens what to do. 'Twas myself recalled the screw steamers running back and forth to Ogdensburg, bringing corn and provisions from the West, and going back half empty most of the time. A deckload of passengers would just be money in their pockets. And who's to give it a second thought—a band of young men off to new jobs, now that the harvest here is over and so many in the States gone off to war? All the lads were needing was a man to go to Ogdensburg to buy the tickets and arrange for them all to be picked up."

"Why, that's brilliant," Erryn said. "Now I'm more tempted than ever. Still, a group of young men off to find jobs can't be travelling armed for war, surely?"

"There's a passenger will be bringing on some trunks. Alone, of course—no connection whatever between him and the lads. They'll have everything they need, even knives for close work if it comes to that."

"My knives, I wager," Erryn said cheerfully. "I bought the best I could find. But damned if I want to wave one at a cannon. Please. Tell me we'll have a little nine-pounder at least?"

"Aye, that you will."

"Thank God. Otherwise . . ." He raised both hands. "Otherwise, I fear it would be another of those glorious expeditions they write sad songs about. 'Alas for the boys who sailed to Johnson's

Island,' and so forth." He paused, just for a breath. "It *is* the island we'll be after, isn't it? The gunboat first, of course, and then the prison?"

Carroll was already compromised beyond any possible salvation, but still he hesitated. Somewhere outside, a dog barked, five or six times.

"You'll not be forgetting your promise, Erryn Shaw?"

"I will not."

"Aye, it's the prison they're after."

"As I thought. Once they've taken the *Michigan*, and the prison is under her guns, the Yankees will have no choice except surrender. And we'll have the steamer and the gunboat both to fetch the prisoners away."

"Jesus, no. The harbour boats will serve for that. The *Michigan*'s a warship. The lads'll take her raiding, and there's nothing on the Lakes that can stop her. She'll be worth a small army, she will."

It was Erryn's turn to be silent. A Confederate raider, armed and unopposed, loose on the lake, with all of Erie's shipping as her prey, and every harbour town from Sandusky to Buffalo in the path of her guns? The expedition launched from Canadian territory, armed with Canadian assistance, planned in part by Canadian agents . . . ? God almighty. He doubted that any political leader, any diplomat in the world, could resolve such a crisis short of war. And war would be the end of them—all of them, their little ribbon of colonies crushed between two empires, precious to neither, sacrificed by both.

And you, Daniel Carroll, what have you learned from your ballads of poor battered Ireland, except how to sing?

"That is extraordinary," he said at last. "With good men, and a bit of luck . . . I dare say it's just about flawless."

"It is, isn't it? I don't mind if I say so myself." Carroll smiled. Some of the tension seemed to be leaving him. He refilled their glasses. "So. A wee drink to your grand adventure, Mr. Shaw."

"Why, thank you."

Erryn sipped his Madeira briefly without tasting it. He had learned enough, he thought, to protect the country's peace. The trick now would be to protect himself. He placed the glass quietly back on the table.

"I fear, Mr. Carroll, that it's altogether too grand an adventure for me. As I said, I don't fancy a Yankee prison, and I fancy an English one even less."

Carroll stared at him. "You don't want to go now? But you said the plan was flawless."

"That's the trouble. It's too flawless. It's going to start a fire too big for anyone to put out. What do you suppose the government will make of the likes of us, violating Her Majesty's neutrality laws in such a fashion, collaborating with a foreign power to bring war upon her colonies—"

"Nobody takes those neutrality laws seriously, for all love. They're lip service. The Confederacy's building her raiders in Liverpool shipyards, right under the government's nose!"

"Of course. But that's just commerce. Things will be a bit different when it turns to war. Especially for Irishmen."

"Irishmen?" Carroll whispered.

"Yes, Irishmen. Fenians. Rebels. That's what it's all about, isn't it? What does a man like you care about a bunch of American plantation owners? Bloody hell, they were all English themselves just a few generations back. But if there were a war between England and America, well, that would be a fine occasion for the Irish to rise, now, wouldn't it? The Fenians certainly think so. They've been organizing for years in the States, waiting for a moment just like this. Didn't you think anyone would make the connection? Violating the Foreign Enlistment Act, that's only a prison offence. But plotting with the Fenians, that's an attack on the Crown. That's high treason."

"For the love of Mary, I don't even know any Fenians!"

"Oh, you probably do; they have a lively chapter here in Montreal. But even if you don't, do you think it will matter? Once our friends start burning Ohio, and the Yankees declare war, all that Her Majesty's government is going to care about is finding heads to roll."

It was, Erryn thought, as though Carroll had been holding a piece of wood or stone that was mutating in his hands, dissolving, running through his fingers. On the wall, the pendulum ticked, slowly and harshly.

"But . . ." he said finally, "but, damn it, they *want* to settle with the Yankees. *Everybody* wants to!"

"Unfortunately, Mr. Carroll, everybody doesn't. And even those who do will prefer to hold up nice clean hands to the people and say: Listen, we didn't start this. It was just a few God damned Fenians, and look, we've hanged every last one.

"This is going to wreck every man who came near it, and I don't fancy being wrecked. Which leaves you with two choices. You tell the authorities you discovered this dangerous little plot—you needn't name names, because if they stop it in time, they won't much care about the names. Or else I tell them, and I *will* name names."

"You'd betray Jack's friends? You want me to betray them?"

"Oh, bollywogs. I want you to save your damn fool neck, and mine while you're at it. Nobody'll get hurt. The Confederates will just sigh and say, alas, another good plan down the river. God knows my heart is with them, but they do bungle." Erryn paused for a fraction and added quietly: "Think about your family, for Christ's sake."

"My family." Carroll got to his feet, far steadier than Erryn expected. He walked aimlessly for a moment and then turned. His face was bitter and grim. "And what do you suppose will become of my family, and myself, once the Southerners learn what I've done to them?"

"Nothing. Without help from England, the Confederacy doesn't have a hope. They can't afford to kill Englishmen." He paused and added quietly, "Our government, on the other hand, can."

He got to his feet, drawing on every inch of height, every thread of acting skill, every echo of aristocratic power that was bred into him or taught to him: pride and rank and raw class arrogance, abandoned yet still in reach, like the flawless Eton English, the marksmanship, the eye for ships, and horseflesh, and clothes. It helped, also, to be unbeautiful, with a face of hard bones and slate grey eyes, and hands like talons, pulling on the finest, richest of kid gloves.

"You have twelve hours to contact the Canadian authorities. I care not how you do it, but make sure you're taken seriously. At the end of that time I will contact them myself. If the matter is known, I will say nothing more. If it is not, well then, you will be for it."

"You are a fiend out of hell, Erryn Shaw."

"No. In truth, I've done you a service. Oh, yes, there's one other thing. I intend to make a record of your involvement in this matter, to be kept by a friend under lock and key. A ransom for my continuing good health, you understand."

He met Carroll's eye very directly. "As for this meeting between us, and what passed here, keep it to yourself. I have profitable dealings with the Confederates. If I were to lose them on your account, then you would indeed discover me to be a fiend out of hell."

"It's all money to you, then, is that it?" Carroll said bitterly. "All bleeding profit and the rest be damned!"

"My dear fellow, it's bleeding profit for everyone—whatever did you think? Let me tell you what the blockade-runners drink to, when they come to town and we all gather at the Waverley to party. May I?" He reached and poured himself a mouthful of Madeira. "Here's to the Confederacy, for buying everything we bring! Here's to the Union, for driving up the prices! Here's to them all, may the war go on forever!"

He raised the glass high, drained it, and placed it calmly back on the table.

"That is what you drink to? 'May the war go on forever'?"

"Of course. It's making us rich. Shall I see myself out?"

"You may see yourself to the devil."

"Well then, good night. And thank you for dinner. It was very fine."

—◆—

It was almost three when Erryn rapped softly on the door of Jonathan Bryce's house on rue Ste-Catherine. No one answered. After a long time he rapped again, a good deal harder. It was a fine night, but cold. An icy half moon hung high above the river, and the crisp northwest wind had a taste of winter in its teeth. He was glad of his bulky disguise.

A voice came muffled from behind the door. "Who is it?"

"Todd."

A grumble followed, perhaps an obscenity or two. Bryce did not let him in immediately. He stared through the half-opened door, a pistol held firmly in his hand.

"Be damned, it is you. What the devil do you want?"

"May I come in?"

Silently, Bryce stepped back, latched the door behind them, and lit a small kerosene lamp in the hall. Its one window, Erryn noted, was carefully draped.

He took an envelope from his pocket. "Sorry to trouble you, Jon, but it's a message for the governor. It should be sent at once."

The policeman shoved a long rag of hair out of his eyes. He was in a rumpled nightshirt and he looked worn to crumbs.

"You want me to take this to the telegraph office in the middle of the fucking night?"

"Yes," Erryn said. "I'm sorry."

"What is it, anyway? One of your hare-brained raids on Johnson's Island?"

"It's information I believe the governor should receive immediately."

"So take it there yourself."

Erryn was completely spent. It took all his willpower to say nothing, merely to stare as an old Eton master might have done. *Really now, Bryce, really . . .*

"Sorry," Bryce said. "I've had a bloody bastard of a day." He took the offered envelope, knowing as Erryn did that only a handful of men in British North America could read the gibberish inside: Erryn himself, Matt Calverley, and a few staff officers at Canada's Government House. "I hope it's worth it."

"Thank you," Erryn murmured, and turned to go.

"Say, Todd . . . ?"

"What?"

"Good luck, eh? Whatever you've stuck your nose into, don't get it chopped off, all right?"

———◆———

Bryce wasn't a bad sod, he thought, leaning back in the carriage with his eyes half closed. Not the sharpest tack God ever made, but not a bad sod. *Don't get your nose chopped off, Todd.*

It was all in Daniel Carroll's hands now, what became of his nose. Would Carroll go to the Canadian authorities? Would he go to Jackson Follett? Would he sit tight and pray for a miracle? Any of these were possible. Other things, too. Things Erryn had never considered, perhaps. Things he did not want to consider.

He was lost in his thoughts when he stepped from the carriage, and so it took a moment before he noticed motion at the side of the hotel, something or someone disappearing into the trees. He saw it so briefly, he was unsure if it had been a grown man, or a street urchin, or even just a dog.

Brownie in the slouch hat, I wonder? At least he's learning to stay out of sight.

You really were too hard on him, you know.

Ah well, he thought, when the war was over, maybe they would cross paths again and he could buy the poor chap a drink. The

Federal agents were merely doing their job, after all, and whatever Reb shenanigans they could foil on their own, it was all to the good. Besides, in this particular quarrel, he was entirely on their side.

He climbed wearily to his room, pulled off his clothing in slow, uneven motions, like a clockwork toy that was just about to quit. Still, he knew sleep would not come easy. Until tonight his work had always seemed to him something of a game. A dangerous game, admittedly, but nonetheless a game: Alexander MacNab singing gold in my pocket and Jamie Orton singing Bonnie Dundee and some pied piper preacher singing darky come home; an air of nastiness over all of it, but also an air of theatre.

No theatre anymore, no game. He felt as though he had been unceremoniously kicked off the stage and out into the street, with a carriage and four coming at him. *The* Michigan's *a warship. The lads'll take her raiding, and there's nothing on the Lakes that can stop her.*

He stared at his ceiling and wondered just how bad it would have been. He wondered what else might be afoot, as dangerous as this, or even worse. He wondered if Carroll would break, and what would happen if he did not.

Without help from England, the Confederacy doesn't have a hope. They can't afford to kill Englishmen.

Well, maybe. A prominent, prosperous chap like Daniel Carroll, probably not. A hired spy, on the other hand, a colonial exile with a made-up name, whose friends in high places consisted of an aging militia colonel, a police constable, and a chambermaid, well, that might be different.

He had a day, he thought, perhaps two, before all the military defences were in place and all the diplomatic manoeuvres carefully made. Then Lord Monck would make it public, and it would hit the front page of every newspaper in North America. A day, maybe two, for Carroll to make up his mind. Then Erryn Shaw would be utterly in the clear, or utterly finished as an agent. Possibly dead. *Don't get your nose chopped off, Todd.*

The sun was high before he slept.

CHAPTER 11

※

The Rainstorm

Alas, I have grieved so I am hard to love.
Yet love me—wilt thou? Open thine heart wide,
And fold within the wet wings of thy dove.
—*Elizabeth Barrett Browning*

ALL AFTERNOON THE RAIN POURED DOWN, hammering on roofs and cobblestone streets, a cold rain laced with a bitter wind. Despite the storm, Sylvie found Erryn Shaw waiting as usual near the old sailors' church—rather like a solitary lamppost, she thought, buffeted but erect, while everything around him was bent over and scurrying for shelter. He was drenched despite his umbrella, but he seemed happy to see her—extraordinarily happy, as though he had feared the storm might keep her away. Clearly, he did not know Madame.

He had a table for them in the little café across the way, he said. Would she join him for *tourtières*, cake, tea, wine, anything at all she might fancy?

"Oh, I'd much rather have a walk," she said, and then laughed softly as astonishment and dismay and concern all flashed across his face, each on the heels of the other. "You're not an easy man to surprise, Erryn Shaw, but there, I think I've finally done it."

He smiled. "*Tourtières*, then?"

"Oh, yes, please."

The little café truly did have anything she might have fancied. The wine she refused, for Madame would know, but there were pies made with chicken and pork, and with fruits of every description. There were puddings and pieces of iced cake, and tempting, miniature creamy things she had never seen before. Erryn bought recklessly, letting her choose what she wanted and then adding more. "Here, you must have one of these, and yes, one of these too, they're exquisite, you can take some back with you, Madame can't possibly object, not to a *pastry* . . ."

He did not eat much. He seemed on edge—as attentive to her as a man could be, and yet on edge.

"Tell me," he said, "how did we come to like each other so much, when I scarcely know anything about you, and you know even less about me? Does that make it fate, do you suppose?"

"Do you believe in fate?"

"I don't know." His hair was very wet from the rain, hanging across his forehead in long, pale strings. Beside him, more rain streamed across the window glass, shimmering each time lightning slashed across the sky. "I believe in chance, I suppose. Sometimes things just . . . happen. Fate seems to imply design, and I have doubts about design."

"So you're not the religious sort, then?"

He shot her a sudden, sharp glance, as though he wondered if he might have said the wrong thing. Nevertheless he answered the question freely and, she supposed, honestly.

"Not in the usual sense, no. When I was at Eton College, reading the Greek and Roman classics, I used to think I'd have made a good pagan. I liked our old churches, the really *old* ones, and the old graveyards, and the dark places in the woods—places where it seemed spirits might be. I could see how a man might want to talk to spirits, or make them an offering, pour wine into the ground or something. Now . . ." He smiled faintly, made a small, dismissive gesture. "Now I don't know what I think. All the answers seem too easy. Have you ever heard of Procrustes?"

"No. What are they?"

"He. He was a chap in one of the old stories. He had a very famous bed. It was rather on the short side, apparently, and when people came to visit him, if they were on the long side, like me, he cut their feet off to make them fit. I think a lot of ideas in the world are like Procrustes' bed—not bad ideas in themselves, maybe, but not long enough, or wide enough, or deep enough. Reality doesn't quite fit. But when we notice, we don't stand back and say, 'All right, we've missed something. Our philosophy, our politics, our religion, has to adapt.' No, we go get the hatchet and start chopping at the world. Sooner or later, alas, the world invariably chops back." He paused as she nibbled one of the creamy confections. "Is that good?"

"It's wonderful."

"Tell me about your life."

"What?"

He put both elbows on the table and leaned his chin against his hands. "I have this deplorable tendency to babble. I'm sure you've noticed. My father used to say my mouth was like a mill wheel: once it started, you had to drain the river to make it stop. But if you talk to me, I'll be quiet and listen. Tell me where you came from."

It was still day outside, but the heaviness of the storm had darkened the café. The poor light softened his bony features, made him almost handsome, what with his youth and the warmth in his eyes and her own irrepressible admiration. It was glorious to be courted. By anyone, she thought, but especially by a man with so much grace and charm, a man who could make her laugh, a man who knew the world and who could—like Madame, but infinitely more so—open doors to all its marvels. Of course, it was a courtship without a future. He was a gentleman, rich and cocky like they all were, and used to having his way. He was an actor—oh, he wasn't *really*, he said, he was only a second-rate amateur; it was *staging* plays that he was good at, as if it made any difference; he knew how to pretend. He could talk the birds down out of the trees and into the cat's mouth, he was so convincing. He was just acting that he liked her; it was just a game, until he got her into bed, and then he would walk away.

And it was not his getting her into bed that mattered, or even, in the end, his walking away. It was the acting itself. It was the *certainty* that he was acting, that he could not possibly mean the things he said and did, even for a little while. Because no man could.

There was the truth of it, the old truth, older than this temporary wild delight. *Wickerface, wickerface, fly away home, go cut your nose off and make me a comb. God almighty, Bowen, what did the cat look like when it was over?*

Tell me where you came from . . .

For a moment she considered lying, making up an entire life history: a loving family, a tragic accident . . . a train wreck, perhaps. Oh yes, a train wreck would serve perfectly, smash her face and kill everyone else, all except Fran, and then the two of them off to the mills because what else could a lone woman and an orphan child do?

The idea died even as it was conceived. She was not at all sure she could carry it off, but more importantly, she knew it would serve for nothing. She did not want him to like some other lass who had never existed; she wanted him to like her, and probably he would not anyway, he could not. So no, there was no point in telling him anything but the truth.

"We lived in a mill town. A place called Darwen. I don't know if you've ever been there—"

He shook his head no.

"It weren't much. Just the factories and the cottages and some fancy houses for the sods who ran the place. And a church, of course, and lots of taverns. You could get your comfort in one place or the other. Nobody cared which, as long as you didn't bring it to work the next day.

"My ma took her comfort from God, and my pa took his from a bottle. He drank everything they earned, and when my two brothers were nine, he put them in the mill and drank everything they earned too. He beat on her at least once a week. Some women left their men when it got bad enough, but she wouldn't. Her husband were her cross, she said, and she must bear it."

Sylvie had been looking mostly at her plate as she spoke, or at her hands, or at the rain-battered window. Now she looked full at Erryn's face, and was surprised to find neither horror nor pity, only a kind of watchful, driven intensity. He said nothing, and she went on:

"I got to go to school for two years. Then he put me in the mill too. There weren't any laws then about how old you had to be; those came later. And that were the worst of it, Erryn, having to leave the school. It weren't the mill, or even the fighting, except for the last bit. But when I couldn't go to school anymore, then I had nothing to look forward to, ever. There were the mill and there were home, and the mill were likely to kill us, and still it were better than home."

"Did your father beat you, too?"

"Sometimes. Mostly the older ones. But Ma always got between them, so she took the worst of it."

She stared at the window again. She had begun her tale without the least reluctance. It was old history, after all; she was past it. So why was it suddenly so hard to go on?

"You spoke of 'that last bit' of fighting," Erryn murmured, very soft. "It ended badly, didn't it?"

"He killed her."

"My God." His hands slid quickly across the table, but she pulled hers away before they touched.

"Please," she whispered. "I don't want to cry."

"Forgive me. I meant only . . . Please, go on. I'm sorry."

"There ain't much more. He went crazy that night. I don't know why, what were different, except something were. We were all screaming—Ma, me, the little ones. I went at him with the water pitcher. If I'd got his head, I might have knocked him out, but he saw me, and so I only broke it on his shoulder. He took it away so fast, like my hands were made of paper."

She touched her fingers to her cheek, half consciously. "He gave me this. With the pitcher. What were left on it. When I woke up, he were passed out on the floor, and Ma were dead. The neighbours got the sheriff and they took him away. He got hanged, and we got scattered around to whatever relatives would take us. My aunt Fran took me to live with her in Rochdale. It were another mill town, bigger and dirtier than Darwen. Fran were so good to me, but the mill were horrid. They paid the women so little, we couldn't hardly get by. It took forever to save enough to get away."

"To America."

"Yes. Like Fran's old friend, Susan. She went years before, when she were twenty or so—she and her brother. He had a bit of money from the navy. One day Fran wrote to the Bishop of Halifax, bold as brass, asking about her old family friend, thinking m'appen he'd know what'd become of her. That's how we found out she were Susan Danner now. She'd made herself a good life, she even had her own inn—a mill girl, just like us. We lived on that for years."

She wished he would give her a clue to his thoughts. But he sat very quietly, leaning back in his chair, one long, thin hand wrapped around his wineglass, the other out of sight on his lap. As though he had backed off. As though he did not know what the hell to say. *Dear God, the girl's nothing but factory trash* . . . well, he would not *say* it, of course not, he would not even let it show. Damn actors, anyway.

"So," she said. "That's where I come from." She made herself smile, and took another sweet from the plate. "Now it's your turn."

"My turn." He shifted in his chair, played some more with the wineglass. He looked troubled, but even while she ran the obvious, hurtful reasons for it through her mind, she did not entirely believe them. His unease seemed born of something else, something older and altogether his own.

He looked up and met her eyes. "Once, many years ago, a friend of mine said to me, 'There's a whole lot of different handbaskets a man can go to hell in.' He said it to be kind, because he'd been through hell and he knew very well I hadn't, no matter how sorry I felt for myself when I set my mind to it.

"I don't know if he was right about the handbaskets. Maybe a little bit. In any case, mine was a gilded one, as I'm sure you've guessed. I had anything a child could want, except companionship. I didn't get much of that. My father was in the army, and mostly gone. My mother was a great lady, and lived the social life expected of her. She kissed me good night from time to time, and told me to be sure to say my prayers. Our tutor was a grand old cove, but he was positively ancient. Our nurse, with whom we spent most of our time, was rather like a brick fence: the protection is nice, but you can't say much for the conversation. So I went my own way, and before anyone really noticed—even me—I'd turned myself into a considerable misfit. By the time I hit sixteen or thereabouts, my father was in complete despair. I'm sure if he'd believed in changelings, he would have thought the trolls brought me."

"Lord save us, why? I think a man'd be pleased to have a son like you."

"Well, that's very kind of you to say. But my father was of the old school. God save the king and the rest of you do as you're told—that sort of thing. There wasn't much we agreed on. But what finished it was my choice of career. Young men of my rank become military or naval officers. They go into politics. Or they take a sinecure, and live like parasites at the country's expense—"

"What's a sinecure?"

"A posting where you get paid for doing nothing. Or almost nothing—reading a few reports and signing a few papers, two, three times a year. I could have done that. I could have taken up the law, or maybe even taught classics at Cambridge. But running a theatre? For my life's work? It was beyond him. It *shamed* him. It was like a daughter deciding to be a courtesan. Inconceivable."

"Didn't he *like* the theatre?"

"Oh, I'm sure he did. He liked a good roast of beef too. That didn't mean he wanted me in a butcher shop." He made a small, bemused gesture and leaned his elbows on the table again. "It was all very mad, Sylvie. He came up to London once, to bring me to my senses. Of course, it was much too late. We did nothing but quarrel. By the time I left England, we weren't speaking at all. We don't write." He paused as though to say something more, and then did not.

"Will you go back, do you think?"

"Never." He spoke without anger, without a trace of defiance, but with an absolute finality. Never.

But, she thought, if he was of high rank, surely there would be land, property, an inheritance? Surely he would go back for that?

"Do you have brothers and sisters?" she asked.

"An older brother, a younger sister. Both married and living frightfully proper lives."

Again he was silent for a time, as if he was considering whether to speak of some matter or not. This time, perhaps, he did.

"You've spoken honestly, Sylvie, so I will do the same. Nearly everyone who knows me thinks I'm doing what young men of the aristocracy traditionally do: they travel abroad for a while, have a few adventures, sow a few wild oats in the colonies, and then go home and take their proper place in the social order. There's a gentleman in Halifax who thinks the burning of the Grafton Street Theatre was the best thing that could have happened to me; now I'll settle down and build my fortune. I don't argue with him, but I mean to have another theatre as soon as I can manage it.

That's where my fortune is, and it's likely to be a lean one. I get a bit of money every year from my father: even an impossible son can't be left to starve in the wilds of America. But I don't expect to inherit much. And I will not, under any circumstances, go back to take my proper place in the social order.

"So . . ." His smile was both easy and a trifle sad. "So I am as you see me, Sylvie Bowen, nothing more . . . and hopefully nothing less."

She was left without words, unable to read the implications in his, everything from honesty and honour to a warning that if she were an adventuress she was wasting her time. She could not be glad for what he had lost; she was not sorry he was here to stay. As for his personal handbasket to hell, how gilded it must have been, to think his fortune a lean one with such fine clothes on his body, and gold rings on his hands, and money coming over from England as a matter of course. Money he was simply given. For nothing. For being somebody's son.

She had no wish to hurt him, or to sound like a fool, and any response she could think of promised to do the one thing or the other. She made a pretence of remembering the time.

"Oh, heavens," she said, "it's getting dark out. Mass must be long over."

He pulled a watch out of his pocket and glanced at it briefly. "For some time, I fear," he said. "Will Madame be more forgiving because of the rain, or more impatient?"

"Madame is never impatient. Well, almost never."

He packed the remaining delicacies into a small box the host had given him and handed it across the table with a smile. "These might do for a bribe."

"She's fasting."

"Oh, right. I forgot."

"Do you make a habit of offering people bribes?"

"All the time."

"And," she said, "I suppose you always tell the truth."

"Miss Bowen, though it embarrasses me to say so, I am a paragon of honesty and virtue. A veritable walking miracle. After the good Lord made me, he broke the mould."

"And a flaming good thing, too. I couldn't imagine two of you in the world."

"Of course not. How would you choose between us?"

"Oh," she said, "I'd sit on a park bench, with one of you on one side and one of you on the other, and let you go on about it. Be as good as going to the theatre."

Amusement danced in his eyes. He reached both hands to capture hers, and this time she let him.

"It's nearly dark," he murmured, "and everybody out there is running heads-down in the rain. If I were to kiss you in the street, will you promise not to batter me with a wet umbrella?"

His hands were warm, lean like the rest of him yet surprisingly beautiful, with the perfect, balanced symmetry of a hawk's wing. She had wanted other men in her life—quite a few of them through the years, always from a distance. She had lain sometimes in her cot and run her own hands across her body, wondering how it would feel to have this man do it, or that one, whoever had caught her attention at the time, because he was nice to her, or handsome, or new in town, or merely because he existed. Sometimes desire was like the wind or the rain, it just came.

She wondered how much her face gave away, if Erryn Shaw could guess what it meant to have his fingers whispering over the back of her hand, to have the offer of a kiss. She wished she were a lady from a novel, or at the very least a woman like Fran, worldly and subtle and sure of herself. There was an art to all of this, no doubt, a raft of clever things such a woman would know how to say.

"It's Madame's umbrella," she said. "What could I possibly tell her if I broke it?"

They went into the storm and were instantly driven together, holding on to each other for safety as well as shelter, laughing as

gusts of wind splashed rain into their faces, yelping with indigna-
tion as unsuspected puddles swallowed their feet, reaching the feeble shelter of the church wall and turning to each other as with a
single mind.

Not laughing at all now. He brushed wet hair back from her
face with one hand. His mouth whispered across her forehead, her
cheeks, the tip of her nose, all of it easy, playful, unbearably delicious. She abandoned Madame's umbrella on the cobblestones
and wrapped herself against him, the heat from his body leaping
through her wet clothing as fire through grass. He smelled of
sweat and wet fabric and a rich, unfamiliar cologne, and he was
still trying, a trifle clumsily, to hold his umbrella over her—an
absurd little gesture, but utterly adorable. He kept saying her
name, saying beautiful things, that she was lovely, enchanting, and
she held him harder and allowed herself, just for a little while, to
believe it all.

They kissed—how many times she could not afterwards have
said, but many—and after a bit she told him to put the bleeding
thing down and they stood with rain spilling over their faces and
dripping off their hair, wrapped in fire. She supposed it was
shameless to embrace a man so. But she would have sold her soul
to have Erryn Shaw, to have him for herself, and all her longing
went into those kisses, all her years of longing, all her certainty
that this was temporary and must be taken with both hands, for
whatever small time it might be in reach.

It was he who ended it, drawing back and cupping her face in
his palms. His voice, always so honeyed, had an edge of harshness
now; it surprised her.

"Sylvie . . . God forgive me, my heart, you are utterly
drenched." He found the umbrella and hoisted it again.

"I'm all right," she said.

"Ah, yes," he said, and brushed another kiss across her forehead.
"But whatever will you tell Madame?"

CHAPTER 12

Departure

Thus, my dear admiral, with victory, and such
a victory, within our grasp, we were foiled . . .
—*Captain Robert D. Minor, Confederate Navy*
Report to Admiral Buchanan, February 2, 1864

FOR ALMOST TEN DAYS Erryn had been hinting to Jack Follett
that he would soon have to return home. Above all things, he
wanted his departure to seem planned, to appear to have no connection with events in the expatriate community except by sheer
coincidence. Still, it troubled him to be saying goodbye the same
day the story hit the papers.

All the papers. The Conservative *Gazette*. The Liberal *Herald*.
The abolitionist *Daily Witness*. The three French dailies. In each,
the slant and the interpretation of the story varied; the facts were
essentially the same. The Canadian government had discovered a
plan to seize a vessel on Lake Erie and attack Johnson's Island.
Governor General Monck, as required by international law
between nations at peace, had promptly notified the Americans.
The U.S. military was sending reinforcements to Sandusky. Ships

operating in the region of the Welland Canal were instructed to refuse passage to any suspiciously large group of men, and to report their presence to the authorities.

He read the story twice in every paper, thoroughly content. The grand plan was all undone. There would be no war with the United States, at least not today. On the contrary, Lord Monck's quick response would soothe many a ruffled feather across the border and encourage a bit of trust to get them through the next Confederate shenanigans. *Listen, lads, we're not your enemies; we want peace, and we're doing our very best to keep it.*

Moreover, a communication had come last night from Latour, who had set a man to watching Daniel Carroll. Early Monday morning—the morning immediately after his dinner with Erryn Shaw—Carroll had sent word to cancel all of his appointments, rushed to the home of his member of Parliament, and remained closeted there for three and a half hours. This could mean many things, he knew, but the likeliest thing was that he, Erryn, was walking out of this free and clear.

A splendid performance, he thought; they could all take a bow. He dressed in his almost-best, went downstairs for a shave and shoeshine, and strolled out into the noonday sun. He was absurdly happy. He was going home, and Sylvie Bowen was going with him. His future lay before him like a rich harbour, filled with possibilities.

He had served well.

It was still there, he noticed, that old hard kernel of duty drilled into him from boyhood. Under the relief, under the gratitude for dangers averted to the country and to himself, there was a fierce and unexpected pride that would not—could not—separate the thing he had accomplished from the man he was raised to be. He had served well.

He wondered what the admiral would think.

It was odd how the old man would turn up, all unlooked for, out of small, quiet corners in his mind. They had never been close. By the time Erryn was grown, making the critical decisions that changed his life, his great-uncle was dead, wrapped in a Union Jack and covered over with stones, another family legend, another stern portrait on the wall. If he knew of all this, perhaps he would approve. "Capital, my boy, capital, a fine piece of work!" Or perhaps he would glower. "Spies? In *our* family? Bloody damned *spies*?"

Well. Erryn sighed inwardly and wiped the smile off his face. Little Richmond was dead ahead.

———✦———

St. Lawrence Hall was a magnificent brick building, five storeys high and taking up a full city block between St. James and Craig Street. It was, without question, the most elite hostelry in the city, with every amenity its guests might require—porters and couriers, reading rooms and private antechambers, a telegraph desk, and of course the very best of food and drink. In England, the well-to-do ate four meals a day. In St. Lawrence Hall, one was offered five: breakfast, lunch, dinner, tea, and supper, all at the cost of two dollars per plate.

Erryn ambled past the dining room, bright with crystal and white linen, and calculated that his yearly stipend from England would feed him, at this level of luxury, for approximately one month out of twelve. Clothing, medicine, books—to say nothing of a roof above his head—would all be extra. Whatever else, he thought, this did say something about the resources of the Confederacy's expatriate elite.

The bar was, as he expected, solemn. What he did not expect was the chill that greeted him. Always before, when he walked into St. Lawrence Hall, the Southerners he knew would welcome him with smiles and pleasant talk, or wave and call him over to their tables: "How are you, Mr. Shaw! Here's a friend of mine who wants to meet you!" Now many of them offered only brief, curt nods. A few pointedly did not look up at all, or looked away.

God almighty, he thought, did they know? Had Carroll betrayed him after all?

He kept walking, half expecting to be challenged, or called a filthy, rotten traitor to his face. But there was no open hostility. A few of his old acquaintances seemed friendly enough, albeit in a quiet, down-hearted fashion. Jackson Follett, they told him, had retired to his room a couple of hours ago, with George Kane and several other close associates. As far as anyone knew, they were still there.

"Thanks," Erryn said.

The staircase was painfully short, and the small length of hallway even shorter. He paused for a long moment by the door, wondering quite seriously, if he went in, whether he would be carried out again in a sack. Perhaps, he told himself, this was the worst possible moment to meet with them. Perhaps he should slip quietly back to Halifax and hope they wouldn't notice.

Then again, perhaps the one safe thing he could do was walk through that door like a man with nothing to hide.

"Mr. Shaw." It was George Kane who answered his knock, the blunt-faced, hard-eyed former police marshal of Baltimore. "Good to see you. Come in."

Everything about Kane's manner was normal, right from the first flash of recognition, as though Erryn Shaw were merely Erryn Shaw, a man he knew, but not particularly well, a man for whom he had no feelings whatever, neither affection nor dislike. Erryn began to breathe a little easier.

The large, well-furnished room had the appearance of a council chamber after the debates were over. A large map hung halfway off the bed; several newspapers lay scattered in disarray. Jackson Follett sat slumped in a huge cane chair by the window, with a glass of whiskey and the freshly opened bottle close to hand. He was thirty-six years old; today, still in his shirt sleeves, unshaven and probably unfed, he could have passed for fifty.

He rose to shake Erryn's hand, offering a drink and the best smile he could manage.

"Jack, how are you?"

"Hello, Erryn. You've heard, I suppose?"

"Yes. A damnable business altogether."

Five others were present in the room, along with Follett and Kane. Two he remembered as escaped prisoners of war, including the young lieutenant he had met at Edmund Morrison's party. They sat at a small table where, along with another Southener, Darius Gavin, they were tearing the *Daily Witness* into pieces and rolling the pieces into various indifferent shapes. The sort of thing you did in a prison camp, he supposed, when you had read the paper fifty-seven times and had absolutely nothing else to do.

"We were this close." Jackson Follett held up his hand, thumb and forefinger almost touching. "The boys were in St. Catharines, all of them, and the boat was due any day." He shook his head and sank back into his chair, staring at the whiskey glass in his hand. "This close."

"It was . . . *your operation*?"

"Well, no. It was Wilkinson and his navy boys that were in charge. But we helped them put it together, George and I."

"Ah, shit!" Erryn made a huge gesture of sympathy and dismay. "Damn it, Jack, that's too bad!"

"Can you think how they're feeling on the island?" Follett went on. "Reading this?" He kicked briefly at a piece of newspaper on the floor. "Knowing how close they were to getting out?"

"I don't even want to think about it," Erryn said. It was the bleak side of his triumphant little mission, those fifteen hundred men on Johnson's Island, locked away without proper shelter or proper food, and a lakeshore winter coming on. "What about the lads in St. Catharines? Are they safe?"

"I don't know. I sent a couple of telegrams first thing when I heard, telling them to scatter. Christ knows what that bastard Monck will do to us next."

Which was, no doubt, what they had been discussing for the past two or three hours—what might lie ahead, and what they should do to shield themselves and continue with their work. Erryn hoped the conversation would return to this question, but instead Follett asked if he had any immediate plans.

"Actually, I do. It's one of the reasons I came by. I'm heading home tomorrow. I wondered if there was anything you wanted me to take. Or anything I can do for you in Halifax."

Follett glanced at Kane, who shook his head. He seemed completely engrossed in what was happening at the table.

"I'll send a couple of letters with you," Follett said, "if you can stop by tomorrow and pick them up. But what I'd really like you to do is look after Wilkinson's boys on their way back through Halifax. See that they have somewhere decent to stay, money for food, a doctor if they need one, all that sort of thing, until they can get themselves on a blockade-runner. Al MacNab has funds for it, but I'll give you a letter of credit in case you need more."

"Certainly, Jack. I'd be happy to do that."

"I had a long talk with Maury Janes yesterday. He left last night on the boat west, never quite said where he was headed." Follett looked up, his gaze thoughtful, speculative. "What did you think of the fellow, yourself?"

"I'm not sure," Erryn replied. "He certainly seemed . . . enthusiastic."

"Yes. He is that, sure enough." Follett drained his glass, offered more to Erryn, and then served himself. "I used to think it was a fine quality in a man, such enthusiasm. Now I've been burnt twice, I'm not so certain."

"Twice?" There was the Reverend Andrew Boyle, of course, with his dream of homesick runaways. That was once.

"Yes." Under the Southerner's melancholy surface was a core of bitter anger. It showed now in his eyes, in the hard line of his mouth. "You remember that Irishman? Carroll? I think you met him. He was all enthusiastic too. Full of grand ideas."

"Right. At Morrison's last week. I spoke with him a bit. He seemed like a nice chap, actually." Erryn paused a fraction and went on, seemingly bewildered. "He hasn't gone off chasing phantoms too, has he?"

"I think he was the one who wrecked this operation."

"God in heaven . . ."

"I can't prove it, of course. But only four men knew every detail of it: Captain Wilkinson, George, Dan Carroll, and myself. Now maybe one of us bungled and never knew it. Or maybe a Yankee spy got into somebody's closet. But judging from what's in the papers, wherever that bastard Monck got his information, he got all of it. And Carroll's packed up his wife and kids and gone off to see her folks in Hamilton. Seems one of them suddenly turned up sick."

"Sounds awfully convenient, I'd say."

"Yes." Follett shook his head. "You know, when he came in with us, I was so impressed. He knew the lakeshore like his own backyard—the shipping, the business interests, the climate, everything. He had contacts from Detroit to the Gulf of St. Lawrence. And he was so . . . *enthusiastic* . . ."

"Was he working for the Yankees, do you suppose?"

"Maybe. Or maybe he just folded. Some do, you know. As soon as it might cost them something, they lose their nerve and quit. Anyway, I wanted you to know, in case he turns up again—"

A loud grunt of satisfaction drew both men's attention to the table. Erryn caught his breath in surprise and then got to his feet to have a better look. Using nothing, as far as he could tell, except wads of newspaper and bits of string, the men had fashioned an impressive paper sculpture: a scaffold with two gibbets. From one of them a small paper figure already dangled. Judging by the large shamrock stuck to its back, it represented Daniel Carroll. Another figure, draped in paper robes, was about to have its cowled head slipped through the second noose.

It took Erryn a moment to understand. When he did, he was both profoundly offended and profoundly relieved. The figure was a monk—or, more precisely, a Monck.

"That's bloody clever, mates," he said, hating himself. "Pity it's not the real thing."

"A great pity," Gavin said. "But what I'd like to know, Mr. Shaw—who is that son of a bitch speaking for, anyway? A man sure has to wonder."

The coolness Erryn had encountered in the bar was more comprehensible now. It had not been personal, merely political. He was English. And which damn side were the English on, anyway?

Gavin hanged the paper governor neatly and tapped the figure to make it sway. It bobbed a little and hung rigid.

"Stiff-necked bugger, that Monck. Doesn't even make an interesting corpse."

That will be Lord Monck to you, Mr. Gavin.

"What's your view of it, Erryn?" Follett asked wearily. "Is he really speaking for London, do you think?"

Erryn shrugged. "Oh, I suppose he thinks he is. But from what I've heard, he has almost no political experience—and none whatever for a situation like this. He's an Anglo-Irish nobody who took the post because he needed the money." *And because he didn't want to bleed it out of his tenants, but we won't mention that little detail.*

"Then why in God's name did they give it to him?" Kane demanded.

"Well, quite a few of the people who should have taken it were afraid of wrecking their careers if things went to hell over here. Monck was handy. He's an old friend of Palmerston's, apparently. And he had no career to wreck."

Dear Lord, Erryn thought, *I'll soon have to join Madame in the sailors' church and do penance for all of this.*

"Patronage politics," Gavin said scornfully. "That's one of the reasons we parted company with the Yankees."

"Yes. An admirable objective." Erryn made a point of pulling out his watch. "I fear I must take my leave, gentlemen. Jack, I'd be honoured if you'd join me for lunch tomorrow. We can go over any last-minute matters."

They shook hands all round, and Erryn left them and walked quietly down the stairs. He felt light-headed and unexpectedly weary, like a man recovering from a fever. How good it would be to have a quiet pot of tea, perhaps at Chez Maurice, and buy a flower, and walk with Sylvie Bowen down to the Irish Stone. "I'll go with you," he had offered, "if you'd like to see it one last time before we leave." Tomorrow night they would take the paddle-wheeler to Quebec, and then the Grand Trunk to Maine, and finally a coastal steamer back to Halifax. Two glorious days to spend in her company, away from the Confederacy and all its works, maybe three if the weather turned bad or Madame needed rest.

Finally he would have his furlough.

But not just yet. Three British redcoats stormed into St. Lawrence Hall just as he was about to leave it and almost bowled him over.

"Why, lookit, lads, it's Erryn Shaw!"

A huge, sweaty hand gripped his and another slapped his shoulder. "Hullo there, Shaw! What bloody good luck! We're off for a drink or two!"

They had already been drinking, obviously. They were loud, boisterous, altogether friendlier than Erryn had ever encouraged them to be.

He knew them, of course. St. Lawrence Hall was not merely Little Richmond; it was also the headquarters of the British army's North American commander, Sir Fenwick Williams, and his staff. The general operated out of a large suite of rooms on the first floor, a small distance down the hall from Jackson Follett.

It was a fine, comfortable lodging, of course, appropriate for a man of his rank. It was central and convenient for his duties. But its presence there led, predictably, to continual fraternization. Any day of the week one might find Southerners sitting in the bar with English redcoats, having dinner with them, going off together for an evening's performance at the Theatre Royal just a block away.

Most of the Englishmen in the Hall were officers, born of the best families; they looked upon the well-bred Southerners as men of their own kind. Inclined already to be pro-Confederate, this ongoing personal contact only made them more so.

"Come on, Shaw. We got to cheer the lads up. I've heard it's a bloody graveyard in there." He nodded toward the bar at the far end of the foyer. "You've read the papers, I suppose?"

His companion did not give Erryn a chance to reply. "Hell, Bob, the whole world's read the papers." Then, to Erryn himself: "Have you talked to poor old Follett yet?"

"I spoke with Mr. Follett briefly, yes."

"What did he say about it? Did he think it would've worked?"

"I fear you shall have to ask him yourself."

The officer guffawed and slapped Erryn's arm a second time. "Course it would've worked. Why else would the GG get himself all in a flap? It's a damn shame he ever found out. We could have had ourselves a fine old dust-up with the Yankees."

"We could have indeed."

"Hell," said another, "even if he did find out, why go running to them first thing? I mean, he could always say the source was unreliable and he had to look into it. A man's got to cover his arse. That doesn't mean he has to give the buggers anything."

"Come on, Shaw. The drinks are on us."

"I'm sorry, gentlemen. I'd love to join you." That was lie number three hundred and eleven for the day, more or less. "I have a prior engagement. With a very charming lady."

"Oh, well, in that case, you shan't join us—we shall join you."

"I think not."

"Selfish bugger, ain't he?" They laughed and parted like old friends.

How typical they were, he thought, watching them go. They were like a hundred others he had known, patrician officers—in England there was no other kind—young, generous, easy to get on with, a trifle shallow, living for the day and the hour. Decent enough men, in their own way, but painfully unaware of what the world was really like for most of the people who lived in it.

We could have had a fine old dust-up with the Yankees . . .

Oh, no doubt. And how many young men riding innocent into town to buy a sack of meal and swept away by the press gangs, never to be heard of again? How many old ones, later, like those he had seen in London, without legs or hands or faces, ragged and shivering in the streets, with a little flag beside their begging bowl? How many asylums full of children with nothing to eat? None of those three men would ever think to ask.

And if it were himself in that scarlet coat, his head full of drums and glory, sitting in a foreign outpost without half enough to do, desperate for adventure and promotion because, if you had made the military your life, what else was there? Then what?

I wouldn't be like that, wanting war for its own sake, not ever . . . which is probably why I didn't go.

Well, he reflected, it was a nice, comforting thing to tell himself, but deep down he was not sure. There were those paintings on his bedroom walls, after all. There was his boyhood hero, the admiral, as mangled as Nelson and almost as renowned, the man he had wanted so long and so passionately to emulate.

The man who swore at him: "Get out of here, God damn you, what the devil are you staring at?"

That was where it began. The first bewildered "oh," the first uncertainty, the first hint of a war god's clay feet. Not recognized as such, not then, not for years, but still the beginning.

Was that why the old man did it? Unconsciously, perhaps, not willing to say the thing plainly, or even to think it, yet driven nonetheless by some hidden and desperate intent: *Don't, lad, don't! Whatever you do, don't follow after me. . . !*

It was this possibility, never considered before, that moved him to buy two beautiful roses to take down to the riverbank later, when he went with Sylvie for a final visit to the Irish Stone. One rose he placed on the stone, alongside Sylvie's small bouquet. For the other he brought a model ship, small and very sturdy. He tied the rose to its single mast and set it adrift in the St. Lawrence. Then he took out his flute and played till the tiny craft was lost from sight.

"Will it reach the sea, do you think?" Sylvie wondered.

"No. Likely as not some youngster will find it washed up in the reeds half a mile away. But . . ." He shrugged. "It's like the old Romans pouring wine in the ground for the spirits . . . or like you said about Nassau, about things going round and coming back again. Maybe it will count for something."

It was a day of peculiar and uneasy perfection, the air hot and sensual with perfume, so warm a human might well be tempted to stretch out on the grass like a sunning cat. All around them the hills lay in a riot of colour, and wherever the autumn light struck the water, it danced.

Yet Erryn sensed the end of it hovering just out of sight. There was an oddness to the light, as when storms were in the air, and he was quite certain that if he climbed to the very top of Mount Royal and looked to the northwest, he would see black clouds prowling in the distance, with wind riding on their backs and the ice of winter in their eyes.

"Will you play another song or two?" Sylvie asked. "It be so beautiful, the way you do it, as if . . . as if you knew magic or something."

He smiled. She was not a lady, as the world measured things. She said "bloody" and even "bugger" and never thought twice about picking up a messy pastry with her fingers. Yet she could pay a compliment as graceful as any lady might have dreamt of, and all the sweeter for being utterly sincere.

He found them a patch of grass that was free of stones and briers. It would have been pleasant to sit watching the river, but he preferred to keep an eye on the path and the docks, just in case.

No one came to trouble them. They sat close, their shoulders brushing warm in the sun. He needed both hands for his flute, and that, he decided, was likely just as well. After three or four pieces he stopped to kiss her, a few gentle, decidedly careful kisses. She returned them equally carefully, as if she knew how dangerous this all was—the flawless day, the utter, deceptive tranquility of the place, the loneliness in both of them. All tinder, he thought. If they were somewhere safe instead of here . . .

But they were here and that was the end of it.

"I wish Fran had met you," she said. "She would have liked you awfully, I think."

"She was a good judge of character, then, I take it?"

"You're not very humble, Erryn Shaw."

"Yes, I am. I'm so humble it doesn't even bother me when people don't notice it."

She smiled faintly and then looked away. Not at the city sprawling across the hill before them, he suspected. Not at anything in particular.

"You have faith in things, don't you?" she said. "I don't mean religious things. I mean . . . life things. The future. Other people. Dreams. You believe when you set out to go somewhere you'll get there, and when you have something of your own you'll be able to keep it." She paused, just for a breath. "It must make the world look very different."

"Different from . . .?" *Different from the way it looks to most everybody else, of course.* That was the sort of thing Matt Calverley used to say to him, when they were just beginning to be friends. *You don't know what it's like. You just don't know!* It was true, at least to a point, but it did not matter nearly as much as Matt expected.

"And you don't have faith in such things?" he asked softly. "Not ever?"

"Oh, sometimes, I suppose. A little. But never . . . never way deep down, the way you do. The way you seem to."

"Why?"

She answered slowly, thoughtfully, as if she were sorting her explanation even as she gave it.

"It's not . . . it's not because I think bad of people, or that I think the world's a horrid place. I don't. Honestly, I don't. It's just that things . . . things *change.* Like ice melting. Or like a fog coming in. You look at something and it ain't what you were looking at a little while before."

He thought about answering, but even as he chose the words his mind was taking a step back, hearing the truth in her own. Things did change. He himself had changed quite a lot in his still rather young life. He waited then, and listened.

"After it happens a few times," she went on, "you get . . . wary, I suppose. When I were a kid, I could believe in anything. Like when I first went to school. I were so happy, as if a door opened, with a whole other world just lying on the other side. And then it were gone, like that, and I got put in the mill, working for Pa's whiskey, living for the day I'd be grown up and could get out. That be freedom, see, being grown up. M'appen I'd go far away, or marry someone handsome and brave, a soldier who'd take me to India . . . Oh, I could dream of anything, I could. Then I got this." She touched her face. "Fran took me to Rochdale, and there we dreamt of Canada. All those years slaving in that bloody mill, we held on to one thing, going to Canada, until I got sick from the cotton and the mill closed because of the war. And then nothing were going to get us out except a miracle.

"We still thought it would happen somehow. Or Fran did, anyway. I weren't so sure anymore. But she were right, it did. One day we found a little notice in the newspaper, about a Yankee ship wanting cabin passengers. We had twenty-one quid between us, Fran and me, and the *Osprey* would take us to Nova Scotia for twenty."

The Osprey? *But the* Osprey *was . . . Oh, my God! . . .* He went taut and unmoving, the way a hare might, sitting quiet in the sun, looking up suddenly into the eyes of a fox.

"You came on the *Osprey*?" he whispered. "Not on an immigrant ship?"

"No. Fran wouldn't go near those ships. She said too many people died on them. She said we had to save for something better, but with one bloody thing and another we never had enough. And then we found the *Osprey*. Oh, she were beautiful, Erryn—you must have seen her in Halifax—she were something from a story-book. We thought we had our miracle, see. We thought we'd made it, and all the bad things were behind us.

"They told us about the Southern pirates before we left. That's why the fare were so cheap. But we had no choice except to go, and anyway, it's such a big ocean . . ."

Erryn felt shaken to his bones. He had wondered sometimes how Sylvie's aunt came to be buried in Nassau. Merchant ships travelled far and wide with their cargoes, but emigrant ships usually sailed straight to a single destination, most often New York or Quebec. For such a vessel Nassau would be hundreds of miles off course. But he had never asked her about it. The subject was likely to be painful, and the explanation as predictable as it was tragic. High winds, no doubt, a damaged vessel blown off course, a quick docking for repairs, just as the epidemic was beginning, before the warning flags were up.

Just fate. Just the hard, cold fortunes of the North Atlantic. Not the war. They had never spoken of the war. He had consciously avoided ever bringing it up.

"So you were on the *Osprey* when she was captured?"

"Yes—"

"Did they hurt you?"

"No. Not . . . that way. But Fran wouldn't be dead if it weren't for them. She'd have the life she worked for all those years—friends, and a bit of money to live decent, and maybe Captain Foxe calling on her like he said he would. They took it all away. They burned our ship and dumped us off in Nassau. We were waiting for another ship out when she got sick."

"Christ, love, I'm sorry. I'm so sorry . . ."

"She were always the strong one, never scared of nothing in the world, except what might become of me. And then she were the one who died." Sylvie turned—almost unconsciously, he thought—to stare at the Irish Stone. "It were so fast. They had a row of white houses along the beach where they took her. A quarantine station. Like this one used to be, I suppose. They wouldn't let me go inside—not even inside the fence."

"Oh, Sylvie, my poor heart . . ."

She drew away from him, brushing off the two small tears that slithered down her cheeks. "Can we start back now? Please?"

"Yes, of course."

He thought she meant to change the subject then, but she did not. Bit by bit, in no particular order, she told him more of it, perhaps nearly all of it, from a grey morning on the Mersey to a windswept grave in the Bahamas. And he saw that she simply found it easier to speak if she was walking, easier to fend off grief with her eyes on the path or the river, with her voice held carefully even, like her steps.

He walked close by her side, asked a small question now and then, and otherwise let the story unfold. Aunt Fran and Captain Foxe and the snobs who wondered where she got her money. The long chase and the failing wind, the *Osprey*'s burning sails tumbling into the sea, and poor Pepper the cat going down with his ship. Nassau glittering in the Caribbean sun, drunk with Rebel gold. The hospital and the terrible waiting, the hope when they told her Fran was better, the blind, reckless, stupid hope. The nurse explaining why she couldn't have any of Fran's things back, not one tiny thing to remember her by.

"You have her love," he said. "You will always have that."

"No," she said bitterly. "I have the memory of it. And a memory ain't the same."

They were almost at the sailors' church. She had talked about it all this long way and she had not cried at all.

"Everybody says we should forgive our enemies. Madame, too. She says if we don't, we give them power over us. But I won't ever forgive the Rebels for what they did to Fran. Not ever. I can't.

"Anyway . . ." She turned, offering him a small, melancholy smile and brushing one hand softly up and down his sleeve. "I don't believe in futures anymore, or anything being sure, or safe, or mine. And it ain't because I don't like you, Erryn. I like you awfully. But I think you know that already."

"Well," he said wryly, "I've rather suspected. But consider the possibility, Miss Bowen, that I may not be especially certain of the future either, or of anything being sure, or safe, or mine."

This, he saw, surprised her. He wondered if she even saw the exile, the thin, unlovely scarecrow, the theatre manager without a theatre, the artist misfit who would not easily find a soulmate anywhere; or if she only saw a gentleman's son, proud and privileged, for whom everything came at the snap of a finger.

"Will you be on the boat tomorrow night?" she asked.

"Yes. That much of the future you can depend on."

"Will you play your flute for Madame? She loves music so."

"And she has a soft spot in her heart for those who play it, perhaps?"

"Perhaps."

"I would be delighted."

He really could not kiss her on the street, not in the bright, sunny late afternoon, with carriages rattling by, and great trundling carts whose bored, curious drivers watched anything about that might be interesting; not with fine ladies hurrying past with their purchases, and worshippers beginning to drift down the street from the sailors' church, some of them still murmuring their prayers. No, it simply would not do.

He did, however, lay a brief, chaste kiss against her forehead, and another, much less brief and chaste, against her hand, and watched her disappear into the old church with a deeply troubled heart.

God help us, he thought, she had endured so much. He ached for all she had endured, the cruelty and the endless work and the betrayals of fate, getting knocked down and getting up and getting knocked down again, as if being poor and cold and hungry were not misery enough all of itself. And then the *Alabama*. Raphael bloody Semmes and his God damn Rebel sons of bitches.

I won't ever forgive them for what they did to Fran. I can't.

Many things about her life were alien to him, things he had never experienced, even remotely; things he could only reach for with his imagination and try to understand. But he understood loss, the disbelief of it, the pitilessness, the darkness in his soul as he stared at Cuyler's wrecked body lying on a slab, Cuyler his best-loved friend, who had laughed and sported with him just two days before, Cuyler who was only twenty-three, with the whole world before him, waiting to be conquered.

Forgive? No, never. Oh, maybe in the Christian sense, letting them be, leaving them to God—yes, he could forgive to that extent; he could walk away, with twelve years behind him and the worst of them dead. But *personally* forgive? Speak to them, allow them into the circles of his life? Never. Sylvie Bowen's bitterness toward the Rebels was something he quite understood.

And what of you, Erryn Shaw, when she finds you among them? What of you?

CHAPTER 13

━━◆━━

On the Saguenay

If there were dreams to sell,
What would you buy?
—*Thomas Lovell Beddoes*

SYLVIE BOWEN STOOD quietly on the deck of the *Saguenay* as the big sidewheeler edged away from the jetty, where a few last faithful stay-behinds stood waving goodbye. Most had already gone, streaming back up the hill on foot, on horseback, or in fine, hurrying carriages that were soon out of sight. The sun was far behind the mountain, and already great parts of the city were wrapped in shadow. The steamer moved easily onto the great back of the river, past the bridge and the railway yards and the abandoned Irish Stone. So small the memorial appeared now, from the deck of the steamer, so very small and lonely; in no time at all it had vanished in the scrub. She wondered if she would see Montreal again . . . if she would ever see any of this again.

She leaned against the rail, watching the bluffs along the shore grow distant and ever darker, and the last traces of the city slip away. It had been a grand adventure, her journey with Madame. She could have imagined nothing like it back in England—this landscape almost savage in its beauty; this new and fascinating freedom, limited by Madame's plans, by Madame's every wish, but nonetheless real, for even Madame could not command the river. Six weeks, a thousand miles, and everywhere unexpected wonders, not least of them a man who smiled at her.

It was ending now. Not over, but ending, like the Indian summer. In three days at most they would be back in Halifax, and she would be back at the Den. She did not look forward to it. Halifax she liked well enough, for all that some found it scruffy. The sea was endlessly varied, what little she saw of it; and the fortress town had a hard, cold splendour that seemed to her the stuff of poetry. But Susan Danner's boarding house was a wearisome and lonely place. It was better than the Lancashire mills, of course it was—no cotton fluff, no smoke, no hideous noise, no dangerous machinery. They had decent food to eat, and as much of it as they wanted. For all of this she was grateful.

But a servant's life was bound to her household. She had no life outside except for a few precious hours once a week—too few, so far, for Sylvie to have made friends in the city. Fran, her lifelong friend, was lost to her, and in the Den she had found none. She got on, day by day, but there was no closeness, not even the militant worker comradeship she had shared sometimes in England, which had mostly been impersonal but always intense. It did not help that she was bookish when her fellows were not; that she was new to the work, and had to be shown things, when they were already run off their feet. And then there was her scarred face, all the worse because she had to wear a stupid white bonnet with her hair tied back. Little Annie MacKay, the timid, illiterate scullery maid, who was terrified of everything from thunderstorms to mice—little MacKay would flinch sometimes when she turned and found Sylvie unexpectedly beside her. She would laugh and try to make it nothing, just startlement, but she never met Sylvie's eyes. There was no hope of friendship there. Dinah Reeve, the housemaid, had a follower and would marry after Christmas; she was interested in absolutely nothing else. Sanders the cook was a proper flaming Baptist, the sort who frowned on every kind of pleasure and never shut up about the Lord. The only man among them, other than the master, was Harry Dobbs. He was twenty-odd and full of himself. He behaved himself under the Danners' roof, but Sylvie never wanted to meet him on a dark road at night.

For weeks she had simply lived from day to day. No matter how quickly she learned, it never seemed to be quickly enough. Reeve could whip a sheet around a mattress in seconds, with every corner tucked neatly out of sight. All of them could run up and down the stairs, wipe, carry, scrub, polish, or pack things up faster and more neatly than she could. Miss Susan might well have dismissed her except that it was summertime and workers were hard to find, domestic workers hardest of all. Nobody wanted to be a servant.

When she was abruptly summoned from her scrub pail to the parlour on a quiet September afternoon, she felt sure it was the end. She was terrified, and almost relieved. Maybe there was something better, somewhere. Maybe.

But her mistress said nothing to her. She spoke instead to the strange woman who sat in the parlour rocker, dressed entirely in black. The woman looked to be sixty or so, and she squinted as though there was something wrong with her eyes.

"This is Bowen," Miss Susan said. "I think she'll suit." She introduced the older woman as her sister-in-law, Louise Mallette.

Louise Mallette seemed decent enough, although she asked a lot of questions. She told Sylvie not to call her M'um but Madame, and she said it differently, with the stress on the last bit, the way the French Acadians did. She knew Sylvie had been in the mills—Miss Susan must have told her—but she wanted to know what sort of work she had done there, and for how long, and why she came to America.

"There were no more work, Madame. We had to leave or starve."

"We?"

"My aunt and me, Madame."

"Ah, yes. Frances. My sister-in-law mentioned her. They were friends once, many years back. Your aunt died in Nassau, I understand. Because the American Rebels took your ship and left you there."

"Yes, Madame."

"A truly villainous business, this war. I'm told you can read, lass."

"Yes, Madame."

"You went to school, then?"

"Only for two years, Madame. But my aunt were always borrowing things for us to read. And there were classes sometimes in the Mechanics Hall, in Rochdale. I went to those when I could."

The woman handed her a small book, the meditations of a saint with a peculiar, European-sounding name. She read aloud as she was asked, losing her nervousness almost at once in the simple pleasure of the words, stumbling over a few that were difficult, but only a few. It was religious writing, different from anything she had heard in church, or anywhere else. She wondered if it might be Papist.

They let her read quite a long bit, and she suspected she was being tested in some way. Perhaps she was supposed to protest. Sanders would, no doubt. Sanders would drop a Papist book quicker than a hot coal, before anything inside could jump out and gobble up her soul.

"Thank you, that will do," Madame said at last. "You read well. Have you ever served as a lady's maid?"

"No, Madame."

"Well, you're obviously intelligent, and my sister-in-law tells me you're well behaved. She's offered me your services for a journey to St. Catharines, in the West. My sight is very poor. You'll have to attend me day and night, take care of my clothing and possessions, look after the travel arrangements, everything. And you'll have to read to me every day; I have few other comforts. Do you suppose you can do that?"

Could she do that? Could she eat strawberries and cream?

"Yes, Madame."

"Well, that's settled, then," Miss Susan said. "You may return to your duties."

It felt like a miracle even then. St. Catharines. It was a long way off; she was not sure how far, but a long way. She would see oh so many wonders, ride on trains and riverboats, meet all manner of fascinating strangers.

"No, you won't," Reeve told her scornfully when they gathered for their supper in the kitchen. "You'll be running and fetching for the old biddy day and night. My sister was a lady's maid for most of a year. Said it was the worst year of her life. Said she'd rather be in the scullery, at least the potatoes didn't call her names."

"She's a Papist, too," Sanders added, "that Miss Louise. She'll turn you if she can. Mark my words, girl, she'll turn you from the Lord, same as she was turned by that awful man she married."

"What awful man?" Sylvie asked. "Who did she marry, then?"

"Ship's mate on some scruffy Yankee freighter," Harry Dobbs said. "A handsome devil, apparently, but a Frenchie, and a real hellion. She went off with him one night just like a milkmaid, got herself taken into the Catholic Church, and married him before the sun come up."

Reeve nodded. "All he wanted was her father's money, and when he saw he wasn't to get any, he left. And got himself sunk. Was years until her father talked to her again. Then he up and died and left her a fortune."

"She's got a nice house," MacKay offered timidly. "On South Park Road. I saw it once, walking by. It's all brick."

"Oh, Miss Louise lives fancy." Sanders finished off a last chunk of stew and wiped her mouth. She was tall and sturdy. She would have been a handsome woman except that she always seemed to be angry about something. "She got servants of her own, too. So why's she coming here wanting one of ours?"

"Her maid begged not to go," Sylvie said. "Her son's awful sick."

"And did the missus say why she picked you?"

"She said I could be easiest spared."

"Well." Sanders looked at her and then at the others, one by one. "That's right fair, ain't it? Them as been here the longest and works the hardest gets to stay and work harder, and this little snippet goes traipsing all over the country."

It was like a punch bowl spilled on the table. Dobbs looked maliciously amused. MacKay lowered her chin almost to her chest, the way she did whenever she heard what she wished she had not.

"No," Sylvie said grimly. "It ain't fair. Not much be fair that I've noticed. But I were nine when I started in the cotton mills, and I been working ever since. So don't act like you got a monopoly on it, Sanders. You don't."

"Watch yourself, girl. I'll take no lip from a lady's maid no more than I'll take it from anyone else."

Sylvie said nothing further. Sanders was the cook and therefore the senior, the one in charge, the same as a foreman in a factory. The sort who could say most anything they pleased, and then nail you to a wall if you answered back.

Why don't you just go bugger yourself, Emma Sanders? Someday, she thought, she would really like to say it, right into the woman's hard, self-righteous face. Only Fran had always said there was no purpose in such things. When you really needed to do it, you did not dare; and by the time you *could* dare, it hardly mattered anymore, it was all behind you.

There was no more talk that night about her change in fortune, at least not in her presence. But in the days that followed, she felt more distant from her fellows than ever. She had been rewarded for being the least valuable member of the household, and they resented it. She was going to be a personal maid, one of those snotty creatures who always had the lady's ear, who got the lady's cast-off dresses, who never had to dirty her hands, who thought she was better than her peers.

They did not seem to care that it came about by sheer chance. They did not seem to notice that it was temporary, that it would never happen again, that only a blind woman would have a body servant with Sylvie Bowen's face. She had been given something wonderful and they had been passed over, and they resented it.

How would it be now, she wondered, when she came back? She was finally healthy. She had lost the last traces of her mill-town cough and gained several pounds; she did not look like a rake handle anymore. There was colour in her cheeks and sparkle in her hair. She had thrived like a young deer on the sunshine and the restful days. Would that seem unfair too?

———◦———

The deck was almost deserted. A cold wind had come up in the northwest, and one by one the passengers drifted away. There had only been a handful. According to Madame, most who made this journey were businessmen. They travelled often; they had seen it all before. The moment they were on board, she said, they would claim their staterooms, or drop a hat or a handkerchief on a berth in the lower level, and settle down to sample the offerings of the bar.

But even those who had come out to watch the departure, or to enjoy a smoke in the last of the evening's light, were gone now. Sylvie remained. She loved being here, but mostly she hoped that Erryn might come to join her. He had seemed so happy yesterday, like a boy on a picnic. Maybe it was because of her. Or maybe it was only because he was going home. She wondered how she could possibly know. She wondered how a woman ever knew, with men—if there were signs you could identify and depend on, or if it was like religion: one day something changed inside you and afterwards you simply believed.

Erryn did not come. The night turned pitch-black; the only light on the deck came through the windows of the grand saloon. It was a gorgeous place, she could see as much even from the outside. Persian carpets as fine as Miss Susan's, and cut glass chandeliers all dazzling with lights. Men in fancy waistcoats and gold watches sitting in the stuffed chairs with their legs crossed, reading the newspapers. A handful of women, not one of them alone. Nary a sign of Erryn Shaw.

At least he was going back to Halifax too. It would not be so dreary, being at the Den, if he were nearby, if he still remained her friend. But would he, being a gentleman's son like he was and she a scrub maid? Sometimes she laughed at herself, bitterly, because the notion seemed so absurd. Other times . . . other times she would think: Maybe. Maybe he had meant the things he said. Maybe he would go on meaning them, at least for a little while.

She would have given almost anything to talk with Fran, and yet she knew exactly what Fran would say. Fran would brush her hair from her face and tell her there was no way to know, no way to be certain of anything. Not with human passions, not with love. That was why everybody kept writing poetry about it— because no matter how much they had said already, they had not said half.

She sighed and finally turned to go, and almost ran into him in the passageway. There was barely any light at all, and no other people, just a beanpole shadow dead in front of her and then his laughter. "Sylvie, my heart, is that you?" In the next breath his arms were around her, no one to see, the cabin wall sheltering them at one side and the great round paddle box at the other. His arms hard around her and kisses to melt her bones.

"You'll not believe who's on this boat," he said when he stopped to speak at all. "We have a travelling German pianist. We have seven members of the glee club from McGill College. We have the esteemed Erryn Shaw, flautist and stage manager extraordinaire, who has just spent the last hour arranging for the biggest, most glorious party to ever brighten the windows of Richelieu's bedtime express. By tomorrow, Miss Sylvie Bowen, I give you my word, I shall have the formidable Madame Louise eating out of my hand!"

He was wrong, but only by some hours. Madame was ready to eat from his hand well before midnight.

———⋙◆⋘———

The Richelieu Steamship Company offered very fine service on its nightly runs between Quebec and Montreal. Those who travelled first class could travel in the height of luxury; they could eat a king's feast off burnished silver, drink the most expensive imported spirits from crystal glassware, and sleep on pressed linen in a stateroom with gilded knobs on the doors. But they could not reserve anything in advance. Thus, even the *Saguenay*'s most elite passengers had to stand in line on the quay, in rain or wind or burning sun, to be assured of obtaining a stateroom at all.

The businessmen could send some lowly clerk to hold a place for them, and wealthy residents could send a servant. But strangers and tourists had no choice except to turn up early and wait like any ordinary chap.

"It is appalling. It is absolutely uncivilized." The speaker was a Frenchman sitting directly at Erryn's left, at one of the long supper tables lit with candles where, just now, a profusion of edibles were being offered: beefsteak braised in champagne, roast venison, *roguet canellas*, braised carrots, potatoes, turnip, chicken pie. The Frenchman had introduced himself as the Baron Pierre Laurent de St. Denis, which may or may not have been the truth; barons and dukes and counts of all sorts turned up fairly often in North America, many of them more familiar with the inside of a jail than the inside of a castle. But in any case, the man was well educated. He spoke flawless English, with only a small accent, the occasional "is" sliding into "ees." Montreal was in the French part of North America, he said; he had expected better.

"Well," someone offered, with an irony the Frenchman altogether missed, "the English *have* had their hands on it for a hundred years."

Across the table, Madame Louise murmured something to Sylvie, who bent her head to listen. In the candlelight, with her hair hanging loose about her face, the scars were barely noticeable. Even in good light Erryn noticed them less and less—or, more correctly, he noticed them always differently, seeing them at times with a shock of recognition and dismay, and at other times barely seeing them at all. They had never robbed her of her prettiness and grace, not even the first time. Now they were becoming simply part of her, a sad part, yes, but more and more peripheral, like a crippled finger or big feet. An imperfection. Who was he, great bony birdlike makeshift that he was, to mind an imperfection when he had so many?

His gaze, he feared, was becoming obvious. He turned back to the Frenchman, who was still talking with great energy and enthusiasm to his other near companions.

"And now this matter we read of in the papers, this . . . this *confederation*. A big editorial today in your *Herald*. 'The time is now,' it says, in letters this high." He held up his hands a foot apart. "I do not understand it. You want to make a country here? Out of all this bush?"

It was lovely to watch, the way every male head in reach of his voice turned and stared at him. The way Madame Louise smiled.

"But why not, m'sieu?" she said. "What is wrong with bush?"

"Oh, nothing, madame, nothing! It is very fine. I have hunted, I have fished, I have sailed all those Great Lakes. *C'était merveilleux.* But it is so empty. You are so . . . *comment dit-on?* . . . so scattered, yes? There is a city, and then there is nothing for a hundred miles, and then there is a town, and then there is nothing again. Your

Nova Scotia is so far away you cannot even get there except by going through the United States—"

"Well, really," said the man at his left.

"Oh, I understand you may take a freighter, and arrive in a month or so. Or you may take a stagecoach and arrive in a fortnight, with all your bones rearranged. That is life in the colonies. I quite understand. But how this can make a country, or why you would even want to attempt it—I confess, *mes amis*, it is quite beyond me."

Fewer than twenty of the *Saguenay*'s hundred and eighty passengers were women. One of them was a certain Mrs. Foster from St. John, New Brunswick, a city that had almost as many Grey Tories as Halifax. She was easily fifty, wearing impressively fine silks and a small fortune in rings.

"You have not been paying attention to the war, then," she said.

"The war?" St. Denis murmured. "You mean the American war, yes?"

"Yes. When the Yankees are all kicked out of the South, where do you think they will come looking for more territory?"

"Or rather," suggested another, "when *they* kick the Rebels out, which is far more likely, and they're stronger than ever, with a good army at hand and nothing more for it to do, our few scattered colonies might look a little tempting. Do you not think, sir, that an established nation, however bushy it might be, would be somewhat more secure?"

"Ah, *oui*, I do see your point. But if you cannot govern it—"

"We'll govern it," Erryn said quietly. "We're a very resourceful people here in Canada."

St. Denis smiled. "Ah yes, I suppose you are. You have to be. So it is this war, then, that worries you? That is the other thing I wish to ask about. Everywhere I have been, men talk about this war, and none of them say the same thing. I should like to hear what all of you have to say—"

"Perhaps later, sir," Erryn interrupted softly. "Not at table. It is . . . it is a contentious subject, sir."

"Ah, yes, forgive me. The curiosity of the traveller, you understand."

"Of course. Now I have a question for you. You found the manner of boarding our steamer somewhat . . . uncivilized, I believe—"

"I meant no offence."

"None was taken. I merely wanted to ask if you ever boarded a steamer at Toronto?"

A ripple of chuckles went up and down the table—chuckles of amusement, yes, Erryn thought, but also of relief. Many others besides himself preferred to leave the Yankees and Confederates a long, long distance from this table.

"No, I have not," the Frenchman said. "And now you are going to tell me it is even worse than here, yes?"

"Oh, much worse. The steamers come all the way from Windsor, most of them, through Lake Erie and the Welland Canal. What with fog and bad weather, they're often late—two hours, four, even six."

"You have experienced that, have you, Mr. Shaw?" Madame asked wryly.

"Oh, yes."

So had several other people, who rushed to tell the Frenchman what departure day was like for those who travelled east from Toronto. Since the time was so completely unpredictable, people simply went on about their business until they heard the approaching whistle. Passengers hunkered down in local bars and tea rooms; those who lived near the waterfront remained in their homes. Shipping agents served their customers and tended their accounts. At the first distant signal, everyone stampeded for the wharf.

The first time, Erryn had had no notion what to expect. In a matter of minutes he had found himself engulfed in chaos, carried by a tumultuous river of humans, animals, packages, and every kind of vehicle invented since the Stone Age, all of them fighting their way toward the jetty—except for those who had obviously lost something, a hat, a portmanteau, a child, perhaps, and were shoving frantically in the opposite direction. The noise rose to the level of a battlefield. Parents shouted after uncontrollable children, porters yelled for passageway, babies wailed, hack drivers cursed their teams, even the dogs in the streets beyond set up a royal howling. He never quite understood, then or afterwards, how everyone and everything was got on board with no one trampled into pudding or shoved off the quay and drowned in Lake Ontario.

"The last time," he told them, "I got a barrel rolled into my shins, without so much as a beg your pardon, and a gust of wind blew my hat some forty heads away. I actually got it back, after. A kind soul took it on board and gave it to the steward to be claimed. But there I was lamenting my vanished hat and battered shins when I felt someone tugging on my hand. It was a lad of five or so, obviously lost and not the least bit frightened. 'Please, sir,' he said, 'you're really tall, sir. Can you see my mother?' I told him even if I could it wouldn't help, since I didn't know her, so I hoisted him up on my shoulders to look for himself. I was turning this way and that way for him when I heard a most outraged, panic-stricken wail behind me: 'You there! What the devil are you doing with my baby? Let him go this instant!'

"I knew if I put the lad down he'd soon be as lost as before. I couldn't get to his mother because the crowd was shoving me in the opposite direction. Of course, he was delighted when he saw her, and made a great commotion waving and shouting. But all *she* saw, I suppose, was her poor darling screaming 'Mama!' as he was carried off by a great shaggy troll, who'd sell him to Barbary pirates or possibly eat him alive. So, of course, she started shouting for the police."

Erryn finished with a wry gesture and a smile. "It was not my finest hour as a good Samaritan."

"But you were a good Samaritan nonetheless," Madame said. "I trust the lady forgave you, once the truth was known?"

"Oh, handsomely," he said. "What was left of me."

Everyone laughed, which delighted him. But the best was Sylvie's lingering smile after the laughter finished, the frank admiration in her eyes. He felt that fortune was riding on his shoulders tonight, that tonight was one of those times, which came to a man once or twice in a lifetime, when he could do absolutely nothing wrong.

—◆—

The concert was a triumph. The lads from McGill were talented and fun-loving, and they had a fine repertoire. They sang sea shanties and old ballads, tender love songs and heart-tugging, melancholy laments. Several songs Erryn suggested himself, which Sylvie had identified as Madame Louise's favourites. One of them happened to be a favourite of his own, and he had learned to play it on the flute some years before—an eerie, dark tale he had first heard at Eton, which had haunted him ever since.

> *I am a man upon the land,*
> *I am a silkie on the sea . . .*

The silkie came to land and found his love, but his story ended—as such stories most always did—with the poor were-creature doomed.

> *And ye shall marry a gunner good*
> *And a right fine gunner I'm sure he'll be*
> *And the very first shot that e'er he shoots*
> *Will kill both my young son and me.*

The chorus faded out, the flute lingering briefly, like a memory, or a shadow disappearing into water. When Erryn looked up, everything was absolutely still—for a moment, a long, wonderful moment before they applauded to rattle the chandelier.

So it went for most of an hour. Yet when it was done, when all the thank yous had been said and the compliments paid, when the performers shook each other's hands for the last time and the pianist and the lads from McGill were gone to their berths and he was left to himself, he felt both restless and ever so slightly sad.

By then the saloon was empty, the great bound bible standing alone on the marble table, the stern windows black against the night. A steward came unobtrusively to darken the candelabra, leaving only two small gimballed lamps. It felt much like the Grafton Street Theatre after a good performance, when everyone was gone—the same satisfying memories of music and applause, the same sudden, unnatural silence.

In that silence he could hear, for the first time, the voices of the passengers in steerage: many voices, the sort of muffled babel one would hear from outside a crowded pub. They had no beds and plenty of liquor. Many would be awake half the night.

He went outside, finding two of them in the passageway by the wheel, smoking and talking quietly in German. But no one was on the rear deck, and for that he was grateful; he wanted no one's company except Sylvie's. A sharp wind was blowing off the river and there was nary a star to be seen. They would hit fog before morning, he thought, fog and rain, perhaps even snow. He looked back immediately at the sound of steps, hoping it might be her. But no, it was just another male passenger, wandering to the rail to have a smoke.

He sighed and turned again to face the wind. The euphoria of the concert had mostly gone, leaving him quiet and reflective. Now, even as he hungered for Sylvie Bowen and lingered over every favourite memory of their time together, he knew that his mind was still divided. A wary, self-protective part of it warned him the whole matter was getting out of hand. He was growing besotted, and if he kept on in this fashion he would finish as a proper romantic fool, of the sort he had met once or twice in London, running about feather-brained and making decisions with their cocks. Another part of him wondered why he could not love a woman from the mills, why such a woman should be, by definition, an unsuitable companion for a man with an Eton education and packs of relatives in wigs. It also reminded him that he was put together like a scarecrow and had but seventy pounds a year with which to entice such women as might be considered more suitable. And finally, with a hard, blunt kick, it reminded him that he was lonely—bone-deep lonely and weary to death of it . . . whereupon the sensible part of him observed, most sensibly, that if mating were at all reliable as a cure for loneliness, the whole damn planet would be happily and permanently coupled. It was nothing but lust he was feeling, and why not? Any man with some fire in his veins would catch his breath at that hair, at those small, pert breasts in their little cage of cotton. Any man might find her on his mind and in his dreams, living in the bloody colonies and alone for so long. He wanted to take her to bed, that was all.

Of course I want to take her to bed. I'd have to be stone dead and six days buried not to want it. But it's not all I want.

You don't know what you want.

And there was the truth of it. He did not know, not yet—and he knew he might never have a chance to find out. Halifax was a small city; it would be hard to keep his links to the Grey Tories out of Sylvie Bowen's sight even if she had no links to them herself. But with Madame Louise being cousin to the Ortons, it was likely to prove impossible. She would discover him cozied up to everything she hated and despised, and walk away. And that would be best for both of them, no doubt. She was still young, and this *was* the colonies, after all. Even with a scarred face she had a fair chance of finding some happiness with a decent man . . . whereupon the damn fool in him leapt straight back up again: *Yes, and why the devil can't that man be me?*

"Mr. Shaw."

He turned sharply, irritably, yanked from his thoughts by a drawling voice, a sudden, faint scent of cheap cigar. The man was standing about four feet away, wrapped in a mackinaw with the hood up, both hands stuffed in his pockets.

Several facts collided in Erryn Shaw's brain in a single instant. As a rule, men did not get this close to him without being noticed, not even when he was being dreamily concupiscent. This man had worked at catching him off guard, coming out for an innocent smoke and then, despite his heavy boots, padding across the timbers as softly as a cat. There was too little light for Erryn to discern his face, yet there was about him a vague, maddening familiarity.

The final fact, the one that truly frightened him, was recognizing the stranger's voice—not its personal identity, for he had never heard it before, but its origins, its tactical identity: the voice was Southern, and cold, so cold it felt like an ice pick levelled at his heart.

Christ, he's come to kill me . . .

He actually considered yelling, *"Help! Murder!"* at the top of his lungs and bolting for the pilothouse. Then common sense returned, albeit shakily. One could hardly go into this line of work and then run shrieking from every stranger who stepped out of the shadows for a chat. Such chats were, after all, central to the business. Nonetheless he was painfully aware of how loud the paddlewheel slapped against the water, how nothing moved inside the grand saloon, how most everyone was probably asleep.

"I know who you are, Mr. Shaw."

This did not reassure him one bit. He shifted to face the man, poised and steady. *I've got length on him, anyway.*

"Then you have the advantage, sir," he said with just the right mix of politeness, curiosity, and hauteur.

"You're the bastard who sold my brother to the Yankees."

Even as the man spoke, he struck. Erryn never saw the knife, only the swift, dagger-like thrust of an arm. He dodged sideways, very fast, but not quite fast enough. The blade seared across his ribs and tore into his side. There was a rough thud as the deck railing slammed against his back. The whole world spun. He would have fallen to his knees but for the man's bulk pinning him, the blade still driven to its hilt.

"You're caught now, ain't you . . . *little robin redbreast?*"

God almighty. It was Brownie. Brownie in the slouch hat. And he must be Brad Taylor's brother, the crazy one, the one who hated all the Brits . . .

"You thought you was so damn smart, didn't you, Mr. Shaw? You thought nobody'd ever cotton on to you. Sneaking out at night in all them funny clothes, as if any damn fool couldn't see how tall you was. My brother had you figured from the start, said you was too perfect by half, and yet you was always around when things went to pieces. Just like now."

You're going to die, Erryn Shaw. In a few seconds it will all be over . . . The thought was unbearable. To die now, with half his life unlived? To die like this—alone and unarmed, like an idiot child gone playing with cobras, caught flat out by a bloody Southern maniac who sneaked up on him in the dark?

You thought you was so damn smart, didn't you, Mr. Shaw?

He gulped with pain as Zeb Taylor pulled the knife free to strike again. He reached instinctively, missing the man's wrist but deflecting the blow. He had no vanity left; he sucked in his breath and shouted, "Ho! Guard! Help!" with all the voice he had. It seemed no more than a harsh, unimpressive croak.

Taylor cursed at him. "Not much stomach for a fight, have you, you little Brit bastard?"

His second try captured Taylor's knife hand. He held on desperately as the man's left hammered at his face and belly—a hand like human steel, fast and brutal. He tried to parry the blows, but too much of his strength and attention was focused on the weapon. At this rate he was going to be battered senseless, and then it would be over anyway: Taylor could stab him at his leisure, cut his head off if he wanted to, toss him in the river, and go back to his bed. Erryn's brief, half-formed intention to somehow disarm the man went out like a snuffed candle. All he cared about now was survival, any way that he could manage it.

He had one chance, he thought. Maybe one. He brought his knee hard into Taylor's groin. It was a clumsy, glancing blow, but enough to hurt, enough to make his attacker falter for a moment. In that moment he grabbed Taylor's left wrist and shoved forward as hard as he could, pushing them both away from the railing. Erryn had always been powerful—thin and oddly proportioned, but powerful, and his great reach served him well now. He swung Taylor around as they grappled, and then bent, reaching fast between the man's legs to lift him bodily. It was like trying to hoist a small horse. He almost buckled, gulping for air and for courage. Taylor was an ordinary man, not fat at all; how was it possible he could be so heavy?

You have to do it, Shaw, somehow you just have to . . . !

Taylor's free hand came at him like a club, more vicious than before. Erryn straightened, clinging to every scrap of will he possessed. Bone smashed into his face, his throat, his side. He tasted blood, but he kept going—heaved, shoved, heaved again, almost losing Taylor's knife hand, almost losing his balance, dimly aware of a growing agony in his side, of the strength draining out of him with every heartbeat, of the hard knowledge that he would once again be a killer. All the while, with a terrible clarity, he was aware only of distances: the few inches between his throat and the knife, the few feet between them both and the railing. Taylor's curses came at him in gulps, snarling and bitter. For the first time Erryn sensed fear in the man, and it heartened him. They hit the rail hard. For a moment they were poised, almost motionless, like dancers. Erryn slammed him backward, bracing for one last mortal heave, and hearing, even as he did so, the sudden, sharp crack of splintering wood.

All his life he had prided himself on his quickness, but his enemy was quicker now, and equally desperate. The knife clattered harmlessly on the deck as Taylor's arms whipped around him, panicked arms made of iron, the man's weight tipping him, folding him like soft taffy as the railing gave way. Erryn had a fragment of time to understand, and another to protest, silently and pointlessly, that it was a mistake, it was not what he intended—!

Then they struck, and the river took them down together.

CHAPTER 14

———◆———

Not Death but Love

"Guess now who holds thee?"—"Death," I said. But, there,
The silver answer rang,—"Not Death, but Love."
—*Elizabeth Barrett Browning*

IT HAD BEEN a glorious evening in the saloon, the sort of evening Sylvie Bowen used to dream about when she was a very young girl, when such evenings seemed barely possible even as a dream. The singing had been as fine as any she had ever heard, even in church. And there was Erryn Shaw's flute, an enchanting thing made—or so it seemed—of wild birds and wind and running water. ("How beautifully he plays," Madame whispered to her in a quiet moment. "We must be sure to thank him for it.") Best of all there was Erryn himself, to watch and admire to her heart's content, as elegant as ever, and here, in the sorcery of the music, looking lean and serpentine and powerful.

He made it all seem easy, winning Madame's approval, talking gracefully with her when she came to thank him, complimenting her, making her laugh. As if he had a gift for winning things,

Sylvie thought, not just good manners or charm but a kind of magic. As if maybe, centuries and centuries before, one of his ancestors had bedded down in the woods with the elfkind and he had just a tiny, tiny whisper of the blood.

⟐

The hard part of the evening came afterwards. It seemed forever before Sylvie was able to get away. After such glorious entertainment no one wanted to sleep, not even Madame. Several of the women remained behind in the grand saloon for a considerable time, enjoying the company of the men. They came back laughing and chattering just when most of the others were ready to turn in.

Any other time Sylvie would not have minded. Indeed, she would have enjoyed seeing Madame Louise so animated, and listened with great interest to the conversations of her betters. It was, after all, one of the few real pleasures in the life of a servant.

There was, for example, a Mrs. Wallis, travelling to Quebec to visit her sister. She thought the singing very fine and the flute exceptional, but she did not approve of making songs about creatures such as silkies.

"They don't exist. And if they did, it would be the wickedest thing imaginable, turning a man into a fish. God made men and He made fish, and He didn't make them to be changing places."

Madame started to reply, but a younger lass was faster. "A silkie's not a fish, ma'am. He's a seal."

"Doesn't matter in the least. He's a perversion of nature."

A perversion of nature? Oh, my, my, I must tell Erryn. I wonder what he'll say.

Then there were the Misses Bedard, trying to decide which of the lads from McGill was the most attractive, and why, for one had finer hair and the other had broader shoulders and a third was said to be very rich. There was Mrs. Foster, the Grey Tory from St. John, thinking it a great pity they hadn't sung "The Bonnie Blue Flag"

as a tribute to the brave, outnumbered heroes of the South—
especially since she had made a personal request for it.

Sylvie sighed, trying to control her impatience. At least an hour
passed before Madame was ready to go to her berth. By then
nearly everyone else had done the same, and there was only the
stewardess to deal with, a sturdy, brisk woman in her late thirties.
She was an altogether admirable stewardess, courteous, thoughtful, and busy. Still, for Sylvie she represented authority, to say
nothing of respectability—those stern, unyielding boundaries of a
proper lady's life. Sylvie tried to imagine their conversation.

"Was there something you needed, miss?"

"No, m'um."

"But where would you be going, then, miss? It's very late."

"Out on the deck."

"But miss, most everyone's abed, except for them"—and here
she would point to steerage, out behind the cargo bay, whence,
even through two sets of doors and mountains of freight, boisterous noises could be heard—"and Lord knows what sort they
might be. You can't be going out on the deck alone, miss."

"Oh, I won't be alone. My young man is waiting for me."

At which point, Sylvie thought, the stewardess would turn pale,
march over to wake Madame Louise, and ask her if she knew that
her servant was playing the harlot behind her back.

No, it would never do; she would have to slip out. Funny, she
thought, how a woman could be done in with factory dust or starvation or disease or drink, and no one would bat an eye, but the
whole bleeding world bent over backward to save her from a
handful of kisses.

———◆———

The ladies' cabin filled less than a third of the middle deck; the rest
was taken up by passenger baggage, freight, and, at the stern, the
cabin for the steerage passengers. Sylvie could hear them clearly

the instant she slipped out into the cargo bay—a general hubbub of voices, children crying, the clattering sound of something being dropped. A frail lamp outlined mountains of boxes and crates piled in uneven rows. But there were no ruffians about, only two immigrants standing by the rail in the passageway, laughing and talking in a language she did not understand. They seemed to be great friends, totally absorbed in their conversation. Sylvie was light, slender, and quick on her feet, and the steady slapping of the paddlewheel was far louder than the soft steps of a woman or the small rustle of her dress. She waited until her eyes had completely adjusted to the darkness, then she crept past them and up the stairs to the deck.

She thought Erryn would be right there, waiting, eager to see her, maybe catching her in his arms even as she appeared. But she could see no one at all; the deck seemed utterly deserted. She fought back her first rush of disappointment. He might be off to the side, perhaps. The night was pitch-black, without a star, and only the gimballed candles were lit now in the grand saloon, leaving small, timid pools of light, no bigger than a pair of pillows, just below the stern windows. It would be hard to see anyone who had wandered more than a few feet away.

"Erryn?"

There was no answer, no movement, nothing but the steady slapping of the wheel and once, briefly, a harsh masculine laugh from the passageway below. She looked through the stern windows into the grand saloon with its rows of stateroom doors, all shut tight like the gates of palaces. She looked up where the puffing funnel was barely a silhouette against the black, descending sky.

Had she missed him? Had he come out and grown bored with waiting and gone off to his bed? She had not been terribly long, an hour and a half, or possibly two, and he knew she had to wait on Madame . . . No, probably he had not come at all. He had shrugged off his promise like a drop of rain and gone to his bed . . or elsewhere. Perhaps he found the other ladies far more pleasing, the ones who gathered around him after the concert, flashing their jewels and their eyes.

Always it was the same, she thought. Always she allowed herself to hope, to imagine that something might have changed, that this time, with this man, it might be different . . . and always she was wrong. Always the hurt was new and unbearable, as though it had never happened before.

She knew he was not there; to imagine otherwise was absurd. Yet she walked to the far side nonetheless, and then slowly back toward the stern, trailing her hand along the rail for balance in the darkness. The tears came slowly, quietly, at first, and then more and more bitterly. For the smallest moment she scarcely noticed the splinter tearing at her hand; it was only another hurt. For yet another moment she felt only bewilderment: what on earth was *that*? She felt at her hand and found it wet, not as with water but with something sticky. She wiped her eyes with her sleeve and looked down. Right beside her, the upper railing was gone, its jagged end thrust out into nothing like a tree trunk broken in a storm.

Oh, my God . . .

She ignored a wild impulse to lean out across the water and scream Erryn's name. Instead, she sped back down the passageway, past the two foreigners who still smoked by the paddlewheel, praying they were honest immigrants and would not try to grab her. She did not knock on the door of the pilothouse, she wrenched it open and yelled at the two men inside.

"Stop the boat! Please! I think something awful's happened! Stop the boat!"

The man at the wheel stared at her as though she were mad. Only later would she consider how wild she must have looked, how totally she must have surprised them.

"Someone's overboard?" he demanded sharply.

"I don't know. He were supposed to meet me on the deck and he ain't there and the rail's all broke! Oh, please, sir, stop the boat!" For the first time she could see her hand in the light. The wetness on it was blood, a great smear of blood, more than ever could have come from a splinter. Her breath caught in a sob of fear.

The pilot still thought she was mad, perhaps, but he reached quickly, yanking on a lever, and shouted at his companion, who promptly took the wheel from his hands.

"Now, tell me, miss, what is this all about?"

Be calm, damn it! If you aren't calm, they won't listen!

"Mr. Shaw. He's . . . he's my friend, and we were going to meet on the deck, and when I got there, it were empty—"

"It's late. Perhaps he's in his cabin."

Where I would be if I were a proper woman, yes, I bloody well know.

She held up her bloodstained hand. "*Someone* broke that railing, sir."

He nodded. "Come."

They swept down to the passageway. Already the motion of the steamer had changed and the paddlewheel was churning to a stop. A great, clanging bell began to ring, and feet were hammering up the stairwells.

The smokers still chatted by the wheelhouse. They were the obvious people to ask who might or might not have gone to the deck, but they spoke very little English. It took all of Sylvie's willpower to stand still while the pilot addressed them—slowly and carefully, as he might have done with children.

"You? See? Anyone? Go? Up?" The pilot pointed emphatically to the deck.

"Go up? *Ja, ja.* I see. Big man." He held his hand well above his head. "Then other man. *Ja, ja.* I see. Go up."

"When?"

The immigrant shrugged, looked at his friend. They spoke together softly, briefly.

"I think maybe . . . *Viertelstunde* . . ." He groped for words, then, frustrated, held up one palm, fingers extended. Once, twice, three times.

"Fifteen? You mean fifteen minutes? A quarter hour?"

"*Ja, ja*. Quarter hour. Maybe more."

"Did they come back down?" Sylvie pleaded. "The men you saw. Did they come back?"

"Beck?" He shook his head emphatically. "*Nein, nein*. Not beck. Still there."

Oh, God. She barely noticed the pilot's muttered curse as crewmen spilled into the passageway, the fateful words already being shouted and echoed. *Man overboard! Man overboard!* She thought about the broken rail, and the blood on its jagged edge, and the immigrant's words. *Maybe fifteen minutes. Maybe more. Still there.*

Only they were not there. They were in the river.

The pilot's hand closed firmly on her arm. "Easy now, lass, easy. Don't be getting in the way."

They waited until the last of the crew ran onto the deck and then followed. Later, looking back, she would realize the response of the *Saguenay*'s men had been efficient and quick. At the time it seemed to be neither. All she could see was a chaos of men running hither and yon, lanterns flaring, boats slowly dragged from their moorings and lowered down the side, over all of it a great shouting, mostly names and commands, and most of it incomprehensible to her even when it was in English. The whole of eternity seemed to pass before the first boat touched the water, an eternity in which to wonder how the railing had been broken, and how far the steamer had gone, and whether anyone could survive in that pitiless river for so long. *Maybe fifteen minutes. Maybe more.*

Or maybe less, she reminded herself desperately. The man in the passageway saw them go on deck. He did not see what happened after. Maybe it did not happen right away.

She turned sharply to a voice at her shoulder. An officer stood by her, breathing hard, as though he had run from the farthest corner of the ship. He touched his cap briefly.

"Marcel Drouin, mademoiselle. I am first mate. I am most sorry, but I must ask you what you know, and make a record."

He wrote everything down, not only her name but her berth

number and where she lived in Halifax. When he had finished, he
thanked her and turned to go.

"Sir . . . please . . . "

"*Oui*, mademoiselle?"

"Will you find them? I mean, *can you*? Has anybody ever . . . "
She faltered.

"You are asking, has anyone ever fallen in the river and been
saved? *Mais oui*, mademoiselle. It has happened many times, if
they can swim."

Could Erryn swim? He had never said. Most of the men in the
mill towns could not. Some even went to sea and never learned.
But rich young men learned everything, surely—to ride and shoot
and swim and do all the other sporting things?

By now both boats were over the side and men were scrambling
down the ladders and rowing away. The captain himself came on
deck, and the mate stood and spoke with him quietly. When the
boats were well away, the captain gave a sharp order for silence.
Those remaining could only watch now, and wait, and maybe
pray. The mate crossed himself. Sylvie's hands clenched hard by
her side. The sudden quiet was startling, no sound except the river
slurring against the sides, the gentle slap of oars, then, starkly, a
voice calling, *"Allô! Allô! Y a-t-il quelqu'un?"* And then silence again,
and the cruel waiting, and then another voice, from another direction, "Is anybody out there?"

There were strong currents in this river, she had been told. It
was dark and the water must be dreadfully cold. What chance did
a man have, going over?

If he could swim, the mate had said. Only if he could swim.

The sailors' lanterns flashed on the water, eerie, like carnival
lights. Most any other time they would have been wonderfully
pretty; now they spoke only of doom. He was dead, she thought.
What else was possible? He was dead, and this was his burial rite,
this last bit of light playing over his grave, all he would ever have, a
stranger and so many miles from home . . .

Muffled voices came on the wind—not the clear, precise calling of the searchers, something else, more like the sounds of men at work. One boat, the farther one, had stopped moving. For a long time it stayed motionless. Then the voices fell away and its lantern swung in a broad arc. Drouin the mate crossed himself again.

Sylvie turned desperately to the man beside her. "What is it? What does it mean?"

"Means they 'as one, mademoiselle."

It was the hardest waiting of all, watching the one small boat make a beeline for the steamer while the other still called and circled, wider and wider, with ever-diminishing hope.

"Steady now, steady, take it slow!"

They brought the man up by inches, with another great flurry of commands. She pushed forward desperately and saw through the mass of bodies that it was Erryn. He was conscious, but just barely, hanging in the arms of the sailors like a long, wet towel, water dripping from him everywhere, one hand pressed hard against his side. She wanted to run and wrap her arms around him in pure thankfulness and joy, but there were too many others in the way. She thought they would take him below, but instead they eased him flat out on the deck, one of them calling sharply over the voices of the others: *"Mon capitaine, il est blessé!"*

The man beside her translated without being asked. "Says he's wounded. Must've been a fight of some kind. That's likely how the rail got broke."

Sylvie's brief flood of happiness melted back into fear. She watched as the circle of men opened and the *Saguenay*'s captain knelt by Erryn's side. It was hard to see what he did, but she could hear fabric tear and rip. A young man came running onto the deck with a satchel. She hoped he might be a doctor, but he merely handed the satchel to the captain and went away. There were mutterings from the men, and once a small moan from Erryn. A few minutes later the captain got to his feet. "M'sieu Drouin!"

"Mon capitaine?"

"I think it would be better if we did not disturb the passengers with this. I should like to take Mr. Shaw to your quarters."

"*Mais oui, mon capitaine.*"

They lifted Erryn onto a board and strapped him down. Two sturdy sailors picked the stretcher up as though it were nothing more than a feather quilt and headed for the passageway. Sylvie hurried over to the captain as he moved to follow them.

"Please, sir, how is Mr. Shaw? Will he be all right?"

Even in the lamplight she could see that he was weary and on edge, perhaps not in the best of health himself. He stared at her as if for the smallest moment he could not remember who she was or what she was doing there.

"Miss." He touched his cap. "Yes, he'll be fine. It's just a flesh wound. I've patched up a dozen worse who walked away laughing." He waved a summoning hand at his first mate. "M'sieu Drouin, I'm placing this lady in your care. And, miss, I want to thank you for your actions tonight. Your quick thinking undoubtedly saved Mr. Shaw's life. If there is anything you would like for your comfort, anything at all, just ask the stewardess to fetch it for you and tell her I said so. It's the least we can do."

"There ain't anything I need, sir," she said.

"Well then, good night." He touched his cap again. "This gentleman will be pleased to escort you to the ladies' cabin. I hope you will have a bit of sleep in spite of it all."

Good night? Lord save us, he was sending her off to her bed like a bleeding child.

"But what of Mr. Shaw, sir?"

"We'll look after him the very best we can. M'sieu Drouin, after you've seen the lady below, take the deck. If there's still no sign of the other fellow, call in the searchers and get us under way."

"*Oui, m'sieu.*"

"Captain, sir." Sylvie stepped forward with a boldness she did not feel. "Please, can I come with you? To be with Mr. Shaw?"

"That's quite unnecessary, miss. He'll be well taken care of."

"Please. Just for a while."

"Believe me, Miss Bowen, it's not a place for passengers." His voice was brusque, impatient. He was worn right out and she was being forward. She was not a wife, after all, or a sister. Why didn't she go back where she belonged and leave him to his duties?

"I don't care what kind of place it be. God in heaven, sir, if it were your son they knifed and pitched in the river, you'd want someone there with him, wouldn't you? Someone he knew, to comfort him a bit?"

He had a son, no doubt. He stared at her for a breath and then looked away. "All right. But mind, you'll have to be quiet and let him rest."

"I understand, sir. Thank you."

◆━◆━◆

The mate's cabin was small and plain as a box. They made her wait outside till they were finished—for modesty, she supposed, as if she had not seen every human body part, male or female, long before she was twelve, and many times since.

Erryn lay very still, covered with a thin grey blanket. His face looked cruelly battered, as if he had been brawling in a tavern. She said nothing, not wishing to wake him, but brushed her fingers very gently across his hair. It was still wet.

His eyes opened. He tried briefly to pull his hand out from under the blanket, then settled for a small, wan smile.

"Sylvie."

His voice was weak, barely his voice at all. It frightened her. So did the ashen pallor of his skin. She fought back the urge to spill out questions—was he all right, did it hurt, what could she do? The captain had not been long patching him up. Did that mean he was not much hurt after all? Or did it mean they did not know, or could not help? They always patted you on the head and said things would be fine. Somebody could be lying with his head six feet away in a ditch and they still said things would be fine.

"Sylvie . . . I'm . . . so sorry . . ."

"Hush, love," she whispered. "Just rest. There's nothing to be sorry for. Try to sleep."

Obediently, he closed his eyes. She stood very quiet, watching him. She heard the paddlewheel start up again, wondering briefly if they had found the other man and who he might have been. Then she forgot him as Erryn shifted on his bunk. He seemed almost to huddle, as if only his wound prevented him from curling himself into a ball. She bent closer and realized he was shaking.

"Erryn?"

"So c-cold," he whispered. "Is there . . . m-m-more blankets?"

She looked around desperately. There was a small sea-chest in the corner, but it was locked, or perhaps only worn and difficult; in any case she could not get it open. There was an old jacket hanging on the wall, and an oilskin lying across the foot of the bunk. That was all. She spread the garments over him, right to his chin, tucking each carefully against his sides. He said a feeble thanks, trying vainly to keep his teeth from chattering.

The captain had said his wound was not dangerous, and maybe it was true. But no one knew how much blood he had lost, how close he had come to drowning. His skin felt dry and cold where she touched it, not just his hands but his chest as well, as though all the life in him were huddled deep inside, trying not to be driven out.

"I'll be right back," she whispered fiercely. "I promise!"

She did not know whom she might find to ask for help, and she did not care. Anyone would do. Her second try found the steward's door. He opened it half asleep, but he said yes, he would fetch the captain right off, and she fled back to Erryn Shaw's side. He was as she had left him, ashen and shivering. The thought that he might die—that he was perhaps already dying—closed like a cold wind around her, turning everything to ice.

Please, God . . . oh, please, please . . .

She had known that she might lose him. Indeed, she considered it all but inevitable. He might court her, even care for her a little, but in the end he would go his own way, perhaps with a laugh and a kiss, or perhaps without a second thought, the way you walked away from a kitten you had cuddled on the street. She would lose him, of course . . . but it had never crossed her mind that she might lose him to death. She had thought him invincible.

She slid her hand like a feather down the side of his bruised face, puzzled by her blindness. How was it possible that she had forgotten death? Forgotten her mother, and the poisoned air of the mill, and the graves scattered right here on the bank of this river? Forgotten Fran, smiling and asking for some oranges, no longer there when Sylvie came back, never there again? Was it because they were powerless and poor? Because wanton, stupid, pointless death was the headsman of the poor? Because however much she liked Erryn Shaw, or even loved him, she had always seen the image of pride and power more than she had seen the man?

Now only the man was left, desperately hurt, broken, shivering with fever. Just a bit of bone and blood. Maybe with a soul, the way the church folks said, or maybe not; but no lord, no elfkind, only another animal as fragile as herself. The yellow jack could take him, or a knife, or the black darkness of the river, and he would be gone just like the others. Forever.

No.

It was empty defiance, of course. God was not likely to listen, nor was anyone else, but she would say it anyway. *No*. She lifted the covers and slid gently into the bunk, wrapping as much of her body as she could against his own, the way Lucy Brady had wrapped her son when they carried him home from the mill in Rochdale. It was cold in the tenement that night, far colder than the *Saguenay*; they could see their breaths like puffs of smoke. Lucy laid her boy on a blanket and covered him with her coat, an old dress, some rags, everything she had, finally herself. Her own warmth, holding back the night.

"It's all right, Erryn. I won't leave you. I promise. You'll be all right."

The captain did not return. He had just left after all, pronouncing the patient fine. What would he think now, except that she was a silly, panic-stricken girl? She fitted the coverings tightly around him again and then lay very still except for a whisper now and then: *It's all right, love, you'll be all right.* She did not care what the ship's men might think if they came in, all proper and appalled: *What the devil do you think you're doing, miss?* Whatever they thought, it did not matter. She wrapped Erryn close, and after a long time she no longer heard his teeth knocking, and after a much longer time she realized he had stopped trembling; his chest was rising and falling quietly against her—unevenly, but quietly— and he had begun to sweat.

She took the oilskin away and stood upright again, barely daring to hope. The captain did come by at last. He was sorry, he said, there was trouble in the engine room. Now, what seemed to be the matter?

When she told him, he did not seem concerned. It was common, he said, just a bit of fever, nothing to worry about. He laid his hand across Erryn's forehead, looked briefly at the bandaged wound, and nodded, satisfied. Sylvie listened until the last of his steps faded down the hall, and turned again to the thin figure on the bunk.

He was asleep. The cold, deathlike thing that closed on him had backed away—maybe not very far, but it had backed away. She watched him, one hand lying soft against his shoulder, until dawn light crept across the windows . . . dawn light, and foggy bits of farms, and finally a harbour, grey and rugged, sodden with October rain.

BOOK FOUR

———✦———

Halifax, October – December 1863

———◆———

CHAPTER 15

Spirit Creatures

For a dreamer he'll live forever,
and a spoiler will die in a day.
—*John Boyce O'Reilly*

THERE WERE ONLY a handful of people by the graveside: a widowed mother, a few friends, three discharged soldiers from the United States Army, who had never met Sandie Douglas but who came just the same to honour a fallen comrade. Matt Calverley stood alone, somewhat apart from the others. He barely heard the simple, familiar prayers. He thought of the years he had known Sandie, the times they had been hungry together or cornered in some rathole, the things they had stolen. They were gifted thieves, back when they were boys. Sandie had joked about it on his last furlough home. Barrack Street was far enough away by then; they could find it amusing being respectable, tramping around in uniforms and earning honest money. "If there was a jail for the squeaky clean," Sandie said, "they'd lock us both up in two minutes flat."

And then he had gone all serious, right in a breath. "You know what I think about sometimes, Matt, old boy? When the camp's gone quiet and most everyone's asleep? I think nothing's changed much at all. It was always a war, surviving. We've just gotten better at it."

He had joined up for a three-hundred-dollar bounty, re-enlisted because he said some wars were more worth fighting than others, survived malaria and Gettysburg, and then took a mortal wound in a skirmish so small no one even gave it a name. Crippled and in pain, he came back to Halifax to die. He was not alone. Every week or so there was a notice in one newspaper or another, someone's son or brother wounded, or killed, or finally safe home. There were thousands of Canadians in Mr. Lincoln's army—or more likely tens of thousands—a fact too often forgotten under the blustering of the Grey Tories. Joseph Howe's own son had gone to fight, and a regiment raised in Boston in '61 had so many Nova Scotians in it they nicknamed it the Highlanders. There were New Brunswickers too, and Islanders, and young men from the West, most of them working in the States when the war began. Others marched across the border for money or adventure or faith in the cause; a much smaller number (again, no one knew quite how many) were taken against their will by dishonest crimps, drugged or bashed on the head, and woke up in a Yankee uniform. All of them were part of it now.

Erryn Shaw, too.

Wind tugged at Matt's sleeves and whipped about his uncovered head, tore spatters of dirt off the grave mound and spun them willy-nilly over the mourners' feet and into the grass. He looked away, out to sea. It was impossible to keep them apart in his mind, the dead and the wounded. It was impossible not to wonder if Erryn might also be coming home to die, this time or the next time, or if one day he might never come home at all.

And it will be your doing.

It would not be, of course, not really. Recruiting men for this work was no different from a sea captain signing up a crew: he wanted good people, the best ones possible, and if one or two were his friends, all the better—they would be the men he could especially depend on. It was not his fault if one day a hurricane swept over them and the ship went down.

Funny, Matt thought, how the logic of the mind and the logic of the heart sat at opposite sides of a man's being, and never quite met in the middle.

Earth fell hard on the wood of Sandie's coffin, a terrible, melancholy sound, one Matt had heard far too often of late. He turned to go, and was surprised to find another man standing alone, even farther back from the others than himself.

"Mr. Romney."

"Constable. Figured I'd find you here."

Jabin Romney was heavy-set and well into his forties, generally unshaven, with the look of a man who rarely slept enough. He was the most important Federal agent in Halifax—that is, he was the most important Federal agent who was recognized as such. That others equally important came in secret, and were replaced when the nature of their business became known or even suspected—this Matt took for granted. Romney's particular role required openness; he was the man to whom anyone could go to trade information for money.

Matt did not envy him this role. To begin with, the use of paid informers was almost universally despised. Worse, in a place like Halifax, Romney's job could drive a man crazy. Like any port, the city was full of transients, people whom no one really knew, people whom no one could vouch for. Like any garrison town, it numbered among its permanent inhabitants many who lived on the edge of the law, in a dirty world where violence, drunkenness, prostitution, and general desperation were the order of the day. Any of these people might stumble on a piece of useful intelligence and rush to sell it for a meal or a bottle or a day's peace. Many were equally capable of inventing information they did not have, and offering the Yankee anything they thought he might be dumb enough to buy, right up to and including General Lee's beard in a brown paper bag.

Matt had encountered similar nonsense himself, but he had the great advantage of knowing the city and its denizens from boyhood; he had a decade of experience as a policeman, and a street rat's instincts for the game. Poor Romney had been a bank clerk before the war. No wonder he looked permanently spent.

Romney nodded faintly toward the gravesite. "You knew him?"

"He was an old friend."

"I'm sorry."

Matt said nothing, and Romney went on: "Did you go to Major Harrington's funeral last week?"

"Now why would I do that?"

"I thought you were an extraordinarily curious man."

Matt laughed a little, dryly. "They wouldn't have liked it much, me and my curiosity turning up. I heard all about it, though. Coach and six, all matched and decked out in black. Parade five blocks long. Half the Halifax Club come to pay their respects, and the Archbishop of Charleston himself saying the Mass." He looked back at Sandie Douglas's lonely grave, at the handful of mourners now drifting away, an even dozen if you counted the minister and the American spy. And Sandie was a Halifax man. Major Harrington was a Southern Rebel, an ordnance specialist sent abroad to obtain weapons. "It could make a man bloody cynical, watching this war unfold."

"You got that right," Romney said. "Most of the time, anyway." He turned his hat around in his hands, brushing off invisible bits of dust. "You wouldn't happen to know a flossie girl named Jessie Bedard, would you?"

"You mean personally?" Matt murmured, and was amused to see Romney blush.

"Oh, no, not at all, constable! I meant did you know anything *about* her—"

"I do. And I was only joshing you, mate."

"Would you believe her if she told you something quite outrageous?"

"Maybe. But only if it wasn't going to come back on her. She wouldn't rat on anyone who might break her head a couple of weeks down the road. Someone passing through, well, that might be different."

Romney nodded faintly, his only acknowledgment. He never said thanks, and Matt was glad of it. They were, after all, only making conversation.

"Captain Wilkinson's back in town, with some of his boys. I suppose you heard."

"I heard," Matt said. "Word on the docks is he's likely to get command of a blockade-runner."

"Wouldn't surprise me. He's a damn fine seaman. Well, good day to you, constable." Romney put his hat back on and moved away, a worn and sorry-looking figure, bending slightly against the wind.

He had arrived in Halifax in the fall of '61. Partly from scuttlebutt and partly from a few casual conversations with the man, Matt had learned that he was—or at least claimed to be—a bank clerk from somewhere in Maine. He had no pre-war experience in dealing with such matters as conspiracy or deceit. He had no legal or investigative training. He had no particular charm or persuasive skills; indeed, he was almost timid toward others. He seemed, on the surface, a most unlikely candidate for his job. Yet, more than two years later, he was still here, and appeared to have the full confidence of the American consul, Mortimer Jackson, who was himself competent, energetic, and alert.

Matt's relationship with Romney was delicate. There was, to begin with, the question of English neutrality, a profoundly slippery question, clear in principle but fuzzy at the edges, shifting its meaning as the balances of power in Europe shifted, and as the war itself became more ferocious and harder to predict. Scarcely anyone who was paying attention was *really* neutral; certainly Matt was not. Yet he considered it his duty to seem so, at least publicly, to do nothing that might embarrass his superiors, whether in Spencer Hall or in London. Secondly, and fundamentally, he was a Canadian, and Romney was the agent of a foreign state. Questions of neutrality Matt would bend from time to time; questions of nationality, never.

So he was careful. He liked Romney, and he had come to respect the man's quiet resolve. But he never hinted that he himself might be anything more than a friendly city constable who thought the Union had the right of it in the war. No doubt Romney knew better. Indeed, it was probably because he knew better that he so readily accepted the boundaries Matt set. There were a remarkable number of things Constable Calverley claimed to know nothing about, and after he had made such a claim once or twice, Romney never asked him again.

Still, Matt shared with the American everything he felt he could, not least his knowledge of the city. He took no money, of course. He merely grinned once and said, "Oh, well, one day I might need your help to catch a footpad." To which Romney solemnly nodded, as if such a request, from an experienced policeman to an expatriate bank clerk, were the most reasonable notion in the world.

———⊰•⊱———

The police station was lodged in the grubby heart of the Halifax waterfront, in the triangle where Upper Water Street veered northwesterly to cut off Bedford Row. It was a busy, noisy, rambunctious part of town. Within two blocks in various directions were the city docks, the market, Her Majesty's ordnance yard, six banks, the customs house, and the provincial legislature, along with scores of ironstone warehouses and all manner of tradesmen and shops: cobblers, tackle makers, a chocolate factory, imported fashions, grog shops, eateries, and numerous taverns and houses of ill repute.

Tucked among them on Hollis Street was a decaying three-storey rooming house with sombre Scottish dormers and creaky stairs. Matt Calverley had taken lodgings there many years before, a scrappy, half-grown youth with his first real job. He held it more than once on credit, for Mrs. Kramer could not bring herself to pitch him out, young as he was and trying hard to make himself a life. Now he could afford something better, but he had no wish to move. He liked the old woman, for all that she was not much of a cook. He liked his room, tucked in the back away from the worst of the noise and the sea wind. And he liked his spiders. He doubted he could move them without half of them getting lost or killed, and he was not at all sure anyone else would let him keep them.

A lot of people thought he was crazy, having those small crawly things around on purpose. They would laugh uneasily if he mentioned it, or make a dumb joke that proved they did not believe him. After all, he was a grown man and otherwise appeared normal. He was a police constable, for God's sake. He kept *spiders*?

Erryn Shaw's eyes had lit up like a boy's. "What a smashing idea!" he had said. "Can I see them?"

It was precisely at that moment that Matt was satisfied they could be friends. Real friends, deep-down-to-the-bone friends, for whom an English manor house and a Barrack Street brothel were merely places they used to live, places that shaped them, of course, but that they had long ago left behind. It was not because of the spiders, of course; they would have been friends even if Erryn Shaw hated spiders, or if he were scared to death of them. But that was when Matt *knew*.

He wondered sometimes if they were fated to be friends or if it was only chance—if it might never have happened at all except for the dust-up in Mahoney's Bar back in '55. He thought about it often, as a man would think about those occasions that completely changed his life. It began on an ugly November night, just after seven. The night guard was coming on duty and Matt was supposed to be going home. But the guards were two men short, with a terrible grippe making the rounds, and word had just come of a robbery over on Bedford Row. The victim, one Colin Downs, had stumbled into the police station severely battered and covered in blood. The men who attacked him, he said, were in Mahoney's Bar, drinking their ill-gotten money as quickly as they could.

Matt did not necessarily believe him. Downs was something of a low-life himself, and not very bright, the sort who might be driven to the law from honest desperation or from thoughtless, stupid malice, or from anything imaginable in between. Still, it required a look, and Stan Coffin and Tom Perreault were the only men at hand. They were both past fifty, decent, ordinary chaps, and Mahoney's was famous for its rough crowd. It was not the worst place in town—that honour was claimed by three or four different ratholes on Barrack Street—but it was, without question, the worst place on the waterfront. Stan turned to Matt with one of the saddest, most hangdog looks he had ever seen.

"I say, Matt, you wouldn't consider coming with us, just for a bit? It ain't but a block, and I'd sure feel better walking in there if there was three of us. Especially if one of 'em was you."

"Sorry, lads," Matt said. "I'm off-duty." He gave them half a minute to feel sorry for themselves and then added, "I might come down to Mahoney's for a drink, though."

They walked in quietly, poor battered Downs hanging close to their sides. He never needed to identify his attackers. Halfway across the room a hulking brute in a sheepskin roared to his feet. "Look! The flamin' little bugger's gone and fetched the guard!"

And the fight was on. The big man overturned his table and came straight for them, howling obscene promises of death and dismemberment. Matt gave him a billy stick across the midsection followed by a knee to the chin as he buckled, and then paid him no more attention. There were three others right behind him. Constable Coffin tackled one to the floor, got a manacle on him, and cuffed him to a table leg. Matt was grappling with another when he heard a panicked yell behind him. "Christ, man, look out!" Then something hit him—something hot, sticky, and reeking of onions, splattering onto his neck and over the back of his head. Furious, he brought a deadly right into his opponent's jaw, and by then Constable Perreault was there to pin the man's arms.

It was one of those moments when Matt hated bars, hated drink, and purely hated men in packs. The whole place rattled with laughter and hoots: *Bloody good toss, mate!—Ten shillings says he can't do it again!—Och, look at the constable, ain't he a pretty sight!*

Hot gravy was running down the inside of Matt's collar. A chunk of greasy carrot slithered out of his hair and sat for one hideous moment squarely on his nose. He flung it aside with his cuff, turning to the crowd from whose ranks, somewhere, the mess had come. He knew it was pointless, but he spat the outraged question nonetheless.

"Who the God damn bloody hell threw that?"

To his complete astonishment, someone answered.

"I did, sir."

It was the bony Englishman from the theatre, Shaw his name was, if Matt remembered it right. A man who never brawled, never made trouble, indeed a man who was rarely seen in ratholes such as Mahoney's. Before Matt could begin to imagine what this meant, the Englishman added, with a small, easy gesture: "He had a knife."

Matt spun round and saw the brute in the sheepskin trying to get to his knees. He had stew all over him, and blood running down from his cheek and his ear. Beside him lay a copper tureen. Nearby, still in reach of his fumbling hand, was an eight-inch blade.

God almighty, I thought I put him out! Matt slammed his boot across the knife and then bent to seize it, remembering the harsh warning shout, realizing that this maniac had been a mere foot or two from his back. He felt chilled all over, as if he had fallen through a frozen lake . . . and been pulled back again, a breath before he drowned.

He walked over to the Englishman and held out his hand. "Thank you, mate. You've done me a damn fine turn. It's Mr. Shaw, isn't it?"

"Yes, and you're most welcome. I'm sorry I splattered you, but it was all I could think of at the time."

They shook hands like old friends.

"It was your supper, I suppose?" Matt asked.

"It's replaceable."

"We have to take these dumb buggers to jail, but if you'll join me after, I'll buy you a better one, and a bottle of the best wine in town."

"That's most kind of you." Shaw surveyed the room: the crowd, volatile as crowds always were; two night guards, neither of them as young as he used to be; four captives, all crazy drunk and mad as hell, quite possibly with friends in the room or in the streets. "If you wish," he added, "I could just as well tag along and save you the trouble of coming back here."

Well, Mr. Shaw, I see you can toss a courtesy as smoothly as a soup tureen . . .

They sat up for hours that night, talking, and from their last weary handshake at four in the morning they never looked back. Still, Matt was cautious. He was intrigued by his new friend, and liked him intensely, but he was nonetheless cautious, always holding back a measure of trust. Then Erryn came to see his spiders, grinned at them, let one of them scuttle across his hand, and the last wall came down.

"Is it your spirit creature, do you suppose?" Erryn asked.

"Spirit creature?"

"Like the Indians have—leastways in the stories I used to read. The creature who comes to a young man in his vision, when he goes off to fast and become a grown-up. An animal comes to teach him and he takes its name. Black Hawk, Running Wolf, that sort of thing."

"I was named after an Apostle, Erryn."

"Oh, that's what our parents name us for, when we're too small to fight back. Saints and ancestors and pretentious virtues. Like Prudence, for God's sake. Who'd ever want to be burdened with a name like Prudence? Or that poor sod in Massachusetts, Increase Mather. Imagine what the other lads must have called him when he was little. Here, Inky. Run, Inky. Stinky Inky. No, the Indians had the right idea—we should take our own names. Would you be Spider-Something, do you think?"

Matt laughed a little, softly, at a loss for what to say, remembering all at once a room over on Barrack Street—a room where half the time he could not sleep because the noise went on all night, a room with a spiderweb in the corner, just below the ceiling, a web he watched sometimes for hours because there was absolutely nothing else to do. The winters came and went, the strange men, the ships, the cholera, the Temperance Society, the Church, the state, the law. The spider survived them all, and so did he.

Spirit creature.

"Do you know much about Indians, Erryn?"

"Bugger all, to tell you the truth. Just books I read as a boy, probably half of them nonsense. I hoped to learn a bit about the Mi'kmaq here, but they seem to keep pretty much to themselves."

"I suppose they think it's safer that way. I been told they were friendly enough when the first of us came. Traded, visited, let us have land all over. Of course, it dawned on them that we kept on coming and more of their land kept going, so they started to fight back. And they got damn near wiped out."

"There was an Indian war here? I never knew that."

"Oh, it was nothing so gallant as a war. There were some skirmishes, of course, an attack here and there. Then General Amherst invited them to a parley and made peace. Said we'd leave them alone, and brought along a whole raft of blankets as a gift. They all smoked the peace pipe and went home happy. Only what Amherst didn't tell them was that his blankets came from folks who had the smallpox."

"Good God."

"They had no resistance, I guess. They died in droves. After that they backed off."

Erryn Shaw looked at him, and then at a spider hanging by the window, and then at Matt again. "Rule, Britannia, eh?" he murmured.

Matt said nothing. Nothing seemed to be necessary.

"Will we ever get past it, do you think?" Erryn went on. "Not just England. Us. Humankind."

"I don't know. But the day we decide we can't, that's the day we're finished."

"You're a frightfully practical man, you know."

People said that sort of thing a lot, but Matt did not think it was true. He was not practical at all; he was a dreamer. The practical sort, growing up as he did, would have taken to crime, or found a likely whore to live off, or at the very least run away to sea. The practical sort would have drunk everything in sight to forget how much he hurt.

The practical sort . . . hell, he thought, the practical sort would be dead by now.

CHAPTER 16

———◆———

The Den

Life means dirty work, small wages, hard words,
no holidays, no social station, no future . . .
—*Wilkie Collins*

THE DEN ON BARRINGTON was bigger than many of the warehouses on Water Street, and plainer than most of them. Every line
of the building was straight and severe, every window a blunt rec-
tangle exactly like every other. The smooth-cut granite face had
no hint of decoration. Sylvie could not help but wonder at the
man who built it; why, with so much money to spend, he would
not have got himself something prettier.

But then, as Fran used to say, the rich were peculiar. Perhaps he
was one of those hard-bitten sods who never even noticed prettiness unless it wore a skirt. Whatever the case, when he died, the
house was sold, and sold twice more before Jack Danner bought it
in '52. The rumour among the help—never confirmed, of course—
was that Danner had mortgaged everything except his immortal
soul to get it, and even so, the Scott family had to stand good for

the loan. If it was true, Sylvie thought, it certainly explained the Danners' driving ambition.

She arrived back on a chilly late October afternoon. As usual, the boarding house was full. She walked through the back entrance into the familiar scrubbed hallway, the smell of chicken roasting, a piano tinkling idly in the boarders' sitting room. But the first person she met was a stranger, a woman slightly older than herself, in servant's dress, with the solid, muscled body of someone raised on a farm and used to plenty of work. She had plain, blunt features and big ears. She looked briefly at Sylvie's face, at the travelling bag in her hand. She seemed bewildered, as if a guest had wandered through the service entrance by mistake.

"Good afternoon, miss. Were you looking for Mrs. Danner?"

"I'm Sylvie Bowen. The chambermaid. I work here."

"Oh, it's you! We were wondering when you'd be getting back." She held out her hand, the same as men did when they met. "Howdy. I'm Aggie Breault. I'm real glad to see you. I've been doing most of the rooms of late. That woman Miss Louise gave us to replace you, she's a sweet little thing, but she's a hundred years too old."

"Where's Reeve?"

"Gone. Miss Susan's in the stillroom, last I saw her. Watch out for her today, she's eating nails."

"Thanks," Sylvie said. She hoped this Aggie Breault would prove a friendly sort, as she seemed. The Den had need of one.

She hurried to the maids' quarters, up three flights of steep and narrow stairs, and changed quickly into her work clothes: plain dark brown dress, white apron, white cap—not a proper bonnet at all, just a silly round cotton muffin pinned to her hair. The room was gloomy as a cave, hunched up under the rafters with only a small dormer window. There was no grate, much less a stove; the only warmth came from the stovepipe passing through from the kitchen four floors below. Sanders had a room to herself, across the hall; the other three women slept here. The smaller, nicer bed was Reeve's—or, no doubt, Aggie Breault's now. The old, lumpy one Sylvie shared with Annie MacKay. Their furniture consisted of one chair, one washstand and basin, one wardrobe, and one chamber pot.

She could not help but remember the fine hotel rooms she had stayed in with Madame, the even finer quarters the Danners had for themselves on the first floor. Soft beds with canopies they could close all around. Fireplaces in every room. Big windows, from which they could see the carriages on Barrington, and the running children, and the pretty stray cats; from which they could see the world, like anyone who lived in it.

This was the dark side of service. Oh, the work was hard, bitter hard, and always the same; but what could break a servant's spirit was that she had no private life, no space that was her own, not even a factory worker's tenement, just a cubbyhole like this one, of which her share was more or less the size of a coffin. If she had free time and wanted to read, or have a friend in for tea, the only place she could go was the kitchen, down in the basement, where there was barely a scrap of sunlight, and where she got in the cook's way at the peril of her life. A servant was discouraged from courting, and sometimes forbidden it; many had no friends at all. In Lancashire the rich went begging for domestics; the women said bugger it and went by droves into the mills.

Sylvie picked up the small mirror on the washstand, saw that her hair was pinned back neatly and the cap positioned right . . . and saw also, even in this poor light, how well she looked compared with a year ago. It was a trade, she thought, the only trade she could have made; the mill would have killed her. That was all she could afford to think about: here she might survive. And maybe, just maybe, she would be able to move on. Every free afternoon now she would go to Madame's house to read. *You're a bright lass, Bowen. You could improve yourself a great deal with a bit of effort. Come every week, and I shall lend you a book to take home with you.*

She would learn all manner of things, and then she would find some other kind of work. Maybe there was something else, even for a woman, even for someone with a ruined face. She *was* bright; that much she honestly believed of herself. And this was Canada, as hard and desperate a world as the one she had left, perhaps, but with one critical difference: the boundaries to a human life were not written in stone. There was a possibility of moving on.

But for the time being, there were only rooms to clean. Her mistress barely took a moment to say good afternoon. The boarders' rooms were in dreadful shape, she said. Miss Louise's housemaid had never been able to keep up, and Breault had too many other things to do.

"I want them done from top to bottom, Bowen, floors, windows, everything. You can manage two a day, can't you, until they're all shipshape?"

Two in a day? One big job was the usual, in addition to her other tasks. Each day, she cleaned out the grates in the ten guest rooms and brought up fresh coals. She heated water on the kitchen stove and carried it to every guest. She emptied and scrubbed their chamber pots while they were gone to breakfast; scrubbed their wash basins; cleaned up whatever they spilled or left about, anything from crumpled papers to men's whiskers and women's bloodstains. She aired out the beds and made them again, with every corner tucked tight and every blanket absolutely straight. She dusted the rooms from corner to corner, even the frames around the windows and the knobs on the bottom of the bedsteads. She scrubbed four flights of stairs and cleaned the servants' privy and washing area below the basement. If the housemaid fell behind, she was expected to help clean the family bedrooms as well.

All of that, and the missus wanted her to shipshape two rooms a day besides? *Watch out for her today, she's eating nails.*

"You can manage that, Bowen, can't you?" It was neither question nor request. Susan Danner rarely bothered with either.

She stood now with one hand on the banister and one foot on the step, as if pausing in flight. She was probably in her early forties—Fran's age, more or less; they had been girlhood friends. She was beautiful, which must have helped a great deal in winning Jack Danner's hand. She was also weary-looking, extremely so, and Sylvie wondered, not for the first time, what sort of bargain the Danners had made with each other when they married. He was a small commission merchant—prosperous certainly, but small; it was the Den that was making them rich. The Den, and the Lancashire mill girl who ran it like a man-o'-war.

"Yes, m'um. I can manage it."

⸺◆⸺

Sylvie was not at all sure how her fellows would receive her back at the supper table, but they were friendly enough, asking all sorts of questions: had Madame tried to make her Catholic, what were the riverboats like, did she see a lot of Indians? The meal was almost over when she got to ask a question of her own.

"So where did Reeve go, then? I thought she were staying till the New Year. Till she got married."

No one looked at her.

"She was let go," Sanders said bluntly.

"Dear heavens, why?"

"That is not your concern, Bowen."

"Oh, tell her," Harry Dobbs said. "She'll find out anyway. Dinah's laddie put himself on a steamer to points unknown and Miss Susan had to let her go."

Had to let her go? Nobody dismissed an experienced servant because her young man left her; more likely they would be grateful. Unless she was . . . *Oh, bloody hell,* Sylvie thought. *Bloody damned hell.*

"He left her with a baby coming, is that it?"

"That's enough!" Sanders snapped. "This sort of wickedness ain't to be discussed at our table. I'll have no more of it. Breault, bring us our dessert."

There was no more of it until the women were alone in their room. Sylvie was the last to get in. She found little MacKay already curled up in the bed and Breault wearily tugging off her shoes in the light of the kerosene lamp. The new woman looked directly at her and spoke, very soft.

"I'm sorry about your friend, Sylvie Bowen."

"My friend?"

"The housemaid. Reeve."

"Oh. She weren't my friend, really. We just worked together for a few weeks. But it's so unfair, what happened to her. She were gone when you came, I guess?"

"Yes. More'n two weeks ago now. Dobbs says he's heard she's in the poorhouse." She was silent for a breath and then added, "Men talk about these things." As if Sylvie did not know.

"Where you from? The States?"

"New Hampshire. My dad's got a big farm over there."

"So how'd you end up here?"

"I lost my ma when I was twelve, and I had to raise all my brothers. I didn't mind. I reckoned it was my duty, being the oldest. But when the last of them hit seventeen, I'd had enough, and I married Charlie Breault. He was Acadian, come down to work the harvest. He was big and shaggy and shy as a mouse, hardly said ten sentences to me before he was ready to head home. Then he up and asked me to come with him. I figured I'd never get a better offer, so I went. He was a good man."

"Was?"

"He died, couple of years back. Drowned in a flood."

"Oh. I'm very sorry."

"Yeah, so am I. Was the saddest day of my life. You're English, right? That's what Sanders says. She calls you that little English snippet."

It sounded funny, second-hand. Sylvie giggled. "She's a bleeding ninny, that one. But yes, I'm English, from Lancashire. I were in the cotton mills, before."

"Was it awful? We've got a bunch of mills in Lowell, across the border in Massachusetts. A lot of the neighbour girls went to work there. Some seemed to like it well enough. They'd made a bit of money, they said, and now they could get married with something of their own. Some couldn't stand it and said they'd rather starve. A few got real sick. I'd've gone myself, I expect, but I couldn't leave the boys."

"It were pretty bad," Sylvie said. "The noise were enough to kill you all by itself. The cotton fluff gets into your lungs and rots them. People died from it. And they got hurt from the machinery too, sometimes killed. We didn't get paid much, either—not the women, anyway. I guess it's better in the States."

"Better, maybe," Aggie said. "But nothing what it should be. Nobody treats working people fair."

It was late and they were tired. They snuggled into their beds, but they went on whispering for another ten or fifteen minutes, easily, comfortably, as if they had known each other for years. Then, quite suddenly, after a small break in their talk, Sylvie heard a quiet snore coming from the other bed.

She pulled her blankets up snug and nestled closer to MacKay for warmth . . . and thought of Erryn, instantly, fiercely—the warmth of him wrapped against her, the scent of him, the glorious animal aliveness that she could never stop looking at, never stop wanting to stroke. It was like a flash of fire, remembering, but on its heels came the other memories, the search boats and the icy river, the thin body lying drunk with fever, carried down the pier to a waiting hack that turned and vanished in the rain.

Please God, let him live, that's all I ask. Nothing else, not to touch him ever again, or to have him for my friend, nothing, just his life, please, please, please, just his life . . .

November came down hard along the coast in the fall of '63. Grey winds howled in from the sea, rattling windows and spinning dirt from the unpaved streets into bent human faces. Grey sheets of rain turned the same streets to mud, and hammered all night on the roofs, until every room in the Den felt as damp and icy as a cave. There was more work to do than ever, for everything seemed to get dirtier, and nothing ever seemed to get dry.

But once every week there was an afternoon or an evening at Madame Louise's fine old house on South Park Road. It was warm there, with a big fire in the hearth, and always, when she came to read, Madame's housemaid would bring them a steaming pitcher of hot chocolate and a plate of tiny, delicious sandwiches. Sylvie never missed a visit, even when the weather turned cold and she had to walk ankle deep through snow.

It was a fortnight or so after their return from the West when Madame brought up the subject of Erryn Shaw. It was not a conversation Sylvie was expecting, for Madame knew little of what had happened on the *Saguenay*. She had been sound asleep in her berth when Sylvie finally left Erryn's side and slipped back to the ladies' cabin. After the ladies were wakened and dressed, the mate came to tell them there had been an incident on board the previous night and one of the passengers had been injured. He would be taken off immediately upon docking, the mate said, but all the passengers must remain in their cabins until the police could be summoned. They would undoubtedly want to question the gentlemen and the passengers in steerage. There would, of course, be no need to disturb the ladies. He apologized for the delay, assured them there was no cause whatever for concern, bowed politely, and left.

Sylvie did whatever Madame asked of her through the morning, and otherwise sat exhausted and numb, barely hearing the whispers and rumours spreading through the cabin. She had no doubt the police would send for her, or maybe even question her here, in front of everyone. Either way, Madame would know. And then anything might follow: judgments and accusations, complaints to Miss Susan, perhaps dismissal . . .

But it proved to be as the mate said: no one disturbed the ladies. Perhaps the officers were grateful to her. She had, after all, saved a passenger's life, a blessing in itself, and one that would spare the Richelieu Steamship Company a good deal of trouble. Or perhaps this was simply how things were done in the world of ladies. Perhaps a lady's personal servant was judged respectable in a way that factory hands and chambermaids were not, and therefore given the benefit of the doubt. *A mere indiscretion, surely; we'll say no more about it.*

And so she was caught off guard when, two weeks after their return to Halifax, Madame brought up the matter of Erryn Shaw. It was a melancholy November afternoon. The entire coastline was draped in fog, and every landmark had vanished from the streets, even the Citadel. On Madame's mantel, beside a statue of the Virgin Mary, a candle burned day and night, an offering for all who were at sea. It was on a day like this, thirty-seven years before, that her husband and his shipmates had gone down off Sable Island.

Madame spoke without even looking up from the piano. She would do that sometimes, come at you from your blind side, like a guilty conscience. "I wonder about that young man from the steamer. Mr. Shaw. It was dreadful what happened to him. Do you suppose he's all right?"

Sylvie held her voice carefully even. "I hope so."

"Yes." Madame paused to rub the back of her hand, slowly, the way she did when it hurt a lot or when she was troubled by something. "You knew him before, lass, didn't you?"

"Before?" Sylvie whispered.

"Before we boarded the *Saguenay*. Oh, don't be silly now and deny it. I may be losing my eyesight, but there's nothing wrong with my wits. It was plain you fancied him—you scarcely looked at anything else all evening. And I will grant you, he was a charming man. But you're a sensible lass, Sylvie Bowen, not the sort to turn all starry-eyed over a total stranger simply because he said a few clever things at table and played a fine flute. Not the sort to be brooding as you are, so much that my sister-in-law has asked me what happened on the journey, that you came back so troubled. Did you think no one noticed?"

Sylvie said nothing and Madame went on. "You are concerned about Mr. Shaw, I think, and although you are a kind lass, as well as sensible, I think you are more concerned than kindness can account for. So I have no choice: I must conclude that you knew the young man already."

Madame did not frame it as a question and yet Sylvie knew she was expected to answer. She had no idea what to say. There was scarcely anything a mistress hated worse from a servant than a lie, even when the question asked was none of her flaming business. But if Sylvie told the truth, would it mean no more visits, no more borrowed books? Would yet another small sliver of hope in her life be snatched away?

She had never known Madame to be cruel. Fussy on occasion, silly about the small things only rich people could afford to be silly about, but never cruel, not in all the six weeks they had spent together. That had to count for something.

"Yes," Sylvie said. "I knew him a little. We met one day while you were in church. He were a stranger in the city, just like me. He came and spoke to me. He were always kind and polite. I saw no harm in it."

"We never do," Madame said. "Never, until it's much too late."

"No harm came of it, Madame."

"You grew fond of him, lass, and there was harm enough. You're troubled now, and your mind is not always on your duties."

"I'm sorry, Madame."

"Easy, lass. I am not judging you for it. But you must understand—surely you understand, my dear?—that you cannot allow yourself any . . . *hopes* . . . in regards to a man like Mr. Shaw?"

"I don't have any hopes, Madame."

"Well, that's good, then, if it's true." The old woman's fingers tinkered with the keys, searched, slid softly into a melody. "It's safer to sail full rigged into a hurricane, Sylvie Bowen, than to love a man who is not of your station."

"Yes, Madame." Sylvie wondered how much the woman's words were rooted in her own experience. She dared not ask, of course, and Madame would never say.

But as for coming to the big house on South Park to read, and borrowing Madame's books, her fears proved unfounded. Madame invited her to come again as usual. Then, three days later, a small story appeared in the *Acadian Recorder*: HALIFAX MAN ATTACKED ON STEAMER. It was a brief account, probably copied from a Montreal paper, but it had the one piece of information she longed for: *Mr. Shaw is in hospital in Quebec, and is said to be recovering from his injuries.*

He had made it. She quietly tucked the knowledge away and savoured it against the gathering winter. He was alive, and would be well again, and that was hope enough.

———◆———

Barrington was a respectable street, much favoured by those who wished to remain close to the shipping and business heart of the city and yet keep their distance from both the waterfront and the despised upper streets around the Citadel. The owners of the Den took full advantage of this fact, maintaining the boarding house as a clean, well-ordered, and reputable residence. Liquor could be ordered at meals and in the sitting room, but those who drank were expected to behave with the dignity of guests in a private home. If they did not, they were asked to leave, something the Danners could do without hesitation, as twenty others were always waiting to get in.

Some boarders were transients, coming and going so quickly that Sylvie barely learned their names. Others had been there for months or even years. Most were ordinary people with good jobs, the sort who could afford the place but were not rich: tradesmen, clerks, a chemist from Mott's Drug Store, a teacher from the National School. Sometimes, if a ship came in when the good hotels were full, they might get anyone—blockade-runner captains, high-ranking officials from England or the United States, European aristocrats travelling for pleasure. And of course, among both the regulars and the transients alike, there were always American Southerners.

Sylvie did not have much contact with them, but Aggie Breault did. As housemaid, Aggie served the boarders' table and tended the sitting room where they spent most of their free time. Few of the Southerners had work, and all of them seemed to find the Nova Scotia weather abominably cold. Among them were two married couples, the Warners, who were very young, and the Mattisons, who had a fifteen-year-old daughter.

"The men go out drinking or plotting or whatever," Aggie told her. "The women just sit. Half of me feels so sorry for them I could cry, and half of me wants to take them and knock their heads together."

The two servants were down in the ice house, a cellar-like room below the basement level where perishable foods were kept on great blocks of ice. Every Saturday it was their job to clean it. The food was carefully moved onto shelves; the old ice was taken away; the floor and the drainage pipes were scrubbed spotless. It was a chilly, bitterly unpleasant task, but now it had a side Sylvie treasured: she and Aggie could talk together freely. And talk they did.

"They just sit," Aggie said again. "Even young Miss Marianne. When I was her age, the only way you could have kept me in a chair for a whole afternoon would've been to tie me there. They keep asking for more coal and more hot tea. It's all I can do sometimes not to tell them, for God's sake, go *do* something. Anything. Go outside and walk. Buy a pair of skates. Take up charity. Just get out of those damn chairs—you'll feel better."

"Is it because they're strangers here, do you think?"

"Oh, partly. They don't like Halifax. I overheard them once talking about what a *dirty* place it was, dirty and common, you had to scratch to find two decent houses in a city block, and there was no society to speak of—"

"Where on earth are they from, then?"

"Charleston, the one who was complaining."

"Where is that?"

"South Carolina. Deep South. Lots of money, lots of slaves. I've never been there, but I know some folks who have. They say it's got places as fancy as anything in New York. I suppose *their* ladies would look down their noses at most anything. But that ain't all of it. I think they . . ." Aggie paused in her scrubbing and looked up. "One of them asked me right out once, where were our Negroes? She'd heard there were lots of Negroes here, why on earth was a white woman cleaning out a grate?"

"Good thing she can't see us down here. She'd faint dead away."

Aggie laughed. "I think they spend all their time in that room because they're ladies, that's what I think. Because Halifax is grubby and it's cold outside, sure, but mostly because they're ladies. Because a lady is supposed to be idle. I mean, all rich folks like it easy, but having it easy ain't the same as doing nothing. Doing nothing . . . to tell you the truth, Sylvie, I think doing nothing day after day would be miserable hard."

"Well," Sylvie said, "I guess it depends how much nothing you mean by nothing. Those women can read all the books they want. They can learn about the whole world if they fancy it. They can play music. They can do a whole lot of things I'd like to do."

"And then what? What do you do with a mess of learning if there's nowhere they'll let you use it? A Yankee lady can educate herself and work at most anything. Some will call her names for it, and a lot of men won't touch her with a big long pole, but if she's willing to put up with the nonsense, she can do it. A Southern lady can't, less'n she moves north."

Sylvie shook her head. She had always known that rich and powerful people built walls and fences around each other, the same as they built them around the poor—thousands of *musts* and *can'ts* and *dare nots*. What she had never understood was why rich people put up with it. With so many resources at hand—schooling and money and knowledge of the world—why didn't more of them just say bugger it and walk away? The powerless had to do as they were told or starve. Surely the powerful could simply walk away. *I don't want to live like this, and you can't make me.*

Or did it get into your blood, being up there at the top? Making the rules, even if those rules bound you as well, because of how it felt inside to make them? Maybe it changed you so you couldn't walk away; you couldn't ask yourself, *What am I doing this for?* You were doing it to be you.

Was that how it worked? she wondered. Was that how it came to a war in the States? Because owning a slave was more than just owning some property, however valuable; it was *being* a certain kind of person?

"Maybe you're right, Aggie," she said, "but I'd still get myself something to read."

"A body can't read all day long."

"I could give it a good try."

"Well, you're bookish. That's what Sanders says, anyway. Me, I like to be up and doing. You about done with that pipe?"

"Yes." Slowly, Sylvie got to her feet. She was cold all through, and thoroughly grateful that, when they finished here, they would get to have some hot tea in a hot kitchen.

"Aggie, when you said the men go out to plot, what did you mean?"

"The men? Oh, those men. They're Confederate agents, most of them."

"You means spies?"

"And everything else. Weapons buyers, couriers, people to preach the Rebel gospel and raise money for the cause. Snoops to keep track of who comes and who goes, and to tell their masters what everybody thinks. Out-and-out plotters too, trying to make trouble between the States and England. They've all got their noses into something."

"I thought a lot of them were refugees."

"That isn't going to stop them from plotting."

"I suppose you don't like them much," Sylvie ventured, a bit uncertainly. "You being from the North, I mean."

"I can't think of one blamed reason why I should," Aggie replied. "Can you?"

"No. Nary a one."

Aggie grinned, a big, warm grin, as comradely as a hug. "Well then, Sylvie Bowen, except for being bookish, I think you and I have a great deal in common."

———◦◦◦———

So the last of autumn passed, and winter came in with gales and fog and finally snow. On the twelfth of December, Madame Louise had her fifty-fifth birthday, and the Danners invited her to dinner.

One might have thought it was a fairly ordinary thing, having an aging relative over to dinner. But no; for three days running the Den was turned all but upside down. In the Danners' personal quarters, all the furniture was moved and all the carpets were cleaned. Every painting on the walls was taken down and the heavy frames were carefully dusted. Every square inch of mahogany and oak was waxed until it shone; every ornament and piece of bric-a-brac was cleaned and polished—and there were, Aggie said, at least two million of them. The best china, already spotless, was taken out and washed again.

God knew Madame was a fine lady and wanted things done right, but this was topping it like royalty. Besides, the poor dear thing could hardly see. This was for the other guests, Sylvie decided, for the Orton and Scott kinfolk; perhaps even for Jack Danner's brother, William.

It was William who had moved the family up; this Sylvie had learned from servant gossip when she first arrived. The eldest son of a small merchant, Will Danner made money and powerful friends as a lawyer. He turned his earnings into a fortune through lucky investments, and won the hand of a Halifax beauty named Mary Scott—the daughter of shipping magnate David Scott; the sister of Louise Mallette; and the first cousin of yet another prominent lawyer and pillar of society, James Orton.

It was for them, all this fuss, but even for them it seemed too much. Polishing silver without a mark on it? Washing immaculate china?

"What are we doing this for?" she whispered at one point to Aggie Breault. "They don't even need china. The place is so clean they could eat off the furniture."

"You haven't had much to do with high folk, have you?"

"Nothing at all," she said, and then thought of Erryn. *Well, maybe a little.*

"The way I see it," Aggie said, "if you're really high, you fuss with things because it's expected, but if you miss something, the world isn't going to end. You have your place. But if you're just trying to get up there, like the Danners, then everything has to be perfect, and more than perfect. You have to be twice as Catholic as the Pope."

"I thought the Danners *were* up there. More or less."

"Oh, William is, pretty much. But for Jack I think it's still 'more or less.' He's just a small commission merchant, after all. As for this boarding house, it looks real fine to us, but to people who own shipping companies and run banks, it's small change. And then there's . . . well, Miss Susan's background."

Ah, yes. Miss Susan's background. You would never guess it if you didn't know, Sylvie thought; she dressed every inch the lady. She spoke like a lady too, not a trace of Lancashire about her, never a hint of North Country dialect or working-class toughness. She had erased it all, and made herself over in their image. But still they knew.

"Will they ever really accept her, do you think?" Sylvie asked.

"Oh, I reckon so. There's a few snots who won't, but most of them will." Aggie paused and then added pointedly, "As long as she never makes a single mistake."

At that point Miss Susan's steps could be heard in the hall and they fell silent. When she had checked on their progress and left again, Aggie had a question of her own.

"Do you ever see anything of the Ortons? At Madame Louise's place, I mean?"

"No. I've never even met them. I saw Mr. Jamie on the street once, but Reeve had to tell me who he was. I know he's all for the South, though. His son went off and joined their army last year."

"Yeah, I heard about that. What does Madame think of it?"

"She's never said. But she's all for the North, so I doubt she thinks much of it. She says slavery is a great sin, and defending it by warfare is a greater one."

"She actually said that? Good. I heard rumours she was on the Union side, but I never know what to make of rumours. Well, we might have an interesting time of it tomorrow night."

———◆———

As it turned out, they did indeed have an interesting time of it, but not for any of the reasons they expected. The guests began arriving around two, all very grand in their finery and fancy stones. Sylvie caught only glimpses of them, seeing them in the hall as they arrived or stealing a look through the parlour doorway as she passed. She tried to picture Erryn among them, in his wine-coloured waistcoat and gold cufflinks and spats. It was like picturing a hawk in a drawing room. A very well-behaved hawk, of course; he would perch with his wings carefully folded and he would never peck a soul. But his bright eyes would not miss a flutter in the curtains, and there would be all that wild energy inside, restless, wanting to take wing, to snatch a choice hors d'oeuvre from the plate and soar away.

God, how she longed to see him again.

And maybe she would, one day soon. It was something to hold on to as she spent most of the long afternoon in the scullery, where Emma Sanders fussed and stormed like a clockwork toy that never ran down. Sanders was an exceptionally good cook. The dainties they sent upstairs by the plateful made Sylvie's mouth water, and the meal they were preparing seemed fit, not merely for a king, but for a god. Racks of lamb, squashes baked with sugar and spices, Yorkshire puddings as light as a cloud, stuffed potatoes, pastries with chicken and cream, preserved vegetables in sauces, a great pot of chowder, duffs and trifles, bite-sized tarts made with brandy and nuts . . . it was truly divine. And this time they would get their share. Usually they ate the boarders' fare, not the household's—a fact that Sylvie accepted without complaint; it was nourishing food, decently prepared, and there was always plenty of it. But if Miss Susan was a hard mistress sometimes, she was also a shrewd one. She knew that her perfect evening required more than the servants' best. Their best she expected as a matter of course. For this she needed perfection, and if she got it, they would get to feast.

So they worked like fiends. They had a bit of help. William Danner had loaned them his butler to help Aggie with the serving. And Madame Louise's only manservant, who was also her coachman, put the horses up at the nearby livery and settled down in the kitchen, whence he would tend to the boarders and their dinner. He was somewhere in his forties, a gentle, quiet man named Jonathan Boyd, who made himself useful every way he could.

Sometime during the afternoon, the sun went down. Sylvie never noticed. She was inexperienced in the scullery and therefore given the meanest jobs, mostly fetching, chopping, and slicing, or washing an endless accumulation of pots and utensils. Nothing she did pleased Sanders. If she worked quickly, she was too careless; if she took more care, she was too slow. She was a ninny, a simpleton, and what in the world was Miss Susan thinking of, hiring factory trash to serve in a proper household, she might as well put an old crow in a birdcage and expect it to sing.

After a while it was like the rattling machinery in the mill: you never stopped noticing, but you kept your mind on what you were doing and tried to shut it out. So it was that she did not hear Aggie's steps running down the stairs, and only half heard her voice as she ran into the kitchen.

"Those dirty bastards have taken another ship!"

Sylvie did hear the cook's response, loud and properly outraged. "See here, Breault, we do not use that sort of language in this house!"

"Language be hanged!" Aggie flung back. "Mr. Orton just came in, Sylvie. He said he's just had word from Saint John. The Rebels took another one of our ships, went on board as passengers and took her over and killed a crewman and wounded a whole lot of others. They took the engine-room boys prisoner and dumped the rest off in Saint John and now they've gone raiding and he says they're Canadians!"

"WHAT?"

At this, even Sanders went motionless, with a spoon half raised in her hand.

"Slow down, Mrs. Breault," Jonathan said. "Start from the beginning. What ship? And what do you mean, they're Canadians?"

"The *Chesapeake*, from Boston. Some passengers took her over on the high seas, they say they're Confederates, but the crewmen they left in Saint John say they're from here—"

"From here?"

"—and Mr. Orton says he thinks it's true, says he recognized one of the names they used. And anyway, Englishmen don't sound like Southerners when they talk, and everybody knows it—"

Sylvie stared at her. "You mean there's our own people gone pirating for the Confederacy?"

"You can't call them pirates!" Harry Dobbs said. "It's war and they got every right to take an enemy ship!"

"We ain't at war," Sanders snapped. "Our lads got no business taking anybody's ships."

"Well, they did," Aggie said. "And they killed the engineer, and the captain says it was plain murder and the whole ocean won't be big enough to hide them."

"Oh, bloody damned hell." Jonathan sat down on a kitchen bench and shook his head. "You know what this means, don't you?"

The answer came from the doorway, where Miss Susan had arrived unnoticed.

"It means we might yet find ourselves at war," she said. "But for the moment, we have guests, and they are your only concern. Is the boarders' dinner ready to serve?"

"Yes, m'um," Sanders said.

"Very well. Boyd, if you would be so kind, see to it. Bowen, you are to help him. As for this matter of the ships, it may be exaggerated, and until we know, it's not our place to be spreading gossip."

Never once had anyone heard Miss Susan express an opinion on the American war. She ran a boarding house where both Northerners and Southerners stayed; she was the soul of discretion. But now there was a bleakness in her eyes and in her voice, of a sort Sylvie had never seen there before—a bleakness she knew she would not find in the eyes of Jamie Orton. To this extent at least, Miss Susan had taken sides: she wanted no part of the Rebels' war.

⊰―◆―⊱

For the next couple of hours, no one had much chance to talk. Two meals had to be served, to thirty-seven people, dining on two different floors, all separate from the kitchen. It was mostly Sylvie and Harry Dobbs who carried the pots and platters up, and the dirty dishes back down. By nine-thirty the Danners and their guests were down to chocolates and brandy. At ten Aggie and Jonathan returned to the kitchen.

"Miss Susan says we can eat now," Jonathan told them. "And Mr. William's butler says we should behave like Christians now, and leave a bite for him."

He was smiling, just a bit. Sylvie glanced at the chowder pot, still half full, at the racks of lamb still lying on the plates. They could all eat twice over and there would be plenty left.

"What're they saying up there, anyway?" she asked. "About that ship?"

"Nothing. Not a peep. They say one thing, they'll get Madame all upset and spoil her birthday. They say the other, and Mr. Jamie'll skewer them for it later."

"How well do you know them, Jonathan?" Aggie questioned. "Are they all for the South, like Mr. Jamie?"

"Madame isn't."

"I know Madame isn't. I mean the rest of them."

He shrugged. "Near as I can tell, they split nicely in three: one batch Union, one batch Confederate, one batch don't-care-poppycock. Trouble is, Mr. Jamie's the head of the family, so the Union sort and the don't-cares don't argue with him much."

"Except Madame," Sylvie said.

"No," Jonathan said, "not even Madame. There's no point. It'd be like arguing with a tree."

"So why's he like that, anyway?" Aggie persisted. "So keen for the Southerners, I mean. Do you know?"

"The rich stick together. Haven't you noticed?"

"Madame's rich," Sylvie said.

"Madame's been through a few storms," Jonathan said. "Makes people think when they get kicked around a bit."

Sylvie shook her head. "In Rochdale, there were big arguments about the war, even in the mills. John Bright came and gave a talk in the Mechanics Hall one night. He's in the Parliament and all, and he's rich. He's got more bloody money than you or I can dream of. And he spoke for the Union and we cheered him and signed this big long letter to send to Mr. Lincoln, saying we were behind him even if it meant no cotton for the mills, because we were working people, and slavery kept working people down, didn't matter where. And when we came out of the hall, some of our own mates called us horrid names, and said why should they go hungry for the sake of some bloody niggers." She paused, searching for words. "It's rich and poor, maybe, but it ain't *just* that. It's . . . I don't know . . . like you said about Madame . . . it's *thinking* . . ." She wished Erryn were here; he would know what words to use. And then she wondered if he bothered his head about any of these things, ever. He never so much as mentioned the American war. Once, she'd asked him very tentatively for an opinion, and he merely shrugged. He didn't know, he said, he hadn't paid much attention. It was one of the few times he had ever disappointed her.

"Let's go eat," Jonathan said. "A meal like this doesn't come every day."

They descended on the nearby table, where the others were piling their plates. Two hours ago she had been dreaming of this feast. Now she scarcely cared if she ate or not.

"You're right, Jonathan." Harry Dobbs sat down expansively before a plate that looked laden enough for two. "Let's eat by all means. It'll be army biscuits next week, likely." The silly ass actually sounded pleased.

"Do you think they'll come here?" MacKay whispered to no one in particular. As at so many other times, she seemed frightened and bewildered.

"Will who come here?"

"The pirates."

"Oh, come on! They're privateers, not pirates!" Dobbs said. "And I rather hope they do come. It would be something to see!"

"And the whole Yankee fleet behind them, I suppose?" Sanders flung back at him. "You'd like to see that as well, would you?"

Dobbs shot her a defiant look, but said nothing. However great an ass he was, he knew, as did every Haligonian who was sane and past the age of five, that every warship in the Atlantic Squadron was gone, sailing weeks ago for their winter posting in the Caribbean.

Except for a few old, unimpressive cannons on the Citadel, the city was defenceless against an attack from the sea.

CHAPTER 17

❖

MacNab

What security is there that . . . in an ill-judged attempt to
quench the American strife, we should in the result
endanger the peace of Europe?
—*The Times* (London), November 17, 1862

FROM THE DECK of the mail packet *Delhi*, Erryn Shaw watched
Halifax glide closer, bit by bit, a ribbon of buildings strung along
a grey shore, with the mound of the Citadel rising hard at its
back. In the winter morning it seemed all black and grey, but at
least it was there, visible, a small miracle after five days of fog and
gales. For a brief while the cloud cover broke, the water sparkled,
and the spire of St. Paul's and the dome of the Town Clock shone
proudly in a pool of winter light. Erryn stayed by the rail despite
the wind, admiring everything he saw. George's Island passed
with its bare slopes and stone batteries, and then the busy
wharves of the South End, Corbett's and Wood's and the West
India Company, all suddenly as familiar as old friends. More than
any time since he had left England, he felt as though he were
coming home.

They docked at Queen's Wharf with barely a bump. As always, Her Majesty's mail sacks disembarked first; he was the first of the passengers to follow. He would have liked to go to his rooming house, have a hot bath and a long nap, and then find Sylvie Bowen and invite her to dinner. But alas, those were the governor's guineas rattling in his purse, and Lord Monck, worldly and dutiful soul that he was, expected him to earn them. He picked his way through the waterfront crowds and the mud to Alexander MacNab's Dry Goods Emporium on Hollis Street.

———✦———

Although other Grey Tories in Halifax were more socially prominent and more personally committed, for sheer energy and usefulness to the cause MacNab outranked them all. He was a large man, almost as tall as Erryn himself, and easily twice his girth. Receding hair and sagging jowls gave him something of a bulldog look, which rather suited him. He had scrapped his way from obscurity into the ranks of the Halifax elite. Now, in his fifties, he was one of the richest men in town, but everything about him was still hard-edged and always slightly challenging. It did not help that he had been born with a hair-trigger temper, and he never made much effort to control it.

Erryn found him already on his way out, his coat wrapped over his arm, talking to a deferential and harassed-looking clerk. Erryn remained discreetly at a distance, but he could still hear anger in MacNab's voice, and numerous references to things amiss, and the clerk saying "yessir" to everything, indiscriminately. MacNab was still talking as he turned away: "I want it packed before you leave tonight, do you understand, before you— Well, I'll be damned! Mr. Shaw. Good to see you back."

"Thank you. How have you been, sir?"

"Can't complain." MacNab had a crunching handshake, and a bear's paw to wield it. His gaze raked Erryn from head to toe, as though he were examining a piece of damaged merchandise. "You look like hell, Shaw. No offence, but I've seen livelier washed up on the pier. What the devil happened to you, anyway? I never could make much sense of it in the newspapers."

"I got myself a knife wound and a very cold bath in the St. Lawrence. They fished me out again, but it was a near thing."

"Did you know the son of a bitch?"

"No. He went over the side with me, and they never found him. Some sod who called himself John Hill was missing from steerage after, or so the police told me, but no one knew anything about him. He was just a ruffian, no doubt, with his eye on my purse."

"You don't suppose it was some damned Yankee agent?"

"Now why would I suppose that?" Erryn murmured, very dry. "What with our neutrality laws and all?"

MacNab laughed and slapped him lightly on the arm. "Why indeed? So fill me in, for Christ's sake. Did you come by Portland? The buggers must be mad as hornets down there."

"I did, and they are, though I couldn't make any more sense out of their newspapers than you could make out of ours. Is it true the men who took the *Chesapeake* were Canadians?"

"Half true. The captain's a naval officer from Kentucky. Duly commissioned, by the way, with a letter of marque, legal as can be. The piracy charge is rubbish. But most of the crew was recruited in New Brunswick, and a few around Shelburne."

"No wonder the Yankees on the *Delhi* wouldn't talk to me."

"It's a hell of a kick in their teeth—and right before Christmas, too. Listen, I was just on my way over to the Waverley for lunch. Come with me. Jamie Orton will be there, and some other lads. They'll be glad to see you."

"Thank you, I will. But first I'd better give you these." Erryn unbuttoned an inside pocket and withdrew two envelopes. "Our friends in Quebec sent some letters for you."

"Ah, good. Give me a minute, will you?"

MacNab flung his coat over a counter and took the envelopes away with him. Idly, Erryn glanced over the store's interior. MacNab's Dry Goods Emporium was large, classy, and profitable. It had made the man a good deal of money before the war, but now, supplying blockade-runners with overpriced goods had raised his profit margin from high to astronomical, a fact he demonstrated by building himself a splendid three-storey mansion—not out on the Northwest Arm, where most of the rich people lived, but right in the heart of the city, on Barrington, where he could stay close to his business . . . and where, of course, the whole world could walk by every day and admire it.

Erryn admired it as well, on the way to the Waverley. It was almost finished, MacNab said; the workmen were installing the floors and the panelling. Erryn judged it a beautiful home, and he said so.

"Well, thank you, lad. You could have one of these yourself, you know, a few years down the road. You've got the smarts for it. You just have to stop drifting and settle down."

Erryn said nothing. He merely gave MacNab a quiet sidelong glance—somewhat amused, somewhat haughty—the glance of a man who had three or four such houses back in England, and finer ones, ready to occupy any time he felt like it. MacNab changed the subject.

━━◆━━

The Waverley House in Halifax, like St. Lawrence Hall in Montreal, was the preferred gathering place of Southern Confederates and their allies—couriers, political agents, businessmen, spies, military and naval officers, and, above all, blockade-runners. New men came with every ship, a fact that must have driven the Union agents crazy. But some in the dining hall were known to Erryn, and greeted him with smiles and handshakes—one of them a man of approximately his own age, with sandy brown hair and a boyishly attractive face, who leapt to his feet and strode full across the room to meet him.

"Erryn! You're back! God damn it, you're a welcome sight!"

"Jack! Good to see you!"

They shared a long, warm handshake, and afterwards Jack Murray gripped his arm, affection and concern both clear in his eyes.

"How are you, mate? You seem a trifle peaked."

"I was fine until everyone started telling me how bad I looked. You lads keep this up, I'm likely to keel over dead."

Murray laughed. "Always the same old Erryn." He nodded to Erryn's companion. "MacNab. I suppose you're dragging him off to the privy council over there?"

"I am."

"I'll join you later, Jack," Erryn said. "I want you to tell me everything that's happened since I left."

"You know about the *Chesapeake*, I suppose?"

"It's all MacNab and I have been talking about."

"It's all anyone is talking about. Later, then." He gave Erryn an airy half salute and walked away.

◆━◆━◆

The privy council, as Jack Murray called it, was an alcove at the back of the dining room, somewhat apart from the crowd, where Jamie Orton sat with four companions. Orton was a Scot, the sort of Scot all the world's twelve-year-olds imagined when they read about Wallace and Bruce and Bonnie Dundee: a giant of a man with red-gold hair and a great roaring laugh. At his side was his friend of many years, David Strange. Both belonged to old, well-established families, and between them had interests in nearly every Haligonian enterprise of importance, from shipbuilding to bank directorships to the choir of St. Andrew's Presbyterian Church. Also at the table were Orton's eldest son, Tobias, and Strange's nephew, Robert Collier, whom Erryn frankly considered a fool. In the place of honour was the English captain of a visiting blockade-runner.

The men were not, as it happened, talking about the *Chesapeake* at all. When the pleasantries had been concluded, Orton turned at once to Erryn Shaw, obviously picking up the conversation where they had left it.

"Well, laddie, we've heard everyone else's opinion. Tell us what you think. What did this damned mess in Tennessee do to the Confederacy's chances?"

"You mean the defeat at Chattanooga, I presume?"

"Aye."

"It's difficult to say." Erryn frowned in the general direction of his plate. He believed, personally, that the Confederates were in a great deal of trouble. They had lost frightfully at Gettysburg and Vicksburg back in the summer. And then in November, just weeks ago, the new commanding general of the Union's western armies, Ulysses Grant, had whipped them and run them headlong out of Tennessee, reversing their brief September triumph at Chickamauga. *There! Thought you were on your way back up, lads? Think again.*

For Erryn, lying in his hospital bed in Quebec, recovering from pneumonia and dying of boredom, it was the best news imaginable. Maybe the war would end soon after all, and the danger would be over. He could live like a sane man again, get himself another theatre, and set about courting Sylvie Bowen in earnest.

Then he remembered the summer. He had felt the same way in the summer, after Gettysburg, and he had been dead wrong. War appeared to be one of those human endeavours where it was damnably, terrifyingly easy to be wrong.

"It's a setback," he went on. "Hell, it's a bad setback. But it's likely to make the Yankees overconfident. And the Confederates have more pluck, we all know that. They'll stay with it until they win. Or until Europe gets fed up with the cotton famine."

"Cotton famine doesn't matter a damn," the English captain said. "We're getting cotton from Egypt now. It's not as good, but it will do. And the Southern cotton that we do get in brings four times what it did before the war, so no one's out of pocket very much. There'll be no intervention over cotton."

"What about intervention over liberty and justice?" Orton demanded. "Damn it, captain, we are the defenders of Western civilization. If England doesn't stand up for the right, who will? And why in God's name don't we think of our own Anglo-Saxon people first? We went into India and China and the bloody Crimea—"

"That's part of the problem, sir."

"I don't follow you."

"The bloody Crimea. It was a costly war, and the Radicals aren't letting anyone forget it. The government is wary now about getting in another. And as long as the Yankees keep winning battles, they're only going to get warier."

"In other words," Erryn said, "the more the Confederacy needs help from England, the less likely she'll be to get it."

"That's about it, Mr. Shaw. As I see the matter."

It was how Erryn saw the matter also, from poring by the hour over English newspapers and English pamphlets, all of them he could get his hands on, and the colonial papers too, which often echoed the sentiments of London. Intervention was dangerous. Quite apart from other considerations, such as the morality of it, or which side one favoured, it was simply dangerous, a potential quagmire that could endlessly eat up lives and treasure, destabilizing the European balance of power and ultimately threatening the empire itself. Prime Minister Palmerston was an interventionist by temperament and a man who leaned decidedly toward the South. But the empire would always come first. "England has neither allies nor enemies," he said once. "She has only interests."

It was a damnably cynical sort of politics, Palmerston's. It was also the best they could hope for, probably. Better a wary cynic in power, just now, than any number of eager defenders of Western civilization.

"Palmerston's too damned old," Robert Collier said. "They ought to put him out to pasture."

David Strange, who was past sixty and still running his shipping line like a well-oiled machine, gave his nephew a very sour look. Then he rose and pointedly changed the subject.

"Gentlemen, let me propose a toast. Here's to a fast voyage and a safe haven for the *Chesapeake*!"

"Hear! Hear!"

"You boys obviously know something I don't," Erryn said when they sat down again. "Everyone I spoke to in Portland seemed to think the *Chesapeake* was still in our own bailiwick, looking for coal."

"She was, until yesterday," Strange told him. "MacNab here sent a schooner out Wednesday night and found her just down the coast, at Sambro. He brought her all the coal she'll need, and a couple of engineers too, so they could let the Yankee prisoners go. Couldn't be the pleasantest thing in the world, standing guard in your engine room all day and all night with a loaded pistol." He glanced at MacNab, who looked extraordinarily pleased with himself. "I expect the lads were on their way by dawn."

"Well," Erryn said, raising his glass again. "You've been Johnny-on-the-spot, as usual."

"What the hell are you drinking there, Shaw?" MacNab grumbled. "It looks like water."

"It is. Doctor's orders. No spirits for a fortnight."

"Christ. Remind me never to get myself thrown in the St. Lawrence."

A waiter came, bringing steaming platters of food. Erryn glanced briefly toward the main part of the dining room and noticed, for the second time, that it seemed emptier than usual. Even now, a group of diners were hastily picking up their coats and preparing to leave.

Ships coming in, he thought. Anxiously awaited ones, no doubt, after five days of appalling weather. Outside, even the boardwalks on Barrington were covered with mud, and broken branches and wind debris lay scattered everywhere. How thankful everyone would be, and how eager, to see their vessels and their cargoes coming home safe.

He turned his attention back to the table, where young Tobias Orton was raising a matter he would have liked to raise himself, but dared not.

"I heard the damnedest thing this morning, talking with Tom Hogan. He's just back from Saint John, and he says the Confederate captain on the *Chesapeake* is named Braine—John Braine, to be precise. There was a chap by that name came through here in the summer, remember? Selling advertisements for a business directory, supposedly for the Grand Trunk Railway. Only the directory never came out. You were frightfully annoyed, Strange, as I recall. Then we found the railwaymen had never heard of it, and Braine had made off with all the money. You wouldn't suppose it's the same man?"

"The captain of the *Chesapeake* is a commissioned officer in the Confederate navy. I'm sure the swindler is a different man altogether. It's hardly an uncommon name."

"Well, I hope you're right. There's been a lot of criticism of the hijacking, even from our own side. It won't help if the man responsible turns out to be a common thief."

"And there are no common thieves in the Yankee army, I suppose?" Orton flung back at him. "Or in our own? Christ almighty, a man's got to look at the issues in a war, not at which side's got the choirboys in the ranks."

Indeed, Erryn thought wryly. *And how I would love to remind you of it the next time you go on and on about Yankee ruffians and Southern cavaliers.*

James Dougal Orton went on about such things rather often. More than any of the other Confederate supporters in Halifax, he was involved in the struggle out of personal commitment. He was a lawyer by profession, a philanthropist by choice, a mover in the world of affairs, a man with an abiding sense of duty. Most especially, he was a man who believed in order and tradition. He neither liked nor trusted the polyglot world across the border—a world, as he saw it, of dishonest traders, shoddy goods, hare-brained ideologies, whiskey-barrel electioneering, and irreligious people, all of it growing worse as immigrants flooded in from the roughest and most dismal rubbish heaps of Europe.

The Southern Confederates at least were gentlemen, well bred and well spoken. They were men who went to church, and who took proper care of their wives and children. Slavery Orton disapproved of, at least in theory, but in practice he refused to pass judgment on a society a thousand miles away that he had never seen. Slavery was already in place, after all, had been in place for centuries; surely it was for the men who lived there to determine what to do about it. The Northerners could not run their own society properly; what right did they have to take cannon and sword and try to run somebody else's? To him, it was England and Scotland all over again. It was more dull-eyed yeomen and brave cavaliers. It was Bonnie Prince Charlie and bloody King George . . .

A voice broke harshly into Erryn's thoughts.

"Mr. MacNab, sir!"

Hurrying over to their table was a clerk from the Emporium—not the one MacNab had bawled out earlier, a different one, but he looked equally distressed. He was shouting even as he came. "There's Yankee ships coming in, sir! Warships! Mr. Doane said come and tell you!"

MacNab's big head shot upright. All conversation at the table ended as if snipped with a knife.

"What the devil do you mean, warships?"

"Two of them, sir. The signals are up on Citadel Hill, and half the town's out running for a look. I wanted to come right off, but

Mr. Doane said no, go up to the hill and make sure. It's Yankee warships, all right. I could see them clear." He patted the spyglass still clutched in one hand. "They got another ship with them. Folks are saying maybe it's the *Chesapeake*."

———◆———

It was just as the young man had said: half the town was out for a look. Business had ground to a standstill on Water Street, the warehouses abandoned except for a clerk or two, delivery teams left drooping in their harnesses, the reins hitched hastily to posts and trees. People were strewn all along the quays and bunched in upper-storey windows. Here and there a spyglass passed from hand to hand. But they were not laughing or dressed in their finery, as they were when they gathered in May, when the Atlantic Squadron came back from the Caribbean. They stared, and talked quietly in huddles, or not at all.

The ships were well into the harbour channel now, passing Fort Charlotte at the tip of George's Island. Erryn waited for a turn with the glass and studied them carefully. In the lead was a steamer he judged a merchant ship. From the descriptions he had heard in Portland, he thought it might well be the *Chesapeake*. Behind her came a sloop, and then a lean, low, speedy-looking sidewheeler with twin masts. Gunboats, both of them.

"Bloody damned hell."

Was it war, then? Had someone already made the irreversible blunder? Or was someone about to make it? Were they going to blow his small grey city into the sea?

Surely not, he told himself; neither government wanted war. Yet he could not stop fear from seeping through him like a winter fog.

He handed the glass back to MacNab. "What do they want, do you suppose?" he asked.

"They want to pay us back," Jack Murray said grimly. He and his dinner companion had rushed out along with the others. He was standing now almost at Erryn's shoulder. "It was our lads took the *Chesapeake*, and they mean to slap us for it. They'll have some outrageous demand to make, you can bet on it, and God knows what they'll do if we don't comply. Damn, I wish the Squadron was still here."

"Quite," Erryn agreed. But he wondered if they might be safer without it.

"Whatever the buggers want," James Orton muttered, "they don't mean us well or they'd be firing their salutes by now."

The ships came on, steady and serene. They fired no salutes, but neither did they fire anything else. More people came and clustered on the waterfront. The Town Clock tolled a quarter of the hour and then the hour. Two in the afternoon, the seventeenth of December, 1863. Would it be written in the history books one day, Erryn wondered, as the day the world ended here?

Surely not . . .

He raised the glass again. On the lead vessel it was now possible to read a name, faint at this distance, but decipherable. It was, indeed, the *Chesapeake*. The Confederates would have painted over any identification when they captured the ship, which meant the Yankees had promptly painted it back again. Yes, he thought, they were rubbing it in.

But they were not shooting, and that was what mattered.

"It's the *Chesapeake*," he said.

Orton snatched the glass from his hand, stared for a long moment, and cursed. He was a steady, churchgoing man; he hardly ever cursed.

"They never got away from Sambro, then," MacNab said wearily. "The bastards must've been waiting for them, right outside the harbour."

"The poor laddies," Orton said. "The poor brave laddies."

Oh, God, have pity on me, please.

Erryn pulled up his collar as something grey and mean from Newfoundland swept in across the channel and ripped at his sleeves and his hair. He wanted to go home and crawl into bed, or, failing that, find a tea room with plenty of hot tea and a big, roaring hearth. Instead, he had to stand in this God-benighted wind, keeping this pack of God-benighted arseholes company . . . *Matt, when this is over, I'm going to strangle you, I swear it.*

"We need to send a man to Sambro, right off," Orton was saying. "Find out whatever we can."

"Shaw's right here," MacNab said. "He can go."

"No," Orton said sharply. "Not Shaw."

Erryn went absolutely rigid. It was not a reasoned fear, but instinct, pure and immediate, knotting his belly and steeling his every nerve, all of it too quick for thought, even as Orton's voice went on without a pause, "For pity's sake, MacNab, he just came from the hospital. He's been two days on the road. He must be dead on his feet. I'll send Harper."

There was honest concern on Orton's face and in his voice, perfectly clear and obvious as soon as Erryn's brain had the few needful seconds to perceive it. Not suspicion. Empathy. Slowly his fear drained away, leaving him utterly exhausted.

"I appreciate that, sir," he said. "I'm not up to scratch yet, I'm afraid."

"Don't worry your head about it, lad."

Out in the harbour, the American ships were dropping anchor some distance from the docks. A small boat pulled away from the sloop, heading for the shore. It was soon blocked from view by the larger vessels lining the waterfront. Al MacNab leaned over to say something to his clerk, who scurried off. Ten or fifteen minutes later he came back at a run. The landing party, he said, consisted only of a petty officer and two guards. They appeared to be heading directly to the U.S. consul's office on Bedford Row.

"Well," David Strange observed, "it would seem they want Mr. Lincoln's permission before they twist the lion's tail."

"They won't get it," Erryn said.

Much of the city appeared to agree with him. Activity was starting again all along the waterfront, unevenly but distinctly, like a great perambulating sigh of relief. Men disappeared back into warehouses, carts began to move, hack drivers jumped onto their vehicles and offered their services to the dispersing crowd, many of whom were in a hurry now, remembering neglected duties.

"Gentlemen," Erryn said, "I'm afraid this vessel is about to founder. If you'll forgive me, I'm heading home."

"I'll not only forgive you," Jack Murray said, "I'm going to take you there myself."

Erryn did not argue. He let Jack hire them a carriage and sank onto the seat like a rag. He tried to listen as Jack babbled on about the sad death of Major Harrington, and what a splendid funeral they gave him; about a certain Mrs. Gentry, who was in town to raise money for medical supplies, such a lovely creature, pity she was married. Most of all he talked about the Yankee spies in town. Every week there were more of them, he said; you could hardly sit down in a restaurant or talk on the street without some damned eavesdropper lurking nearby.

That's what I used to worry about too: eavesdroppers. Now Jamie Orton says don't send me to Sambro and I think my life is forfeit before he can even explain why.

He wondered if it would always be like this now, if every wrong word would freeze him in his tracks. If he would always be looking over his shoulder, till the end of the war, maybe till the end of his life. If he had lost a part of himself forever.

He knew it was not Zeb Taylor's knife that lay at the heart of his loss, but Zeb Taylor's words. *My brother had you figured from the start.* He had always liked Brad Taylor. They had shared meals, joshed each other, even spoken of the theatre, of a play Brad had seen in Kentucky and how awful it was. Yet through it all, Taylor had been watching him, doubting him, waiting for him to make the inevitable, fatal mistake . . . and the possibility of it had never crossed his mind.

You have faith in things, don't you? Sylvie told him by the Irish Stone. *I don't mean religious things. I mean life things. You believe when you set out to go somewhere you'll get there, and when you have something of your own you'll be able to keep it . . .*

Maybe not, anymore. Maybe never again.

CHAPTER 18

Muffinry

There is a great mass of cool judgment and plain sense
on the side of freedom and humanity, but the ardent
spirits and passions are on the side of oppression.
—*John Quincy Adams*

"Well, it's going to be war now for sure."

Sylvie, still on her knees by the drainage pipe, sat back on her haunches and stared at Harry Dobbs, who had just tramped down the stairs with the first fresh block of ice and was now shoving it into place with a huge grunt of satisfaction.

"What the devil are you talking about?" Aggie Breault demanded.

"I'm talking about the bloody Yankees, that's what," Dobbs said. "They didn't catch the *Chesapeake* at sea like we figured. They went right into Sambro harbour. Do you believe it? Right into the harbour, and boarded the ship and took it over. And that ain't the half of it. There was a schooner there from Halifax, and they boarded it too, at gunpoint, and they got a bunch of prisoners now, and they're going to hang them as pirates—"

"And they come and told you all about it, I suppose," Sylvie said scornfully.

"It's all over town. Timmins just come with the ice, and he heard it from half a dozen people already. He says for sure it means a fight. And the Yankees bloody well know it. There's two more of their ships come in this morning. We got five of the devils in the harbour now, and one of them's a bloody *frigate*. Oh, it's war all right."

Sylvie threw her scrub rag back into the bucket and wrung her hands to warm them. She wondered how a man could pass on news like this and be stupid enough to sound pleased about it.

"It don't have to mean war," she said.

"Course it does. Sailing into one of our harbours like that and taking ships? Taking Englishmen prisoner? That's an act of war. There's no way we're going to stand for it."

"You don't know the prisoners are Englishmen," Aggie said. "You couldn't possibly know."

"They were all from here, what took the *Chesapeake*. Every one of 'em but the captain. That's what Mr. Timmins says."

Miss Susan's voice came sharply down the stairwell. "Dobbs! What are you doing down there? I don't want this ice melting in the hallway!"

"Yes, m'um. I'm coming."

"Lord," Aggie muttered when he had disappeared up the stairs, "that boy don't have the sense God gave a flea."

Sylvie got to her feet, emptied her bucket, and brushed loose hair from her face with her sleeve. "I wish I knew what be going on out there, I really do."

"Well, we know one thing," Aggie said. "We know those American ships poor Dobbsy is so worried about were trading salutes with the Citadel this morning. Odd how he didn't hear it."

"Maybe he thinks it don't mean anything."

"Yeah, but when the *Dacotah* didn't salute yesterday, he thought it meant everything."

"Do you suppose it happened like he said?" Sylvie asked then, very soft. "They went into Sambro harbour?"

For a time the only sound in the cellar was Harry Dobbs's boots tramping back down the stairs, the thump of another block of ice on the fresh-scrubbed stone.

"I don't know," Aggie said at last. "But even if they did, those men are pirates. England wouldn't start a war over a bunch of pirates, would she?"

No, Sylvie thought. Not over pirates. Not over a harbour violation either. Wars might be set off by trifles, but the trifles were never the real reason, they were only the excuse; that much she was sure of. But what the powerful people in both countries really wanted—now there was a whole other question. There were men here who hoped for war; probably there were Americans who did too. Every now and then a colonial paper would reprint some flaming editorial from New York or Chicago, howling insults against England and talking like all of North America was United States property by divine decree. And the nitwits here were just as bad, hating the States because they had overthrown the lords and put government in the reach of ordinary people, and that meant the end of human civilization.

How plentiful were such men in either country? She did not know. But she doubted they cared a fig about the *Chesapeake*, or Sambro harbour either. They cared only about themselves.

＊

More news came to the Den as the day went on, and it soon became clear that Harry Dobbs, as usual, had only part of the story. Aggie Breault learned more from conversations overheard in the parlour and the family quarters, and passed it on to Sylvie in the hallway.

Yes, she said, the Yankee gunboat *Dacotah* had sailed into Sambro harbour, seizing both the *Chesapeake* and the coaling schooner that Al MacNab had sent with supplies and two local engineers.

"But the Rebels saw the ship coming," she went on, "so of course they all bolted into the woods. It seems the only prisoners our boys got was a fellow they found sleeping on the schooner, and the two engineers, who never bothered to run."

"Why not?"

"I guess they thought they were safe, being Canadians. And they hadn't really done anything yet."

Sylvie cocked an eyebrow at her.

"Well, legally they hadn't," Aggie said.

"So they're all somewhere down by Sambro? The pirates?"

"All except Captain Braine. Apparently he ran out on his crew a couple of days before and nobody knows where he is." She paused and added quietly, "I guess some folks here are hopping mad because we took your lads, and they'd maybe make trouble if they could. But Miss Susan says the men in charge intend to talk. On both sides. That's what she's heard, anyway."

"Do you think it be true?"

They could hear their mistress's steps approaching on the stairs.

"All we can do is hope," Aggie said, and turned to go.

——◆——

It was a good thirty-minute walk to Madame's house on South Park Road, past St. Paul's and the marble yard and the Catholic convent; past the corner at Spring Garden Road where, for no reason whatsoever, not even the smallest curve, Barrington started calling itself Pleasant Street; and finally westward, away from the wind. Her hands grew painfully cold, clutching the parcels Miss Susan had sent along with her, but otherwise it was lovely to be outside.

She found Madame sitting in her favourite chair by the fire, wrapped in a shawl to her knees. She had a touch of the grippe, but mostly she seemed depressed. She wanted Sylvie to read poetry for her—Gray's "Elegy," and Wordsworth, quiet, meditative things with a lot of sadness in them. Twice Sylvie saw her nodding in her chair, and after an hour or so she said it was enough.

"You read well, Sylvie. You are improving all the time. What would you like to take home with you?"

"Another of Lord Lytton's, if I might, Madame."

"Take *Harold*, then. It is his best."

Sylvie crossed the room and plucked a beautifully bound volume off the bookshelf. She had read Lord Lytton's *Pelham*, because it was about a young aristocrat; she thought she might learn something of their lives. But no matter how hard she tried, she could not picture Erryn Shaw in Henry Pelham's world. Oh, in little things, perhaps: the fine clothing, the ways of speech, the careful attention to small courtesies. But otherwise, no. Despite its pleasures and comforts, Pelham's world seemed shallow to her, even silly. She did not see how a man with spirit could ever be content there.

But then, he had not been content, had he? *I went my own way, and before anyone really noticed, even me, I'd turned myself into a considerable misfit.*

She straightened the shelf a bit and turned back to Madame. It was still early, but already the parlour window was dark. Thick snowflakes swirled endlessly against it, catching the light from Madame's seven lamps.

The old lady was fussing with her reticule. "Did Susan give you anything extra?" she asked. "For bringing the parcels?"

"No, Madame."

"Here, then. Take this." Her outstretched hand held a ten-cent coin. "Go on, take it, lass. You had a long way to walk in the cold. And watch yourself on the streets now. Even in a blizzard there are villains out, and few decent folk around to be watching them."

"Thank you very much, Madame."

Ten cents, what marvellous good luck! A week's pay, after board and lodging, was all of thirty. She slipped the coin into the pocket of her thin coat and walked out into the wind. A carriage waited in the street, the driver huddled under a cape, the horses standing with their heads down. Snow clung to their harness and lay draped like a blanket across their backs.

Odd, she thought, and wondered whom they might be waiting for. Madame was not going out, as far as she knew, and the house across the street was dark. She slowed her pace as she approached, remembering Madame's warning, and stopped altogether when the carriage door opened and a figure stepped out, draped in an immense hooded cloak.

It was almost dark. For a moment the figure was only a tall silhouette in the falling snow. It could have been anyone, yet her heart leapt with hope. Then he flung his hood back and bowed with a flair and grace she had only seen in one man, ever.

"Miss Bowen, it's an utterly abominable day for a lady to be walking. May I offer you a ride in my carriage?"

Erryn!

She took two running steps toward him, then caught herself. Weeks had passed, after all; perhaps she was no more than an acquaintance to him now. And he was not, as Madame said, of her station.

"Mr. Shaw! Oh, it's so good to see you! Are you all right?"

"A bit the worse for wear, my heart—but yes, I'm all right. And you?" He took her hands. Even in the poor light he seemed thinner and bonier than she remembered. "Miss Susan and Madame are treating you well?"

"Oh, yes."

"I've thought of you every single day since I left the *Saguenay*. I feared it would take forever until I might see you again, and thank you properly for what you did. Be hanged, but that's a mean wind. Let's get inside."

He helped her into the carriage and pulled the door shut with a satisfying whack.

"Winter," he went on, "was invented by the devil. Thought he could bottle it up and pack it back to his own bailiwick, cool things off a bit. He was a dumb sod. He didn't do himself one scrap of good, and he made all the rest of us miserable. What are you smiling at?"

"You."

"Oh, dear, I'm babbling again, aren't I? Here. I brought you a present."

He picked up a wrapped parcel from the seat beside him and handed it across to her. A large parcel, in fine paper and ribbons, of the sort Miss Susan sometimes brought home. She took it wonderingly.

"Go ahead, open it."

"Here?"

"Please."

She would have preferred to open it in her room, slowly and with infinite care, savouring every moment. But she untied the ribbons and peeled back the paper, and caught her breath. Inside was a cloak, hooded like his own but designed for a lady, long enough to reach her ankles, and made of the most exquisite wool, soft and thick and impossibly rich. She could scarcely imagine what it must have cost.

"Oh, my heavens . . ." She stroked it ever so lightly, conscious as never before of how thin her little mantle was, how the wind sometimes cut through it like a knife. "It's beautiful, Mr. Shaw, and awful kind of you. But it's so . . . so grand, and you hardly know me . . . I mean, perhaps I shouldn't . . ."

"Oh, but you should. If a man is delivered from death by his friend, what can he possibly do except bring her something grand? Otherwise it might seem he did not value *her* gift—and hers was more precious than any." He smiled, but his gaze was intense and serious. "Take it, my heart, and wear it contented. You've earned it."

For a moment she said nothing, overwhelmed by his generosity, and also by the enchanting thought that it might be more than generosity or even gratitude. She thanked him repeatedly and then, unable to resist, slipped out of her mantle and put the cloak on.

"Ohhh . . ." She snuggled like a kitten in a muff and saw that he was pleased. "I feel like I've just grown fur."

He smiled. "You look utterly dazzling, Sylvie Bowen. Will you join me for supper? I have a table reserved at Compain's, and for once we can talk to our hearts' content, and not be sent running by a church bell. Will you come?"

Sylvie was not vain, but she felt like the grandest lady in the world, walking into Compain's famous eatery on the arm of Erryn Shaw, wrapped in her beautiful new cloak. Compain's was the smallest of the city's good hotels, but everyone said its restaurant was the best in all of Nova Scotia. It was still early, tea time really rather than supper, but because it was storming outside, all the chandeliers were lit, and everything shimmered in their brilliance.

Erryn ordered wine for them. Survival, he said, was a proper cause for celebration. But he had shadows under his eyes now, and a worn look about him—not haggard, precisely, but damaged and spent.

"Are you sure you're all right, Erryn?" she asked softly. "You look awfully thin."

"I was born thin."

"Well then, thinner."

He smiled, laid the menu down, and reached across the table to take her hands. "I'll be fine, Sylvie. Really, I will—thanks to you."

"I only did what anyone else would've done."

"I'm not sure the Richelieu Steamship Company would agree. One of their chaps came to see me, you know, in the hospital. He said you were a most resourceful young woman. Said if you'd made even one mistake, like going to find an officer instead of running straight to the pilothouse yourself, I mightn't have survived.

"I can scarcely tell you what it was like in the river, Sylvie. Those ages and ages, holding on to that broken piece of wood—I'm sure it measured out in minutes, but it felt like all eternity—watching the *Saguenay* sail on, so fast, so indifferent. Knowing no one could hear me shout. Knowing I could have made it, that he hadn't killed me, that he was gone, but I was going to die just the same, because the benighted boat was leaving me behind . . ." He shook his head. "It was like screaming into an abyss, 'Please! I'm here! I'm here! *Please!*' And nothing answers. Nothing cares. I felt . . . oh, the absurdity of it all, the sheer absurdity . . . but more than that, Sylvie, I felt such despair . . . I don't know what kept me fighting then, staying afloat. I was so cold, and there seemed to be no point in it—"

"Maybe he did," she said very softly.

He stared at her. "What?"

"Your great-uncle. Maybe he were there. In the river. In the little ship you sent him."

He studied their linked hands for a very long time. "Do you think that's possible?" he said finally.

"Do you?"

"No. Not for a second. Not in my wide-awake, rational mind, that is. The rest of me . . . the rest of me isn't nearly so sure as to what's possible and what isn't. Not anymore. Whatever else, the old cove was a fighter. He never would've sunk till he was stone dead." He lifted her hands to his lips and kissed them each in turn. "But it was you who got me fetched from the river. It was you who stayed with me all night. And for one poor, drowning scarecrow, that was miracle enough."

Supper came a few moments later, a glorious supper, strips of beef in a wine sauce, roasted potatoes, carrots with a glaze that tasted of honey. Erryn had ordered chicken and offered her a slice in return for a strip of beef, an exchange that felt playful to her, and also strangely intimate.

For a time they said little, content to revel in their food. He seemed exceptionally hungry; she wondered if he had been getting enough to eat.

"Did they take good care of you?" she asked. "In the hospital?"

"Oh, quite," he said. "But I turned up with a frightful grippe, from being chilled so badly, I suppose. And then pneumonia, and then a cough that simply wouldn't stop. I wanted to leave anyway, but the nuns told me to get back into bed and be quiet. So I did."

They ate every crumb, and drank every drop of wine. By then all the old enchantment was back. She found it difficult to do anything except look at him, difficult not to reach across the table and stroke his face. And yet something had changed. There was an easiness between them now—not trust, exactly; she would not go so far as to call it trust—but a kind of certainty nonetheless . . . or perhaps just a lessening of uncertainty.

"They have a delightful custom back in Quebec," he said. "It was dreamt up by the men of the garrison, I'm sure, but now everybody does it. At the start of the social season, each young man will ask a girl to be his companion for the season—to go sleigh riding and skating, and to the theatre and the balls. She doesn't have to promise to love him or to marry him or anything—she can be someone else's companion next year. But if she agrees, then he has a lass to take to all the entertainments, and she has a young man to take her, and so she becomes his muffin."

"His *muffin*?"

"That's what they're called. Muffins. Because they're sweet and warm and comforting, I suppose—"

"Every muffin I ever met got eaten before the day was out."

He laughed right out loud, as though it tickled him enormously to have her throw some pleasantry back at him.

"These muffins never get eaten. Honest. It's against the law. They get fed, though, all sorts of good things, ices and pastries and great chocolate truffles. They quite enjoy their . . . what do you suppose they call it? Muffinry? Muffinage? Muffinhood? In any case, I think it's a grand custom, and we ought to import it to Halifax." He inclined his head very gracefully. "Would you be my muffin for the winter, Sylvie Bowen? I would be so very pleased and honoured."

She could find no words to answer him. In itself, the offer was wonderfully sweet and flattering. But beyond this small circle of candlelight and dreams, it was absurd. He knew nothing of the world she lived in, she thought, nothing whatever. They had not grown closer on the *Saguenay*; they had merely, in the face of death, forgotten their separation.

"Erryn, I couldn't—"

"Oh. Do you have . . . another friend?"

"Another . . ? Dear heavens, no. But I . . . even if I had the clothes and pretty things to go to balls, there wouldn't be any time for it. I have my half day Fridays, nothing more, and part of that goes to Madame. Most nights we're busy till we fall into bed. And if we ain't, Miss Susan lets us read or sew, or maybe even have a friend come by for tea, but we can't go off anywhere. We might be needed, see. So . . ." It hurt to finish. How fine it must be to be Isabel Orton, to receive such offers as a matter of course, to accept one or refuse another purely as she chose, as if she were choosing between peach or strawberry pies. "So I can't. It's good of you to ask, it is. But I can't."

"And what of Fridays? Shall I not even have a muffin on Fridays?" He asked lightly and yet as though he meant it. "There are pleasant things to do sometimes on Fridays. And there is always dinner."

It was as hard as anything she had ever done, not simply saying yes.

"I'll go with you, Erryn, any time I can. You only got to ask. You don't have to make promises."

"But . . . but it's not a promise! It's just . . . muffinry . . ."

He leaned back in his chair. For a small moment she thought he was angry at her, and she unwished every word. But when he spoke, there was no anger in his manner, only quiet speculation.

"Well, it *is* a promise, I admit. For the winter. But you're uncommonly fine company, Sylvie Bowen, and I'm selfish enough to want every bit of it I can get. You wouldn't consider it? I know I'm a great ugly troll, but I'll do my best to please you."

"You're not a great ugly troll! You look as nice as anyone, and if you didn't, who would I be to care, with my face, and you always so charming and so good to me? I'd promise in a minute, I would, only . . ." She looked up, forced herself to meet his eyes and say it plain. "You be gentlefolk, Erryn Shaw, and I'm a scrub maid."

"Ah, yes. My flaming relatives in wigs. Of course." He made a small restraining gesture with his hand. "Wait, love! Please. Let me say this. I know you work as a scrub maid. I may go on like a blathering idiot sometimes, but I *had* noticed. And I know that, to most everyone, a friendship between us is unthinkable. No man of my rank would lower himself to such a thing, no woman of yours should be so foolish as to expect it. Et cetera, et cetera, et cetera.

"Only . . . only people are more complicated than that. Odder, too. Oh, they can live by such notions, of course they can. It's how my family got to be rich and important, and how I got to be born. But it's like the old chap Procrustes I talked about—if any part of you doesn't fit his bed, somebody chops it off. And if you let them, after a while there isn't much of you left.

"So I don't care a lot about rank anymore. Maybe in some things; a man can't leave his whole past behind, I suppose. I'll puff out my feathers and play the silly peacock like the rest of my peers, once in a while. But as a way of living, it's not worth it. You get bored, and frightfully lonely. Besides, we're not in England anymore.

"So . . ." He reached across the table once again and took her hands. "So, I would be very happy to have you for my muffin. We'll be together when we can, and be happy, and those who disapprove can simply go and chase themselves. What do you say, my heart?"

His touch was playful yet sensuous, enchanting. It made her remember the day of the rainstorm, the way they had embraced, the blind, animal things she had felt. She wondered if what he had said was true. He meant it, at least for the moment, but was it true? And if it was not, did it really matter very much? Wasn't a little happiness better than none at all?

No doubt Madame had asked herself the same thing, running off with her seaman. Now, year after year, she burned candles for her folly, and for his. *It's safer to sail full rigged into a hurricane, Sylvie Bowen, than to love a man who is not of your station.*

No doubt. But she could swim the whole bleeding ocean easier than walk away.

"I'd like that," she said. "I'd like it more than anything."

CHAPTER 19

Queen's Wharf

. . . Our fossils, our remnants of antiquity, our devotees of Church
and State alliances, entertain the liveliest sentiments of regard for
the slave-aristocracy of the South, while Liberals are inclined to
sympathize with the free North.
—*The Globe* (Toronto), February 20, 1862

IT HAD BEEN, in Matt Calverley's opinion, one miserable, bleeding bugger of a night. He shoved yet another piece of wood into
the cast iron stove and shook the coffee pot irritably, as if rearranging its contents would make them heat faster. He had been
working for almost thirty hours, and the day had just begun.

Across the room, François Dufours sat with his feet on his desk,
leaning his chair back. Two constables from Ward Three stood by
the stove, still in their greatcoats, trying to warm their hands; and
Constable Neary was painstakingly writing his report of a stab-
bing yesterday evening in a tenement on Barrack Street.

They had not slept recently either. The entire police force had
been on duty throughout the night, manning the station and
patrolling the streets in case the *Chesapeake* pirates turned up. It was
a reasonable precaution; had he been the man in charge, Matt

would have given the same order himself. This in no way prevented a small, cynical voice in the back of his head from telling him that mermaids and unicorns were going to turn up on the streets of Halifax sooner than Captain John Braine or his men.

"Those pirates got any sense at all," Dufours said, "they'll go to ground for a month or two. Leastways till it all blows over and the Yankees go and get mad about something else."

At the stove, young Johnnie Delft turned a pinched face toward the room. "You figure it *will* blow over?"

"Sure," Dufours said. At fifty-six he was the oldest of the city's twenty constables. He had rheumatism in his hands and knees, and he was very heavy—hardly the sort to chase a thief or subdue a pack of drunken sailors. But he was a skilful detective, and, like Matt, he was respected as a mentor by the less experienced men.

"The Union's got the Rebels on the run," he went on. "They'd just be shooting themselves in the foot, starting a scrap with England. Besides, from what I've heard, everybody's talking. The Yankee consul was back and forth all day yesterday, going out to the ships, and back to the lieutenant-governor and the mayor, and telegraphing Washington. They'll be sensible about it, and if they are, there's no reason for us to start something."

"What about them going into Sambro harbour like they did?" Delft asked.

"What about us building Rebel raiders in Liverpool?" Matt replied. "We got dirt on our fingers too, mate. Seems to me we should all just say sorry, call it even, and walk away in opposite directions."

Delft looked unconvinced, but before he could pursue the matter, Dufours went on, "Matt, when you was in Sambro yesterday, did you learn any more about this Captain Braine? Is he really the same sod was here in the summer, taking money for that directory what never got printed?"

"Well," Matt said with a grin, "he ran off on his mates at La Have and took the ship's strongbox with him. Sure sounds like the same man to me."

"You were one of the lads was sent to Sambro, Matt?" The question came from Delft's companion, Ed Grover. "I didn't know that."

"Yes. Neary and me, and Phineas Praed from the county office."

"They only sent three of you? To arrest twelve armed men? What was that supposed to accomplish?"

The coffee pot was rattling on the stove. Matt poured a cup for each of them and fetched a pitcher sitting on the windowsill. The milk came out with little slivers of ice in it. He drank half his coffee at one go before he spoke.

"Well," he said, "we might've got lucky and found one of them asleep, like the Yankees did."

"Fat chance," Neary grumbled over his notebook. "It was the whole constabulary we were needing, or better still, the militia. Sending the three of us was a joke."

"Not a joke," Matt said amiably. "Just politics. Nobody's about to send the whole constabulary anywhere just now—nor the militia neither. And it looked bad for us to sit here and do nothing, with those rotters running free just a few miles down the coast."

"You're saying it was all for show?" Grover said, disgusted.

"No. Not as far as I was concerned. I'd have damn well hauled them back here, any of them I could get my hands on. But . . ." He shrugged. "I knew unless we could arrange for a miracle or two, it wasn't going to happen."

"Did you even get close?" Delft asked. "Did you see them?"

"We got close enough to think twice about getting any closer. They shot in the air at first, called us names, told us to go bugger ourselves and our bloody Yankee friends while we were at it, before we got our bloody stupid heads blown off. Then they started peppering the ground right in front of our feet. There was local lads mixed in with them too, so even if we could have found some decent cover and given them a fight, we'd have been shooting at men whose only crime was being related to the bastards.

Nobody was keen on that. Praed said there was nothing for it but to climb back on our sleigh and go home."

"That's a real shame, you know," Grover said. "Three against twenty-odd? You could have been heroes. Could have had yourselves a nice funeral parade and a fifty-foot monument right in front of city hall."

"And poems, too," Matt added, "just like those poor buggers at Balaclava: 'Pistols to the left of them, pistols to the right of them, volleyed and thundered—'"

"God love you, Matt," Neary said, "you keep on like this, you'll be getting as daft as that mouthy Englishman you used to hang about with."

It was like a cloud passing over the room. No one responded. Neary ducked his head back to his report, quickly, like a man wishing hard that he were ten miles away.

The subject of Erryn Shaw was not one Matt wished to discuss with his mates. The friendship was over; he had made this clear to them months ago. He had no use for fair-weather patriots, or fair-weather friends, and even less for fair-weather radicals who were all for justice and other people's rights as long as it was only talk. Erryn had gone over to the slavers and their Grey Tory friends, so be damned to him.

And if he had done it? Matt wondered. *If it weren't a pretended choice, but real—how would I feel then?* The question, considered seriously, seemed unmanageable, absurd. Erryn *wouldn't*.

But what if he had?

Erryn's own words played across his mind now, words he had spoken of Jack Murray: *He didn't really change, Matt; it was simply that I never knew him.* What if he, Matt, had never known his best mate as well as he thought he had? What if those eight years of talk and theatre and laughing at spiders were only a part of Erryn Shaw, and now, in a crisis, a different, more essential part emerged? How did people deal with such discoveries? For Erryn and Jack Murray, it was no great matter; they had never been more than casual friends. But what if it were the person a man loved best in all the world?

In the States, he knew, some people steeled themselves and broke the bond outright. They burned the photographs, threw away the gifts, cut the name from the family bible. Others grew quietly apart, and found themselves one day on opposite sides of a chasm, a chasm they would never cross again, neither enemies nor strangers nor friends, but some improbable combination of all three.

And others stood and held. As he hoped he would have done. *You're God damn bloody wrong, Erryn Shaw, but you're my best mate still.*

He fetched another cup of coffee and drank it black, only half listening to Dufours and Grover wondering what would become of the *Chesapeake* pirates if they were captured. Dufours said they were a sorry lot, and whatever they got, they deserved it. As to most of them, Matt thought, Dufours was undoubtedly right. The erstwhile captain, John Braine, was a common swindler whose list of victims stretched from Halifax to Ohio. His followers had taken the *Chesapeake* in a hail of bullets, and shot a civilian engineer point-blank in the face, a man who was almost certainly unarmed. Even some of the Grey Tories stood apart from them, calling them criminals and a disgrace to the Confederate cause.

Al MacNab thought they were bully good lads.

And what would I think of Erryn, if Erryn said the same? My best mate still?

God help him, he thought, but as to that question, he would damn near choose to die rather than have to answer it.

———✦———

City hall took up half of the same stone building that housed the police station, but it was decidedly the better half. Among its many well-furnished offices was that of City Marshal Gabriel

Hauser. It was there, sometime after eleven, that Matt was ordered to report, along with Constables Grover and Neary. They found the county sheriff already there. Both men looked extraordinarily pleased with themselves.

"Gentlemen," Hauser said. "Do sit down." He was well into his fifties, with a face like a prizefighter and thin red hair turning slowly grey. He was, in Matt's considered opinion, much more a politician than he was a peace officer.

"Sheriff Cobb and I have just returned from a meeting with Mayor Bond and officials of the provincial government. You'll be happy to know that a satisfactory agreement has been reached with the Americans."

From the beginning, Matt had expected this. He was surprised now to find himself overwhelmed with relief.

"That's bloody good news, sir."

"Yes. They're turning the *Chesapeake* over to us. It will be up to the Admiralty Court to decide what becomes of it, whether the former owners in Boston are to have it back or whether the Confederates will have it as a prize of war. And at one o'clock this afternoon, the three prisoners will be brought to Queen's Wharf and turned over to us as well. Which is where you men come in." Hauser puttered briefly with his papers. "Two of those prisoners, as everybody knows, are local lads, who went out to the *Chesapeake* three days ago to hire on as engineers. They're obviously guilty of nothing whatever, and will be unconditionally freed. The other, however, is one of Captain Braine's men. George Wade. He's the one the Yankees found sleeping on the coaling schooner. They say he shot the *Chesapeake*'s engineer, and they've asked that he be extradited to the States to face charges of piracy and murder. The lieutenant-governor agreed, and a warrant has been issued for his arrest."

Ah, Matt thought. *So we're both being reasonable, thank God.*

"But there's a catch," the marshal went on. "The Yankee consul's lawyer picked up on it right away. It seems, if Wade goes straight from their hands to ours, he might have to be released on the grounds that he was arrested unlawfully in Sambro—as of course he was. So he's to be turned loose on the wharf and allowed to walk around for a couple of minutes before we pick him up."

"Oh, for pity's sake!" Neary protested. "He'll just bolt into the crowd, and we'll not see hair or hide of him again!"

"There won't be any crowd. The lieutenant-governor has ordered troops to the waterfront. Nobody is getting onto Queen's Wharf, or off it, without passing through a cordon of infantry. One thing everyone is determined on, gentlemen, and Mayor Bond most of all—this matter is going to be resolved quietly. We damn near had a riot on the wharf yesterday, when it got out to the public who the prisoners were. The Americans going back and forth to their ships had to pass under armed guard. This is *not* going to happen again.

"So. Sheriff Cobb, you will take the men down just before one, so as to attract the least possible attention. Take custody of the prisoners, release them, rearrest Wade after a couple of minutes, and bring him in. In the meantime, nothing of this matter is to be discussed with anyone. With a bit of luck it'll be over and done with before anyone knows it's happening."

———⋅◆⋅———

There was indeed a cordon of infantry around Queen's Wharf that afternoon—such an excellent cordon of infantry that Matt was inside it before he saw them, the whole benighted pack of them: MacNab, Orton, Collier, Strange, and the rest. He scanned the wharf with growing astonishment and anger. Some government officials had come down, including the solicitor general and the provincial secretary. The United States consul was there with his attorney, and so were a handful of other people who had, or might have had, official business. The rest of the crowd of fifty or so were members of the Halifax elite, most of them Grey Tories.

It'll be over and done with before anyone knows it's happening . . .

Sheriff Cobb seemed not to notice anything amiss, not even when Matt demanded of him bitterly, "What are those sons of bitches doing here?"

"Who?"

"Orton and his lot! I thought this was all supposed to be kept quiet! How the devil do they know about it? And why were they let in?"

"Oh, now really, Calverley. The order was to keep the riff-raff out. Those gentlemen aren't the sort to start a riot."

"They're Rebel supporters. They're damn well the sort to start something."

Cobb looked at him and looked away, with a small shake of his head. Matt could readily guess what he was thinking. Cobb had always been a man with an overly high opinion of respectability— not rank as such, but respectability. His background was almost as destitute as Matt's, but his family had been law-abiding and decent, indeed heroically so. He was therefore convinced that those who made up the low-life of a community were inherently different from those who did not. It was not poverty or bad luck that took them down; it was heredity, or some other essential flaw. They were—so he had said more than once—the detritus of society. They could be helped occasionally; he was all for supporting the City Mission and the SPC. But such people would never really be like decent folk.

To Cobb, the streets below the Citadel were as low as the low-life got, and hiring the likes of Matt Calverley as a peace officer had appalled him: this was bringing Barrack Street back to city hall to live. It made no difference that years of honest work and quiet living stood between the street arab and the aspiring police constable. Young Calverley was still a whore's brat; a vicious, dirty fighter, a long-time petty thief who would have ended up in Rockhead except he was always too smart to get caught. What the devil did the Halifax constabulary want with a man like that?

"Well," François Dufours supposedly had said, "maybe we want a man who knows how it all works, up by the Hill. All I can ever do, most times, is guess."

Perhaps the city officials of the day agreed, but Matt always suspected that a shortage of candidates had been the real reason he was hired. The constabulary was undermanned, dismally paid, and routinely exposed to every sort of weather and every sort of insult, including violence. Men were not exactly lining up in droves for the job.

Now, twelve years later, not even Cobb could seriously doubt Matt's effectiveness as a peace officer. But the sheriff would always doubt him as a man. The sheriff would always believe that, somewhere inside, Matt carried a flawed identity that would never be eradicated, and that might show itself at any moment, like hereditary madness or disease. He did not trust Matt's judgment on anything, least of all on the subject of his betters.

You have such a grudge against Orton, he said once, *you could see him rocking a baby and you'd think it was plot.*

There was a fragment of truth to the accusation. Matt was generally inclined to believe the worst of an enemy. This was a fault with some practical value in the streets—it had saved his life a time or two—but it was a fault nonetheless, a prejudice. He reminded himself of it now, and warned himself to be careful. *If something starts here, Matt old boy, you damn well don't want to be the one to start it.*

Quarters were close on the wharf. The Grey Tories clustered loosely at one side and talked among themselves. Matt watched them relentlessly, but he sensed nothing of the edgy hostility that usually built up in groups of men when they were contemplating violence.

"What do you suppose they're about?" he muttered to Constable Grover.

"Nothing much. Showing the colours, likely. Making sure their poor Mr. Wade knows he's got friends here."

Matt said nothing. His common sense confirmed Grover's words; his instincts still resisted, bitterly.

"I think Cobb's right, mate," Grover went on. "This is the sort of thing gets fought out in a courtroom. And God knows the buggers might win there, too. The Yankee consul closed one loophole on them; they'll do their damnedest to find another."

So they'll be watching like hawks for any misstep on our part.

This made sense, especially coming from Grover. The man was experienced, and on the subject of the American war he was as close to a genuinely neutral observer as Matt had met.

Matt scanned the wharf again and then looked out to sea, to the five American vessels anchored in the channel. The harbour looked as it did on most any winter afternoon, with clusters of vessels anchored all along the waterfront. The Dartmouth ferry was heading out; a few fishing boats were drifting in. None of this held Matt's attention for longer than a second—only the launch from the *Ella and Annie*, approaching fast. Orton's people were watching with attention now, but otherwise quiet. Behind him, Matt knew the military cordon was solid. Unless several of them had been suborned—not one of them, but several—no one was getting George Wade through.

The launch docked quietly.

"We won't crowd them," Matt said softly. He did not believe that a legal definition of George Wade's freedom depended on how much room he had to walk around in, but he had heard some very strange arguments raised in courtrooms from time to time. So, fine, he thought, the pirate could have his two minutes of liberty undisturbed. He could talk with his Grey Tory friends, with Jamie Orton, who was already stepping forward to shake his hand.

Sheriff Cobb drew aside to give them room for their courtesies. The men were milling a little now, and laughing. Wade took Orton's outstretched hand, leaned forward a little to listen to something he was saying, then, between a breath and a breath, stepped over the side of the jetty and disappeared.

"Bloody damned hell!"

It was almost too quick to be comprehended. Matt lunged forward, using elbows and shoulders on everything in his path, including Cobb, who was staring vacantly like a fish who had been whacked on the head. Matt plowed through to the edge of the pier and cursed savagely. A skiff was pulling fast away, with Wade hunkered down in it and two men on the oars, rowing like very demons. Matt cursed again, for he knew them: John Elworth Payne and Harry Gallagher, rowing champions for the entire province of Nova Scotia.

"Stop!" he shouted. "That man is under arrest!" Even as he shouted, he drew his pistol, knowing they would not heed him. "I'm a policeman! God damn you, Gallagher, stop or I'll shoot!"

One warning shot over their heads, and then Wade . . .

The warning shot tore into the grey sky as Jamie Orton's big hand knotted over the gun.

"You'll nae be killing anyone today, you damned Yankee hireling!"

Orton had height on him, and reach, and seventy-five pounds. It made no difference. Matt spun in his grip like a cat and rammed his knee into the man's crotch. Astonishingly, even as Orton buckled with a cry of pure anguish, he managed to keep his hold on the gun. For a moment they grappled, the weapon pinned perilously between them. Another second or two and Matt would have wrenched it free. Then the full weight of a man's body slammed into his back and a wiry arm closed around his throat. The voice was Robert Collier's, almost pleading, "Let go, God damn it, let go!"

"Bastard!" Matt spat, and slammed his elbow backward and up, hitting something, he did not care what. By then Jack Murray was on him as well, grabbing at his arms and his clothing. They were not trying to fight, only to hold him, but they were strong, and he was mad as a bitten cat. He struggled savagely, cursing them with the ugliest words he knew, words he never used in ordinary anger, not buggers and bastards and God damns, but the worst gutter talk of the brothel. The gun clattered onto the wharf and some-one kicked it into the water, but now, like men who had taken hold of a wolverine, they dared not let go, until finally all four were tumbled to the timbers in a snarling, dishevelled heap.

Constable Grover and various Grey Tories rushed over, peeling the men off one by one, helping them to their feet. Matt was on the bottom.

"Keep your bloody hands off me," he snapped. They did, but two of them stayed resolutely between him and Jamie Orton, a fact he noted with quiet scorn. He rubbed his wrist. It hurt cruelly from being twisted, but otherwise the Grey Tories were far more dam-aged than he was. Collier's nose was streaming blood and Jack Murray was holding his stomach and hobbling on one foot. Not that it mattered; they had won. The skiff was well out of range. Even as Matt stared after it, the fugitive waved, cupped his hands around his mouth, and shouted, "Thank you, boys, and God save the Queen!"

The Grey Tories cheered. Matt pointedly ignored them. Despite what Sheriff Cobb or anyone else believed, he was not a man who carried grudges. He valued his small, stubbornly acquired place in the world too much to wager it for the sake of malice or revenge.

The Grey Tories milled around him, all of them very pleased with themselves, MacNab laughing and slapping Jack Murray on the back, Orton still grey-faced but nonetheless smiling. There would be many a toast raised in the Waverley tonight, and in the Halifax Club.

Matt did not promise himself that he would bring them down. After twelve years, he knew better. Bringing one of these bastards down was like seeing a comet: it happened, but not very often. But he promised them a fight. With the hard anger that brooded softly in the bottom of his soul, an anger kindled and nurtured in his boyhood, which he had learned always to contain but which never altogether left him, he promised the Grey Tories of Halifax the fight of their God damn miserable lives.

CHAPTER 20

After the Chesapeake

We hold that the independence of the South is the
true and sure means of extinguishing slavery.
—*Pamphlet of the Southern Independence Association, Manchester, England*

No bill of attainder or ex post facto law, or law denying or impairing
the right of property in negro slaves shall be passed.
—*Section 9, Article 4, Constitution of the Confederate States of America*

ERRYN SHAW KNEW nothing of the Queen's Wharf affair until it
was over. He woke up Saturday morning feeling feverish and
exhausted, came out to the kitchen for a hot cup of tea, and crawled
back into bed. His landlord was determined he should stay there.

Erryn got on well with his landlord. Gideon Winslow was a
widower now and past sixty, but in his prime he had been a fine
tailor, and with his wife had raised three hardy sons. All of them
were off in the world now, being sailors and farmers and Lord
knew what, sending money home so he might live decently. He
rented his spare room cheap, mostly for the comfort of having
someone in the house.

He was not fond of cooking, and in any case Erryn never kept
regular hours when he ran the theatre; nor did he keep them now.
So the two men formed a simple understanding: Erryn was not to

expect regular meals as a boarder might, but, on the other hand, if he came home hungry, he was to help himself freely to whatever he found in the kitchen. Winslow always made sure there was something substantial—at the very least, a loaf of good fresh bread and cheese. Erryn appreciated the old man's kindness, and also his flawless discretion. Winslow only asked about his background once or twice, very delicately, and when Erryn evaded the questions just as delicately, he never asked again.

For his part, Erryn tried to be a good tenant. He wiped his boots, he never smoked or spat tobacco, he did his drinking elsewhere, and he always paid his rent on time. From time to time he brought home delicacies to share—chocolates, fine sausages, oranges in the wintertime—and the old man would smile like a boy.

They were, therefore, more like friends than landlord and tenant. Winslow, proud as he was of his fine sons, never made the mistake of thinking Erryn Shaw was one of them. Still, he could be surprisingly protective. When Jack Murray came by on Saturday morning to take his friend down to Queen's Wharf with the others, Winslow would not so much as invite him in.

"The lad's sick in his bed," he said. "You oughtn't to be fetching him out, not on a day like this."

Jack nodded sympathetically and went away. When Erryn rose shortly after noon, Winslow fried him up a plate of scrambled eggs and potatoes, and told him what he had done.

"Why, thanks," Erryn said. "I would've gone, I suppose, but frankly, I'm glad I didn't have to."

Monday morning, when he learned of the prisoners' release in the newspapers, he decided Winslow had done him a greater kindness than he knew. It would have been hard to see three men go at Matt Calverley, with himself standing by and pretending not to care. He was not at all sure he would have managed it.

He read the story again very carefully, assuring himself that Matt was, in fact, unhurt. He read the editorials. He went out for a breath of fresh air and bought up all the other papers, poring over them with the same care. It was too early, perhaps, to speak of a pattern; this was only the first day. But except for a handful of the strongest pro-Confederate journals, a pattern was already emerging.

Halifax was not impressed.

Halifax, this supposedly Grey Tory town, this bastion of blockade-runners and spies, was raising its editorial eyebrows at the behaviour of James Dougal Orton. Whatever had the man been about? they wondered. Offering insult to the Queen by preventing the exercise of her lawful warrant? Attacking a peace officer in the performance of his duty? Helping an accused murderer to escape? Surely these were not the actions of a leading citizen and a man of the law. One after another the editors found themselves at a loss, unable to understand the descent of a gentleman of such lineage and reputation into what was scarcely better than the act of a hooligan.

"Welcome to the world, lads," Erryn murmured, laying the paper aside.

He did not allow himself to feel too reassured; the only thing more changeable than the moods of the press were the winds of the North Atlantic. Still, it comforted him. The Grey Tories were a powerful minority; it was easy to forget sometimes that they were only a minority.

One week later, James Dougal Orton was arrested. The word on the grapevine was that Sheriff Cobb was feeling mean as a weasel, seeing how he had made a fool of, and went over to the Northwest Arm in person to pick him up.

⟞⬦⟝

The cells beneath the police station were gloomy, dirty, and cold. Today they contained the usual assortment of brawlers and drunks; a woman named Malone, charged with keeping a common bawdy house; and a fourteen-year-old pickpocket who reminded

Matt rather sadly of his younger self. James Orton had a cell of his own, next to that of Malone and the women prisoners. He was sitting on his wood bunk with his coat wrapped around his shoulders, looking dignified and altogether untroubled.

As well he might, Matt reflected. He would be bailed out in an hour or two, and the odds were high he would never return. Matt pulled a chair into the cell, locked it again, and sat, resting his arms on the rickety chair back. Orton glanced at him without hostility, but also without much interest.

"I'd like to ask you a question or two, Mr. Orton."

"There's nae a thing I can tell you, constable, that Sheriff Cobb has nae heard already."

"Well then, let's just say if a lie is big enough, I prefer to hear it with my own ears. First off, the release of the *Chesapeake* prisoners was private information. Who told you about it?"

"I was nae told a thing about it. I went down to the waterfront to look after a wee bit of business. There was a crowd gathering, and I went by for a look. A few of the lads said they thought there might be something afoot with the *Chesapeake*, and so we stayed about to see."

"And they were all there on business too, I suppose? Your lads?"

"It was nae my concern why they were there, so I did nae ask."

"And the rowboat, with champion rowers on the oars?"

"For that, you must ask Mr. Gallagher and Mr. Payne."

"Oh, I did. It was a pleasure outing, they tell me. They brought their boat all the way round from the Northwest Arm just to scuttle along the stinking jetties, and listen to the fishmongers scream, and dodge all the traffic coming in and out, purely because they enjoyed it. Man does that for pleasure, he belongs in the crazy house."

Orton said nothing.

"How much did you pay them, Orton?"

"I paid nae man for anything."

"Send him over to us, constable," the bawdy woman Malone suggested. "We'll soften 'im up for ye."

"Now there's a thought," Matt said cheerfully, and saw the quiet indifference in Orton's eyes harden into offence. The man's moral priorities were curious, to say the least.

"So," he went on, "we're supposed to believe it was all . . . what's that wonderful word they use in books? . . . oh, yes, serendipity. It was all pure serendipity, you being there, and all your friends, and even a rowboat just when you needed it. As for you jumping on me and knocking me down, I suppose that was serendipity too. You took a fit, I suppose, standing out in the wind?"

Orton refused to be baited. "I could nae let you shoot a man down in cold blood, constable."

"What about Orrin Schaffer?"

"Who?"

"The engineer on the *Chesapeake*. The one George Wade shot in the face. In cold blood."

"We can nae say he did it, constable. The man's nae been tried."

"No, he hasn't. And you made damn sure he won't be. You puzzle me, Orton, do you know that? Most times, a man might think you were a decent sod. You've done a good deed or two in this town, you talk as though you got a conscience. And yet you don't seem to care a damn if you and your Grey Tory friends drag the whole country into someone else's war—and not just in it, but on the wrong damn side. What the devil do you like about the Rebels, anyway? Do you think it makes men special, keeping other men as slaves?"

"Ah, for God's sake," Orton said sharply, "that's nae the question at all—"

"Question or no, they're still the side with the slaves."

"And that's a great misfortune, constable, I've never denied it. But it's been around a long time, slavery has, and when the lads tell me it's nae a thing to sort out easy, and that the Lord will make his will known in the matter in his own good time, it seems to me they have the right of it."

"Well. I ain't a godly man like yourself, but if I was, I'd have to wonder if maybe the Lord *did* make his will known, when Abe

Lincoln was elected president. Maybe the Lord nudged all those Yankee chaps to say, 'Enough now, this slavery thing has gone far enough.' Ever consider that possibility?"

Orton was a damn fool, but he was not altogether witless. "It's possible," he said. "There's nae a man alive kens the will of the Almighty for certain. But I'm thinking when he wants slavery done away with, he'll bring the wisdom of it to the slaveholders."

"Ah. And when he wants thieving done away with, he'll bring the wisdom of it to the footpads? Damn. I wish I'd known that before I took up an honest living."

A rough laugh erupted from Malone, and a ripple of giggles from the other women. The prostitute got to her feet and ambled over, putting both rough hands on the bars. She was a few years shy of forty, already haggard and thin. Matt supposed she was sober from time to time, but he had never seen it.

"It's a right sharp laddie you are, constable," she said. "And handsome, too. You can come by and ask me questions any time you fancy."

Strange, Matt thought, how some things never left you. He had walked out of Perrin Cray's bar for the last time twenty-three years ago, with nothing of his own in the world except the ragged pants he wore and a shirt with one sleeve torn off, tied across his butchered arm so he would not bleed to death.

Cray's was the bottom, the last in the downward spiral of his mother's homes, if anyone could call such a clapboard ruin a home. In front, it was a broken-down tavern where even soldiers rarely came anymore, only the worst of the low-life; in back, a bare room that reeked of excrement and shuddered with every gust of wind, where the women took their trade and where they all slept afterwards on the floor, Cray and his horrid wife and their sons and daughters and nephews and grandchildren and Jane Calverley and her boy.

Time had taken the edge off most of his memories, even muddied some of them. But there were a handful of things that never

left him, that held, and always would hold, an immediate, shattering familiarity.

*You're a right sharp laddie, and handsome, too, come by any time you
like . . .*

He would never forget the voices—any of the voices, but most
especially his mother's. It was not the words that gnawed at him,
or even the intent. It was the desperation, the emptiness he always
heard beneath the coaxing or the mockery, the vulnerability of
someone who had been beaten down too often and was never,
ever, getting up again.

There were boys who whored on Barrack Street. The folks
from the City Mission never talked about it in public, and neither
did anyone else, but it went on just the same. Matt took up thieving instead. He neither blamed nor judged the others, but for himself, anything was better than such absolute vulnerability, even
Rockhead Prison.

Even a bullet in the streets.

For a long moment he studied Susie Malone's drab form against
the bars, remembering why he sometimes wished he had put a
thousand miles between himself and his past.

Next to him, James Dougal Orton's polished, arrogant voice
reminded him why he had not.

"You twist my meaning, constable," Orton was saying.

*Your meaning? Ah, yes. God will bring his wisdom to the slave-
holders.*

"Sorry. Like I said, I ain't much for religion. But I've never seen
the Lord come lecture us with trumpets and poster signs. Maybe
it's different in the South, I've never been there. But looking
around me here, it seems like whatever the Lord's trying to do,
he's got people out doing it for him. Asking questions. Calling
meetings. Considering how we live, and how we treat folks, and
trying to change things if there's need—"

"There's nothing godly about trying to change men's minds
with a cannon."

"Except it wasn't a cannon at the outset. It was an election, remember? It was their own fellow citizens saying the time had come for change. The Rebels were the ones who broke up the country and fired off the cannon."

"They were being invaded."

"They were not. The Yankees were merely bringing food to the garrison at Sumter."

"The South had declared its independence. The garrison should have been withdrawn."

"Right. And if Yorkshire declared its independence, and fired on Her Majesty's troops for the wanting of their dinner, what do you suppose Her Majesty's government would do?"

"Don't be ridiculous. That's nae the same thing at all."

"Maybe not, but where do you draw the line? How do you decide this nation is a real nation, and not for carving up, and that one ain't? How do you decide this election should stand, if a free vote means anything at all, and that one we can just walk out on? How do you decide, Orton?"

"Justice is how you decide, constable. Did that wee fact never occur to you?"

"Justice?"

"Aye. The right of every man on earth to be lord of his own destiny, and be treated fair, and have nae stranger riding into his yard, taking the bread from his mouth and telling him what to do. That's how you decide."

"So tell me, how does a slave get to be lord of his own destiny?"

Orton got to his feet, throwing out one hand in a gesture of frustration and disgust. "What is the point of talking with you, then? You nae listen to a thing a man says. They'll deal with slavery when the time comes. It's nae the business at hand—"

"No, of course not. States' rights is the business at hand. That's what they're telling us, anyhow—"

"Aye, they are. And like you said, constable, you've nae been to the South. Do you really have the gall to say they're lying?"

"Most everybody lies when they're cornered. You did yourself, just five minutes ago. The Rebels need English help. We don't approve of slavery, mostly, so they tell us it's not what they're fighting over. But it ain't exactly what they tell themselves."

"How the hell would you ken what they tell themselves?"

"Their constitution. That's where folks write down what really matters to them, you know. They write it in stone. And the Confederate constitution says anyone's got the right to keep slaves, anywhere in the country. You're a lawyer, Orton, you know what that means. If a constitution gives you a right, no local government can take your right away. Which means nary a one of those states who're all dying to be lords of their own destiny can abolish slavery inside their own borders, ever, short of changing the bloody constitution. Why do you suppose they'd agree to that, if states' rights was really what they cared about most?"

Orton glared at him for a moment. Then he laughed. "So now the likes of you is an expert on the Southern constitution? How very impressive. Lord knows we'll have an archbishop from the upper streets next."

Matt bit back his rush of anger. After all, what else should he have expected?

He got to his feet. "Laws are public information, you know. Some lads here went to the trouble of finding out. Obviously, you didn't."

"No, I didn't," Orton said coldly. "I judge the South by her men, Calverley, men who are honest and brave, who want their freedom like all proud people do, who win battle after battle against the odds—"

The last of his words were drowned out by the cell door clanging shut. Matt locked it, rattled it to make sure it was fast, and then said quietly, "Orton, you're an idiot. There's no army ever marched that didn't have good men in it. If you think that proves anything, you don't have the sense to know your brain from a bunghole."

All the time they had been talking, only traces of hostility had shown in Orton's eyes. Now it flashed out, quick and savage. Had

Matt still been inside the cell, Orton might well have struck him to the floor.

"Oh, it's a grand feeling, isn't it? Being able to stand outside these bars and insult me? The Barrack Street bastard's little hour of glory! You simply can nae bide it there's men in this town who'll stand up for things they believe in, when you've nae stood up for anything in your life!"

"You're not standing up for shit, Orton; you're about to stand down. You want to fight for that damn pack of slavers, go fight for them. Put on your grey uniform and go. I'll God damn kiss you goodbye! But you're not taking us with you. We're going to make a country here, all for ourselves, and we'll be damned if you're going to blow it out from under our feet. And you can tell your Grey Tory friends the same. There's more than one proud people in the world who ain't about to be told what to do!"

Orton shouted a rude name at him as he walked away. He did not care, or answer. He was aware, but only vaguely, of voices in the other cells, Malone's among them, laughing. Sometimes he regretted joining the constabulary; it required him to behave himself. Years back, he would have left James Dougal Orton lying in a heap on the floor—somewhat damaged, perhaps, but peaceful as a pile of rags.

BOOK FIVE

———◆◆———

Halifax, 1864

CHAPTER 21

Spies at the Den

The gathering of knowledge by clandestine means is
repulsive to the feelings of English Gentlemen.
—*Lord Raglan*

SYLVIE HAD NEVER thought of Aggie Breault as a person with
secrets. So it surprised her when, on a quiet January afternoon,
she slipped upstairs to change a badly soiled apron and found
Aggie in their small attic room, bent close to the lamp, with a letter. The room was icy cold, and the lamp no better than a candle.
No one, she thought, would read here instead of in the kitchen,
unless they were reading something very private. As if to make
the point, Aggie immediately tucked the letter into her pocket
before Sylvie had even closed the door.

"Oh, hello," Sylvie said. "I didn't think anyone were up here."

"Just wanted a breath of time to myself," Aggie said. "I get so
tired of young Dobbs going on. He's barely twenty and already he
knows everything. Are you all finished?"

"Almost. I got one room left."

"Sit for a spell, then. But open the door, would you, so we can hear the bell?"

Strictly speaking, they were not supposed to rest or visit until all their tasks were done. But it was Sunday, and unusually quiet. Miss Susan had gone calling, and most of the guests were out. Gratefully, Sylvie settled onto the edge of her bed.

"So what's Dobbs going on about?" she asked.

"You recall they caught some of the *Chesapeake* pirates in New Brunswick? Well, he's saying how unthinkable it would be to send them off to the States to stand trial—as if being British gives them some kind of immunity to other people's laws."

"I thought what they did were against our laws too," Sylvie said.

"Sure. But all an English court can charge them with is violating the Foreign Enlistment Act. If they're going to be charged with anything serious, like piracy or murder, it has to be in the States, because they did it on one of our ships. Leastways, that's how I understand it."

"You think it'll happen? A trial in the States?"

"Sure. When pigs fly and mice go hunting cats."

The women shared a small, cynical smile.

"You must despair of us sometimes," Sylvie said.

Aggie shrugged. "Actually, I don't. The Union has a lot of friends here. They aren't sitting in the highest places, but I think if we counted heads, we'd be surprised at the numbers."

A door opened and closed somewhere below. Aggie paused, listening for a summons, but all went still again.

"So," she went on lightly, "what about your beau? What does he think about the war?"

"My beau?"

"Your young man, or follower, as you call them here. You do have one, don't you? You've certainly been showing all the signs."

A woman of nearly thirty, Sylvie thought, should not blush as foolishly as a girl. Perhaps in the poor light Aggie would not notice.

"What do you mean, showing signs?"

"Really, Sylvie. You rush off on your half day as though the world were ending, and you stay out as late as Miss Susan allows. You've been looking right happy, too, these last few weeks, like a girl with something nice on her mind. Just because you aren't talking about it doesn't mean I wasn't going to notice."

Sylvie was at a loss for what to say. In the weeks since Erryn's return she had not mentioned him to anyone. She did not believe, consciously, that everything would melt into smoke if she spoke of it. And yet her world seemed so far from his, and his friendship so improbable and so precious, she could not imagine explaining it, even to Aggie. Besides, she knew what people were likely to think.

"There's a chap I met a couple of times," she admitted, "but he isn't my . . . we aren't . . . We're just friends, Aggie."

"Oh, I'd say he fancies you some, judging by his presents. They are presents, aren't they? Your pretty cloak, and the sweets and all? Charlie was like that too, always bringing me something. Said he wanted to thank me just for being there. Don't worry, Sylvie, I don't have a big mouth. Sanders already asked me where you got the fancy cloak, and I said last time I looked it was winter out, and I reckoned you bought it."

Sylvie smiled. "Thanks."

"So," Aggie went on teasingly, "do you fancy him, too? Lie awake at night, scratch his name on tree trunks, that sort of thing?"

"I fancy him a bit," she said. "He's a real nice man. If he wants to offer me a bit of company, course I'm going to take it. But it's just . . . it's like ships passing in the night, see? Nothing to make a fuss about."

"Well, you're a cautious one," Aggie said. "Seems my whole life long, all the girls I knew were bragging about their beaux. It made me right jealous, sometimes. Till I met Charlie."

She looked down suddenly, staring at a spot beside her feet. Sylvie wondered how she bore it, having been so lonely for so long, and then, against all the odds, finding the love of her life . . .

and having someone come to her one day, a day like any other, to tell her he was dead.

"You miss him a lot," Sylvie said, very softly.

"All the time. But I'm kind of used to it now. Anyway, you never told me what your young man thinks about the war. He ever say?"

"He said he doesn't think on it at all—doesn't really have an opinion, I guess. A lot of folks in England were like that too. I remember one sod at the mill asking me, if some big scrap were on between a couple of warlords in Timbuktu, which one would I speak for? I told him America weren't Timbuktu. And he said damned if he'd noticed." Sylvie noted the housemaid's expression and added hastily, "Oh, my friend's not like that—not snotty about it, I mean, not at all. But I guess he sees it as something happening far away that ain't his business."

"Well," Aggie said, "it's an honest perspective, I suppose. But you support the Union, don't you? I mean really, deep down? You think we're right, and it matters whether or not we win?"

"Course I do. You know that."

"Then I want to ask you about something. But first I need you to promise you'll never tell anyone I mentioned it."

"Oh, come on, Aggie. Why would I tell anyone what we might talk about, the little time we ever have to talk by ourselves?"

"Ordinarily, I expect you wouldn't. But I need you to promise anyway."

"All right, I promise. So what is it?"

"Would you help the Union, if you could?"

"Help . . . ?" She tried to frame an answer that would not be rude. *Me? Help the Union? When I'm up to my neck in chamber pots and it's a bleeding thousand miles away? God almighty, Aggie Breault, where did you find the key to the wine cellar?*

But even as the words were taking shape, she thought about Aggie tucking her letter away so quickly. Aggie, smart and well schooled as she was, taking work here at the Den when she could surely have got something better. Aggie telling her about the

Southerners in Halifax: *They're Confederate agents, most of them . . . spies, weapons buyers, couriers . . . out-and-out plotters, too . . . they've all got their noses into something.*

If the Rebels had agents all over town, and if the Federals were not incompetent or sound asleep, then . . . ? Then there were Federal agents here too. Maybe even at the Den. Maybe right in this room.

"What do you mean, help?"

"Just little things. And just once in a while."

"Yes, but what?"

"You're the chambermaid. You can go into their rooms, and you can . . . well . . . snoop. Me, I got no business upstairs. If someone even sees me in a hallway, they'll wonder right off what I'm doing there, and my being a Yankee won't make them wonder less. They see you there, you're just doing your job."

"Miss Susan finds out, she'll put me out on my ear."

"You're sharp, Sylvie. Whatever you do, I expect you can do it quick and cover your tracks. Anyway, we can pay a little. To make up for the risk."

"We?" Sylvie whispered.

"I didn't dream this up all by myself, you know."

"Good Lord."

Sylvie rubbed a bruise on her hand, stealing little glances at Aggie Breault as she did so. Such an uncomplicated soul, the housemaid was . . . or seemed. A sentimental widow who never stopped remembering her Charlie. A sturdy farm woman, still shy, at the age of forty, about her big ears. A good worker, respected by everyone.

A foreign agent.

No point mincing the words, Sylvie thought. She was a foreign agent on British soil.

So, likely as not, were some of the people to whom she served dinner every day. Some of the people whose beds Sylvie made up every morning. And they came here first. They came looking for a way to spread the war. Aggie told her the local Rebels might be spies, but no one had to tell her they wanted a bigger war; for that, she needed only to read the papers, listen to people talking, look at the posters on the street. *Why the South Deserves Our Aid. Christianity and the Great Confederate Cause. Free the* Chesapeake *Heroes.* Et cetera, et cetera. If this lot had their way, there would be blood and fire running through the streets of Halifax tomorrow.

"What sort of . . . *snooping* . . . did you have in mind, Aggie?"

"That fellow who came on Wednesday, calls himself Theodore Manley? Can you see what he might have with him—documents, messages, things like that? You might not have time to copy anything in detail. Just take notes or, better still, memorize it if you can. And look for anything what might hint at his real name—a personal letter, a prayer book, engraved jewellery, that sort of thing. They often have secret pockets in their clothes or their cases. Look as thoroughly as you can, but don't undo anything you can't fix. And always have an explanation for why you're in the room."

"You've been doing this for a while." Aggie merely shrugged, and Sylvie went on, "A spy wouldn't do that, would he? Use a false name and then carry around something with his real one?"

"A lot of them are green," Aggie said. "There's things they just never think of. And it's a good thing, too, because we're about as green as they are. Did you know General Washington had a huge network of spies, in the Revolution? Your Lord Wellington too, so I've been told—he turned it into an art. These days, a lot of folks look down on the very notion. It's dishonourable, they say, a relic from the old corrupt states of the Continent, completely beneath the dignity of a white, Anglo-Saxon gentleman."

"Well," Sylvie said wryly, "the dignity of gentlemen really ain't something we need to worry about, is it?"

—◆—

She thought she would be frightened, going through Mr. Manley's belongings, and perhaps she was, at the very outset. But in a matter of moments the intensity of the search absorbed all of her attention. According to Aggie, he had mentioned at the breakfast table that he was going over to Dartmouth for the morning. This was reassuring, but only slightly. He might change his mind and return. Or Miss Susan might come into the room for some reason. Sylvie worked very quickly.

There was indeed a false bottom in his portmanteau, but all she found beneath it was money, almost a hundred dollars in United States paper, which she left exactly as she found it. But in the desk drawer was a pouch of pipe tobacco, and nestled at the bottom, under the tobacco, was a small key.

There was nothing it seemed to fit—nothing in the case or in the dresser; nothing under his mattress; nothing in the closet. Whatever it was, she supposed he had taken it with him, which did not make a great deal of sense. One might leave a box and take the key, but why would anyone do the opposite?

All around the room, as she scanned it, were various spots where a small item could be tucked out of sight. She noted them and rejected them in turn: they were all places she cleaned every day. Except for one. Beside the hearth was the coal bin—the coal bin she kept so carefully supplied that it was never, ever, empty.

She put everything she had moved back in its place, fetched an empty bucket, and emptied out the coal—and there it was, a small metal box to which the key fit perfectly. Inside the box was a single piece of paper. The message was simple and was probably in code.

Robert. We will buy the horse on Tuesday, at the warehouse. Bring the money. L.W. Deans.

She scribbled it onto a piece of notepaper, replaced it, and fled to her regular work, taking a long moment to check that she had, in fact, left no traces of her search.

She had done well, she thought; in a part of herself she felt quite triumphant. And in another part of herself she felt more and more uneasy. The message was simple enough to be memorized and destroyed; why would the man keep it? Why would he leave his money in the portmanteau, even under a false bottom, when there was plenty of room for it in a locked and well-hidden box? And why did he not keep the key on his person?

A lot of them were green, Aggie said. Well, maybe. Only this one did not strike her as green, just very, very peculiar. She slid her own little slip of paper under Aggie's pillow moments before the others came in to bed, wondering if the American woman would ever tell her what she made of it all.

Friday came wrapped in fog. Not just a bit of fog, the sort one expected along the coast in the wintertime, but great, drowning blankets of fog, so thick you could not see across the street. Now and then as she worked, Sylvie glanced at the windows, hoping it would clear as the sun rose higher. It seemed rather to thicken instead. Last week Erryn had promised to rent a small boat on the first fine Friday afternoon they had, and take her out to George's Island or down around the Point. It would not be today.

She was finishing the kitchen stairs when Aggie Breault found her. Aggie looked quickly in both directions before she spoke. No one was in the hallway above; in the kitchen, Sanders was making enough noise with her chopper to drown out an army.

"I'm going downstairs," Aggie murmured. "Come with me for a minute."

"Going downstairs" was proper talk for using the toilets. She followed Aggie into the basement, where the water closets were discreetly tucked away. Instead of entering one of them, Aggie turned to face her.

"You did good yesterday," she said. "I'm impressed. Tell me, how long did it take you to find the key?"

"The key? I found the key right off. It were the box I couldn't—oh, rot it, anyway!" She stared at Aggie in the dim light, running the search through her mind in a moment, its implications clear now that she considered them. "That stuff were all . . . it were all bait, weren't it? You put it there yourself! You just wanted to see if I could find it!"

"Well, partly," Aggie said. "Mostly I wanted to see if you were careful. If you didn't leave signs. And if you were—no offence, please, but we have to be sure—if you were honest."

"And poor Mr. Manley?"

"A good, loyal American who was willing to do me a favour."

"What if I'd bolted with all his money?"

Aggie shrugged. "It wasn't his. It's . . . operating money."

"Well, bloody damned hell."

"It's a serious business, Sylvie. It's not a game."

"I never thought it were."

"I didn't figure so. But a friend of mine got stung real bad last year, trusting someone he shouldn't have. So I try to be careful." She smiled then, warm enough to burn the fog from the streets. "Are we still friends?"

"Course," Sylvie said. "You gave me a turn, that's all. I ain't mad. Comes right down to it"—here she offered a quiet smile of her own—"I'd a lot sooner work with someone who's careful."

"Good. You're off to Madame's now, I guess? Jonathan's brought her carriage. He's in the foyer, waiting for you."

Madame had sent her carriage? Sylvie was astonished at the old woman's kindness. She was a rare one, Madame Mallette.

"Is it him, then?" Aggie asked her.

"What?"

"Your follower. Is it Jonathan? It was clear as day at her birthday dinner that he fancied you."

"Jonathan fancies me?" Sylvie whispered. "Go on."

"Well, of course. Are you telling me you didn't know?"

"You're imagining things."

Aggie laughed softly. "You're a right smart girl, Sylvie Bowen, but you don't read men very well."

Was it so? She went over the matter many times on the long ride to South Park Road. It was almost impossible to see. On Barrington, the few carriages abroad were lit as though it were night. Pedestrians picked their way carefully along the boardwalk, many carrying lanterns in their hands. Back in England, Sylvie recalled—back in the mill country—a fog like this would mix with factory smoke and turn the air to poison. Here it rolled in clean from the sea, eerie and dangerous, but clean.

She settled back in the carriage, watching bits of Halifax come and go, stone buildings turned to spectres, appearing and disappearing in a breath. Were men so strange to her, so mysterious? She thought not. She had lived and worked among them all her life.

But she had never been courted, at least not by anyone she trusted enough to accept his courtship—never until Erryn Shaw. And perhaps to that degree Aggie Breault was right. Perhaps she did not read those particular signs very well. Did Jonathan Boyd fancy her? The notion had never crossed her mind. Now, when they reached Madame's house, he thoughtfully held out his arm for her as she stepped from the carriage. She could not resist looking into his face then, trying to read it. He had always been kind to her, but he was mostly kind to everyone, so she had thought nothing of it.

"Careful, lass," he said. "There's a bit of ice underfoot."

His eyes gave nothing away—nothing she could read—but they lingered on her, just a little, and so did his steadying hand. He was older than she was, well past forty, she thought, and sturdy as an oak. She judged him a man who had lived a bit and knew what he wanted. Was it possible that he wanted her?

She hoped it was not so, for his sake, and yet she could not help but be pleased. It was, after all, so very rare.

She read to Madame Louise as usual, and listened for a while as the old woman played the piano. Madame seemed melancholy today, and tired. Sylvie wondered if it was fog and memories of shipwreck, or if it was her rheumatism, and the grippe she had had for weeks that would not go away. At one point she stopped playing and kneaded her fingers as though they hurt.

"Do not get old, Sylvie Bowen," she said. "It's very bothersome."

"I've never heard it could be prevented, Madame."

Madame laughed. "I fear you have the right of it, alas. Pour us some more tea, would you please? Now tell me, have you gone down to Tobin's and read the memorial to Mr. Lincoln?"

"Yes, Madame."

The old woman nodded. "Tobin has stirred up a tempest in this town, God bless him. 'We see no acceptable outcome to this war except the restoration of the Union and the destruction of slavery. All real lovers of liberty and of humanity support you in your struggle.' Brave words, Sylvie, and it's high time someone stood on his feet and spoke them in public. We let the other side do all the talking for much too long."

"Harry Dobbs says Tobin will have his nose bloodied for it."

"By whom?" Madame scoffed. "Harry Dobbs? John Tobin has powerful friends, as many as Al MacNab does, and maybe more."

On reflection, Sylvie thought this might well be true. The Irish activist was a member of the Nova Scotia assembly, wealthy and respected. Among the scores of signatures on his memorial were many names as distinguished as his own. His nose was probably altogether safe.

"What do you think will happen in Saint John?" Sylvie asked. "At the hearing? Will they send those pirates to the States, do you think?"

"Extradite them? I don't know. There are always loopholes in the law, if men want to find one, and probably they will. I expect there's a great deal of talk about it at the Den?"

"They hardly talk about anything else. Some of the Rebels are so angry at us, you'd scarcely believe it. Yesterday one of them called us a nation of snakes. He didn't know I were just outside, scrubbing the hallway. It's peculiar, ain't it? At the start of the war England were doing all sorts of things she shouldn't have, for the South, things that weren't neutral at all. Now we're having second thoughts about it—not doing things for the Yankees, just saying maybe we shouldn't be doing them for the Rebels, and already they're calling us backstabbers and betrayers. They were building rams in Liverpool, for heaven's sake—*rams!*—and the government won't let the Rebels have them now, and so we're a nation of snakes."

"He who is not with me is against me."

"I suppose so." Sylvie cupped her tea in both hands. It was hot, and purely delicious. It was such a luxury, she thought, to have real tea, fresh, instead of the used leaves that were sold off from the kitchens of the rich, which was all they could ever afford in England. At the Den, the cook sold theirs. Sylvie wondered who finally used them, if they went to the poorhouse, perhaps, and filled the cup of Dinah Reeve.

Madame's voice broke her dark speculations. She would be going out soon, she said. Would Sylvie like to choose a book for herself and then Jonathan could drive her home?

"Thank you, Madame, I'd love to have a book. But there's no need to trouble Jonathan. I can walk back."

"Not in this fog. It's nigh as dangerous as the dead of night. Some ruffian could snatch you off the street and no one be the wiser."

"People are out, Madame. I saw them."

"No doubt, lass, down by the shops and hotels. Not here. It's out of the question. Jonathan will take you."

To Sylvie, this felt like an excess of caution. To Madame, no doubt, it was a matter of being responsible. Either way, it left Sylvie to tell a lie or a truth when she wished to do neither.

There was no point in the lie. She would never be able to sustain it. More importantly, she did not want to. Louise Mallette had always been good to her; it would be shabby to pay her back with lies.

"I am being met, Madame."

The woman went absolutely still. Even her lips scarcely moved when she spoke. "Met?"

"Yes. By a friend. I'll be perfectly safe."

"A gentleman?"

Sylvie wanted very much to look at her hands, or at the window, or the fine furniture. She did not. "Yes, Madame."

"And does this gentleman have a name?"

"He is Erryn Shaw."

"As I thought."

"Please, Madame, I knew you'd disapprove, which is why I never spoke of it. But he's never been anything but good to me! He's been a true friend, and I have so few!"

"Yes. That's precisely the trouble, that we have so few friends. Loneliness is the bane of every woman's soul. I trust God understands it as well as I do. Come, Sylvie Bowen, don't look at me as though I were the hangman. I disapprove indeed. I think you are a great fool. But my father railed at me and locked me in my room, and all he did was make me headstrong. So . . ." She made as if to smile, but she did not manage it. She looked wearier and more melancholy than before, as though the world had suddenly and bitterly disappointed her. Again.

"So I'll say only this. It is very rare for a man of Mr. Shaw's background to marry a woman of yours—not absolutely unheard of, but very rare indeed. Do not judge by the Danners. Mr. Danner was only a shopkeeper's son with four years of schooling when he married Miss Susan. The gap between them was tiny compared to yours. I hope you are not using it for a measure."

"I am not, Madame."

"No. Perhaps not." She sighed faintly. "Well, go fetch yourself a book, lass. And Sylvie?" She got to her feet, slowly, majestically.

"I've always thought well of you, since the first day I met you. You have a future here, a simple one, but decent and secure; you can live the rest of your life at peace with man and God. I should be very sorry to see you throw that away." She paused and added softly, "I helped at the City Mission for years, you know. I've seen the alternatives."

"I understand, Madame."

"No." The old woman shook her head. "No, lass, you don't. No one ever does, until it's much too late."

CHAPTER 22

---❖---

To Love or Not to Love

How say you? Let us, O my dove,
Let us be unashamed of soul,
As earth lies bare to heaven above!
How is it under our control
To love or not to love?
—*Robert Browning*

"WELL, MY HEART," Erryn said, "it's too foggy to walk, too early to sup, and too cold to sit under a tree. Shall we go and have tea?"

She said tea would be lovely, and smiled at him as their carriage rumbled gently into the fog. He seemed in the best of spirits, and he looked well at last. The ashen pallor was gone from his face and the brightness back in his eyes. "You're all better," she said.

"Oh, much," he agreed, "except for a nasty scar and some very bad memories. And what of you, Sylvie? A week is such a long time not to see you. Are you well?"

A week is such a long time not to see you. Sweet words, she thought, but ever so slightly hollow. In the six weeks since he had been back, he could have come to the Den a time or two, to visit. He knew the maids were not permitted to go out except on their half day, but they could have a bit of company of an evening if their work was done. He had never come, not even once. Unwillingly, she thought of Madame's words, not as a moral or a practical warning, but as a reminder of her social place. *The gap between the Danners is tiny compared to yours . . .*

And he seemed inclined to keep it so. In Montreal they had spoken sometimes of themselves, of things they feared or valued in the world. Now, increasingly, he spoke of things that touched him only distantly or not at all: his life at Eton, or people he had known in England, or funny, silly stories to make her laugh. He encouraged her appetite for knowledge; he would explain the workings of a man-o'-war or the habits of a snowshoe hare, or anything else in the practical world she might be curious about. But she knew little of how he spent his time when he was not with her. If he had close friends here, she had no idea who they were. She had asked him once about his mate who kept the spiders, and he only shrugged. "Oh, we're not mates anymore, haven't been for years."

He was sealing his life away from her, treating their time together more and more as play—as an escape, she supposed, from the world where he really belonged, a world where she had no place.

All of this was perfectly predictable; she had expected nothing else. Yet sometimes, when they held each other, she believed that she was precious to him in spite of it; a diversion, perhaps, but one he wanted very much.

It could not all be acting, could it?

Most times when they went for supper, he took her to Corey's, a plain little eatery on Hollis Street, where the food was delicious, plentiful, and cheap, and where he always had a table set aside for them in a quiet wedge at the back. But Corey's was not open for afternoon tea, so they went to Compain's fine hotel. It was as lush and elegant as she remembered it, the chandeliers already lit against the fog, and all the silver glistening.

"Are you hungry?" he asked.

"A little," she admitted. She knew if she said yes, he would think her starving and order everything in the place. They settled on bits of lamb in pastry puffs, and something called paté that she had never tasted before but that Erryn said was wonderfully good; with a small carafe of wine, and sweets. The tea came in a great china pot. He was just lifting it to pour when the voice of a woman caught them both unawares—a young woman, dressed to the very nines, with rich chestnut hair falling to her shoulders. She swept toward their table like a princess, accompanied by a young couple as elegant as herself. Sylvie had seen her only once before, briefly, through a dining-room doorway, but she recognized her at once: Isabel Grace Orton.

"Why, Mr. Shaw. What a marvellous surprise."

Erryn put the teapot back on its pad and rose smoothly to his feet.

"Miss Isabel, good afternoon. How nice to see you. You look perfectly divine, but then you always do."

Well, she did, Sylvie thought, and no one could deny it. Isabel Orton had the peach-perfect face artists dreamt of, flawless, symmetrical, winsome with youth, and yet proud, the face of a lady with a place in the world. Sylvie could well understand why she was pursued by half the young bloods in town.

Erryn was gracious and at ease, as most always, and yet Sylvie sensed he would have preferred to avoid this encounter. He introduced the two women, and then Isabel introduced her companions, a brother and sister, two of her cousins visiting from Saint John.

"Welcome to Halifax," Erryn said. "I trust you're enjoying our fine city—what you can see of it, that is?"

"Oh, very much," the young man said. "How could I not? We're being treated like royalty. Everyone feels sorry for us and invites us to everything."

The two men chatted briefly. Miss Isabel offered a few appropriate pleasantries, but her eyes scavenged everything of Sylvie she could see: the plain rubber boots and rough woollen dress; the cloak no servant girl could possibly afford; the scars that even loose hair could not hide entirely in daylight. She would have heard, if only in passing, about Susan Danner's new chambermaid, the one with the dreadful face.

"I fear we must be off," she said, "or we'll keep our host waiting. Mr. Shaw, how nice to see you again. Papa spoke of you just this morning. I must tell him I saw you."

The young man held out his hand. "It was a pleasure, Mr. Shaw. Perhaps we'll see you at the club on Sunday?"

"Perhaps."

"I'll look forward to it. Miss Bowen, good afternoon."

Isabel seemed to float rather than walk, weaving among the tables and out into the foyer and away. Yet she floated quickly, almost hurrying her companions, as if she could not wait to tell them. *You won't* believe *who that creature is, sitting there with Mr. Shaw!*

"I didn't know you knew the Ortons," Sylvie said noncommittally.

"It's a theatre connection, mostly. In a garrison town, the officer corps are among the theatre's best patrons—and some of its best amateur performers too. They always put on a production of some sort every winter. In fact they're doing another one this year, even though we have no theatre. They're using the Masonic Hall. The Ortons are very much part of that circle. So yes, I know them all."

He glanced toward the foyer door, where Isabel's party had vanished. Perhaps he too could guess what she would be telling her kin. Each time he and Sylvie had been together before, they had met people who knew him, but the meetings had been brief, the people mostly ordinary. None of them knew who she was; they had no connection with the Den. No doubt they noticed that she was of a lower rank than her companion, but they did not seem to care much.

"Well," Erryn said lightly, "we're grist for the gossip mill now. I'll give her twenty-four hours and everyone in Nova Scotia will know of us except the fish, and they'll be hearing rumours." He poured tea for them and handed her a cup. "And in case you're wondering, my heart, if I care poppycock about it, I don't. I thought it would happen a lot sooner, frankly. Ah, look, the paté!"

The paté was, as he had promised, wonderfully good. After the first few generous mouthfuls, he picked up his tea and leaned back a little in his chair.

"There was a great commotion around Miss Isabel the summer before last. One of the artillery officers was courting her—a real sharp fellow, the sort who'd pick up a pistol after it misfired, peer down the barrel, and pull the trigger again to see why it wasn't working. But he was dashingly handsome. He didn't have so much as a crook in his finger that wasn't perfect. Miss Isabel liked him. There was talk it might be serious, until he raced their buggy down Barrington so fast he lost control of the horses and put her through a haberdashery window."

"Dear heavens! Horses, buggy, and all?"

"No. Just buggy and all. The horses ended in a heap on the boardwalk."

"Was she hurt?"

"She broke her arm. She was lucky. If they'd hit a wall instead of a window, she might have been killed. Needless to say, Mr. Jamie was a trifle roused. Told the young fool he wasn't to come within a mile of his daughter ever again. I don't know how *he* felt about it, but Isabel didn't seem to take it badly. She's always had more suitors than she knew what to do with."

"And were you one of them?"

Sylvie asked the question lightly, playfully, but she did ask, remembering how Isabel had approached them, as if Erryn Shaw was, at the very least, an old friend.

To her surprise, he laughed. "Me? Hardly. She likes her lads wealthy and well made. I fail on both counts. Do you know what she said about me once, to a friend who wasn't as discreet as she should have been and passed it on? The friend had said to her, more or less, 'Isn't Mr. Shaw from the theatre so very talented and clever?' And Miss Isabel said, 'Well, perhaps, but he's such a long, stringy thing, they must've hung him out to dry before he was set.'"

"Why, that were a bleeding mean thing to say."

"I suppose so. On the other hand, it does get me out of the dock. I can look in the mirror every morning and think: I'm not to blame for any of this. The blighters hung me to dry before I was set."

He spoke lightly, with a ghost of a grin, and she could not help but smile a bit herself. Yet she understood that under his amusement lay a considerable measure of regret.

People never said much about beauty in relation to men. Their gifts in life were practical things: property, authority, competence. If they had those, it was not supposed to matter how they looked. But perhaps for some of them it did, especially those who were sensitive and artistic. Erryn *was* bony as a rake; his limbs were too long for the rest of him and his head was too large. His face was carved all uneven, and bony as well, with a hooked nose that must have been broken more than once. She did not care. She had liked him from the first, back at the Irish Stone, liked his delicacy of manner, his grace of movement, even his fine clothes. All the while her mind was being cautious, backing away, her instincts were reading him with approval. Nice, they would have said if they had had the use of words. Very, very nice.

But for others, perhaps, it was different.

The waiter brought the rest of their food. Everything was delicious. They nibbled it to the last bite, and lingered over their wine. As always, he encouraged her to talk about her own life and about affairs at the Den. He seemed pleased that she had found a friend in Aggie Breault. He was always willing to hear about the guests as well; he had a lively taste for gossip, especially if it was funny or bizarre. So an hour passed, or more. Finally he reached across the table and took her hands.

"Well, my heart, was there something special you fancied doing today, or seeing . . . given that we can barely see across the street?"

She could not have said what it was about his voice that troubled her, but she knew he wanted her answer to be no—no, there was nowhere she wanted to go. And then he could take her back to the Den and go off about his own affairs.

And next week, perhaps, he would not come at all.

It was all she could do to smile, to keep her voice entirely even. "No, Erryn. There were nothing I had in mind."

"Then would you consider coming home with me? I have the house all to myself. The landlord's off to Yarmouth to spend a couple of weeks with his boys. We could make a big fire and play music and talk to our hearts' content. It'll be quite safe, I promise you. In this fog I could take the Royal Artillery home and no one would be the wiser. I know it's . . . it seems . . . improper . . . and if you want to whack me on the head now, I have only myself to blame. But I wouldn't ask except that I want to be with you more than anything else in the world."

She had not expected anything like this. Her astonishment must have shown as distress, for he looked at his hands and then at her again, more troubled than before.

"I only meant . . . oh, be hanged to it, Sylvie, if it were summer, we could go off in the woods and sit under a tree . . . I only wanted some time with you, just the two of us . . . I'm sorry, I meant nothing more, I'm sorry—"

"Erryn." She freed her hands and used them to capture his. "You said once the world weren't laid out neat and clear, with everybody following the rules. Well, you're right, it ain't. I'll go home with you if you like. And I ain't cross at you for asking, either."

"You aren't?"

"No."

"Not even a little bit?"

"No. Not if you keep your promise and play some music for me."

The fog deepened as the sun went down, making the streets through which they passed grow ever more mysterious and strange, and the house seem like an island on the far side of the world. It was a small wooden house, snug and utterly still. Erryn lit a single kerosene lamp. In no time at all he had a splendid fire burning in the hearth, and a glass of dark wine for each of them.

Sylvie had never lain with a man. She had pleasured one once, under duress, crouched on her knees like a dog, but she had never lain with anyone. She did not know what it would be like. She was not even certain she would do it, this time.

Only it was so easy. There was a bear rug in front of the fire, with a thick quilt laid over to make it soft as a bed. There was firelight dancing all over them, elfin and wild. There was her own loneliness, and hours of time, a feast of time in a world as secret as a cave. It was so easy to sit and laugh with him, to reach over and brush a bit of nothing from his hair, and then, because she purely could not help it, to play the back of her hand across his face and kiss him. He was smooth and graceful in everything he did; caressing her with scarcely any restraint, even to play his hands across her breasts, and once, for just a moment, his mouth; yet doing it with such sweetness that it did not seem an act of boldness at all, but a gift. Once, for a long time, he did not touch her at all. He took his flute from the cabinet and played love songs, one after another, "Greensleeves" and "Shenandoah" and "Mary Morrison" and finally the one she liked best of all, the song of Eriskay:

> *When I'm lonely, dear white hart,*
> *Black the night, all wild the sea*
> *By love's light my foot finds*
> *The old pathway to thee . . .*

He sat, easy as a gypsy, one elbow braced against his raised thigh, his eyes half closed, his fingers light and quick as butterflies on the slender instrument. The music, though simple, was utterly enchanting. It was like kissing him, hearing him play, as though the songs were fingers running across her skin, touching her as his had never dared, not yet, making her wet and soft and so hungry that she wanted nothing in the world except to stroke him, every lean, wild, scarecrow bit of him, forever and forever.

This is what they mean when they talk about lust, about the sins of the flesh.

He stopped playing, wiped the flute lightly on his sleeve, and laid it aside.

"That was beautiful," she whispered.

"The pied piper of Halifax"—he bowed as deeply and elegantly as a man could do, sitting on the floor—"at your service, Miss Bowen. Mice, rats, bugs, ghosts and ghoulies, barking dogs, rude neighbours, bill collectors, unwelcome suitors, just call me"—he made an airy, flamboyant gesture in the general direction of the waterfront—"and I'll whistle them into the sea."

"I believe you could do it, too."

He smiled and held out his hand. And that was the end of her; she went to him as one half dead of cold might reach for fire.

He laid her back against the quilt, brushed her hair away from her forehead, stroked her face, even the scars. He said she was lovely, oh so lovely, and of course it was not true, but he spoke as though he meant it, at least for now. They reached as one for a kiss, and there was no end of them then, kisses to burn up all the fogs of the North Atlantic, and his hands on her, as wanton and sweet as his flute. For a small time reality intruded, the many reasons why it was probably a bad mistake—a sin, of course, but mostly a mistake—but it was so good, so impossibly beautiful, that she could not bear to end it, not yet, maybe in a moment or two, but not yet. After a time her clothing was all a disorder about her, opened and slid one way or the other, or slipped off altogether, and ending it was no longer a remote possibility.

——◆◆◆——

Afterwards there was only wonder. When it began to fade and she realized what she had done—not the sin of it, or the so-called shame, none of those things the preachers and the proper people talked about, only the surrender—she felt utterly defenceless. He could shred her to pieces with a word now. With a look.

But he did not. He lay beside her and wrapped her in his arms, drawing the quilt close around and shifting his limbs so they could nestle like kittens. Now and then he stroked her hair or her back; mostly he just held her, his long arms sheltering and fiercely possessive. She clung to him, wanting nothing in the world except to be held. Only much later, weeks later, did she consider the possibility that he might have felt as vulnerable as she did.

He fed the fire a couple of times and poured them a second glass of wine; otherwise he never left her side. As the hours passed, she discovered a number of things about love and lovemaking she had not expected—for one, that in the course of a long winter evening it was possible to do it more than once, and that the first time was not the best time. The second was better, and the best, for all she knew, was still ahead of her, for the thing seemed full of barely imagined possibilities.

Once, in the languor between pleasures, she half sat, half lay beside him and traced the lines of his face with her fingers, then the curve of his shoulder and the taut sweep of his rib cage and his belly, to the mound of his genitals and on down his thighs, right to his feet, to all ten of his very ticklish toes. She thought how Isabel Orton had dismissed him, calling him a long, stringy thing. For the first time, she felt sorry for Isabel Orton. Because he was glorious to look at, like a wild and splendid young animal. And maybe a woman had to be poor to see it, to understand how precious it was. Maybe she had to remember the faces and bodies of a mill town, the wrecked faces, the smiles without teeth, the hands ruined by machinery, the endless coughing, the sores that would not heal. To be past the age of thirty and undamaged, vibrant with sheer animal health and potency . . . that was to be beautiful.

Erryn Shaw was beautiful. And as she stroked him and admired him to distraction, and thought to herself: *Mine, mine, all mine, maybe only for now, but all mine!*—even as she did so, she thought also that beauty had very little to do with it.

"Are you happy, Sylvie Bowen?"

"Yes." She thought perhaps "happy" was too small a word. She settled on one elbow and played with his hair. "And you, Erryn?"

"Utterly, except for one thing: I shall have to take you off to a cold attic room in the Danners' boarding house, and come back here and sleep alone."

"I fear there's no help for that," she said.

"We could get married."

She stared at him, wondering if she had misunderstood him, knowing she had not. *"Married?"*

"Why, yes," he said wryly. "People have been known to do that sort of thing, when they like each other well enough."

She almost believed it. In truth, she believed it more because he said it lightly, as a thing between friends, than if he had thrown himself on his knees with protestations of love. She felt a flash of savage, overwhelming joy. It faded as comprehension came. He was being, of course, the perfect gentleman.

And did it matter? she thought darkly. She could accept him anyway, take what happiness there was to be found in it, try to make him happy in return. End the mortal loneliness, the ache that went right to her bones sometimes, for someone to be close to, someone to touch and to love.

But there was her face. There was the question of rank too, but it did not matter here the way it did in England. And he was never going back; he had made that very clear to her more than once.

Whatever else she doubted in him, this much she was sure of: he wanted his life in the theatre more than he wanted his social place. And she could learn the ways of the higher folk, perhaps, if she really tried, just as Susan Danner had. But the scars . . . no, the scars would never go away.

She remembered how one of the boarders had regarded her yesterday, the new one, Mr. Janes. He looked offended, as though she had no right to be standing there, young and otherwise desirable, with such a face; as though it were unfair to *him*. And there had been so many others down through the years: the fascinated ones who stared, the pitying ones who could not wait to look away.

How would a man feel ten years hence, a man as proud and gifted as this one, having bound himself to such a face? Merely out of duty, and forever?

He caught her hand and nuzzled it. "What do you say, then, Sylvie Bowen? Could you love this poor lonely scarecrow well enough to marry him?"

"I love you more than anything," she told him, very soft. "I would marry you gladly, I would, only . . ." She touched her cheek. "Only there's this, see? Aunt Addie told me once there'd be no sense my getting married, because there weren't a man on earth could wake up every morning of his life looking at this face."

It was hard to read his eyes in the firelight, but it seemed that something darkened in them.

"I think," he said, "it is a very bold soul who speaks for every man on earth." Lightly as a feather, his fingers played across the spot she had touched. "The first time I saw you, on the rue St-Antoine, stepping out of a carriage, I thought you were enchanting. Nothing has made me change my mind. You have scars on your face, yes, and that is a cruel place to have them, but they're not what I see when I look at you. I see your hair, and all I want is to touch it. I see how your body moves like running water, and how, when you laugh, it lights up the whole lonely world. I see *you*, my heart, and you are all that matters. Only you."

If he had been someone else, someone who was less a magician with words, it would have been easier to believe him. Even so, she almost did.

"Do you know what I grieved for," he went on, "when I was lost in the river? Besides the thought of dying? It was that I would never have your love, never know you as I wanted to. Never lay down beside you. I know we're . . . different . . . in some ways. You've lived in a world I can scarcely imagine, and you aren't at all sure what to make of me. But in spite of it, we seem to love the same things in life, and I think we love each other. Leastways, I love you."

"And I love you, Erryn; I do! You've been everything to me a lass could wish for! At first I thought you were just being kind, but I know now it be more. Only I . . . I don't want for you to ever feel beholden, see? I don't want you spending time with me, or laying down beside me, except because you want to. I know what it's like now, to have that. I don't ever want less. I don't want . . . duty. Not from you, Erryn—it would purely break my heart."

His eyes fell for a long, brooding time. She wished she could take her words back, trade them for something harmless and vague. But it had always been her way to be honest, most especially with people she cared for.

"Duty?" he murmured at last. "You fear it would come to that?"

"I don't know. It weren't that I . . . I'm sorry, Erryn, I just . . . don't know."

To her astonishment, he smiled a little then, and drew her to nestle close against him. "And how could you, after all? Everything you ever put your faith in was taken from you, one way or another. So why should you put any faith in this? I do see it, love, I do. And I can wait. God knows I expected a lot, asking you so soon. But you haven't said, 'No, go away, you big bony troll,' so I'll wait. I'll walk out with you Friday afternoons, and babble at you, and take you to bed every chance I get. And I'll ask you again, as often as I have to, and one day you'll be sure."

She wept then, fast in his arms, more tempted than ever to tell him yes. But he had spoken the truth: she had no faith in it, not deep down. She adored him; she believed him honest; she believed, even, that he loved her in some measure. But she had no faith that it would last.

As long as they were free, she could take whatever love and happiness he offered in the certainty that it was real, and whatever became of it, became. Maybe she would grow sure of him, like he said; maybe they would marry. If they did not, if in the end he did not want a mill girl with a ruined face, he would wish her well and walk quietly away. And then all this sweetness would never turn to poison—to sorrow, yes, but not to poison, not to mere icy duty or bitterness or cruel names.

It was hard beyond bearing, but there was no other way.

CHAPTER 23

———◆———

At the Waverley

He seemed to me a man with just enough of intellect to
be a villain . . . and just enough of daring to make him
indifferent to the dangers of guilt . . .
Edward Bulwer-Lytton

EVER SINCE MORRISON'S party, back in Montreal, the image of
Maury Janes's face had remained clear in Erryn's memory—plain
and rather square, with a thin line of mouth and straight, dull
brown hair. An altogether forgettable face, except for who he was
and what he had promised: *If this goes off like it should, it's going to
end the war . . .* Half a million men were trying to end the war and
could not. Such a promise made Janes impossible to forget.

Erryn spotted him immediately on arriving at the Waverley. He
was standing somewhat aside from the crowd, talking quietly with
Al MacNab and a burly brute Erryn recalled well from Montreal:
George Kane, the one-time police marshal of Baltimore. Jackson
Follett's right-hand man.

*God almighty. Two of them already, and I just got in the door. I think
it's going to be a long night.*

"Mr. Shaw! Good to see you again! How are you?" Janes strode over to him at once, smiling like an old friend, shaking his hand as though he meant to wring it off and keep it.

"I'm well, thank you. And yourself?"

"Just fine, sir, just fine. Glad to see you're still in one piece. I heard you got knifed on the boat coming over. Damn rotten business. Did they ever get the son of a bitch?"

"They didn't. I did."

Janes laughed roughly and clapped him on the arm. "I guess you Brits are tougher than you look."

"Positively indestructible," Erryn murmured. He leaned closer. "Did you just get in?"

"No, we came Saturday. I know you said to call on you, but it was just my luck Mr. Kane was heading off to Halifax the same day I was. Made everything right simple. Soon as we landed, he took me over to meet Al MacNab. Hell of a man, MacNab, but I reckon you know that. Never saw anybody get more things done in less time. He got us a nice place to stay, told me to come by Monday morning and he'd get me all set up, and damned if he wasn't as good as his word. I do appreciate your offer, though. I'll say one thing for you folks up here, you all are damnably obliging."

"Well, the offer still stands, Mr. Janes. If I can help in any way at all, be sure to let me know."

"That man," Jack Murray muttered over his punch, "is a mouth on wheels."

Erryn smiled faintly. "Men have said the same about me once or twice."

Jack laughed. "Yes, but you're *interesting*, Erryn. Janes is . . . to tell you the truth, when I first met him, a couple of days back, I thought he was dumb as a brick."

"And do you still think so?"

"No. I'd say he's rather shrewd, actually, in his own horrid Yankee trader sort of way. Sam Slick in person, and all that. His father was from Massachusetts, did you know?"

"Yes, he told me."

Erryn would have liked to say more, to remind Jack that it really did not make a lot of sense to judge men by their origins. But the entire Grey Tory community judged him by his own, and therein lay much of his security.

An aristocrat, his best friend Cuyler had said to him once, *an aristocrat is like God. He doesn't need to explain his existence; he simply is.*

The comment was cynical and irreverent (Cuyler was often both), but it contained a good deal of truth. Sons of the English ruling class turned up routinely in the colonies, doing nothing in particular, merely travelling and socializing with their peers. When Erryn Shaw arrived in Halifax, no one doubted that he was one of them. He had a princely education and impeccable good manners; he had an intimate knowledge of aristocratic life. When he spoke, casually and in passing, of a party at Windsor Castle, of dukes and duchesses come to tea; of seeing, through the window of his boyhood study, the great Lord Wellington old and sad, walking in his father's garden in the rain, it was obvious that he spoke from lived experience.

Oh, people wondered about him, he supposed—wondered just how blue his blood really was, and why he would spend his time on something so dubious as a playhouse, and why he never went home. But as long as he did not aim to marry one of their daughters, or involve himself in their business affairs, the Canadians would neither pry nor judge. Financial difficulties could strike the best of families; and everyone knew there were not enough military commissions and political appointments to go around. Some members of the aristocracy, younger sons in particular, *did* spend part of their lives like God, simply being there. Halifax was content to take him as he was.

Season after season, the business lords and their families patronized his theatre. The garrison officers worked with him on amateur plays and concerts, and bought him drinks and took him out to dinner. Because he liked to be companionable, he rarely discussed politics in social situations. Still, he never made a secret of his distaste for American slavery, or of his admiration for English Radicals such as Cobden and Bright. The whole town knew of his long friendship with Constable Calverley, an unrelenting leveller of the meanest possible origins.

So, when he shrugged it all aside and involved himself more and more on behalf of the Confederate elite, it seemed to him that someone should have asked him some hard questions. Had the circumstances been reversed, Matt Calverley would certainly have done so.

But the Grey Tories took him at his word—or rather, he supposed, at his blood. They did not believe he was returning to the world of his peers; they believed he had never really left it. All the rest had been temporary and trifling, merely the sort of thing young gentlemen did—consorting with low-life a way of learning about the world, running a playhouse a mere diversion, like seducing ballerinas or chasing the great auk in Timbuktu. Now there was something important at stake, and he, as the best of his kind always did, was showing his mettle when it mattered.

Jack Murray had done the same, done it easily and naturally, without the slightest consciousness of anything amiss. If Erryn were to ask him how the values he once embraced could have led him here, he would look at his friend in pure bewilderment. He would find the question absurd.

And that, Erryn Shaw, is your great good fortune. Don't bloody grumble about it.

"So," Jack murmured to him, very low, "I hear it said you're courting."

"Have you, indeed."

"Well, are you?"

"I took a young lady to tea. Does that constitute courting?"

Jack laughed. "Oh, all right, Erryn. I'll mind my own business. But you were seen with her before, you know. Collier didn't think twice about it, the first time. He didn't know who she was—"

"And now he does think twice about it? Rather presumptuous of him, wouldn't you say?"

"Easy, mate. I didn't mean anything."

"No, of course you didn't. Sorry. I have an old, well-entrenched dislike for gossip when I'm the object of it. Petty of me, I know, but there you are. Can I get you some more punch?"

Well, he thought, to show himself so touchy on the matter, he might as well have admitted to being hopelessly in love. He filled Jack's glass very generously, handed it to him with a flourish and a smile, and changed the subject. He was irritated by his own naked reaction; but mostly he was irritated by them, by all of them, collectively. He knew how they would speak of Sylvie Bowen, and how they would evaluate her, noting her scars and her age and her place in the world—most especially her place in the world—wondering what could possibly make her worth it, even for sport. It would have to be for sport, of course; no other possibility would cross their minds. An aristocrat might well seduce a servant. He might, if he was truly besotted, set her up as a kept woman. He did not marry her. In England it would lose him both his friends and his position. Here, at least in some circles, it would make him a laughingstock.

⬦

Dinner was eventually served, at a long table draped in pure white linen and glistening with silver and candles. The guests from Montreal were seated in the places of honour next to their host. Erryn, seeing Maury Janes well out of reach, was both sorry and relieved. He knew he had to seek Janes out at some point and spend some time with him, but he did not look forward to it in the least. He felt a powerful distaste for the man. He had felt it almost the instant they met, back in Montreal: the hackles going up all over him, along with a powerful, gut-knotting wish to be somewhere else. He knew, when he thought about it sensibly, that such antipathies simply happened between people, as did their opposite; he had come to love Cuyler in a day. He knew also that he could sometimes be a snob, not as to rank, but as to qualities of mind and spirit; and Maury Janes had a certain shabby crassness about him that represented, perhaps, the complete opposite of what Erryn admired in other men. Yet, when he accounted for all of this, something still remained, something cold and repugnant, like old rubbish, something that made him look repeatedly down the length of the table and think: *Watch that one, Erryn Shaw. Watch him like a hawk.*

"Tell me, does it ever get warm in this place?"

The words came out like taffy, sticky and slow, with most of the *r*'s left behind altogether. *Evah. Wahm.* Erryn smiled, turning back to his tablemate, a worn and shaggy Southerner who was, in Jamie Orton's words, "the best blockade-running pilot in the game." His name was Taber Hague and he was, he had said, from South Carolina. He had obviously never encountered a northern winter before, not even the tolerable Nova Scotian variety. He was wearing his outdoor jacket to the table, with a heavy scarf around his neck, and he still seemed cold.

"Warm?" Across the table, James Orton responded to his question with a chuckle. He was his old aggressive self, having spent less than twenty-four hours in jail for his part in the escape of George Wade. The local justice simply refused to hear the case against him, holding it over to the spring session of the Supreme Court. That was months away, and Erryn knew that the longer they dallied, the more it all became past history, the less likely would be any sort of conviction at all.

The Grey Tory leader spoke proudly now to Taber Hague. "There's no a bonnier spot in the world than this one, come summertime."

"I'll take your word for it, sir," the pilot said.

"No need to take my word for it, lad. There's thousands to tell you the same, and it's the good Lord's truth." He was sitting several places away. He planted his elbows on the table and leaned well forward, the better to affirm the good Lord's truth. "As ye know, lad, the sun never sets on the British Empire, and that makes for many a garrison town, and many a soldier lad to man them. And do you ken what they all pray for, when the hot sun's killing them in Nassau and the cholera in India? They pray to be posted to bonnie Halifax the next time round. So they do, lad, every last one of them."

The pilot smiled and reached for his whiskey glass. There was, after all, no accounting for the strange tastes of Englishmen. There was also no arguing with James Dougal Orton. Every time he spoke, he was like a train coming at you. You didn't argue; you got out of the way. Erryn Shaw had known several such men in his life, the first and most memorable being his father.

He took a small sip of port and studied his companions. There were some twenty of them, in a strange mix of the very elite and the decidedly raffish—men who, under ordinary circumstances, would never be found eating and drinking together. There was a Virginian named Evers who had been in Halifax since the start of the war, writing newspaper articles, organizing lectures and meetings, and generally promoting the Confederate cause. He was highly effective; Erryn often wondered why the Union never troubled itself to send a man of its own to do the same. Along with Evers were eight other Americans, including Confederate naval captain John Fallon. The remaining guests were Englishmen and local Grey Tories. At the far end of the table, one of them was just rising to his feet.

"Gentlemen, a toast."

Everyone fell expectantly silent. They had already paid tribute to the Queen, to the Confederate States of America, and to their host, Alexander MacNab, who was paying for this exceptional dinner. At some point there would be a toast to Jefferson Davis, may his government soon be recognized by the world, and another to Robert E. Lee, the finest general since Wellington. Someone would remember His Excellency the Archbishop, who was doing as much as any man could to keep God on their side. They would drink to dark nights and safe voyaging, and Erryn himself would raise his glass "To the ladies, God bless them!" if no one else did. By midnight, he thought, most everyone should be well and thoroughly drunk.

"Gentlemen. To Captain John Fallon, and all the brave seamen who run the blockade!"

"Captain Fallon!"

As usual, Erryn found ways to drink much less than he appeared to, a process that became easier and easier as the evening wore on. Thus the toast to Captain Fallon was duly consumed, or not consumed, and the company sat down again. The conversation shifted to the exploits of the blockade-runners, those canny rogues, as Alexander MacNab described them, who ran in and out of the beleaguered Southern ports. They ran out with cotton, coveted in the starving mills of England, and with naval stores—pitch, turpentine, and oakum—coveted in every port city in the world, including Halifax. They ran back to the South with food, shoes, and clothing; with weapons, ammunition, and other materials of war . . . and with luxury goods. Mostly with luxury goods, as Erryn gradually discovered. They were entrepreneurs, after all, not patriots, something canny Al MacNab quite understood.

"It was priceless to see, sir. The look on his face!"

Erryn leaned forward a little to identify the speaker, even though he was sure he recognized the voice. It was Tremain, mate of the ship *Marigold*, whose captain, William Ross, had for some reason not attended this dinner. Tremain was smiling broadly, looking about to catch everyone's attention, with the air of a man who had a tale to tell.

"The captain walks into his store—he'd walked past four or five different ones already. None of them was big enough, he said. Then he walks into MacNab's and looks around, and this little clerk with spectacles hurries over. 'Yes, sir, and what might I offer you today, sir?' and Ross says, 'All of it.' The clerk just blinks. 'I beg your pardon, sir?' 'I want all of it,' says Ross. You should have seen the poor man's face."

Tremain glanced about, toward those few who were recently arrived in Halifax and might have no idea how impressive Alexander MacNab's Dry Goods Emporium really was.

"There was rows and rows of shelves," he went on, "eight feet high, loaded with bolts of wool, and silk, and the finest cotton broadcloth. There must've been a thousand miles of lace. There was boxes of whalebone corsets and high-button boots and fancy embroidered whatnots for the ladies, and boxes of scarves and shawls, and God almighty knows what else. I think Mr. MacNab couldn't tell us himself without hauling out his books. And Captain Ross says to the clerk, just like he was ordering a pair of gloves: 'I'll take it all. Give me a price.' The poor chap didn't know what to do. I'm sure he thought we were taking him for a fool. But he was polite as anything. 'I shall have to speak with Mr. MacNab, sir,' he says, and scurries away like a mouse with his tail on fire."

"And did Captain Ross take it all?" someone asked.

"He stripped the place bare. Those old monks who went fasting in the desert could have moved right in and felt at home."

A small chuckle went around the table. Not surprisingly, someone proposed a toast to Captain Ross. Afterwards, Erryn murmured to the pilot who was sitting beside him: "Where is Captain Ross, do you know? I'm surprised he isn't here."

"Well, if you had a choice between dinner with a beautiful lady and dinner with us, which would you choose?"

"Us, hands down."

The pilot grinned. "You're the first Englishman I ever met who had a sense of humour."

"Englishmen come in many shapes and sizes," Erryn told him. *Altogether too many shapes and sizes,* he added silently, rearranging his legs beneath the table, carefully, so he would not kick the man opposite. "Captain Ross is a dull sort, then?"

"Ross is so full of himself, there ain't no room left for anything else. He acted like he was doing me a great favour, going out of his way to pick me up in Nassau, even though they paid him extra for it. We got that sort in Charleston too, a few of them—treating white men like they was niggers just because they don't have the fine ancestors or the fancy clothes. A real gentleman don't do that. General Lee, now, they say he's a real gentleman. He'd have the time of day for any ordinary fellow, same as for the high ones. And you, Mr. Shaw . . ." He lifted his glass in a small, discreet salute. His hand, Erryn noticed, was not steady. " . . . you are a real gentleman."

"Why, thank you."

Dessert had finally arrived: a generous serving of plum pudding in a thick brandied sauce. Erryn dipped into it thoughtfully, considering his choice of words.

"It must be bloody tricky, piloting a ship under these conditions. With the blockade, I mean. Having to find the channels with no moon, no lights, making barely a sound. And I've heard the Southern ports are treacherous, what with river currents shoving the sandbars one way and the ocean currents shoving them another."

"You heard right. I piloted for sixteen years before the war started, and every trip was different from the one before. A harbour's like a woman, Mr. Shaw: the first time you think you really know her, the first time you take her for granted, bang, there you are with your nose in the mud and your arse on a sandbar."

The logistics of this were difficult to picture. Erryn tried briefly and gave up. "That ever happen to you?" he asked.

"Twice, years back. But I never lost a cargo or a passenger."

"That's impressive. How many times have you run the blockade?"

"I've took five ships out and four back in. The last run, I got so sick I couldn't hardly stand up. That's why they left me in Nassau. I recall them taking me off the ship in a blanket and waking up a week later in a hospital. They said it was malaria."

"That's most unfortunate."

"Wouldn't wish it on my worst enemy."

They talked on, perhaps for an hour or so, interrupted by numerous toasts and by waiters with great pots of coffee, for which Erryn was supremely grateful. Eventually their host tapped his glass for attention and rose to his feet.

"Gentlemen," he said, "it's been a mighty fine evening, but it's late and time for me to go home. Those of you who are leaving tomorrow, I wish you good sailing, and good luck."

On behalf of the company, Captain Fallon thanked him, followed by hearty applause and three cheers for Alexander MacNab. The gathering began to disperse then, mostly toward the bar. Captain Fallon approached the pilot, his greatcoat over his arm.

"I'm heading back to the ship, Taber. Are you coming?"

"I'll stay a bit, captain, sir—iffen you don't mind."

"Very well. But we're raising anchor before dawn. I'll be riled if I have to come and fetch you."

"He'll make it back, captain," Erryn said. "I'll see to it." He held out his hand, wishing the captain luck, and then turned back to his companion. "I didn't know you were sailing tomorrow. In that case, let me treat you to a drink or two."

This suggestion received no argument whatever.

——◆——

The Waverley Hotel was one of the best in Halifax. It was not luxurious by the standards of either the English or the American upper class, but it was large and well furnished. The bar had a fine piano, around which a body of men were now gathered, singing a mix of sailors' songs and Scots ballads. It had a great, roaring stove, but all the tables near it were taken, occupied by consumptive-looking regulars who had probably been there since lunch. Unfortunately for Taber Hague, it also had a door that opened to the street. Customers kept coming and going, and with each of them a little bit of winter entered.

The pilot picked his way to a corner as far from the door as possible. He pulled his jacket and scarf close around him. He was not in the best of health, Erryn suspected, and all that liquor did not make him warmer.

"I don't want to say anything against your fair city," he said. "I mean, really, I don't, but I wish to hell I was in Nassau."

"Couldn't you have stayed if you wanted to?"

"I suppose. But it's war, after all, and Captain Fallon asked for me special."

"So it's no shipload of silks and caviar you're taking, then."

"Not in one of our own ships, not likely, sir. Captain says there ain't an ounce of fripperies in her, 'cept he brought himself a novel to read while we're waiting on the moon."

Erryn took a small, gentle sip of port. "I got the impression once or twice tonight that Captain Fallon doesn't especially admire the . . . ah . . . commercial runners."

"Well, maybe he don't, sort of. And maybe I don't either, sort of. They bring in too much stuff that nobody really needs, just fripperies, like the captain says. And they charge what the trade will bear. But that's how the world works, ain't it? Captain Ross, now, you know what he makes on a run? What the owners in England pay him? Six thousand Yankee dollars for a round trip, or as much in gold or sterling."

"I can hardly believe that."

"Believe it. They paid me three thousand." He raised his glass again, unsteadily. "Think about it, Mr. Shaw. I got four years of book learning, that's all. I spent my whole life piloting boats for hire, and I ain't never owned but one good suit. I never owned a slave. I got more money now than I ever had in my life. That make any sense to you?"

"You have a rare and valuable skill in a desperate and critical time. I suppose that's the sense it makes."

"You use words real nice, Mr. Shaw. But you got it all wrong. It's folks getting other folks between a rock and a hard place, nothing more. Captain Ross said it plain. The whole world is eat or be eaten. Says it's all in a new book by some Englishman—Darren, Dolan, I forget now—"

"Darwin?"

"Yeah, that was it. Darwin. Survival of the strongest, something like that. Ross says— Well, damn it and speak of the devil. Here he comes."

Erryn looked up and his whole body went rigid with shock, like a skater on a frozen lake hearing the ice begin to crack. A man was moving through the barroom, casually yet imperiously, nodding to this one and that one, smiling the bland smile Erryn had come to know so well in important men, the smile that never reached their eyes. He wore a frock coat of impeccable cut, with trousers to match, all in the finest grey worsted; a white linen shirt with gold and diamond cufflinks; knee boots of gleaming leather—gleaming so beautifully he might have used them for mirrors—and a gold watch fob and three gold rings. All of this, however, Erryn noticed only later, for his gaze was riveted on the man's face: a round face, pale and somewhat plump, with small, watery eyes. All the Ambersons had those eyes. Slimy little pig's peepers, Erryn had called them in one of his meaner moments, and then decided he was being cruel to pigs.

It was too late to run, and useless, no doubt, to slide drunk beneath the table; Taber Hague would thoughtfully haul him up again. He could only wait, cursing silently and pointlessly like a small boy kicking at a stump. *Not that bastard, oh damn it to bloody hell, not him, not now, oh, damn, damn, damn, damn, DAMN!*

Ross paused beside their table. "So, Hague, I see you're being well taken care of."

"Yes, sir. This is Mr. Shaw. Erryn Shaw. Captain William Ross. He's English too."

"My pleasure, Mr. Shaw."

They shook hands, Erryn responding with a pleasantry he could not afterwards remember. He was actor enough to be satisfied that his face betrayed nothing, neither his first moments of sheer icy panic nor his drowning relief as it became apparent that Ross did not recognize him.

He certainly recognized Ross. Or, more correctly, Lieutenant Hailey Bryce Amberson, Jr., of Her Majesty's frigate *Lancaster*; not, as far as he had heard, on half pay, and therefore on leave. On leave, and captaining a blockade-runner for six thousand Yankee dollars a run, under an assumed name, against a country with whom Her Majesty's government was at peace.

Well, Erryn reflected bitterly, why should he be surprised? Since the start of the war Englishmen in official positions had been violating their government's neutrality for personal gain. Most everyone in power knew it, and they cared to precisely the degree by which it might embarrass the government. A naval officer engaged in blockade-running would be well beyond the pale—unless, of course, he used an alias and could pass himself off as just another private entrepreneur . . .

Yes indeed, Erryn thought, the Amberson clan was running true to form.

"You were much discussed at supper tonight, captain," he said.

"Not too unfavourably, I hope?"

"Not at all, sir. Quite the opposite."

"Have a good voyage, Hague," Ross said amiably. "Mr. Shaw." Then he was gone, like a king through his court, collecting homage.

Erryn settled back into his chair, more shaken than he wanted to admit. Yes, this was the other side of the Atlantic, and more than a decade had come and gone. His dangerously familiar first name, in the mouth of the Carolinian, had dissolved into a soft, unrecognizable purr: "E'hn." Still, Bryce Amberson had met him a dozen times at least. Bryce Amberson had married his first cousin.

"Snotty bastard, isn't he?" Hague murmured. "Bet he thinks he pisses rosewater."

"Yes." And that, Erryn supposed, was a considerable part of it. Ross had not recognized his kinsman because he had not really seen him. All he had seen was a backwoods pilot and some colonial he happened to be drinking with. Useful people—or at least the pilot was—and so he would make the proper gestures of politeness. But he would not really *look*. Otherwise . . . well, otherwise he might have noticed.

Even in an empire the sun never sets on, there aren't likely to be two of me.

CHAPTER 24

Best Mates

You are green, it is true, but they are green also.
You are all green alike.
—*Abraham Lincoln*

BACK IN HIS ROOM in Gideon Winslow's house, Erryn lit a candle and opened his trunk, rummaging wearily till he found what he wanted: a long, black, clerical soutane. It was one of three costumes that had not burned to ashes with the Grafton Street Theatre because, two days earlier, he had brought them home to mend. He pulled it on, fitted the stiff priest's collar around his neck, and added a hideous black bowler hat. A hand-held mirror confirmed his expectations: he made an entirely believable clergyman—tall and austere, almost cadaverous, with an air of raw exhaustion that was absolutely genuine.

Just don't breathe port all over anyone.

It was well after midnight. He had sent the hack away, of course, and now he had to walk back to Barrington, perhaps all the way to the Waverley, to hire another. He wondered if ruffians would attack a priest, and decided not to think about it. He had to see Matt in person. So far, since he returned from Montreal, his communications had been mostly routine, and he had left them in a letter drop near Cheapside. Tonight that simply would not do. He checked his pistol and slipped it into the pocket of his cloak, looked wistfully at his neglected bed, and went out into the cold.

It was, in truth, a miserable night, ugly enough to make most any man wish he were in Nassau. Even the ruffians appeared to be staying in. He kept himself alert as he walked, and watched the streets all around, but once he was inside a carriage again, he gave himself over to gentler thoughts, to the memory of Sylvie's body naked in the firelight, to her rare, beautiful laughter and the soft hunger in her eyes. He had wanted her so desperately, and yet desire had only been part of it. The other part had been . . . something else. He was not at all sure what to call it: an attempt to bewitch her, perhaps—or even, if he chose to look darkly on it, a sort of manipulation. *If we are close enough, if we are promised, if she loves me utterly, she won't turn on me when she learns the truth.*

To what extent he had bewitched her, he had no clear idea. But he had certainly bewitched himself; opened a door he had scarcely known was there, out of which had spilled a flood of hunger and tenderness and dreams, one dream fiercer and more driven than all the others: to give her a life. To stand between her and everything she had so far known, brute hands and scrub pails and those dark, deadly mills. To wipe it all away, as with a spell, and hold out to her a world of music and books and soft, warm beds.

That he loved her he had known for some time. Or rather, he had imagined that he knew it when it really had been nothing more than possibility. Now it was knowledge. Now he could scarcely imagine an alternative. If he lost her, it would not simply grieve him; it would wreck him forever. Leave him, he thought, as a cripple, with half his body gone and half his soul, walking through a world of empty streets and empty rooms, looking for the pieces.

Matt's rooming house was a forbidding old monster—also, at this ungodly hour, absolutely dark. Erryn let himself in with a back-door key Matt had given him and picked his way to the stairwell. The building was made entirely of wood; the stairs and hallways groaned with every step. An advantage of sorts, he reflected: no one was likely to sneak up on Constable Calverley in his sleep.

The constable did not answer his first gentle rapping, so Erryn rapped again. A voice spoke from somewhere beside the door, Matt's voice, very soft and very flat. "What do you want?"

"It's Canby."

The door opened quickly and was eased shut and bolted behind him. Only then did Matt strike a match and light the small kerosene lamp on the cabinet beside his bed. He turned, shoving tangles of black hair out of his eyes, and smiled.

"Damn, but it's good to see you, mate."

"Likewise, my friend."

He was not surprised at the warmth in Matt's eyes, only, per-haps, by the intensity of it. Mostly he was surprised at himself, at his sudden powerful wish to put an end to this lunacy he was liv-ing in. It was months since they had stood face to face and smiled; two years since they had walked together down a street, or laughed across a table of Corey's fish and chips. They were the dearest, the very best of mates, and they lived month after month like enemies.

Matt looked him over from head to foot and grinned his wry, wicked little grin. "Come to give me the last rites, have you?"

Erryn laughed. "No. Just some news. How've you been, then?"

"Me? Other than fed up to the gills with the Southern Con-federacy and all its works? Capital, really." He kicked his one chair over to Erryn and settled on the edge of the bed. "What about you? I've heard you're all over that wound you took on the *Saguenay*, but I'd rather hear it from you."

"Everything's healed but my pride. I still wince when I look back on it all." Erryn shook his head. "The bastard was following me all over Montreal, you know, and I never took him seriously. I thought he was a Yankee. I even baited him. Can you believe it? I dared him to try and catch me. And so he did."

"Tell me," Matt said quietly. "Tell me all of it." It was less the suggestion of a friend than the bidding of a spymaster. Erryn told him nothing of Sylvie Bowen, but otherwise he recounted the entire affair, without any attempt to justify himself. At the end of it he was once again shaking his head.

"He caught me on the deck of that steamer like a fish in a barrel, and do you know what he said before he stabbed me? He said, 'You thought you was so damn smart, Mr. Shaw.' He was right. I thought I was getting rather good at the business, and I was nothing but a bungling amateur."

"We're all amateurs," Matt said calmly. "Him, too. A proper agent would have stuck his knife in your back and pitched you in the river, with nary a word said. You'd have died without ever knowing why."

"Christ, that's comforting."

"Yeah, well, we all get a bit of comfort now and then. I knew this sod once who had four years in the constabulary behind him, to say nothing of a lifetime in the worst part of town, and he still turned his back on a lunatic. All that stood between him and a daisy patch that night was a bungling amateur and a bowl of hot stew. Do you happen to remember?"

Erryn smiled in spite of himself. "I do."

"I rather thought so. You *are* good at this, Erryn. Damn good, actually, for someone raised all honest and civilized. And I ain't the only one who thinks so. Colonel Hawkins was in Quebec a couple of weeks ago, had himself a fine dinner with the GG and a nice quiet chat by the fire after. His Lordship is very pleased with us, apparently. With all of us, but especially with you, for stopping the Johnson's Island raid. He told the Hawk to pass on his personal compliments for . . . how did he put it? . . . 'a difficult task impressively well done.'"

"He actually said that?" Erryn murmured. "Well, my pride is much mended. Thank you."

"My pleasure, mate. But I should tell you, if you do something that bloody dumb again and survive it, I'll be tempted to drown you myself."

They laughed together briefly, softly. Erryn glanced about, noting spiderwebs as always in the corners of the walls. The creatures themselves appeared to be sensibly tucked away to sleep. He was silent for a time, unsure if he should ask the question he wished to ask or if he should let the matter be.

"You know," he said finally, "I've always wondered about Brad Taylor—who killed him that night, and for what. Did you ever learn anything about it?"

"Beyond the usual crazy rumours, you mean? No, nothing at all. I doubt I ever will."

Erryn nodded. It was the answer he had expected. Nobody knew. Nobody was ever going to know. There was a certain comfort in it, he supposed—the sort of comfort one might find in the cold anonymity of a battlefield.

"So," Matt said, "I know you love me dearly, but I don't suppose you'd be here unless you had news. What are the bastards up to, then?"

"Something quite interesting, I think. The blockade-runner *Moravia* is sailing at dawn, Captain Fallon, Confederate Navy, with a cargo so precious they fetched a pilot specially from Nassau to take it in. Officially, their destination is Bermuda, but the pilot's from Charleston, and he's good—Orton says he's the best in the game—so there's no question that's where it's going. And it's all war supplies. Not an ounce of fripperies, I'm told, except a novel the captain brought along to read."

"Fallon's been commanding the *White Fox* for years. How did you find out he's changed ships?"

"The pilot was feeling cold and altogether miserable. I bought him some drinks to cheer him up. And being a kindly sort, I made sure I got him back to his ship safe and sound, just like I promised."

"Well." Matt leaned over to rummage in the small cabinet beside his bed. "That deserves a drink, mate."

"Please, no," Erryn begged. "But thank you."

Matt shoved the bottle back unopened. "It'll make a grand story for the papers, won't it? 'To Charleston with Guns and Glory. The Gallant *Moravia* Runs the Blockade.' And hidey-ho and fol-de-roley-roley-la. They love that sort of thing, the papers do."

All they shared was a small, quiet smile. They knew, as did most everyone, that the Union navy could not hope to stop every blockade-runner on the seas. But if the Federals learned of a ship with a particularly important cargo, and knew its destination . . . ? All the rest would follow like daylight after dawn. Ten minutes after a newspaper hit the streets, it would be in the hands of the United States consul. That was a perfectly ordinary and reasonable thing. And if he was good at his job, as Mortimer Jackson happened to be, he would promptly whip off a coded telegram to Washington. That was a perfectly reasonable thing too, and nothing to concern a pair of young Canadians. And if, shortly afterwards, a steamer went hot-chugging out from Hampton Roads to find the Atlantic Blockading Squadron, well, that would concern them even less.

It was the most innocent form of espionage imaginable, and the most delicate diplomacy. Not, perhaps, angelically neutral (as if anyone in this bloody, murderous muddle was), but neutrality and peace would hardly be served if Halifax became a gunrunners' paradise. Of this Erryn was entirely satisfied, and satisfied also that the governor would agree—although, being next to angelically neutral himself, Lord Monck would probably not say so, not even to himself.

"There's something else," Erryn said. "A matter I'll need some help with, if you can manage it. There's an Englishman here, calls himself William Ross. He's captain of the runner *Marigold*."

"Ah, yes," Matt murmured. "The greedy sod who bought out MacNab's entire Emporium. He'll make his owners a fortune if he gets it through."

"Quite. To say nothing of a bit for himself. I know him, Matt. He's actually a naval lieutenant named Bryce Amberson. He's also . . ." Erryn paused, redirecting his thoughts. "The man I killed was his cousin. Devin Amberson. They were good friends since they were boys."

"He doesn't know, does he? I thought the whole affair was pretty well hushed up?"

"There's always rumours. Whatever else, Amberson has to know how Cuyler was killed, and how I must have felt about it. He won't blame his mates, of course, but he has to know what happened. And he knows my family, too, a whole lot better than I'd like: five years back he married one of *my* cousins. Which means he's likely heard by now, however vaguely, that the earl's younger son didn't simply go off adventuring. That something happened, something serious. And then there's the timing: Cuyler's death, and Devin's, and my sudden and apparently permanent departure, all within the space of a fortnight. Even Bryce Amberson might make the connection eventually. I dare say he was just about the last man in the world I wanted to meet again."

"He saw you?"

"Spoke to me, even. But he didn't recognize me, at least not yet. I think I can stay out of his sight until he sails, and if we're lucky the Yankees will send him home with his tail between his legs and he won't be back. Otherwise we'll need to do something. It might be useful to find out who owns the *Marigold*. And if someone could bring me word the minute she returns, so I can duck for cover, and not end up sitting next to him at one of MacNab's fancy dinners, that would be useful too."

Erryn looked up, meeting Matt's gaze dead-on. "The Ambersons are a shabby breed," he went on. "Everything you think of when you imagine the ruling class at its worst—venal, undisciplined, and above all, utterly callous—every one of them I ever knew fit the pattern. And I was the one who knew them, Matt—Cuyler didn't. They crossed his path because of me."

"That doesn't make you responsible."

"No. But it makes me a trifle shaky. I don't know how long I could stay in the same room with one of them and be a friendly Grey Tory. And that's the truth, mate. I really don't know."

Matt took this in stride, as he took most everything Erryn ever said to him.

"Fair enough. I'll do what I can to keep him out of your way."

"Thank you."

In the bit of silence that followed, Erryn considered the many things he wanted to say to Matt, but it was close to three in the morning and he was altogether spent. He wanted, in particular, to ask Matt's opinion of the Confederation project, whether it would succeed and how it might unfold. But such questions wanted hours of discussion; to begin now would be like opening a bottle of excellent wine when there was only time to have a sip of it. Better, he thought, to just get to his feet and say goodbye. But Matt was speaking again, his voice no more than a murmur.

"Don't take this the wrong way, Erryn, but I heard the damnedest thing a few days back, and I don't know what to make of it. I heard you were the sorry sod who helped John Braine escape."

Erryn looked up sharply. "You have the most amazing ears, mate."

"Not really. I just put them to the ground in peculiar places. Is it true?"

"I fear so. Are you appalled?"

Matt shrugged. "I'd be a liar if I said it made me happy. But I know you walk a tightrope sometimes. I'm sure you had reasons."

"MacNab asked me to my face, Matt. He said Braine was stranded in Truro and needed to get to the coast. He said I was the best possible choice, because I could use my theatre experience to disguise us both. I didn't see any choice but to go. I could have betrayed the scoundrel, of course, but I wasn't sure there was much point in it. We'd throw him in jail for a month and make a lot of law-abiding noises, but in the end we'd let him go, just like the others."

"Oh, you *are* cynical," Matt murmured.

"There's more. Back before he was killed, Brad Taylor told his brother he didn't trust me, because I was always around when things went to hell. What if he told other people too, not just his brother? I could have found a way to get Braine caught, but all the way to Truro I kept thinking about it. What if Taylor's words were still sitting quietly in some Grey Tory heads? Not a suspicion, not yet—they think I'm a great cove. But they've heard it. Then Braine goes down on my watch and they say, 'Hmmm. Curious coincidence, that.' Then I wreck something else, something I have to wreck, because it matters, and now it's twice . . . So, to put it simply, I said, 'Bugger this. The bloody pirate isn't worth it, let him go.' I fetched him cheerily to Halifax and onto a blockade-runner, and come morning I woke up a hero. It made a grand impression on the Johnny Rebs. They can't do enough for me now. So you see, mate," he finished with a wry smile, "cowardice has been duly rewarded."

"Well." Matt rubbed his knuckles idly across his bearded chin. "I'd call it prudence, myself. I'm glad to see it grows in your part of town; I was starting to wonder. Sure I can't tempt you with a drink?"

"Thank you, but no. I should go, before you have to carry me down the stairs." He got up, shoved the bowler clumsily back on his head. "You know what we're going to do when this is over? We're going out to dinner and staying for a week. Just us. Just to talk."

"I'll take that as a promise." Matt rose easily, smoothly, like an uncoiling spring. "You watch your back now, Scarecrow. I'd find it bloody inconvenient having to replace you."

Scarecrow. It was a name Matt called him only now and then, on those special occasions when another man might have said, "my dear, *dear* friend . . ."

"You can't replace me. You said so yourself. The most perfect natural spy you'd ever seen—remember?"

They shook hands. Then, with an animal spontaneity that was sadly rare among the young men Erryn had grown up with, and that he utterly adored, Matt pulled him close and hugged him.

———◆———

CHAPTER 25

At the Halifax Club

We walked too straight for fortune's end,
We loved too true to keep a friend;
At last we're tired, my heart and I.
—*Elizabeth Barrett Browning*

AGGIE CAME IN late from her half day on Thursday. Sylvie looked up to see the housemaid, still in her street clothes, crossing the kitchen floor with a farm woman's stride. Sylvie closed her book with a smile, thinking her friend would have stories to tell. Then Aggie sat down across from her, and for the first time the light fell clearly on her face. Sylvie felt her smile quietly die.

"Aggie, what is it?"

For at least a minute the woman said nothing at all. She looked at her hands, at Sylvie's face, at her hands again. When she finally spoke, her voice was flat, as if she were holding in a torrent of anger.

"Let's go upstairs. We need to talk."

"All right."

In their attic room, Aggie challenged her even before the door had properly closed. "Your gentleman friend is Erryn Shaw. Isn't he." Despite her choice of words, it was in no way a question.

"Yes," Sylvie admitted, "but he's not really my—"

"Erryn Shaw is a Confederate agent."

Aggie was joking. She had to be. Such a lunatic statement could not be anything except a joke. But there was no lightness in her manner at all, no laughter. Her face was rigid with anger.

"That's crazy, Aggie! He doesn't know anything about the war. He's never cared enough to find out—!"

"That's what he tells you. Or maybe it's just what you decided to tell me. What did he really say, Sylvie Bowen? 'Go make friends with the big Yankee woman at the Den and find out what she's up to'?"

"How can you say a thing like that?"

"Well, what should I say, with you carrying on like you're all on our side, and hanging about with a miserable Rebel hireling behind my back?"

"Now you bloody listen, Aggie Breault! I don't know who's been telling you what about Erryn Shaw—"

"Nobody had to tell me anything! I've known about him for months! Every Union agent in the colony knows. He's one of MacNab's flunkeys—has been from the start. He couriers for them, helps them raise money, goes to all their dinners at the Waverley, and drinks toasts to Jeff Davis. God in heaven, Sylvie, it's no secret! Your walking out with him was the damn secret!"

It was a rare wind-still night, not even a whisper tugging at the eaves. Somewhere in the walls a mouse scurried and squeaked; nothing else moved at all. Sylvie sank onto the edge of the bed, knotting her hands in her lap.

Nobody had to tell me anything! I've known about him for months!

It was not that she believed it. She could not—would not—believe anything so shattering simply on another person's word. It was that the words explained so much: Erryn's vagueness about his activities and his friends; his preference for spending their time in quiet places; his supposed indifference to the war, an indiffer-ence she found astonishing in a man so apparently passionate about everything else in the world. It explained nearly every-thing . . . and left an absurdity that nothing in the world could explain: Erryn Shaw himself. The man who spoke to her so many times of his separation from the privileged world of his family and his peers. *My father was of the old school. There wasn't much we agreed on . . . I will not, under any circumstances, go back to take my proper place in the social order . . . I don't care much about rank; as a way of living, it's not worth it.*

A man did not abandon the world view of position and privilege without a good deal of thought. He might lose his place in the world through misfortune, or be forced out of it by his enemies, but he did not discard its principles blindly; in the ordinary course of things they offered him far too much. He had to look beyond the ordinary to discover what they took away. *It's like the old chap Procrustes I talked about—if any part of you doesn't fit his bed, somebody chops it off. And if you let them, after a while there isn't much of you left.*

Erryn wanted his freedom. He wanted to make his own deci-sions and choose his own friends. He wanted a life in the theatre, whether it was appropriate to his breeding or not. He wanted nobody chopping at him, ever. This much Sylvie believed without question. Whatever he might have lied about, he hadn't lied about that.

So how could he support the Grey Tories and the Southern slave keepers? He had seen their sort of world close up, and he had walked away from it. Was he foolish enough to believe the war somehow *was* for freedom, beyond the freedom of the few to go on controlling the many? Could he possibly be so naive?

"Are you really telling me you didn't know?" Aggie said.

"He wouldn't work for the Confederacy, Aggie. He just wouldn't."

"He does. He's gone to the West three times now, carrying mes-sages, meeting with traitors like Vallandigham and Jackson Follett.

And he helped John Braine get out of the country, too—we're all but certain of it." The housemaid chewed on her lip a little and went on, very softly: "Folks will do a lot of things for money, you know. Things we might think they'd never do."

"*For money?*"

"That's right, Sylvie. Money. Young Mr. Shaw's been living pretty high since the war started, despite his theatre being gone—"

"He gets money from his father!"

"And he hasn't touched it. Two years running now, he's just cashed in his father's notes and put it all in the bank. And now and then a little extra, too."

"I thought that sort of information were private!"

Aggie shrugged. "I'll tell you what a friend of mine thinks, Sylvie—you can make of it what you like. My friend figures Mr. Shaw has some natural leanings to the Southern gentry, being a gentleman himself, but mostly what he wants is to live well and somehow get his hands on another theatre. He isn't trained for any real work, and if he was, we all know what real work pays. So the war's his golden opportunity. He can live off the fat of the South— sleep late, drink the best liquor in town, eat at the good hotels, *and* stash his old man's money away to buy himself his own playhouse."

"No," Sylvie said. "I know him. He wouldn't." But bit by bit the tears began, and she could not force them back.

Aggie sat down beside her. "Did you tell him anything?"

"What do you mean?"

"About the Den. About me."

"No. I promised I wouldn't say anything about you, remember? And anyway, he never asked."

But he did, she remembered now. Every time they met, he asked about the Den—casually, of course, as though he merely wanted to share her life, but he always asked. The remembrance was sharp and cold as a knife.

"If you saw for yourself," Aggie said, "would you believe it then?"

Sylvie said nothing, and the other went on quietly: "There's a man in town named George Kane, come in a few days ago from Montreal. He's a Marylander, and a diehard Rebel—one of the top men they've got up here. The Grey Tories have been treating him like a king. They gave him a seat at the opening of the legislature, and a big, fancy sleighing party. Sunday night there's a farewell dinner for him at the Halifax Club, before he heads off to Bermuda. I been told it's very exclusive, only for the inner circle. Erryn Shaw is going to be there. You could trade half days with MacKay. She'd be glad to be free when it isn't Sunday for a change, and the shops are open—"

"And what then? I should go down to the Halifax Club and see for myself? It's a men's club; they wouldn't let me in the bloody door. And if they did, and I saw him there, what would it prove? Nothing more than that he socializes with those people. It doesn't prove he works for them."

Aggie muttered something under her breath and got to her feet, throwing her arms up in frustration. "For pity's sake, those aren't just social gatherings! They're . . . they're *meetings*, really. It's where they all share information and make deals and talk strategy. God almighty, girl, that's how your ruling class does it, how they've always done it! They run the world from their banquet tables."

"And your ruling class doesn't?"

Aggie laughed then, just a little. "They try. We make it as hard for them as we can. It's one of the reasons the Southern lordlings don't like us." She shoved the chair close and sat again, facing Sylvie. "Anyway, what are you going to do about this? About your gentleman friend?"

"Talk to him. Ask him. What else can I do?"

"Ask him how, precisely? 'Oh, by the way, the Yankee spy over at the Den says you're working for the Rebels'?"

"No, of course not. I'll just say I heard it."

"From who? He knows what a chambermaid's life is like, Sylvie, he isn't stupid. The only reason he could hide this for so long is because you live like a hermit. You see us, and Madame Mallette, and him—that's all."

"I see the boarders sometimes."

"And they have as much reason to start talking to you about Erryn Shaw as they have for running down the stairs in their underwear. Even if *they* happen to know him, why on earth would they think *you* do?"

Sylvie had no more answers. She knew, even as she offered them, that the few she had found were as feeble as old straw. Now they were gone, and she sat like a mouse in a corner, waiting for the cat.

"He's a good man, Aggie."

"Never said he wasn't. Trouble is, he's their man." The house-maid leaned forward, her eyes like agate, her work-hardened hands like chunks of tree. There was no cruelty in her, Sylvie thought, merely a relentless toughness, of the sort the world kept pretending to find only in men. "I need to know where you stand on this, Sylvie Bowen. And I don't reckon you can know yourself until you're satisfied as to the truth."

———✦———

It was as hard as anything she had ever done, writing the letter, telling Erryn she was sick—nothing serious, just a bad case of grippe, but Miss Susan said she had to stay in bed. She was very sorry; she hoped to see him Friday next. Aggie gave it to one of the boarders, along with a coin and a plea to pass on both to a good, reliable messenger boy.

The day was all but intolerable. It did not get better when, around noontime, Aggie passed her in a hallway and murmured: "Mr. Shaw came by with a basket of fruit for you. I put it on your bed." She ran up to the attic the first chance she had. On the top of the basket, under a bit of tissue wrapping, was a darling cotton pussycat with a striped tail and a bonbon in its paws. Under it, and all around, were more chocolates, and a half-dozen oranges—

fresh off a ship from the Caribbean, no doubt, and probably too costly for words. There was also a note.

> *My dearest Sylvie,*
> *I was devastated to learn that you are unwell, for the truth is, I lived all week for this day. But though I shall miss you terribly, I care only that you should be healthy again, as fast as ever is possible. If you are in any difficulty, or need anything, anything at all, please, please send me word.*
>
> > *Your devoted and adoring*
> > *Erryn Shaw.*

She picked up one of the oranges, stroked it lovingly, wiped away the tears that kept spilling over it. He was so good to her. From the very first, walking into the scrub by the Irish Stone, wanting not to frighten her, he had been always, unfailingly, good to her. As the sun sank away behind the Citadel, she could think of nothing except him, wondering how they would have spent the afternoon, what they would have talked about; wondering if his landlord was still in Yarmouth, if they would have gone to his house, if they would even now be lying on the rug in front of the fire. Their time together was the only beautiful thing she had; how could she have given any of it up?

I have to know. Her mind kept repeating the words, holding on to them as to a post in a storm. She had to know. Only she did not want to know, because her mind also told her that Aggie was worldly and experienced; Aggie probably had a large circle of Union agents around her, agents with all manner of links and ties and ways of knowing who was doing what. If they said Erryn was working for the Rebels, then probably he was.

Still, she had to know, and because of it she did all these things it should have been impossible to do. She lied to the person she loved most in the world. She gave her precious, irreplaceable half day away. She stood Sunday evening in the weak kerosene lamplight of the cellar while Aggie wound a long scarf tightly around her breasts, tied her hair up, and helped her into a pair of Harry Dobbs's trousers and a loose hooded jacket. Last of all, Aggie taped a bandage over her scars and hung her left arm in a sling.

"There," she said, holding up a small mirror. "Just a poor messenger who fell on an icy street."

At any other time, for any other reason, the disguise would have intrigued her; now she found it shabby. She found the entire business shabby. It was acceptable, perhaps even admirable, to spy on one's enemies. It was horrid to spy on one's friends.

<hr />

The Halifax Club was as magnificent as any building in the city, three storeys tall and wonderfully ornate. It reminded her of pictures she had seen in books, of the marvellous palaces in Europe. The club had opened only a year ago, and still had everywhere the look of fresh-cut stone, the scent of fresh-cut wood. It was, of course, a male domain, so utterly a male domain that the porter gave the thin young messenger with the bandaged face and broken arm only the barest, mildly sympathetic glance—unable, Sylvie thought, even to imagine that the messenger might be other than he seemed.

"I have a letter for Mr. Shaw, sir. Erryn Shaw. I was told to bring it here."

A thousand times Sylvie had played this moment over in her mind. She would tell him about her letter—whomever it was she had to tell—and he would frown and shake his head. *I'm sorry, Mr. Shaw is not among our guests tonight.* Or better still: *Erryn Shaw? I'm sorry, I'm not acquainted with the gentleman.*

"Mr. Shaw is at dinner. I will see that he gets this. Are you expecting a reply?"

"Yes. But it's not urgent."

"Very good."

"Sir?"

"Yes?"

"It's frightfully cold out there, sir, and I been walking for hours. Do you have a water closet?"

Almost anywhere this would have been a perfectly reasonable request. Whether it was reasonable here, or shockingly inappropriate, she had no idea. The porter merely nodded and led her down a hallway and around a corner, motioning to a door. She slipped inside, waited until his footsteps had faded away, and slipped out again.

The dining rooms, Aggie had told her, were on the second floor. She crept down the hallway. When the porter was looking elsewhere, she ducked down an adjoining passage to search for a way up. It was easy to find, a magnificent winding staircase that again made her think of palaces. She passed a pair of well-dressed gentlemen, who glanced curiously at her but kept walking. Perhaps they assumed that anyone who made it past the porter had business here of some sort. A liveried servant seemed more curious still, but he also seemed in a frightful hurry, so he kept going too.

The place was truly beautiful. For all that her mind was on hard and troubling things, she could not help but notice. Everything was of fine wood, mahogany perhaps, polished until it shone. The lights were all in graceful cornices.

She came to what was clearly a dining room, with many tables and groups of men, and the wonderful smells of good food wafting out of it. But a moment of scrutiny was enough to tell her it was not the room she was looking for. The guests were scattered, some entirely alone, lingering over a cup of coffee or reading a newspaper. She hurried on, trying doors very gently, finding most of them locked. Then a burst of loud masculine laughter came from the far end of the hall.

She edged the door open just a crack, recognizing the voice even before she saw him. It was Erryn's voice, cultured, powerful, filling the room like an orchestra.

". . . can be no response to this heroic struggle, on the part of the people of British America, except our wholehearted and unconditional support. We share more than our common English heritage, for by now, in this modern world, we share our English heritage with many. But with the men of the South we also share tradition, and a love of tradition. We share a talent for military brilliance—no one, surely, would deny that General Lee is the Wellington of our day. We share a common history. Thousands of our people had their fill of Yankee bullying seventy-five years ago, and they haven't learned to like it any better in the interim—"

Laughter and applause swept round the table. Sylvie stood rigid, staring. Erryn always dressed well, but he was clothed tonight in garments finer than she had ever seen on a man except in photographs; he looked like a prince. The gathering was small, perhaps fifteen men, all richly dressed as well, the table shimmering with crystal and silver. She recognized James Orton, and another who had come to Madame's birthday dinner but whose name she had never learned. The rest were strangers, most of them in their fifties. This was the elite, she thought, just like Aggie said. The inner circle. The leaders of the Grey Tories.

And Erryn was with them.

She crept away and waited for him in the anteroom by the entrance. She thought she would challenge him the moment he appeared. She would say, "I hate you, you lying hypocrite!" and stalk away. But his face filled with concern when he saw her—with astonishment first, for he saw through the disguise in seconds, and then with concern—taking in the bandaged face, the left arm hanging limp in a sling.

"God in heaven, what's happened? Are you hurt?"

"No. I'm perfectly all right." She got to her feet. She could not meet his eyes; she could not bear to see the emotion in them. She swept past him into the hallway and out into the street. The sling went into a tangled knot in her pocket, the bandage with a wrench onto the ground. By then Erryn had caught up with her, still pulling on his coat.

"Sylvie, my heart, what's happened?"

She stopped still and faced him. "What are you doing here, Erryn Shaw?"

"Doing here? Nothing. Having supper. Are you all right, love? Why on earth are you dressed like that?"

"How else would I get into your cozy little Confederate club?"

"Confederate . . ? Sylvie, this is the gentlemen's club—"

"I'm not talking about the bloody house! I'm talking about that pack of Grey Tory plotters you were with. How can you work with those people, Erryn? *How can you?*"

"We were only having supper—"

"No, you weren't! I heard you! I heard you telling them how noble they were and how the whole of British America were on their side. And I've heard other things too, before tonight. That's why I came— because I didn't believe it. I didn't think you could do such things—"

"You were upstairs?" he asked, very soft.

"Yes, I—"

"Let's get a carriage, shall we? For a bit of privacy?"

The club, like the big hotels, usually had two or three coaches waiting for customers around the supper hour. Erryn led her to one of them and helped her inside.

"Morris and Birmingham."

"Very good, sir."

He climbed in, gently pulling the door shut.

"I'm not going home with you," she said.

"I had to tell him something. It doesn't matter. We'll go wherever you wish."

She waited to see if he would speak, if he would explain himself. He said nothing, merely looked at her, his thin face all bones and shadows.

"Well," she said finally, "we have privacy now. What do you have to say for yourself?"

Instead of answering, he had questions of his own. "Are you really all right, Sylvie? You're not sick?"

"No."

"Then won't they be missing you at the Den? I thought you weren't allowed to leave except on your half day."

"I traded my half day."

"I see."

That hurt him, she saw. It hurt him quite a lot, and angry though she was, she could not help but feel sorry.

"And the clothes?" he went on.

"We have a lad working there," she said. "I took some of his." She paused and then leaned forward desperately. It was only fair to tell him, to explain. "I had to know, Erryn. There were a big story in the papers about Mr. Kane, and all the fuss they be making over him, giving him a fancy farewell party. And then I heard a couple of the Southerners in the parlour talking about it, and they mentioned you. That you'd be there, see. That you were . . . well, one of them. And I had to know. So I got Sunday free, and sneaked some of Harry Dobbs's clothes out of the laundry—"

"And put a bandage on your face to hide the scars, and put your arm in a sling to explain the bandage, and got yourself past the porter with some wild story or another." He smiled then—a small, sad smile, but altogether genuine. "My compliments, Miss Bowen. I dare say you've done it well."

"What are you doing with those people, Erryn?"

He ran his hands over his face, slowly, like a man who had no idea what to say. "It's a small city, my love. You can't stay in society and avoid them. Half the men who signed John Tobin's memorial belong to the Halifax Club, you know. They do business with Alexander MacNab. They doff their hats to James Orton on the street. There's no way around it."

"They don't stand up in public and talk about the glorious Confederacy and how we owe it our undying support!"

"No. But preaching to the converted never changed the price of tea, so far as I've ever noticed."

"Are you telling me you didn't mean the things you said?"

"You asked me, back in Montreal, what I thought about the American war. I said I really didn't know. What I should have said is that I think all wars are destructive and stupid. There's right and wrong on both sides, and where you end up is just a matter of where you were born. If my wonderful old great-uncle had been born French, he'd have fought for Napoleon. Would that have made him wicked? Or were we the wicked ones? It was the kings and lords of Europe who wanted the French Revolution crushed. They were scared silly that its ideas might spread, and they might lose their power—"

"That's very clever, Erryn, but if you really believed it, you wouldn't touch the Southern Rebels with a ten-foot pole. You weren't born there. You were born in England, and England is neutral. Anyway, you can say what you like about right and wrong on both sides, but there's a whole lot more wrong on theirs. They broke up a country that didn't need breaking up, just to keep their slaves. They started the bloody shooting. Now they're up here trying to drag us into it too! If you think war is stupid and destructive, why are you helping the people who want to start another one?"

"It'll never come to that. There's a few hotheads who want it, maybe, but most of the men I was with tonight simply think the Confederates are rather like us and they want to cheer them on."

"And what do *you* want, Erryn Shaw?"

He thought for a time before he answered. "I want my life back. I want a theatre, and the work I was born to do. I could go to Montreal or New York and hope somebody would hire me— probably somebody would. But the only home I have left in the world is here. All my friends are here. *You're* here.

"I get work from MacNab from time to time. A shipment goes astray, he sends me to Saint John to find out what happened to it. He wants a good new dealer on the Lakes, he sends me to Montreal to line one up for him. So I make a bit of money. I stay on good terms with the people who'll be my patrons a few years down the road. Sure, a lot of them are Grey Tories, but the fact is, even the hotheads among them aren't going to start anything. They aren't strong enough. And whatever happens in the States is going to happen with or without the participation of one long-legged English troll. So . . ." He shrugged. "So I drink a few toasts to Jeff Davis. It makes the old coves feel good. Ten years from now no one's going to care a fig."

She stared at him, wordless. A part of her almost accepted it. He was not *really* a Confederate supporter. He was not *doing* anything—not anything that would matter much. Attending a few dinners, making a few speeches to men who already believed everything he said. Not especially admirable, but not beyond forgiveness either, in a pitiless world. Just surviving, just riding out the storm.

The best liars, Fran always said, were the ones who told you as much of the truth as they could.

"What else are you doing for them, Erryn?"

"What do you mean?"

"I saw that room," she flung back bitterly. "That weren't just a few old coves having supper. That were men with money to burn, men as own shipping companies and banks and God alone knows what else, all decked out to the nines with a table they'd set for the Queen. So they give you work sometimes? You go off to Saint John to find out what happened to a shipment? That be clerk's duty, Erryn Shaw, and nobody gets asked to dinner by the likes of them for doing clerk's duty! Even a chambermaid knows as much!"

"No," he said, a trifle sharply. "I get invited because I have a pack of relatives who run around in wigs. I'm quite aware of that." He laughed then, one of those small, soft laughs he tossed out sometimes, like a boy who never stayed serious for very long. "I'm very fine company, too, you know. That always helps."

Oh, yes, it helped. It could make his every word seem reasonable. The trouble was, his terribly reasonable words felt . . . they felt *rehearsed*, she thought, as though he had known he would face these questions sooner or later, and carefully made up the best answers he could. Worse still, his answers, good as they were, were not quite good enough.

She knew scarcely anything of the lives of the upper classes— how they behaved among themselves, their social rules, their games, the meaning they might attach to a kindness or a snub—it was all uncharted territory. But she felt she knew a few things about power, things that cut across social lines, and probably across centuries and nationalities too; things that held for the ruffians in the streets of Rochdale and for the silk-clad lords of the mills. The powerful never gave you something for nothing. Favours were passed out in return for favours received or in expectation of favours to come.

What did Erryn Shaw have to offer the princelings of Nova Scotia?

He was gentry, yes; he had the blood. But nothing she had ever seen of his life, nothing he had ever said or done, nothing anyone had ever said about him, suggested in the smallest way that he had usable *connections*. On the contrary, he had gone to considerable trouble to make it clear to her that he did not. *I am as you see me, nothing more.* It surprised her, having just met him, but the Halifax elite had known him for ten years; surely by now they guessed as much themselves. He was well bred, gifted, charming; socially he was one of them; he would be welcome at the young men's drinking parties, at their sleigh rides and concerts and birthday celebrations. But did he have any real power, anything he could offer to those men in the upper room, most of them twice his age, rich enough to buy him and sell him for pocket money? Did he still have influence with some of those relatives in wigs? Everything she knew argued against it. And yes, he could *pretend* to have influence; he could pretend most anything for a while. But he had been cuddled up with the Grey Tories since the fall of '61, Aggie said, more than two years. All that time, living well without his theatre, without a cent of his father's money, dining at the Waverley and invited to the Halifax Club, dressing like a prince, buying her oranges in the dead of winter . . . Long before now, those men in linen and gold watch fobs would have been wanting something back.

There it lay. No matter what he said, no matter how much she wanted to believe him, there it lay. They would be wanting something back. If he was not of real, substantial use to them, then he was just a hanger-on; they would have edged him to the margins long before.

"You helped John Braine to escape, didn't you? Fran is dead because of pirates like him, and you helped the bloody sod go free!"

She had learned young to watch her father's eyes. They were easy to read, muddied sometimes by drink but otherwise naked and open. Erryn's were difficult, the eyes of an actor. But she saw a small flash of dismay, like a flinch from a blow, instantaneous, desperate. *How in God's name does she know?*

"Sylvie! What on earth—"

He stared at her, all bewildered innocence now, but it was too late. She had seen. She felt cold all through.

"You carry messages for them. I suppose you spy, too. Is it just for money, Erryn? Is that all you care about?"

"I don't know what you mean, love. I'm not a spy. I wouldn't know how to be. I just hang about with the lads and pick up a bit of work—"

"*Stop lying!* God almighty, do you take me for an idiot? The whole town knows! You're doing work for the Rebels, real work, the sort they'll pay you for, and I want to know why! How can you do it? You know what they are! How can you?"

In the silence that followed, she realized the coach had stopped. It shifted slightly as the driver swung down and opened the door.

"Your destination, sir."

"Wait a moment, please," Erryn said, pulling it shut again. "Sylvie, I'm not . . ." He met her eyes and looked away. After a breath he began again. "I'm not doing anything that really matters. Wars get settled on battlefields. Most of these men . . . they're dreamers, Sylvie, they—"

"Stop the fancy talk, all right? Just bloody stop. I ain't asking about them. I'm asking about you. Why are you helping them? Is it just the damn money?"

He made a small, defeated gesture. "Does it matter so very much?" he asked softly. "We all get on as best we can. I could work for ten years on the docks and not equal what I've made in two. We can get married, use my father's money to set up a theatre—"

"Do you think I'd marry you now?" she said bitterly.

"I thought you loved me."

"No. I loved a man who never existed. I don't know who you are, Erryn Shaw. I don't know what you are. Tell me, what else would you do to get on as best you can? Keep slaves? Run a cotton mill?"

"No, of course not—"

"Why not? The mill in Rochdale ran on Southern cotton. Somebody's slaves worked themselves into the ground to grow it and we rotted our lungs to spin it and the planters and the mill owners got on as best they could! You helping them now, so's they can keep everything after just the same as before, how's that any different?"

Erryn Shaw could talk the stars right out of their moorings most days, but he had no answer for her now. He looked at her, and at the carriage door, and at his knees; on his face and in his manner was a tangle of emotions she had never seen in him before. For a moment she feared he would rail at her or put his fist through the wall, but instead, when he looked up, there was in his eyes an intense, astonishing tenderness.

"What do you want to do?" he asked.

"Do?"

"Now. Will you come in? The house is empty, but if you wished, we need do nothing more than have a cup of tea. I would be honoured."

She almost said yes. In spite of everything, she almost said yes, for the sake of the warmth in his eyes, for the wish to run her hands across his dear bony face just one last time.

"No."

"Have you had supper? We could go to Corey's if you like."

"I want to go back to the Den."

———•×•———

It felt like the slowest journey she had ever taken, and the quickest. Twice Erryn made a feeble attempt at conversation and fell silent again when she did not answer him. She had feared so many endings to their friendship, but never this one—this melting away of the man's identity into something she could not recognize and did not understand. She thought he would fail her in the predictable ways: he would grow bored, or choose another, more desirable woman. She never imagined that she would be the one to walk away.

After a time she watched only the street. It was late. All along Barrington the stores and warehouses and factories were dark, their stone and timber storefronts a long wall of silence. A few carriages passed them, a few men on foot. Now and again a fine, fancy house showed lighted windows. Finally, on her left, there was nothing at all, just the empty Grand Parade, where the soldiers drilled and their bands came to play on Sunday afternoon. The Den was just beyond, its bright-lit windows the only cheer it held.

She felt tears rising, and fought them. She would cry herself half to death, but not now, dear God, not now. She puttered with her gloves as the carriage pulled to a slow, gentle stop.

"Sylvie," Erryn said quietly, "I know nothing I can say just now will make any difference, but I'm sorry I've disappointed you. I'm sorrier than I can possibly say."

"I'm sure you are." She was, she discovered, past anger, past everything except despair. "Thank you for the fruit. It was kind of you to send it."

He smiled faintly. "It was my pleasure." He paused, as if searching for words. "Sylvie, I . . ."

"Don't," she said. "There is nothing to say. I want to go in. Please."

He nodded. "Friday, then? It's still your half day?"

"I'm not walking out with you anymore, Erryn."

"You're not . . ? Sylvie, you can't mean that!"

She said nothing. She rapped on the roof for the driver to open the door.

"Sylvie, please! Don't just . . . don't just walk away! I love you! I'll find a way to make things right—"

"You can't make it right. Everything you showed me of yourself was a lie—everything that matters—what you're doing with your life, what you believe in, what you care about. How can you possibly make it right?"

"I never lied about loving you. And the rest—the rest I only lied about so you wouldn't hate me."

She rose as the door opened, took the driver's offered hand, and stepped down. Erryn followed, silent. He opened the big iron gate of the Den and walked with her to the servants' entrance at the back. She paused with her hand on the door and turned.

"You were good company, Erryn Shaw, and I thank you for it— for all the good times you showed me, and your kindness. You made me happy, and I'll never say different to no one." One last deep breath, a tiny bit more courage . . . "Goodbye, then."

"Good night, my heart. I'm not going to say goodbye."

The door opened, closed. The hallway was dim. Voices came from the parlour above, from the kitchen below, the soft voices of late evening. She scurried into the cellar and stripped to her under-things. She fetched her dress from the laundry bin, flung Harry Dobbs's trousers back in, clothed herself again, and shook down her hair. The masquerade was over.

All the masquerades were over . . .

I could have let it be. I could have told Aggie I didn't believe her and just let it be.

She sat on a wooden bin and wrapped her arms around her knees. All around her, the cellar stank of coal, a harsh smell that stuck in the throat like dust. Coal dust killed men in the mines; cotton dust killed them in the mills. Or machinery did. Or something else. Nobody cared. We're all cattle, her father said to her once, reeling on his wooden chair with his bottle in his hand. Just bloody God damn cattle. Something had broken that day in the mill, he said. There was a boy underneath when it broke, screaming for help, but the foreman refused to shut the machine down. It would waste too much time, starting it up again.

There were so many ways to grind people up, and they were all different—and they were all, in one way, alike. Someone who had the power to do things differently chose not to care.

How, then, could she forgive Erryn Shaw for not caring? For having so many gifts, so many advantages, for knowing everything he knew about the world, and then not caring? A good and decent Southerner might fight for his home and friends, regardless of the cause; a sheltered English lordling might be dumb enough to believe the cause was just. Either one she might have gone on lov-ing. But Erryn was neither, and he knew what was at stake. He could not have lived the life he lived, and said the things he said, without knowing. And he did not care. The Rebels paid him well for his service, so he chose not to care.

There was the barrier she would never cross. To be mistaken was forgivable. But to simply smile and shrug it all aside, to expect it all to come out in the divine wash, ten years down the road it wouldn't matter a fig . . . no, that was beyond forgiveness. That was a man without a soul.

That night, for the first time in months, she heard Sanders snoring in the room across the hall; she heard every late carriage that clattered down Barrington. Earlier, arguing with Aggie Breault, she had thought about practical things, facts and arguments and her own experiences. Now it was hard to think of anything except Erryn himself, the man who laughed and played music and lay with her, the man whose love she wanted almost as much as life itself. Whose love, perhaps, she might have had . . .

She cried softly for hours, so softly that little Annie MacKay never woke, huddled close though she was for warmth. Long after midnight, the sea wind came at last and whispered her to sleep.

———◆———

The next day was all but intolerable. Never had the buckets she carried seemed so heavy, the chamber pots so rank, the disorder in the rooms so tiresome and so eternal. To be a chambermaid, she thought, was to be the worst sort of drudge. Even a scullion could see food at the end of her labours, good things to eat born of the endless scrubbing and peeling. All Sylvie could see was the guests coming back and soiling everything again. At one point, kneeling at the top of the stair, she wrung out her scrub rag and turned to look down. She wondered what it would feel like to toss it all, to watch the water splashing over the furniture and hear the pail going thumpety-thump down the staircase. She had had similar thoughts in the mill sometimes, pictured the great rattling monster crashing to a stop with wrenches and two-by-fours rammed into its guts.

People with nothing lived on hope. They lived for the small things that waited beyond the present—a child's laughter, a gathering with friends, a ship to America. They survived the intolerable because there was something to survive it for. She imagined, just for a moment, year upon year spent scrubbing the Den, shut in almost as a prisoner, as even the mill girls were not—better off, oh yes, much better off, well fed and no cotton dust to breathe, likely to live to a hundred, scrubbing stairways, cleaning grates, remembering that once, for a small while, she had tasted love and would never taste it again. Each of her hopes, so few as they were, either met or annihilated, and nothing to replace them. She understood now, in a way she never had before, why Annie MacKay went through the days like a frightened mouse, why her own father surrendered to drink. To go on, you needed hope. What happened when you no longer had any?

———◈———

The days bled one into the other. Aggie tried to talk to her, to cheer her; she listened politely and said nothing back. Outside, in the streets, everything was mud; inside, everything was damp and cold and the work was endless. When the first bit of grippe came on, she paid little attention. On a bleak Saturday morning a few days later, Aggie dragged her from the ice house, burning with fever and coughing as though she would die.

She was aware of very little that came after: mouthfuls of soup and bread; a man's voice, harsh and tired, talking about her as though she were not there; someone crying out in the hallway, MacKay perhaps, nobody else had that soft, scared little whimper; Aggie Breault's strong hands wiping her face, straightening the covers, lifting her when she needed to use the pot. All the time, when she was conscious enough to want anything at all, she wanted Erryn. But he never came.

———◆———

CHAPTER 26

Separation

O what to her shall be the end?
And what to me remains of good?
To her, perpetual maidenhood,
And unto me no second friend.
—*Alfred Tennyson*

MARCH WAS HALF GONE, but the nights still came early. Outside, for endless miles in all directions, there was only forest—snow to a man's knees, and bare trees, and silence. Perhaps a few wolves. Inside the stagecoach depot, dim kerosene lamps barely held back the darkness, and the fire burned sputtery and pale. Erryn glanced once around the room and sighed. Weeks before, at a candle-lit table in the Waverley Hotel, he had wished for a chance to spend some time with Maury Janes. He had proof now, if he ever needed it, that a man should be bloody damned careful what he wished for.

The depot called itself Miller's Inn, but it had no chambers to let, or even beds. Most of it was a long wood-frame house belonging to a family presumably named Miller. At the front, for the use of the stage passengers, was a large, drafty room, rather

like an ill-kept mess hall in a frontier fortress, its windows
rattling in every gust of wind. The room had a fireplace, a table
where the passengers could eat, and some pallets they could
spread out on the floor. Millers of both sexes and various ages
appeared from time to time through a back door, to sell drinks
and eventually supper. They were always friendly and polite. It
was, Erryn thought, the only good thing to be said about the
place.

He picked at his supper. The food was stale, and in any case he
had no interest in it; his mind and his heart were elsewhere.

Across from him, Maury Janes lifted a last forkful of stew
halfway to his mouth and glared at it. "What d'you figure they
made this out of, anyway? Skunk?"

"No," Erryn said. "Skunk is meat. If there ever was any meat in
that pot, it jumped out and ran home at least a week ago."

"Ha." Janes put the offending mess in his mouth, wiped off his
plate with a piece of bread, and gobbled it down too. The man
could eat anything. He could sleep anywhere. He was one of the
few Southerners Erryn had ever met who seemed indifferent to
northern cold. If he had any weaknesses at all, Erryn had yet to
discover them. Even his tendency to talk too much proved harmless, for he never talked about his work. He talked about his boyhood. He talked about the things he disliked in the world, and
how to fix them. But more than anything, Janes talked about
women, including the young Miller who came to fetch away the
plates when their meal was ended.

"Made just like a willow, ain't she?" he remarked. He watched
her brazenly until she disappeared through the door. "Damned if
she don't remind me of that chambermaid we got back at the
boarding house in Halifax. She'd be a real tasty morsel too, except
she's got the most godawful scars down one side of her face. Top
to bottom, like this." He ran his fingers over his cheek as he spoke.
"I seen sailors cut up like that, but never a girl. She must've got
herself in one hell of a cat fight."

Erryn took a long sip of brandy and put the glass carefully down. The man would dare, by God? She tended his fire and packed away his filth, and he would make sport of her? He of all the maggots in the world?

Erryn would not say it; he must not. But neither could he let the matter be.

"I always thought the Danners ran a respectable place," he said with all the amiability he could manage.

"Oh, I'm sure they do. I've never had a thing to say against the Danners."

"But you can't possibly keep a respectable place without respectable servants. I'd rather think the poor lass must have been in some kind of accident, wouldn't you?"

Janes stared at him for a moment as if puzzled, and then he shrugged. "Might be," he said. "I don't see as how it makes any difference." He glanced briefly down the table, where one of the other passengers had taken out a deck of cards. "You're an odd fellow, Shaw. I keep trying to figure you, and I can't."

Erryn did not like the sound of this at all, but Janes went on, "Sometimes you seem like an ordinary fellow—a lot like me, actually, down to earth and all, with your head on straight. And then, for no damn reason I can see, you turn all . . ." He made a wide gesture in the air. "I don't know, all full of . . . *notions*. All proper, like the sort what think truffle ain't truffle if you don't eat it with the right spoon."

"Surely not that bad," Erryn said. He managed a watery smile.

"No. Not quite that bad. Orton tells me you come from a real fine family in England, and went to college and all. That true?"

"It's true."

"And then you ran the theatre in Halifax, till it burned down?"

"That's right."

"Why'd you want to do a thing like that?"

A talent for the theatre, and all it might imply, was the last thing in the world Erryn wanted to discuss with a Rebel agent.

"Well," he said, "do you know a better way to meet pretty actresses?"

"Can't say as I do." Janes laughed a bit and leaned back in his chair—satisfied, apparently, at least for the moment. An appetite for women was something he understood.

After more than a fortnight travelling with the man, Erryn could still not decide if Janes was the most skilful professional operative he had ever met, or simply an adventurer who had spent his whole life playing for the main chance and was now extremely good at it. What Erryn did believe by this point was that Janes had about him nothing of the actor. Everything he seemed to be, he was—coarse, ambitious, highly intelligent, cold. A man who would talk cheerfully to anyone who crossed his path and afterwards, never mention them again. A man who scarcely seemed to live in his body, who never cared what he ate or where he slept or how long the road was. A man who resented bitterly his lack of social place, not because of the pleasures and opportunities he had lost, but because others were able to look down on him. And therefore, more than anything else, a man who meant to rise in the world, so he might look down on others in his turn. This he showed without pretence, as he showed his frank approval of slavery. Cream just naturally rose to the top, he said. The folks who were running things were mostly the ones who knew how, who were best at it. And sure, once in a while some worthless scalawag made it in. Hell, just look at Abe Lincoln. But Lincoln would never have made it on his own; he found himself a pack of riff-raff to hold him up, folks who thought they could climb by tearing other people down.

Mile by mile, Janes had explained America to Erryn, two days back when they had the coach to themselves for a time. He explained the North and the South, freedom, slavery, all of it. Abolition was not about freedom, he said; abolition was about tearing other people down.

"Getting freedom's like . . . like getting young ones: when the critter's growed up enough, it simply does it. Like those countries in Europe, kicking out the Turks and the Russians one by one. They had to be ready first. Now some folks figure the niggers will be ready for freedom someday, couple of hundred years maybe, but I don't think so. I think they'll always be slaves."

"Always?" Erryn said. "That's pretty grim."

"Not really. You like books and such things, don't you? And the opera? Well, the way I see it, you can't have those things less'n you have a class of men with nothing else to do. Your friend Shakespeare didn't write his plays grubbing in a cottonfield, now, did he?"

"Indeed not."

"So look at history, Shaw. Where did all the great cultures come from, all those famous writers and philosophers? They came from slave states—Greece, Rome, the aristocracies of Europe. The Europeans called them serfs, and couldn't sell them, but they were slaves just the same. The world is like . . . it's like those old cathedrals, you might say. You can't build yourself a cathedral without putting a lot of stone face down in the mud. There'll be high and low in the world, or there'll be nothing but low. Nothing but savagery and stupidity."

Erryn had heard this argument before, of course: slavery made possible a cultured elite, from whose ranks would come the finest thinkers and artists, just as in the past. But those who argued it never told him which idle slave owner painted the Sistine Chapel, or wrote the Unfinished Symphony, or observed how the earth moved around the sun. They never explained why Mozart was dead at thirty-one, thrown in a common grave and covered over with lime.

Nor did anyone ever explain why so little art was coming from the slaveholding South. The region certainly did not lack for brilliance. For decades it had provided the nation with talented statesmen, lawyers, and military leaders. Its people designed magnificent homes and public buildings, and made food to tempt most any Englishman into never going home again. But where was the literature, the painting, the music? Why did their brilliance and creativity stop so sharply, so abruptly, at the boundary of the imaginative arts?

Was it perhaps *because* those arts were imaginative, because the imagination never abided walls? It wanted to experience everything, to answer the whys and hows and what-ifs of all eternity. Why did this happen? What does it mean? What would it feel like?

What would it feel like to be a slave?

The Great Wall of Dixie, right there in a single question, solid stone and a hundred feet high. Picture it, he thought: the blossoming artist and the question. Maybe a friend throws it at him, or the rain at midnight, or the sound of someone crying, but the question is there and his imagination must answer it. What is it like to be a slave? To own nothing, not even the rough shack you sleep in or the shapeless clothes on your back? To be sure of nothing, not your food or your safety or your dearest affections? What is it like to be flogged for a trifle and never call it cruelty, to be used as a whore and never call it rape? What is it like to hoe and scrub and mend and carry, hour upon hour, day upon day, nothing else, no books, no symphonies, no theatre, just work, till your eyes are ruined from the sun or your joints from the cold, till your back cannot straighten and your hands fumble when they pick up a piece of bread? To know there is no end to it, and no escape, not for you, not for your children, ever?

To imagine these things, and then to give them form—to paint them or write them or set them to music—would tear the institution of slavery apart. To imagine these things and not to give them form would tear the artist apart.

For the young Southerners were not Greeks or Romans, or even children of the Renaissance. They did not have the world view of the medieval Church, which made it Christlike to be downtrodden and oppressed. They did not have the paradigms of pagan Fortuna, reminding them how a lord might become a slave, or a slave a free man, in the turning of a single battle. Aeschylus could weep for Hecuba in chains; she might easily have been himself.

Now the world was different, no longer a world of virtuous suffering or arbitrary fortune, but one where men governed themselves under the authority of a just God in heaven, where life, liberty, and the pursuit of happiness were inscribed as inalienable rights. In such a world slavery was unthinkable, unless the slaves were slaves by nature—no tragic queens, no conquered children of Israel, no possible other self, no there-but-for-the-grace-of-God-go-I, but rather someone, or indeed almost some*thing*, utterly different from oneself.

At which point, of course, one could stop wondering what it might be like to be a slave, since for oneself the question had become meaningless. Unfortunately, for a youthful searching mind, a whole other set of questions came into play. If the slaves are base and alien, what makes them so? If it is merely the fact of slavery itself, then how can we possibly condone it? If it is race, then what is the difference between a free black and a slave, except an arbitrary piece of paper? How is it that free blacks can prosper, and even acquire slaves of their own? If it is race, what happens when you mix them? What does it mean when we cannot even tell? And if they are so different from ourselves, why do we trust them with our children and our sick? Why do we lay down with them?

No, Erryn thought, the contradictions of democratic slavery simply ran too deep, were too unmanageable. He ached to his bones to point this out to Maury Janes, sitting in the stagecoach mile by mile, listening to the man blather on. Instead, he merely smiled and pretended to be impressed.

Now he had to do the same wearisome thing at Miller's Inn. Mercifully, the other passengers were gathering for a card game and noticed Janes eyeing them hopefully.

"Care to join us, gentlemen?"

"That's real obliging of you," Janes said, getting to his feet. "How about you, Shaw?"

"Thanks, but no. Not tonight."

The one luxury in the depot was a large hearth. Erryn pulled a chair up close to it and fetched a book from his portmanteau. After ten minutes or so he put it back, just as he had the night before and the night before that. He wished he had brought his flute, even though he knew why he had left it behind: he was too desolate to play it without weeping. For a time, indifferently, he watched his fellows at the table. The logic of poker interested him well enough; the spirit of gambling did not. He understood playing to win—playing *anything* to win—but wagering money seemed completely beside the point. All of his peers did it, of course. It was a badge of aristocratic manliness, like downing absurd amounts of spirits and fighting over trifles. Risk lay at the heart of it, he supposed; risk practised as a way of life, as a pretended readiness for war.

And he himself, now, so wise and so worldly—was he any less a gambler, or any less a fool?

You've lost her, Erryn Shaw. You wagered something far more precious than money. You wagered the only woman who ever loved you, and you lost.

In every moment of quiet he found himself thinking about all that he had lost. He turned his memories of her over in his mind as he might have turned the pages of a book, lingering now on this one, now on another. The way she laughed sometimes, so precious, at small, unexpected things. The way she kissed him in the rain. The way she sat by the Irish Stone and talked about the mills, and the dream of a New World that died on the *Osprey*. But two memories, more than all the others, haunted him: a steamer cabin in the dead of an October night, the ice of death already in his blood, and Sylvie wrapped soft against him, sheltering him in her warmth and in her voice. *I'm here, Erryn, I won't leave you.* That night she gave him back his life. And in Gideon Winslow's house she gave him meaning for his life, a centre it never had before. Every moment of their mating was alive in his mind—her long hair lying spilled on the quilt, shimmering in the firelight; her thin body in its plain woollen dress, smooth as a gazelle's, discovered one whisper at a time, one tiny button. She had been so uncertain, lying with him, and yet so eager. He had been utterly undone by her eagerness, and by her eyes after, when she gazed at him and stroked him softly, all over, as if he were the finest and most precious thing she had ever touched.

Now she was gone.

At first he had refused to believe it. They had quarrelled, yes. She was angry at him, and said she would not see him anymore, but people said such things in anger all the time. He sent a letter to her at the Den, as tender and apologetic a letter as he knew how to write. The following Friday he waited for her outside, thinking to walk with her to Madame Mallette's house. Maybe she would still be angry. Maybe she would refuse to go to dinner with him, or anywhere else. But they would talk; they would take the first cautious steps back to friendship.

She wanted nothing to do with him. She walked like a pillar, rigid and silent. When he fell in step beside her and tried to speak, she wheeled and faced him. "You are cruel, Erryn. There is nothing to talk about. For God's sake let me be!" And so, reluctantly, he did. He told himself the very ferocity of her rejection was proof she loved him deeply, but there was no comfort in the thought, rather the reverse; rather a reminder of how much he had wagered and lost.

I should have told her the truth.

Always he came back to the same conclusion: he should have told her he was working for the Crown. But every argument of common sense and policy stood against it. Secret operations were by definition secret; therein lay their whole reason for existing. Matt had been adamant when on one occasion Erryn had suggested confiding in a mutual friend, a strong Union backer who was bitterly disappointed in him. No, Matt had told him. Don't tell anyone. Absolutely not. Never.

People let things slip, Matt said. Of course, they didn't mean to, it just happened; often it was some little thing they didn't even notice. But whatever they let slip, it was sure to be passed on. Secrets were like water: once they were out of the jar, there was no telling where they would run, so the only thing to do was keep the damn jar shut. Besides, he added, if the staunch Unionists in town were disappointed in Erryn Shaw, all the better for his image as a good Grey Tory.

Erryn might have told her anyway, despite Matt's warning. But his brush with death had shaken him—and reminded him, insofar as he needed reminding, that neutral soil was no protection for a spy. Whatever niceties were observed by day, in the shadows enemies were merely enemies; murder cared not a fig for citizenship. He did not want to end in a waterfront alley with a bullet in his back.

He also did not want to fail in the work he had taken on. That was part of it too, that old hard kernel of duty drilled into him from boyhood. He wore no uniform and carried no sword, but the piece of paper hidden in his shoe was still a commission. It bound him to serve as faithfully as any of the warriors he once hung on his bedroom wall.

So he kept his secrets, and lied to Sylvie Bowen, and watched her stalk away, ignoring the small voice inside him that wailed, *No! Come back! It isn't like that!* Then Al MacNab sought him out, all unexpectedly: "Listen, lad, we've got a wee problem come up in Woodstock. Janes said he can handle it, but we need a man to go with him, and right now there's no one else. Any chance you could help us out?" Erryn nodded, the same voice protesting bitterly, *Now? It's not possible. I can't go anywhere NOW! I need to win her back!*

But he went. And sat tonight in a makeshift inn on a dreary road in the midst of godforsaken nowhere, terrified that she would be lost forever when he got back.

One by one the passengers lifted pallets from the pile and laid them out near the hearth, curling up in their coats or in the scruffy blankets offered by the station keeper. Erryn lay awake for a long time, listening to the quiet sounds of the house, to Maury Janes's peaceful snoring. Deliberately, to keep his mind off his own misery, he went over recent events, and all that he knew and did not know about his companion. When they first met in Montreal, the Carolinian had said he needed someone to do a job for him, a delivery across the border. He never hinted as to what would be delivered or where it was coming from, except that it would come by ship. Later, at the Waverley, he assured Erryn that Al MacNab had taken care of everything. *He told me to come by Monday morning and he'd get me all set up, and damned if he wasn't as good as his word.*

That was weeks ago, and nothing had happened since. Once, Janes had grumbled bitterly but vaguely about delays, about God damned foreigners who could not be depended on (present company excepted, of course). Clearly, the mission had encountered some sort of snag. Janes was entirely willing to go to Woodstock, though the trip would take a fortnight even in good weather. And he should not go alone, MacNab insisted to Erryn. No one should—not with some twenty thousand dollars in captured army payroll waiting to be carried back.

"Some irregulars took it off the Yankees in Kentucky," MacNab told him. "Canada was a whole lot closer than the Southern coast, so they sent three men to take it through to Halifax. They came all this way, it seems, and then one of them turned on his mates."

"For the money?" Erryn asked.

"Probably. It's not entirely clear. What is clear is that there's only one left, and he'll not be travelling any time soon."

That was an understatement, Erryn thought, remembering the young Rebel they found in Woodstock, thin as a stick and pale as the sheets he lay on. He had walked some fifteen or twenty miles in the dead of winter, wounded. They'd had a sled, he explained, but the horse got spooked in the fight and ran away. So he walked all that long way. The doctor had to cut his foot off, and three of his right fingers. But he had the money. He looked eaten up with pain and fever, but very proud: he had kept every dollar safe. He was, Erryn thought, not a day past seventeen.

"You'll get it out, won't you?" he had pleaded. "They need it so bad."

The money was in a carpet bag now, sitting innocently on the floor by the shoulder of Maury Janes. No doubt Janes would get it out; Erryn saw no way to prevent it, short of betraying himself or murdering the miserable sod.

Then again, if the gods were kind, Janes might decide to steal it. The Rebel agent coveted an independent fortune. Maybe he would take this one, buy himself a fancy house, and set himself up as the gentleman he longed to be. And Erryn Shaw would not have to worry about him anymore.

Right, he told himself. *And maybe pigs will fly.*

CHAPTER 27

———◆———

The Return

Is it indeed so? If I lay here dead,
Wouldst thou miss any life in losing mine?
—*Elizabeth Barrett Browning*

HALIFAX LAY draped in fog. The stage from Windsor, due in the mid-afternoon, did not arrive until after supper—late enough that chores at the Den might be over, and early enough that a visitor might still call. Erryn knew it was foolish simply to go there unannounced, but knowing made no difference; he had to try. He had been away for weeks. Maybe she was not angry anymore. Maybe she had missed him enough to want to see him in spite of everything. Maybe, maybe, maybe.

Mrs. Breault greeted him at the door. When he had called at the Den back in February, to bring a fruit basket for Sylvie when he thought she was ill, the housemaid had been polite but not particularly friendly. She was even less friendly now. She opened the door only a small bit and gave no sign that she might invite him in.

"Good evening, Mr. Shaw."

"Good evening, ma'am. I wonder if I might have a brief visit with Miss Bowen this evening. I'm quite willing to wait if she's still at work."

"I'm sorry, sir. Miss Bowen does not wish to see you. I believe she's told you as much herself."

"She did, ma'am, but that was some time ago—"

"Nothing has changed, Mr. Shaw. She's made it quite plain. She won't meet with you, and we're not to take letters from you, either. Frankly, I'm surprised you'd come to this house and expect to be received."

"I do not . . . *expect*, Mrs. Breault. I merely ask. Please, will you at least tell her that I'm here?"

"I'm sorry, but no. It would only distress her."

"Mrs. Breault, please—"

"Good evening, Mr. Shaw." Gently but decisively, she closed the door in his face.

He did not take a carriage home to Gideon Winslow's house. He walked, brooding and bitter. For the first time since they had met, he felt anger toward Sylvie, mostly at the thought of what must have passed between her and Aggie Breault, at the way they might have talked about him. *I never want to see the miserable sod again! I don't want his letters! I don't want anything of his! If he ever comes near me, throw him out!*

But by the time he reached home, his anger, never very strong, was mostly spent. It was the housemaid's duty to deal with callers, to receive the welcome and send away the inopportune. Even the Danners had to confide in her to that extent. A poor chambermaid who wished to be left alone could hardly do otherwise. Besides, she had told him Aggie Breault was her friend.

Her only friend, now.

He lay awake for a long time, staring at the darkness. He wondered what options he might have left, and discovered none. He could appeal to Mrs. Danner, but anything he said would only be his word. She did not know him personally; she had no reason to be confident that his heart was generous or his intentions pure. What kind of creature would she be if she overruled the wishes of a defenceless servant girl and allowed a rejected suitor to pursue her in her own home?

No, he told himself, Sylvie was gone. He should just accept it. They were terribly ill matched, after all. And perhaps she had never loved him very much. Perhaps the ferocity of her rejection was not grief, as he had imagined, but self-contempt, anger at herself for being seduced, for being deluded by the charms of a lying aristocrat, when she, if anyone, should have known better. *Let it go, Erryn Shaw. It was a mistake from the beginning.*

And if it was such a bad mistake, then why were we always so happy?

Maybe the housemaid had lied.

He did not think so, not really, but it was a possibility. Aggie Breault was a Northerner, a staunch Unionist, one of several Matt suspected of passing information, at least occasionally, to consular officials or to agents such as Jabin Romney. If this were the case, then a link between Sylvie and a known Confederate like Erryn Shaw would seem to her not merely objectionable, but dangerous.

So maybe she lied. Maybe Sylvie *had* changed her mind, at least a little bit; maybe she was willing to see him. Maybe, come Friday, she would let him walk with her again. Maybe they could find a bit of ground to stand on till the war was over. Till he could tell her the truth.

It was a lean hope, small and skinny as a wing bone from a sparrow, but it was all he had.

Friday did not come for a very long time. The hours went on for days, and the days for decades. When Friday finally dawned, he was, for a while, absurdly happy. Sylvie usually left the Den around two. Just before one he arrived at Boone's Tavern, about half a block down Barrington, where he got himself a small glass of beer and a table by the window. Now and then a male guest strolled away from the boarding house; now and then a delivery wagon pulled up at the service entrance. Two o'clock came and passed, then three. He told himself there must be some reasonable explanation, and waited. It quietly turned four, but Sylvie did not appear.

At five he went into the street. He could no longer delude himself: she was not coming out. Perhaps she had guessed what he meant to do and traded her half day for another. Or else she had simply stayed inside, spending the afternoon curled up with a book.

He stared at the Den's graceless facade, at the tiny lower windows that allowed scraps of light into the basement kitchen where the servants passed their free time. Sunlight burned warm on his sleeves and spilled like water through the streets. White gulls wheeled above the harbour, shimmering. On the Common, he knew, the first early flowers played. It was an exceptional spring day, the sort they rarely saw even in April. Nothing on earth would keep Sylvie Bowen shut inside on a day like this . . . nothing, perhaps, except himself.

Dear God, he thought, if she was so weary of him, so bitter, then in truth it was over. Then he had no hope at all.

Maybe it's something else entirely. Maybe it's just a case of the grippe.

He considered this quietly, because he knew he should, but the thought had no more power to persuade. If it was not over between them already, it would be soon. Not merely the evidence convinced him, but also something inside himself, a darkness, a sense of closing finality. This was not a separation he was going to repair.

You can still tell her the truth.

And he might have done it right then. He might have marched into the Den and made whatever outrageous demands he had to make to see her . . . only what if it was already too late? What if she handed his little piece of paper back to him, her eyes bitter and empty, and asked him: "Why now, Erryn Shaw? Why are you showing me this *now*?"

He took a carriage home. He would have preferred to walk, but he had no wish to meet or speak with anyone he knew. He offered a mumbled greeting to Gideon Winslow and fled to his room. He barely stirred from it the next day, pleading illness. By Sunday noontime he was hungry—no less unhappy, but very hungry— and wonderful smells of roasting chicken were drifting through the house. Gideon had probably cooked the bird to tempt him— he was a sly old cove, that one—but Erryn knew it was only decent of him to come out and eat it.

They were lingering over tea when the old man asked very casually, "Is there anything I can do for you, lad?"

"Do? No, not at all. Why?"

"Erryn, I may not be the smartest man God ever made, nor the most worldly, but even I can recognize a broken heart when it's sitting at my dinner table. You're grieving hard over something, lad. If there's aught I can do for you, I will."

"Thanks, Gideon, but no. I am troubled, I won't deny it. But it's all my own fault, and there's nothing anyone can do."

They might have said more on the matter, but they could hear steps coming up the walk and then a rapping at the door. It would be some flaming Grey Tory, no doubt, and right now he wished every last one of them packed off to Greenland and left on the ice.

If it's for me, I don't want to see them. The words formed in his mind, but he said nothing. When the bastards wanted him, he would come out. And God help them when he did.

Gideon came back with Jack Murray at his side.

"Erryn, how are you? MacNab says you've been back for days. Have you been sick?"

"Under the weather a bit. Nothing serious. Good to see you."

They shook hands, and Gideon said cheerfully, "Sit down, lad, sit down. Have some chicken."

Jack said he had eaten, but he accepted a glass of wine. He exchanged a few pleasantries with his host and then turned to Erryn.

"I've got Ames and the coach outside, Erryn. We're off to the yacht club—thought maybe you'd like to come along. Collier's got himself a fancy new skiff he wants to try, and there's a party at his uncle's place after. Most of the lads'll be there."

"I'd like that," Erryn said. "Thanks." Perhaps it would help, he thought, a bit of sailing, wind and water and not too much on his mind for a while.

But they had hardly settled into the Murray family's classy carriage when Jack said quietly, "Have you been over to the Den since you got back?"

Erryn shot him a quick, hard glance, but Jack's face was serious and thoughtful. He was not, it seemed, making any sort of sport.

"No, why?"

"Well, I thought . . . when we talked before, I thought you seemed rather fond of the lass there . . . Miss Bowen . . . and seeing you haven't been out at all since you got back, I wondered if you'd heard."

"Heard what?" It was appalling how many dark things could flash through a man's mind in the fragment of time between a question and its answering. She had sailed for parts unknown. She was marrying another. She was dead.

Please God, no . . .

"She's been sick," Jack said. "I mean, really sick—close to dying, I guess. Will Danner says her lungs are wrecked from the mills. I don't think he'd have mentioned it, except now his brother might be needing a new chambermaid. It's the worst time of the year, of course, with all the country folk going back to their farms, so he's been asking all of us, don't we know anybody, can't we help? That's how I found out."

There were a thousand sounds coming through the open windows, dogs and children playing, carriage wheels and hooves, a quickening wind. It was, nonetheless, as silent as a grave.

"You didn't know, did you?" Jack murmured.

"No."

"I'm sorry, mate. I thought . . . I thought you'd prefer to hear it from me rather than over a punch bowl."

"Yes. Thank you."

"Is there anything I can do?"

"Yes. Drop me at South Park Road. I won't . . . I can't come with you to the club. I'm sorry."

"I didn't think you would. South Park it is, then. And by the way, if there's anything we can do for you, just ask. Christ knows my father and I are scrapping all the time now, over the war, but if I told him there was a poor lass without family needing help, he'd be the first man out the door."

"Yes, I know. And you'd be right behind him. Thank you."

——◆◆◆——

He saw nothing of what he passed, walking to the house on South Park Road. He knew what he would do, and beyond that he thought of nothing except Sylvie and what Jack had said of her. *She's been sick . . . close to dying, I guess . . . her lungs are wrecked from the mills . . .*

Back in England, through all their years of friendship, he had never feared for Cuyler. He knew the world was filled with peril, but he had been too young, too sheltered, too damn fool cocky to fear for Cuyler. They were best mates, smart, talented, ambitious; the whole world was their oyster. He would stage the plays and Cuyler would play the leading roles. They would take London by storm.

Instead, a rain-soaked grave and a brigantine to Canada.

And now here, with all of that behind him, he had not feared for Sylvie either. Even when his own instincts warned him of a terrible finality, a separation he would not repair, he had not feared for her—oh, no, he had been far too busy fearing for himself, his sad exile's life, his poor broken heart, poor, poor Erryn. And all the while, dear God, she had been lying on a fever bed, coughing her life out, alone.

CHAPTER 28

The Letter

What I do
And what I dream include thee, as the wine
Must taste of its own grapes. And when I sue
God for myself, He hears that name of thine,
And sees within my eyes the tears of two.
—*Elizabeth Barrett Browning*

THE FIRST THING Sylvie noticed when she wakened properly was bright daylight; the second was the soft, cuddly warmth of her bed. It took a moment to realize where she was—not in the attic, but in the sickroom on the first floor, just next to the family quarters. It was a small room, but wonderfully pleasant. It had gay wallpaper flecked with orchids, and a hearth and a window—not the tiny, dormered mouse hole they had in the attic, but a real window, with real sunshine spilling in, catching flecks of dust in a beam beside her bed, and lying in a small bright, puddle on the floor.

I'm still alive, she thought in wonder, and promptly fell asleep again.

A whole week went by in the bright little room. The fever diminished, but the cough remained, deep and harsh. Her strength crept back by inches, by halves of inches; and sometimes, when the coughing grew worse, it crept away again. Aggie brought her food and looked after her needs, and offered sometimes to read to her. No matter what Aggie read, it always made her sad.

"The doctor thinks I'm going to die, don't he?" she asked once.

"He thought you would, before," Aggie said. "Now he isn't saying what he thinks."

"I had a friend in Darwen, first good friend I ever had. She got sick from the mill. She were sick all winter. Sundays I'd go to see her when I could. She were so weak and skinny—always lying on her little cot, she was. First of May she died."

"You aren't going to die," Aggie said sternly. "So stop thinking about it."

"Thing is, you know, I don't mind much. Oh, don't look at me so, Aggie. It ain't that I want to. It's just I won't grieve over it, see? Everything I was like to grieve over has already happened."

Aggie made as if to speak and then did not. Perhaps she understood there was nothing useful she could say. She finished her chores and then, with a smile on her face that was somewhat less than steady, she bent and brushed her hand across Sylvie's face.

"You're strong, Sylvie Bowen. Strong inside, where it counts. You'll make it."

The other staff of the Den were not allowed in, lest they get sick too; but no one told Madame Louise whom she could or could not visit. She came with fruit and treats from her kitchen, and all manner of good advice. The third time she came—at least the third time that Sylvie was conscious enough to notice—it was on a Sunday afternoon. She picked her way across the room and settled in the chair by the bed.

"Sylvie, lass, how are you?"

"Much better, Madame, thank you. I was up for a bit this morning."

"Good. I am glad to hear it." The words seemed little more than a formality. The old woman's eyes were troubled, and Sylvie could guess why. This morning, when she was up for those few minutes, she had looked in the mirror on the wall, and she had been frightened by what she saw: a woman so wasted and thin as to seem a child, with sunken eyes and hands like small, spent claws.

"Sylvie . . ." Madame was rarely at a loss for words, but she hesitated now, rubbing her thumb across her fingers. "Sylvie, do you still have . . . feelings . . . for Mr. Shaw?"

She could not meet the older woman's eyes. "That be over, Madame."

"Yes, I know. You ended your friendship because of his political activities. I quite understand. But do you still care for him? If, let us say, you had by chance been wrong about him—"

"I weren't wrong, Madame. He admitted it himself."

"Lord preserve us, you are a stubborn child! I never said you were wrong. I only ask about your feelings, and I would not ask without cause. Do you still care for him?"

Tears welled in Sylvie's eyes. "Oh, Madame, how could I not? He were so good to me. And smart, too, and full of life. He could always make me laugh, when it seemed there were nothing left for laughing in the world."

"Well then, that's good. I have brought him to see you. He's waiting in the parlour."

Sylvie could only stare, swept by a blind animal joy, immediate and utterly astonishing; swept by hope and even by desire—and then also, as clear thought returned, by a wrenching sense of betrayal. Not now, dear God, she had no strength to face this now!

"Oh, Madame, how could you?"

"I would like you to see him, Sylvie. Just this once. Listen to what he has to say. He has promised me he will say it only once, and whatever you choose to do then, he will accept it. If you tell him to go away, he will go, and never trouble you again. I have his word."

And what is that worth, Madame, when his whole life has been a lie?

"I have no faith in Mr. Shaw's word," she said bitterly.

"Do you have faith in me?"

The tears spilled faster. "Yes, Madame."

"Then see him. Just this once."

It was impossible to refuse Madame. It was perhaps more impossible to refuse herself, to forgo the chance to look on him again, to hear him laugh, to have, perhaps, a few last caresses. Nothing was going to change. She would not stop loving him, not for years, so how could it matter very much?

"I will fetch him for you, then, shall I?" Madame went on.

"Yes," Sylvie whispered. "Thank you."

She scarcely noticed Madame Mallette after, when the old woman returned through the door with Erryn behind her. He was exactly as she remembered—the same hawk's face, the ragged blond hair, the fine, stylish clothing. Only the laughter was gone, utterly gone now, replaced by a distress so great it seemed almost to be grief, twisting his mouth and turning his eyes to grey water.

"Sylvie, oh my love, my poor, poor love . . ." He took her reaching hand and kissed it, brushing his other across her cheek, desperately, all the time saying her name, asking if she was all right, she was so thin, weren't they taking care of her, Oh, God, he was sorry, he was so sorry . . .

Somehow she found the strength to wipe her face and try to speak. "I'm all right, Erryn. I mean, I'm getting better. They're kind to me here. Really, they are. I'll be all right."

It was so good to see him. It was like food on an icy winter day. How did a starving person take a handful of it and shove the rest away?

"Why did you come, Erryn?"

"Because I love you. I would have come sooner, if I'd known you were sick. But I had gone away."

He'd gone away. He wouldn't have let me die alone. He'd gone away.

On Confederate business, no doubt.

She looked past him, to Madame Mallette sitting in the stuffed chair by the window, counting her beads; to the bright sunshine sparkling beyond, and the bleak, dead trees. It seemed such a contradiction, the bright sunshine and the dead trees—much as her life would be, she thought, if she went back to him. In time, something inside herself would break, perhaps her courage, perhaps her love. Something vital.

That was why she could not do it. But she could have today. She could have this time with him, just have it and keep it as a gift of fate.

"Are you well, then?" she asked him. "You look very dashing."

"I'm well, thank you." He gave her a small, wan smile. "I've brought you something."

She recalled, vaguely, seeing an object in his hands when he came through the door—perhaps the basket that she noted now, sitting on the dressing table behind him. She supposed he would fetch it for her, but instead he did something most peculiar: he bent forward and began to unlace his boot.

She watched him, too bewildered to see any meaning in it except that he might be hurt. Or perhaps it was just a piece of gravel, for he took the boot off altogether and reached inside, groping as one might for a stone. But what he extracted was a long piece of foil. He opened it and pulled out a folded piece of paper. He handed it to her gravely. "Would you do me the honour of reading this?"

It was the most official-looking piece of paper she had ever seen, with a coat of arms printed at the top. She thought it was the Queen's coat of arms, but she was not sure. Below, in fine black script, was printed: *Colony of British North America, Office of the Governor.*

She looked at Erryn in astonishment, but he said nothing. She read what followed:

> *Know all men by these presents that the bearer, Mr. Erryn Shaw, has been engaged under my authority as an agent of the British crown, and is specially entrusted with making such enquiries and investigations as may be necessary to protect the neutrality and peace of these colonies during the present conflict in the United States. All*

civilian authorities, and all officers of Her Majesty's army, navy and colonial militias are hereby requested and required to offer Mr. Shaw all reasonable assistance, and to respect absolutely the confidentiality of his mission.

Monck
Governor General

Engaged under my authority as an agent of the British crown . . . Awed, she stroked the paper softly, briefly, and then handed it back. She felt dazed with happiness, and at the same time painfully small. She had judged him so ill.

"You're . . . you're a . . ." She hesitated, glancing uncertainly at Madame.

"A spy," he finished calmly, "just as you thought. But not for the Southern Rebels. For us." He leaned forward. His voice was still quiet, even gentle, but she had rarely seen more passion in his eyes. "I wanted so much to tell you. The night you came to the club—the things you saw and heard there—I could see how much they hurt you. But of course we were told to keep it from everyone, no matter what. I shouldn't have listened, I know as much now. I should have told you everything. I'm sorry, my heart. I'm sorrier than I can ever say. Can you forgive me?"

Could *she* forgive *him*?

She reached for his hand and, when he gave it, drew it close and covered it with kisses. For a small time they huddled together, each of them rushing to speak, swearing they had been wrong, that the other had absolutely nothing to forgive.

"I was so cruel," she said mournfully. "All those dreadful things I said!"

"No, my heart. You took me at my word, and everything you said was right. I was so proud of you then, you have no idea—"

"*Proud of me?*"

"Utterly." He brushed her hair back from her face, kissed her cheeks, her nose, her forehead. "Devastated, I'll admit, little pieces of me lying all over the carriage floor. But proud nonetheless, and thinking, God, how strong she is, and how courageous! I mustn't lose her! I simply mustn't!"

It astonished her that he would say such things. She had no idea what to say in response.

"Whatever did you tell Madame?" she asked. "To persuade her to speak for you?"

"She left me no choice. I had to tell her the truth."

"All of it?"

"All of it."

"Then you've trusted both of us with your life."

"Yes," he said simply. "But if I hadn't, I would be spending the rest of that life knowing you hated me. And every time I thought of it, it seemed quite as horrible as dying."

"I never hated you, Erryn. I couldn't."

"You were trying hard," he said. "I was afraid you'd get better at it with practice."

She laughed then, a tiny cat's laugh that ended in a cough. It hurt, but it felt wonderful. She had not laughed for so long.

He wrapped both of her hands in his own. "I still want to marry you," he said. "Just so you know. Nothing has changed. Someday soon, when you're all better, I shall take you to dinner, and tempt you with bonbons and rich wines, and we'll go walking in the moonlight by the sea. And then, who knows? Perhaps you'll say yes."

Yes, perhaps I will. I adore you, Erryn Shaw. Whatever happens in the end, whatever becomes of us, I adore you, and I will until I die.

CHAPTER 29

The Rising Storm

Confiding special trust in your zeal, discretion and patriotism, I hereby
direct you to proceed at once to Canada, there to carry out such
instructions as you have received from me verbally, in such manner
as shall seem most likely to conduce the furtherance of the interests
of the Confederate States of America . . .
—*Jefferson Davis to Jacob Thompson, April 1864*

FOR DAYS ERRYN'S most constant companion was fear. Fear
stalked him in the streets, and huddled night after night in the
shadowed corners of his room. It sat brazenly on the window
ledge by Sylvie Bowen's sickbed, tormenting him in every breath
of silence: *She could die. Her lungs are wrecked from the mills, and she
could die* . . . Twice a week he went with Madame Mallette to visit
her, and each time he found her much the same, thin and pale,
with a cough he feared would shatter her to pieces. Sometimes,
after leaving, he could do nothing more than slip away to a quiet
spot by the sea and put his head in his hands and weep.

Only his work took his mind off his fears, and he was grateful
when Matt Calverley sent word to arrange a meeting. It would be
good, he thought, to talk for a while about the public world. It
would be better simply to see his friend.

They could no longer meet at Matt's boarding house, even in the dead of night. A Confederate operative had moved in—for no other reason, Matt was certain, than to keep an eye on him.

"It seems I have a reputation among them," he said. "'That God damn Yankee-loving son of a whore—he plots, he lies, he follows us everywhere. The bloody bastard's always up to something.' You've heard, I suppose?"

"Oh, quite. I've heard you're on Jabin Romney's payroll, too. Come to think of it, maybe all your new neighbour really wants is to sneak in your room some night and steal the wad of Yankee greenbacks you're hiding in your mattress."

"Maybe I should leave him a note."

In a heartbeat Erryn recalled another note, the one he left on a bench in Place Viger: *Little Robin Redbreast sat upon a tree. . .*

"No," he said. "No notes. I tried that once, remember?"

"I wasn't serious." Matt reached a little and turned up the wick on the kerosene lamp. They were in a small, ill-furnished office just off the waterfront. The one window was heavily curtained. Outside, since it was spring now and the weather pleasant, a drunk took his ease near the door, wrapped in an old, half-ruined blanket—a drunk who, when the men inside had left, would quietly go home, bathe, and return to his ordinary life as a member of the Halifax constabulary.

"So," Matt went on, "what can you tell me about these two chaps who turned up last week? This Captain Carson, as he calls himself, and his mate Lacey? I know Carson's left already, but I wondered what you might have heard."

Erryn cocked an eyebrow at his friend. Southerners came and went here all the time, and Matt was always interested in anything he might learn about them. But he had never before arranged a meeting to ask about someone so recently arrived.

"Why do I get the feeling you already know more about them than I do?"

Matt only smiled and waited.

"I can't tell you much," Erryn said. "They were both supposed to go directly to Montreal—I do know that. But Lacey decided to stay on for a week or two. Apparently he isn't well."

"Is that a fact or a pretence?"

"A fact, I think. He looks like death on a stick."

"You've met them, then?"

"Just once," Erryn said. "They were fairly discreet, but they did talk a lot about how war-weary the Northerners supposedly have become, and how much support the Rebels have in places like Ohio and Illinois. So it wouldn't surprise me if they're thinking about another Northwest uprising. And they came well supplied with money; they did let that slip."

"How much money?"

"Carson left five thousand behind just to keep his mate warm and cozy till he feels better."

"Five *thousand*? Jesus. D'you ever have the feeling we're working for the wrong government?"

"All the time."

Matt laughed. "Anything else?"

Erryn shrugged. "Just gut instinct. But Captain Carson is no soldier, no matter what he calls himself. And they're men of substance, both of them. That I could spot from a mile off. Add it in with their impressive bankroll and I'll wager they have high connections."

Matt nodded. "The very highest, probably. Lord Lyons has been hearing some interesting rumours down in Washington. Seems Jeff Davis has chosen himself a pair of so-called commissioners to come up here, name of Jacob Thompson and Clement Clay, politicians from away back. Thompson was Minister of the Interior under President Buchanan, and Clay was in the Alabama senate. The descriptions we have fit Carson and Lacey pretty well. And everything you've just told me fits too."

"Commissioners for what?"

"Well, that's the question. The Hawk's been back and forth with Governor Monck for days, and I gather he's been back and forth with Lyons. Depending who they ask, Thompson's role is purely diplomatic. According to others, it's the usual sort of trouble-making."

"Diplomatic?" Erryn murmured. "That could get rather boring for him."

"Rather. There's no way Monck will meet with them. So I'd vote for the troublemaking role myself. Things are likely to get lively in the West." He smiled then, just a little. "Don't look so gloomy, mate. I'm not sending you to chase after them. I need you here, and even if I didn't, Bryce has a solid team behind him now, he can handle it. And Hawkins says a lot of ordinary chaps have started paying attention too—keeping track of the Southerners, and reporting anything that don't look right. They make a lot of mountains out of molehills, he says, but it's worth it. They keep the buggers off balance." He dug about in his pocket and retrieved a battered muffin wrapped in newspaper. "Do you mind? I haven't eaten since breakfast."

"No, please, go ahead."

"You know Mason packed up and left England? The Con-federate envoy? He damn near set off a war getting over there, on the *Trent*, and when the Rebels didn't get their way with those rams in Liverpool, he just said bugger it and left town."

"Yes, I know. Kind of reminds you of the 1860 election, doesn't it?"

Matt laughed and bit off a great chunk of muffin.

"So tell me," Erryn went on, "this plan that's afoot for uniting the provinces—what do you think about it all? I've wanted many times to ask you."

"I like it. Some are scared, of course, thinking the West is so much bigger and going to gobble us up. They might even be right, to a point, but I don't think we have a choice. I gather the Southerners like the idea, most of them?"

"Oh, quite. They have this vision of an independent Con-federacy all arm in arm with an independent Canada, and the poor humiliated Union squished in the middle. Just the other day, one chap was describing to me the fabulous resort trade they'll bring us after the victory, since they'll never want to spend their summers in New England again. Oh, and we'll soon be building mills, too, for the cotton. We'll replace Lowell as the textile capital. Hell, in a few years we'll replace Manchester."

"Really?" Matt murmured. "And what about this uncomfortable little business of the Underground Railroad?"

"Nobody ever mentions it."

"No, of course not. Doesn't it occur to them that if they *do* win, it might be Canada and the Union standing shoulder to shoulder to keep them in line?"

"God knows what occurs to people, Matt—or what doesn't. I used to think we were reasonable sods, most of us. Since this war started . . . I don't know. There's times I think reason is something we take off the shelf and play with when we've nothing else to do."

"And here I thought I was a cynic." Matt licked the last crumbs of muffin off his fingers. "So how are you, mate? You look rather wrung out, if you don't mind my saying so."

"I'm all right." Erryn hesitated, knowing he had to go on, knowing also that his friend would be sadly disappointed in him. "I've fallen in love."

Matt considered this for a moment. "Have you now?" he murmured.

"Well, yes, and the thing is, I had to tell her what I'm doing."

"I was afraid you were going to say that."

Erryn wondered sometimes if Matt had learned his quiet, dangerous patience from his spiders; or if he came to fancy them because he saw in them some shadow of himself. Matt waited for Erryn to continue. Only his eyes betrayed how seriously he was taking this.

Briefly and simply Erryn told him the facts—how he and Sylvie Bowen had met and become friends, how she had turned against him when she learned of his work with the Grey Tories, how he had come home from Woodstock and found her gravely ill.

"I couldn't leave her so. I simply couldn't. She's alone in the world, except for me. I had to see her, make it right with her if I could. And for that I had to talk to Madame Mallette."

"You told both of them?"

"Yes." Erryn made a small, apologetic gesture. "I know you're wanting to call me a romantic fool, and maybe worse. But I love her terribly, and quite apart from that, I owe her my life. It was she who got me rescued on the *Saguenay*."

Matt examined his boots. "What do you want me to say, Erryn? If we were making bets, I'd give you decent odds—you're a good judge of character. Hundred to one, maybe, that both of them can keep their mouths shut. Trouble is, mate, it's still your life on the table. And maybe some other lad's as well."

"I know. And I weighed the risks, really I did. But how do you walk away in such a case? When it's someone who loves you, someone you owe your very life, who needs you now, who's maybe dying—how in God's name do you walk away?"

Silence fell, troubled only by bits of sea wind sighing past the windows, and once, briefly, the scampering of mice somewhere in the walls. The lamp flickered, shifting the dark shadows on Matt Calverley's face. He was almost forty, and for the first time Erryn could remember, he looked it.

"I hear stories," Matt said at last. "Oh, I know most of it's rubbish, just whiskey talk and old gaffers trying to make themselves important. But a man can't get his head kicked in on Barrack Street anymore without someone telling us he was selling information to the Yankees, or to the Rebs. Anyone who turns up dead is a spy. And you can't help wondering if there ain't a few grains of wheat in all the chaff. I watch my back now like I never did when I was running the streets and thieving for my bread.

"So . . ." He looked up and met Erryn's eyes; his own were unyielding. "So you'd best not take this any farther. She knows who you work for, so be it. She's not to know more—no names, no places, not a solitary move you make, nothing. And that's not a suggestion, Erryn, it's an order."

Matt had never, ever, stood on his authority before. Most of the time neither of them considered the fact that he had any. They were best mates, after all; what else was necessary?

"Yes, sir," Erryn said.

"And don't God damn call me sir, either."

It rained the next day, great drowning sheets of rain that slammed against the carriage windows and ran like rivers down the streets. Erryn's fear lay over him as dark as ever, but at the Den he found Sylvie sitting dressed in a chair, reading. He found a brightness in her face and a strength in her voice that astonished him. Soon, she told him, she would be back to her chambermaid's duties, and the servant girl they had borrowed from the Ortons could go home again.

It appalled him to think of her staying on, with the work so brutal and the days so long, with nothing but a garret room to sleep in, sunless and cold as a barn. Yet he dared not tell her of his fears. He dared not say to her, "Sylvie, for the love of God, marry me now, today, and leave this place while you can!" She would see it as protectiveness, or even pity, rather than as love, and she would back away. She would marry him when she was convinced that he meant it, that he knew his own heart. Till then . . . till then, he thought, he could only go on loving her, and wait.

On one thing, however, he was determined: they would continue their courtship as before, and be damned to the war. At first she objected. Everyone who worked at the Den knew how her aunt had died, she told him. They knew she backed the Union. They knew she had been friends with the Yankee woman, Aggie

Breault. Surely this would get back to his Rebel friends sooner or later, and then they might come to doubt him.

"I want to see you," she said fiercely. "I want to more than anything! But if you were to come to harm because of me—"

"I won't come to any harm," he said. "Whatever there is to know, they know most of it already, ever since that day at Compain's when we met Miss Isabel. If I continue seeing you, it won't matter. I mean no offence, my heart, but the Grey Tories will never take you seriously. A gentleman's son could have only one possible interest in a servant girl, and it most assuredly is not her political opinions. I fear it's your reputation that will suffer, not mine."

"That be true for most of them," she agreed, "but maybe not for all. Even one's enough to make you trouble."

Oh, yes, he thought, one might be quite enough. One like Brad Taylor, or even Maury Janes. But it made no difference. Till the day he died, he would never forget the shock of Jack Murray's words; the image of Sylvie lying on her sickbed, wasted almost to shadows; the fear that shot like ice into his soul. He might have a lifetime by her side, or he might have a mere ten years, or five, or two. He was not surrendering a day.

And so, every Friday they walked out together as before, to Corey's for tea, or to the Common, where there were concerts sometimes in the evenings. If it was not raining in the afternoon, they might wander down to the Point, and sit with a picnic basket by Fort Ogilvie and watch the ships go by. This she seemed to enjoy more than anything, especially if he brought his flute along. For two perfect weeks he imagined that his life was unfolding as it should.

By then it was May, the warmest May the city had known in years. Even her attic room was cozy now, she told him, and her work was easier, too, since it was not raining every day.

"Easier, perhaps," he said, "but still hard enough, I expect. Are you managing all right?"

"Oh, yes. Miss Susan's made the others help me some. And she don't say nothing when I'm not as fast as I were before. She's an odd sort, she is. Being around her every day, you'd think there weren't a soft spot in her anywhere. But she'd come in the room sometimes, when I were sick, and she'd look at me, specially if I were coughing bad, and her face would go all sad and haunted. She ain't forgot the mills, I think. She left it all behind, that world, but she ain't forgot."

The sun was low. All the food they had brought with them was gone, and most of the wine. He watched her as she poured the last of it into the small silver goblets he had borrowed from his landlord. He wanted her almost more than he could bear. He wished they were in Gideon's house, or in the woods—somewhere, anywhere, where they could lie together.

There are places in the city, Sylvie—quite disreputable places, I will admit, but well kept and discreet—where a gentleman might come quietly to an unlit door, accompanied by a lady with a veiled face, and there he takes a room for a couple of hours, so they might be together, alone.

She handed him a goblet, smiling. Across the channel, a church spire in Dartmouth gleamed in the last of the sun, but here the shadows were already gathering.

Did he dare to ask her? Would she think badly of him for it? Most women would. But then, she was not most women. She was Sylvie.

They touched goblets lightly, sipped. He could not look at her and sort out his thoughts. He looked to the water, where a small sailboat was drifting in, lazy as a cloud.

"Is there anyone you specially want to know about, Erryn? At the Den?"

Her voice was soft, scarcely more than a murmur, and his mind was still on other things. He answered idly, without much thought.

"I don't think so. Why?"

"I mean Rebels. There be a dozen of them in the place if there be one."

"Rebels?" In a breath he forgot the sailboat. He forgot even his own desire. "Whatever do you mean?"

"I'm the chambermaid, remember? I go in their rooms."

"You *clean* their rooms—"

"That don't stop me from doing other things. I done it before."

"You've done what before?"

"Go through their things. For letters and such. Names. Anything that might be important."

He stared at her, and saw that she was utterly in earnest. He opened his mouth, and closed it again, defeated. For one of the few times in his life, he truly had no idea what to say.

"There ain't much good about being a scrubmaid," she went on softly, "but there's this much, anyway. I can help you."

"No."

"Erryn—"

"Absolutely not. It's too dangerous."

"No, it ain't. They never know I look at their stuff. And if they ever find out, all they can do is complain to Miss Susan. They ain't going to drown me in my scrub pail."

"For God's sake, it's not a matter for joshing!"

"Sorry. But they ain't, just the same."

"You've been . . . you've been doing this for someone else?"

"Till a while back. Till it got out that I was seeing you."

God in heaven. Doing it for Aggie Breault, no doubt: Matt was certain the housemaid was one of Jabin Romney's agents.

"I see." He scrambled for something useful to say. "Sylvie, I'm asking you to forget about this. Please. I don't want to be afraid for you, my heart. I don't want to lie awake every night wondering if you're all right. I don't want to think of some bastard like . . . oh, God, like any of them, walking into his room and finding you going through his mail. It's that simple, Sylvie. Let it be. Please. For me."

She said nothing for a time. She looked at her hands, and then at him, and at her hands again. "And if I were your best mate, Erryn, the one with the spiders you told me about, you'd be scared for him too, wouldn't you? But you wouldn't tell him to let it be."

He could almost hear Matt's voice murmuring at his elbow, soft as it had been that night at Corey's, affectionate, persuasive: *You know, mate, the old man is looking for some spies* . . . God almighty, but Sylvie Bowen had a deadly aim.

"I'm scared for *you*, Erryn. I been scared ever since I saw you with those people at the Club. I thought you were on the other side then, but it didn't matter; the other side's dangerous too. So I don't see as how I can let it be. How I can walk through those rooms every day thinking you might need some little thing I could just pick off the table, need it desperately, maybe, and I be just walking by, too much of a scaredy-cat to look." She paused. "I can't do that, Erryn. I know you're being gallant and all, but I can't. Besides, I don't want a war here either."

"But if something happened to you—"

"Nothing's going to happen. I'll be careful. And it's safer for a woman, anyway. Southerners are full of all these silly notions, treating women like we're made of glass—"

"Southerners," Erryn said grimly, "come in all shapes and sizes, just like Englishmen. And those who are up here plotting our ruin aren't likely to be their best."

"No." She played her fingers across the back of his hand, over and over, her touch as cool and gentle as silk. "I lost Fran because of them. I'll not lose you too, if there be anything I can do to stop it. I'll bring you what I find. It might not be much. It weren't, before. But it all helps. That's what I were told, anyway. It all helps."

There was nothing he could say. It was clear she had decided on the matter before she ever spoke of it. It was clear also that she considered it a duty, something she owed not only to Erryn Shaw, because she loved him, but also to Fran's memory, perhaps even to life itself. *I don't want a war here either.*

There was nothing at all he could say.

———◆———

CHAPTER 30

Maury Janes

The bane and curse of carrying out anything in this
country is the surveillance under which we act.
—*Jacob Thompson, Confederate Commissioner to Canada*

IN THE WEEKS SHE had been away from it, Sylvie had almost
forgotten what the ice house was like—the cellar room damp and
chilly as a grave, the ice blocks so cold they hurt her fingers right
down to the bone. She had found it bearable before, because of Aggie
Breault's company, because they could talk and laugh together and
be friends. But Aggie was not her friend anymore, merely a polite
acquaintance, a faultlessly correct workmate who made a point of
being too busy for conversation. She passed on Miss Susan's orders
without a smile or a trace of affection; she came as late as possible
to their attic room and feigned sleep the moment she was abed.

Now in the ice house they worked together in absolute silence.
Like mules on a coal cart, Sylvie thought. Five minutes, ten, fifteen. It grew unbearable. Disheartened, she sat back on her heels,
rubbing her fingers together, trying to warm them.

"Won't you talk to me anymore, Aggie?"

There was no reply.

"Aggie, I just want to—"

"I don't see as how we have much to talk about, Sylvie Bowen."

"There be a whole world to talk about, last time I looked."

Aggie said nothing.

"I ain't changed my mind about anything," Sylvie went on. "Just because I care for Mr. Shaw don't mean I can't think for myself. I won't do anything to hurt your friends. I promise you, not ever!"

"I'd like to believe that," Aggie said grimly, "but I don't. And I reckon you wouldn't either, if you were me."

"Maybe not. But you're the only friend I got here. And you were so kind to me, when I were sick—it don't seem right now, us never talking, never laughing anymore."

Aggie picked up a half-melted block of ice and slammed it savagely onto the shelf.

"Aggie, *please . . .* !"

The older woman made as if to continue working and then stopped abruptly. "All right, tell me this. When you found out what he was doing, you told me you couldn't accept it. You said mill owners and slave owners were all of a kind, getting fat off other people's blood, and a man who was helping them was no man you could love. So what the devil's changed, Sylvie Bowen? Why can you love him now?"

"I never stopped. I tried to, but I couldn't. I mean, if you'd found out Charlie were doing something wrong, you couldn't've stopped either—"

"Doesn't mean I'd have stayed with him, or left him and then took him back!"

"He says he wants to marry me."

Aggie threw up her hands. "Right. I'll believe *that* when I see it. Anyway, even if it's true, after what you told me, why would you want to marry *him*?"

Sylvie looked away. "I'm scared, Aggie."

The hardest thing, saying it, was knowing it was true. It was irrelevant; it had not affected her decisions, and she hoped it never would. But it was nonetheless true.

"Scared? Scared of—"

No doubt Aggie was going to say "Scared of what?" and then remembered. She started moving ice again.

Sylvie went on, very soft. "I'll never get other work, not with this face. Never get another offer either, 'cept maybe from some old brute who just wants a servant he don't have to pay. So it be this, Aggie—" She made a wide gesture, taking in the dismal ice house and everything around it. "It be this for all my life, whatever I got left, or it be Mr. Shaw."

"And the money the Johnny Rebs are paying him."

"I don't care about his money. I want a bit of living before it's over. A bit of being happy. I never had any yet, 'cept for that time I spent in the West with Madame, and sailing on the *Osprey*, before they burnt her. All the rest's been work and people fighting. It were mill clatter screaming in my ears for years on end, and now it's chamber pots and scrub pails. Nothing sweet. After a while a body could die for the taste of something sweet."

"And you suppose I don't know that?"

"I suppose you do, Aggie Breault. Better than most anyone."

In the stillness that followed, they could hear voices at the door upstairs, and tramping feet. It was Mr. Timmins with fresh ice, no doubt. Soon young Dobbs would be packing it down and their time alone would be over.

"Look," Aggie said finally, "if you want me to say I like what you're doing—well, I don't. No matter what you say about which side you're on. But . . ." She glanced up the stairwell, wiped her sleeve across her face, and sat on the pipe beside Sylvie. "I'm not passing judgment. I'm not God. Wouldn't want to be, to tell you the truth—I'd be too damn confused. I can't be your friend the way I was before. We can't . . . we can't *talk* the way we did. Surely you know that. But we can be . . . I guess a bit like two lads who used to know each other, sitting on opposite sides of a picket line, trading coffee and tobacco. You say good morning, I say good morning. You don't shoot, I don't shoot. Fair enough?"

It was not what she had hoped for, but she knew it was the best she would get. "Fair enough."

⟫⟪

Maury Janes travelled light. Although he always paid two weeks' rent in advance, he kept with him only a single medium-sized carpet bag. It contained no secret pockets, or anything else of interest to a spy—or at least, Sylvie corrected herself, nothing of obvious, suspicious interest. Many travellers carried firearms; two boxes of bullets in Janes's pack proved only that he was one of them. He carried a map of the United States, but it was not marked in any way, and he was, after all, an American. Indeed, the oddest thing about the man was that he had been here so long and yet had nothing personal around him—no books, no letters, no trifles of any sort, nothing to suggest a life beyond his room. He was not poor. He had decent clothing, money to buy spirits in the parlour, money to socialize with the likes of Alexander MacNab and the Ortons. He had spoken of them at meals, Aggie told her, back when Aggie was still telling her such things. He had even described for the other boarders Jamie Orton's splendid mansion out on the Northwest Arm. He described it, Aggie said, like a man who was fixing to get himself one like it. And yet he travelled almost as if he were a fugitive, ready to bolt at a moment's notice and leave no trace behind.

Nothing else about him bothered her. She did not like the way he looked at her face, but this was true of half the men who had ever crossed her path, and many of the women. It was something she no longer cared about much. Janes made little mess and few demands. From a chambermaid's perspective, she would have traded half the guests in the Den for more of him.

But when she returned from her illness, she sensed a change in the man. She did not see a great deal of the guests now that it was summer. She might pass him in a hallway, or bring something to his chamber after supper. It was the briefest possible contact, yet she knew he was watching her differently than before, specula-tively, measuring her in some way. Then little MacKay, fascinated that Sylvie had a follower, took to passing on bits of gossip about Erryn Shaw. It was very little, and most of it came by way of Harry Dobbs, who believed everything he heard, indiscriminately. One thing he had heard was that young Mr. Shaw was awfully good friends with their boarder, Mr. Janes. They were always out drinking and sporting together, Dobbs said. And did she know that back in March, when Mr. Janes was away, he was off to New Brunswick with Mr. Shaw?

"Dobbsy thinks it was something about the war," MacKay whispered.

"He thinks everything's about the war. A dog couldn't cross the street to mess a post but he'd think it was about the war."

"Sanders says it might come here. The war, I mean. They scare me sometimes, her and Dobbs. They're always talking about it. Do you think it will?"

"No." She reached carefully and drew the blanket to her chin, wishing, as she always did, that it were Erryn lying warm beside her. "It won't come here. We got good leaders. They'll see it doesn't happen."

So that's why Janes is watching me: he knows now that I'm Erryn's friend. Erryn had never mentioned the man. They talked a great deal about the war, but always in its broader aspects: the news from the States or from England, the political climate here. He never asked her about anyone at the Den, not even once. He took the small bits of information she brought him with a graceful mixture of gratitude and sublime indifference; he praised her courage and cautioned her to be careful; he never gave anything away.

But he was interested in Maury Janes—he had to be. And Janes, therefore, was interested in her.

So she was not especially surprised when, a few days later, she found him still in his room late in the morning. She offered the usual polite knock before entering to do the room, and stepped back quickly as he opened the door.

"Oh, I'm sorry, sir. I'll come back later."

"No, come in. I'm not going out today. You might as well do it now."

He did not busy himself with papers at his desk or pick up a book. He sat boldly in his chair, watching her. She knew he would speak to her; he would start something unpleasant. He did not even wait very long to do it.

"Your name's Bowen, ain't it?"

"Yes, sir."

"I hear it said you're a real little Yankee."

She stopped working long enough to glance at him. "Don't know who told you that, sir. I'm English."

"You know what I mean. I hear you want the Yankees to whip us. Take all our niggers away. Blow the good ship *Alabama* right into the sea. I hear you're real cozy friends with that Yankee woman who serves us dinner. Is that true, Miss Bowen?"

He did not get this from his Grey Tory friends. Whatever they knew about her aunt's death or her probable loyalties, they did not know all of this. Nobody *could* know it, unless they sat at the downstairs supper table every night.

Damn Harry Dobbs and his runaway mouth. Damn him anyway.

"You've been talking with young Dobbs, have you?"

"Why d'you say that?"

She laughed, a small and slightly scornful laugh. "He's got Yankees and Rebels on the brain, that one. To listen to him, there ain't a soul in town who ain't all tangled up being one thing or the other."

"You saying it ain't true?"

"Depends what you mean by true. I get on with Breault. You got to work, sir, you get on with your mates if you can—don't matter where they come from. But I got nothing against your countrymen, sir. Nor against you."

"You got something against the *Alabama*."

"Dobbsy told you that too, did he? Well then, did he tell you why? My aunt Fran is dead because of the *Alabama*. She were all the parents I had, and she took sick in Nassau and died. We never would've been there except they burned our ship."

"I'm sorry about that," he said. "But sometimes, in a war, innocent people get caught in the middle. No one meant for your aunt to be hurt."

"So people tell me. But were it someone you loved, dying like that, m'appen you'd be a time forgetting too."

She went on with her work, quietly, methodically. If one thing useful ever came from her father's drunken rages, she thought, it was this: she could move around a man as though he were not even there. Dust, sweep, carry; empty the basin, straighten the bed. Notice nothing, least of all his attention.

"But if you had your druthers," Janes persisted, "you'd want the Yankees to beat us down, ain't that true?"

She gave the bedcover a wicked two-hand tug. "If I had my druthers, Mr. Janes, I'd have a nice easy job and a room with a fire and a mess of books. That'd be my druthers."

"Maybe so," he said, "but it ain't what I asked you."

"I can't answer what you asked me. Back in England, when I worked in the mill, a lot of my friends kept saying the North were right, and I thought m'appen it were true. Now I come here and a lot of people be saying the opposite. What's a poor soul to make of it, then, between scrubbing stairs and fixing beds and staying out of Miss Susan's hair? I ain't like Dobbsy, sir. I don't know everything yet."

He laughed then, just a little. "You're a plucky little snippet, ain't you? I reckon that's what Shaw likes about you."

She straightened sharply, turning to him with what she hoped would seem to be the right sort of silly, girlish surprise. "You're acquainted with Mr. Shaw?"

"Yeah."

His gaze went over her, top to bottom, returning to her face, evaluating everything, not even troubling to hide the fact. *Plucky, my ass. You're a she-cat in bed, I expect, and not bad to look at from the neck down. That's what he likes, same as any man would* . . . She dropped her eyes and turned away.

"Mr. Shaw and I are good friends," he went on. There was a warning in his words, but it was not, she thought, particularly political. It was a man's warning to a whore to remember her place.

❖

She knew he was not altogether reassured, neither as to her real opinions nor as to her possible influence on Erryn Shaw. He was undoubtedly a smart man, and the relentless bareness of his room suggested that he was a cautious one—extraordinarily cautious, in fact, leaving nothing to chance, assuming nothing was safe. Even a tiny misstep would make him suspect her, and perhaps Erryn as well.

Yet now, she thought, she dared not let him be. He was one of Erryn's targets; he had to be. Erryn would never be friends with such a man. He would not touch the sorry bugger with a pole unless there was a reason for it. Each time she cleaned his room, she searched it. He was human like everybody else. Maybe once he would leave something. Maybe just once.

But he never did.

June was almost gone. In the States, three huge battles had been fought, battles everyone talked about, their names as common as the days of the week. The Wilderness. Spotsylvania. Cold Harbor. Bloody slaughters, all of them, and nothing had been decided. Now the armies were dug in at Petersburg, and the Confederates and their friends began to speak again of victory.

The Union campaign was a total failure, they said; General Grant had achieved nothing except a stalemate, and this at an appalling cost. The Northern population would never tolerate such losses. Elections were coming in November and Lincoln would be turfed out. An independent Confederacy was only months away.

So it surprised Sylvie, passing Aggie Breault in the hallway one quiet, rainy morning and seeing a smile on her face. Aggie paused, glanced around, and said, very softly: "Have you heard? We sunk the *Alabama*. It's all they're talking about in the parlour. I guess it was in the morning papers."

"*What?*" Sylvie whispered.

"Yes. Just outside of Cherbourg harbour. Seems she went in for repairs and couldn't get out again before a Union warship caught her there. Semmes was stuck. He could come out in the open and fight, or he could hunker down and hide till the war was over. He came out, and he got beat."

"They sunk her?"

"Lock, stock, and barrel. And we didn't lose a man. We had some wounded, but no one killed."

It seemed impossible to Sylvie, recalling that lean grey shark of a ship, set low in the water and bristling with guns.

"And do you want to know something else?" Aggie went on. "Our ship had some chains draped around her hull, covered up with planks. And now Semmes is whining to all and sundry that the fight wasn't fair. He says Captain Winslow should have told him about the armour."

"*Told him?*"

"Yeah. Told him. You know: Hello there, Captain Semmes. We know you've sunk a couple of hundred of our merchantmen and whalers and poor little fishing boats, none of them armed with anything bigger than the captain's pistol and a skinning knife for the cook. But one mustn't be unfair, so before you come out to fight us, we have to tell you . . . Do you believe it, Sylvie? Do you bloody believe it?"

She believed it. Back in Rochdale, every time the workers wanted something, however little, the mill owners howled that they were being ruined, that the very bread was being snatched from their babies' mouths. For men who went through life with every advantage, "fair" was merely more of the same.

"Did they get the bugger?"

"Captain Semmes? No, he got rescued. He's safe in France. But I reckon he's out of the war. Nobody'll be crazy enough to give him another raider."

"Well, that's something. Thanks for telling me, Aggie. It's the best news I've had in a while."

"Dobbs is out running errands. I told him to buy me a couple of papers. I'll leave them on your bed when I'm done."

"Thanks."

For the first time in months they both truly, full-heartedly smiled.

———◆———

The papers were there as Aggie promised when Sylvie went up after evening chores were done. She considered taking them down to the kitchen, where the light would be better, and then decided no, she wanted to read them undisturbed by other people's conversations, or by Harry Dobbs's silly Rebel nattering. She settled on the bed as close to the little lamp as she could, leaving the door open in case she might be wanted.

It was, she thought, a small bit of justice at last. In New Brunswick, the *Chesapeake* pirates had walked laughing from the courtroom. Here, George Wade had made it clean away. Jamie Orton went up against the Supreme Court for helping him to do it, and did not get so much as a rap on his well-bred knuckles. But the *Alabama*, at least, was at the bottom of the sea.

She was pleased when she heard Aggie's heavy steps on the stair. Perhaps they would talk; perhaps they would begin to be friends again. But Aggie did not come to the attic. She turned down the hallway on the boarders' floor and rapped smartly on one of the nearer doors.

Sylvie recognized at once the voice that answered. "Yes, what is it?"

"There is a messenger here for you, Mr. Janes. I offered to bring the letter up, but he said he was to place it personally in your hands."

"I'll be right down. Thank you."

"Very good, sir."

Sylvie blew out her lamp and slipped onto the landing, watching as Aggie wearily returned downstairs, as Maury Janes emerged from his room, carefully locked it, and rushed after her. Whatever his message was, she thought, he wanted it very badly.

Never had it seemed so difficult to creep down a stairwell, so clumsily time-consuming to turn a key. Thankfully, the light was on inside. Janes too had a *Chronicle*, but he had not been reading the news of the day. It lay flung open on the shipping news. She searched the columns desperately, but nothing had been marked. She lifted it aside. Beneath it was a piece of notepaper. It had been folded many times, as though he normally kept it tucked away, perhaps in his pocket. She copied it frantically and laid it back as she found it, knowing she dared not look for more. She replaced the newspaper and slipped to the door. There was no sound in the hallway. She opened the door a crack, saw no one, stepped out, and sped to her room like a ghost. She had not yet stopped trembling when she heard Maury Janes return.

After a while she lit her lamp again and reread what she had found: merely three names and three addresses, each of them in a different Northern city. Nothing more. No hint as to who these men were or why they mattered to Maury Janes.

But matter they did, she was sure of it, and even surer after she passed it on to Erryn. She did not tell him how she had come by it, only that Janes had left his room and forgotten it.

He took it carefully. He was a good actor, but she was coming to know him rather well. He was, she thought, both pleased and appalled.

"Sylvie, you didn't . . . he wasn't still in the building, was he?"

"Yes. But he were busy."

"Oh, God . . . Sylvie . . . Sylvie, please, please don't do anything like that again! Not with any of them, and most especially not with him!"

CHAPTER 31

———◆———

Setting the Snare

One does every day and without a second thought, what at
another time would be the event of a year, perhaps of a life.
—*Henry Adams*

EVERY TIME Matt saw Jabin Romney, he looked older and more
tired. Today was no exception. His last shave had obviously been
days ago; his last haircut, sometime before Christmas. His voice,
as always, was quiet and bland, as if everything he said was of
equal and minor importance.

"You're in search of a —what the deuce do you call them here?
Oh, yeah, footpads—it's a better word than 'ruffians,' isn't it?
You're looking for a footpad, are you?"

Matt smiled faintly. He was both amused and impressed by
Romney's recollection of a conversation they shared more than a
year ago.

"Yes," he said. "And I thought, given your line of work here, it
must be a simple matter for you to send messages back and
forth to the States? In some sort of code, I mean? And that your

superiors there could . . . ah . . . find something out for you if you asked them?"

Romney's sagging, world-weary manner did not change so much as a whisper. "I've done that from time to time," he said.

Matt passed him a paper on which he had written the names and addresses found in Maury Janes's room. "I'd like to know who these men are and what they do. Criminal records if they have them—or the opposite. Rank, money, positions of power, whatever. Anything you can find out. But quietly, of course. Very, very quietly."

Romney read the paper. "These folks appear to be Americans, constable."

"Yes, that's the problem. Do you think you could help?"

A great black crow flew into a nearby tree and screamed at them. Romney watched it for a time.

"Why do you want to know anything about a man in Philadelphia?" he asked. "Or Baltimore? Places like that? They're a long ways from Halifax."

"We think they might be planning a crime here, but we don't know what it is. They have a . . . an accomplice in the city. Of course, we could send a man down ourselves, but it would take time, and as you can see, they're in three different cities. And we might be running out of time."

"So just arrest him. Your accomplice."

"And charge him with what?"

Romney scuffed grass.

"It ain't much I'm asking, Mr. Romney."

"That depends on who those men are, don't it, and why you really want to know. And don't take offence at that, constable. I consider you an honest man, down to the bones. It's your government I have doubts about."

"Our governments have doubts about each other," Matt said amiably. "Why should I take offence? However, since I'm an honest man, I'm willing to pay for what I get."

"And how would you do that?"

"There appears to be a certain commissioned officer in Her Majesty's Navy who was given indefinite leave, took himself a made-up name, and is now serving as the captain of a blockade-runner. And this blockade-runner just happens to be owned by the company whose major partner is the admiral who gave him his leave in the first place."

"I see," Romney murmured. This interested him, and he allowed it to show. "My government will find this most useful information."

They would indeed, Matt thought. They would take it straight to the British ambassador in Washington, and Lord Lyons, properly outraged, would send it to London, and London would make all manner of apologetic noises and insist they hadn't known a thing about it but they would put a stop to it immediately . . . It was a real pleasure, once in a while, to get two birds with a single stone.

"I could certainly take this as proof of your good intentions," Jabin Romney went on. "On the other hand, you might want to do this bugger in on your own account. Old enmities, perhaps? Or a simple respect for your country's laws? You do see my point, constable?"

There was a reason this hangdog, unshaven, said-to-be former bank clerk was still the Americans' resident agent in the toughest post in British North America. He was just plain good.

"I do see your point. I trust you see mine."

For a tiny moment Matt considered telling Romney the entire truth—that it was not a criminal conspiracy he feared, but a political one; that the matter deeply concerned the Americans themselves. From where he was standing, it seemed a perfectly reasonable thing to do. But Erryn was the man on the spot, and Erryn said no. Absolutely no. One wrong move, he said, and Janes would spook and run. Matt quietly laid the temptation aside and went on, "I need help. I'm offering fair payment, but I can't offer more than I have."

"Frankly, you're offering way too much, and that makes me damnably curious. Tell you what, constable. Give me the names of your naval men and I'll ask all the questions you want, and I'll give you what answers I can. But I warn you, I'll keep back anything I figure is none of an Englishman's business. And if you don't mind too much, I'd like the names now."

"Will you give me your word?"

"I'll do my best, and I'll play you fair. On that you have my word."

Matt sighed. It was less than he wanted. It was as much as he would have offered in Romney's place. He held out his hand.

"Then we have a deal, Mr. Romney."

＊

Romney was not merely competent; he obviously had good connections as well. In less than three days Erryn was summoned back to the waterfront warehouse where he and Matt had met before. There, after the briefest of greetings, Matt handed him a small piece of paper, neatly printed by hand.

"From Romney," he said.

Erryn read, with growing disappointment: Hans Ludwig Schultz. Age fifty-two years. Married to Maria Schneider of Evansburg in 1825. Seven adult children. Owner of second-hand store at 732 Field Avenue, Philadelphia. Lutheran. Attends church regularly. Member of the Oddfellows Club for twenty-three years. No police record or known criminal contacts. No known political affiliation. Has never held elected or appointed office of any kind. Net worth about three thousand dollars.

The others were of a similar sort. Raymond Hill, thirty-one, unmarried, auctioneer, no religion, no police record, no connections of importance, net worth about two hundred dollars. Zebediah Turner, forty-three, married, haberdasher and dry goods merchant, Episcopalian, no police record, one term as city alderman, net worth about five thousand dollars . . .

Erryn looked at Matt, who said nothing. "These are Janes's contacts?" Erryn demanded.

"Apparently."

"God bleeding almighty. Two small merchants and a bloody auctioneer? All completely respectable, with no political affiliations—"

"What did you expect? Fire-eating Copperheads? Sworn members of the Sons of Liberty?"

Erryn waved an arm at nothing in particular and then sagged in his chair, defeated. "I don't know. I suppose I did."

He had not, actually. But he had expected . . . *something*. Something that would leap off the page, that would have immediate, recognizable implications. Something that mattered.

"This is useless," he went on, laying the paper aside. "Those men don't have a thing in common, except for being males and living in the States."

"They have one thing," Matt said quietly. "They sell stuff."

"Why, thanks, mate. I hadn't noticed."

"Don't be an ass, Erryn. Think about it."

"Sorry," Erryn said. "I didn't mean to jump on you. But what's to think about? Millions of people sell stuff."

"No, think about it. Two stores and an auction mart. What better place could you want to hide something, or to stash it away until it's needed? Merchandise comes and goes, people come and go, nobody pays attention."

"So they're just another set of middlemen?"

"That would be my guess."

"Well then, like I said, it's useless. We've added a link, that's all. The chain still doesn't lead anywhere. We don't know what Janes is planning. We don't know what he's delivering, or when, or what it's going to be used for. We don't know anything that matters." He linked his hands and stared at them. "Worst of it is, Matt, I think we're running out of time."

"Has he said anything?"

"No. But he's been . . . different . . . the last while. Edgy. Ever since the night that message came. If I had to wager, Matt, I'd say his shipment is coming soon."

"Well then, I think it's time for you and I to have a talk with the old man." He made as if to go, and turned back with a small, tired smile. "We'll get one thing out of this, mate. We'll get Captain William Ross on a ship back to England."

———◆———

Colonel Hawkins stepped into the warehouse out of midnight fog, quiet as a ghost despite his solid two hundred pounds. He nodded to Matt Calverley, taking off the shabby slouch hat that hid most of his face, and turned to Erryn.

"Mr. Shaw." He shook hands warmly, but he did not smile. "I'm glad to see you. I take it the good constable here has told you how pleased we are with your work?"

"Yes, sir. Thank you."

"Good." He settled into the first chair he found. "So tell me about this Janes chap, will you? All of it, from the beginning."

He listened attentively, interrupting only with an occasional question, frowning when Erryn explained the involvement of Sylvie Bowen, but saying nothing until he had finished.

Then he asked, very quietly, "Do you trust this woman, Shaw?"

"Yes, sir. Entirely."

He nodded. It was not, Erryn thought, a nod of approval, merely an acknowledgment of fact.

"Calverley tells me you spoke with the so-called Confederate commissioners when they passed through Halifax, and you thought they might be looking to start an uprising in the northwestern states?"

"That was certainly the impression they gave me, sir. They talked a great deal about how discontented the people were in places like Illinois and Ohio, how much support the Sons of Liberty had. All that sort of thing."

"So, if there's an armed rising in the works, your man Janes might be bringing in weapons to support it."

"He might," Erryn agreed. "But if those three names we have are destinations for the shipments, they're all on the east coast."

"Way stations," Hawkins suggested. "Or a diversion—a move to trigger panic. What would the government think if a rebellion broke out in the west and suddenly there was fighting in places like Philadelphia and Baltimore as well? They might well believe the Copperheads to be ten times more powerful and dangerous than they really are."

"Now there's a nasty thought," Matt said.

"Indeed."

"So what do you suggest we do?"

"Well, I can tell you what we don't do. We don't let that cargo leave Halifax if there's any way on earth we can stop it. Mr. Shaw, it seems your man Janes has been fairly close-mouthed about the whole operation. How likely is it you'll wake up one morning and find he's gone? That his contraband came and went without you ever knowing?"

There was an even nastier thought. Erryn ran it through his mind very carefully, and weighed it against everything he knew of Janes: the man's ambition, his shrewdness, his nouveau riche sense of self-importance . . .

"It's very possible, sir. But I think . . . I think there's a chance he'll tell me when it comes."

"Why?" Matt challenged him. "Wouldn't such a cautious man simply take his cargo and slip away?"

"If he hadn't told me anything about it back in Montreal, when he thought he needed to—then I think he would. But I already know a little. I already know he's part of this extraordinary mission that's going to change the course of the war, and that makes me the one person he *can* tell. Not the details of it, no—he's shrewd enough to keep those tucked safe away. But that it's finally happening? That it wasn't all just talk, just Maury Janes playing the big man? What with me being his best mate and a genuine blue-blooded English gentleman to boot, the sort who can appreciate *real* merit in a man? He'll be awfully tempted, I think."

Hawkins looked to the constable, who shrugged. "Shaw knows him, sir. I don't."

"Well." The colonel spoke again to Erryn. "If you're right, and God willing you are, then at least we can impound the vessel and search it for contraband."

Matt shook his head. "That's not a very good solution, sir."

"I know. We'd likely compromise Mr. Shaw, and lose his valuable services."

"If you'll forgive me for saying so, colonel," Erryn murmured, "I'm rather more concerned about Mr. Shaw's valuable head."

"Also a consideration," Hawkins agreed. "You tell me Janes never leaves anything in his room. So he might have some papers with him—a bill of lading, at the very least. Surely you can find some excuse for searching him, constable."

"It's a port city, sir. Hundreds of men carry around shipping papers for one thing or another. Why should I pay any attention to his, unless someone betrayed him? And that someone could only be Erryn. It's the same thing, sir. Search him, search the ship—either way, we're hanging a millstone around Shaw's neck and pitching him over."

"Then fabricate something. An accusation of theft, perhaps—"

"Footpads," Erryn said quietly. "That's what we need. Footpads."

Matt's face brightened with interest. The colonel frowned. "Explain," he said.

"We get attacked on the street. At night. You knock the bugger senseless. He'll think it was thieves."

"And after we've used his papers and claimed the shipment, then what will he think?" Hawkins asked grimly.

"Oh, bloody hell. All right, forget I mentioned it."

"No," Matt said. He leaned forward eagerly, his elbows on his knees. "It's a damn good idea. Only we don't knock him senseless, Erryn, we knock *you* senseless—"

"Now wait just a minute—"

"Only for show, mate, only for show. You play dead. The colonel here and his fellow thieves get scared off, what's Janes going to do? Likely he'll hunker down and be grabbing at you to see if you're dead or not. That could look right suspicious to a policeman just coming on the scene, couldn't it? Or he could leave you lying there and cut and run—well, that's even more suspicious. Either way, I have grounds to arrest him, search him, and keep whatever I find—leastways till poor Mr. Shaw comes to his senses and tells us it was all a terrible mistake. That could take days. And who knows what I'll do in the meantime, being a sod who thinks the worst of the Johnny Rebs on principle?"

Hawkins frowned. "You can't lay a man out for days and then have him turn up without so much as a bump on his head."

"Well then, we can give him some bumps."

"You're so kind," Erryn said, "but I have a better idea. When I wake up and tell you it *was* thieves who attacked us, you start to wonder what he's smuggling. Well, wouldn't you? He's a diehard Southerner. He's up to his neck with the Grey Tories. Now a ship's just come in with cargo for him, and the day is barely gone before he's nailed by thieves. Damned curious coincidence, don't you think?" He turned to Colonel Hawkins, who did not seem the least bit impressed, and then back to Matt. "What did the robbers want so badly? Wouldn't you wonder, Matt? Wouldn't anyone?"

"They wanted your purses," Hawkins said.

"Most likely," Matt agreed. "Then again, given the men involved, given the circumstances, I think the possibility of contraband might cross my mind."

"Would the Rebs believe that? It's for their benefit, remember, not mine."

"They might," Erryn said. "As the constable told you, sir, he thinks the worst of them on principle."

"Well." Hawkins looked from one to the other, gravely. "It's rather thin, gentlemen. But we may not have a lot of time, and at the moment I don't have a better idea. The question is, though, Mr. Shaw—when the time comes, can you lure Maury Janes to some appropriately dangerous spot late at night?"

"I shouldn't have to lure him, colonel. If I play my role right, he'll be luring me."

CHAPTER 32

———◆———

The Vessel of Retribution

He must have iron nails who scratches a bear.
—*Edward Bulwer-Lytton*

I THINK HE'LL FIND IT hard not to tell me.

Erryn thought back on his words many times over the next three days, days as difficult as any he had ever lived through. His judgment of Janes had been instinctive, based on his knowledge of the man rather than on practical good sense. He knew he might be right. He knew also that he might be deluding himself again, reading all the wrong signs, misjudging an enemy just as he had done on the streets of Montreal, and afterwards on the *Saguenay*. The possibility chilled him to his bones. *Little Robin Redbreast sat beneath a tree, along came pussycat and crunch went he . . .*

Not funny, Shaw. There's more at stake here than your head, dearly though you value it.

There was altogether too much at stake, which was why, even though he was bored to desperation by the man, his heart lifted every time he met Maury Janes on the street, every time he spoke with someone who had just seen him. As long as Janes was in town, he still could hope. Sunday passed, and Monday; he found excuses to spend time near Al MacNab, hoping for a drop of news. Tuesday morning he was on his way to the emporium when he spotted Janes through a Hollis Street shop window. He raised his hand in greeting. Janes dropped whatever he had been doing there and dashed into the street.

"Shaw! I was hoping I'd run into you!" For days the Carolinian had seemed a man with something very serious on his mind. Now all the tension in him was gone, replaced by a buoyant energy. He clapped Erryn warmly on the shoulder and fell in step beside him, steering him onward. "Come," he said. "I want to show you something!"

Erryn kept his voice amiable and calm. "You're in a fine humour today."

"You got that right."

At the next corner they turned toward the harbour, and then Erryn allowed himself to hope. He said nothing, however, letting Janes play out his moment of triumph as he wished. The wind coming off the water was fierce; wild gusts tore at their sleeves and tossed dirt into their faces. His companion steered him onto the pier of Taylor's Wharf, where an aging, graceless steam freighter lay at anchor.

"There she is, Shaw," Janes said proudly. "The Vessel of Retribution."

Erryn looked at the man, at the ship, back at the man. "Well, I'll be damned, you've done it!" He held out his hand. "Congratulations! Though I don't mind telling you, I was expecting a more —well, shall we say a more impressive-looking vessel."

Janes laughed. "So was I, once. The lads in Nassau had a nifty blockade-runner in mind for us, but it turned out the captain wasn't interested. That's why everything took so damn long. Tell you the truth, Shaw, there were times I thought I'd never see this day."

"Waiting can be the worst thing in the world," Erryn told him. "Especially when matters are in someone else's hands." A lesson he had just finished learning for himself, unforgettably. He paused, and added with a touch of well-feigned regret, "I suppose you'll be leaving us now."

"Couple of days. Maybe tomorrow if all goes well. Listen, let's go have a drink to celebrate. Then I have to see MacNab."

"I have a much better idea. This deserves a *real* celebration. You shall be my guest for the evening, yes? Dinner at the club at least, and maybe something after? Dear Lord, Janes, this is something you've planned for and waited for so long. We must do it up right!"

———※———

Some thirty hours later, Erryn was sitting on the floor of an empty shed in the ordnance yard, waiting for Matt Calverley to turn up. Hawkins had already arrived, having left Matt to handle the administrative details. Matt was the peace officer, after all; there was no reason for Hawkins to be involved, except for such reasons as they preferred to keep to themselves.

The shed was large and bare, but it was safely away from the curious eyes of the public. It was also conveniently divided into two compartments, allowing Erryn to slip out of sight when Matt and his men brought the contraband in. Supremely practical, the place was, but dreary to sit in, hour after hour. Erryn filled up the time by going over every detail of the previous night: his dinner with Janes at the Halifax Club, the carefully staged attack on Grafton Street, the papers Colonel Hawkins had shown him in the carriage. There was a letter—the same letter, no doubt, that had been delivered to Janes late one night at the Den. *Your trunks will arrive Dover early July. You will need this.* With the letter was a page from *Great Expectations* torn in half.

He remembered also the colonel's wry assessment of the documents: *The captain of the* Dover *likely has the other half, and will only*

surrender the cargo to the man who has its mate . . . or, of course, to an
officer of the port authority with a lawful warrant.

They had him, Erryn thought. Unless something unusual and
dreadful occurred, they had Maury Janes. And he, Erryn, stood an
excellent chance of coming out of it alive.

The trouble was, sitting here waiting, a man could readily
think of fifty unusual and dreadful things that might occur. Thus,
most of eternity had passed before he heard the sound of wheels
and horses drawing up outside and a knocking on the shed door.
He stepped into the next compartment. It had, he discovered, a
few small cracks in the wall, allowing him a limited view of the
other room.

Hawkins walked to the outer door and stood beside it, obviously weary but very much alert. "Identify yourself."

"It's Calverley, sir."

He pulled the bolt and opened the door. "Well, constable, what
did you find?"

Matt and young Connor walked in, carrying a large steamer
trunk between them. Two other constables followed with a second trunk. Astonishingly, when they had returned with a third,
Matt dismissed them.

"Thank you, lads," he said. "I'll be here awhile. Don't send for
me unless we're being shot at, or the city's burning down around
your ears."

"Very good, sir."

The door closed. The wagon clattered away. Erryn stepped
back into the room with the others . . . a room grown extraordinarily and painfully quiet. Hawkins was staring at the trunks as
though they were beetles on a piece of toast. Eventually his gaze
shifted back to Matt Calverley's face.

"For God's sake, constable, didn't you seize the entire shipment? Where is the rest of it?"

"This is all of it, sir."

"This is all of it?" The colonel's voice was altogether too calm.

"Yes, sir."

"Calverley, do you know *anything* about combat?"

"Mostly the street variety, sir."

"That's rather what I thought. God damn it, do you actually think someone is going to change the course of the American war with such weapons as he can stuff into three God damn *steamer trunks*?"

"I suppose that would depend, sir."

"Depend on what, for God's sake? If these are all the guns you need, you can buy them in the States. You don't have to smuggle them from England to Nassau to Canada first!"

"Sir, if you'll forgive me," Erryn said, "we don't know what Janes was bringing in. All he ever talked about was a shipment. But it has to be war contraband of some sort, and dangerous. To that extent we had to take him at his word."

Hawkins threw out his arms and let them fall again. "Oh, I suppose you're right. Well then, let's get on with it."

Matt offered Erryn the keys. "I guess the honour is yours, mate."

Erryn dropped to one knee by the nearest trunk. The key fitted poorly, and had to be rattled and jiggled to get the lock open. He snapped open the catches and raised the cover cautiously. A sickeningly powerful stench wafted out, like old, half-rotted clothing, only worse. The trunk was packed to the rim; folded carefully over everything was a worn grey blanket. He lifted it and turned his face away.

"Whee-eew! Lord Jesus almighty, what a stink. They must have wrapped a dead dog in it for a week."

"Well," Matt said, "that's one way to discourage snoops."

"Just about enough to discourage me."

There were more old blankets underneath, obviously used to wrap and protect the important cargo. He peeled them off, carefully; they all stank. Underneath were a mass of garments—a great many shirts, several pairs of women's drawers, nightgowns— more blankets, a rag doll, a bedsheet, a bible, a diary, a lady's reticule, a child's frilly dress. The others merely stared as he pulled up one harmless thing after another, all of them old and smelly, as used belongings would become, packed for weeks or maybe months inside a trunk. Old, but harmless. Finally he was scrabbling in the bottom for one last ragged shirt, and the trunk was empty. He saw total bewilderment on Matt's face; he supposed his own looked much the same. They turned the trunk upside down. They tapped it and poked it, testing for false bottoms, hidden compartments. There was nothing. It was empty.

"A decoy?" Matt suggested.

"Possibly."

Erryn found the right key for the next trunk and tossed the remaining one to Matt. "Here, constable, make yourself useful."

"In a minute," Matt said. "Let's see what that one looks like first."

It was the largest of the three. Erryn unlocked it easily, but for a long moment he could not bring himself to lift the cover. He was, he realized, quite absurdly afraid, and part of what he feared was that this one would look exactly like the other.

It did. So did Matt's.

Nobody said a word. Carefully he and Matt picked their way through the contents, trying not to gag at the smell, trying not to think very hard about how idiotic they looked, and felt, poking about in the bedclothes and underwear of strangers, holding long fluttery nightgowns up against the light to see if bombs or pistols or dispatch cases would fall out of them. When they were done, three shabby piles of used clothing lay on the floor, and nothing else. No weapons, no contraband, no papers, no money.

"I don't bloody believe this," Matt said. "Where did you find this Janes arsehole, anyway? In a circus?"

"They must have suspected you, Calverley," the colonel said. "They gave you the wrong cargo. I'll wager there's a few tons of weapons still sitting in the *Dover*'s hold."

"No, sir, there isn't. I thought it was a mistake too, but we checked everything. We examined the hold, the warehouse, the cargo manifests, everything. It all matches. That ship was full of cookstoves and hammers and cheap brandy and such, nothing else. Besides, Janes's letter says 'trunks.' We've got the right cargo."

"Well then, gentlemen, you've been had. The man is obviously a lunatic. Give him back his trash and let him go." He took out a fine linen handkerchief and wiped his face. "And now, if you'll excuse me, I'm going to go home and find out how much Madeira it will take to get this stink out of my throat."

"No," Erryn said sharply.

"What did you say, Shaw?"

"I said . . . Damn it to hell, sir, we can't just quit. Not until we know for sure there's nothing here."

"There *is* nothing here."

"We don't know that, sir. All we know is there aren't any of the things we were expecting. There might be something else. Janes never told me what was in the trunks. We just guessed. Obviously we guessed wrong—"

"Obviously."

"We have to search everything, piece by piece—"

"Looking for what, Erryn?" Matt asked. His voice was quiet, almost gentle. He wasn't challenging, just asking.

"I don't know. Messages. Stuff that's valuable but small— medicines, maybe. An ounce of morphine's worth a fortune in the Confederacy."

"These aren't going to the Confederacy, remember?"

"Bloody damned hell, let's just look, all right?"

"All right," Matt said. "One pile apiece, mates." He took off his jacket, hung it over a chair, and carefully rolled up his sleeves. "When I get home, I'm going to take a *bath* in Madeira."

"Calverley, there's no point in this—"

"We don't know that yet. What I mean is, sir, I think Mr. Shaw is right. We haven't really looked at this . . . *stuff*. We just tossed it aside looking for weapons. God knows what might be inside linings and hems, or slipped in the pages of that bible there."

The colonel glared at him.

"If I might say something, sir," Erryn put in. "I spent a lot of time with Maury Janes. He's been working on this project for months. He sent a man to the States to find just the right spots for his bloody trunks. He waited here for weeks for the ship to arrive. Janes isn't crazy, colonel. Or God knows, maybe he is crazy, but he isn't stupid. He didn't do all that for a pile of blankets and under-wear."

"Maybe he did it for a ruse," Matt suggested.

"What?"

"Maybe it's a sham. A ruse for the Yankee agents . . . and for us. Maybe what he's really doing, and really waiting for, is something else."

Oh, *shit* . . . ! Erryn rubbed his forehead with his palm. "I never thought of that," he admitted.

"So what do we do?"

"We search."

What followed was barely endurable. He picked up one dreary item after another, studied them inch by inch until his eyes burned; noticed a small rent in one, a stain in the other; ran each hem carefully between his thumb and forefinger; laid the bed jackets carefully over his lap and patted every inch of lining. Several times he thought he had found something: a lump in a pocket that became a shilling wrapped in a handkerchief; a piece of paper carefully tucked away that, when unfolded, said only *Saturday. Buy fish.* He sliced open the rag doll, but there was only cotton inside. He turned every page of the bible. He read the five brief pages written in the diary, a young girl's chatter about friends, about a boy who walked her home from the market. The last entry read: *Susan came to visit me this afternoon. Mother is sick today so we couldn't play the piano or sing. Tomorrow is Susan's birthday and she will have a big party.*

That was all. Just bits and pieces of other people's lives, small and passing and innocent. Just things they sold or gave away or left behind. No things of war at all.

His head hurt. He leaned it against his hands for a bit, trying to think, and trying not to think—trying most especially not to think about his growing certainty that he would find nothing, either because there was nothing to find and he had made an idiot of himself or, worse, that he would not find it because it was so small, so cunning, so hidden he would never notice it, and they would pack it all up again and give it back to Maury Janes, and he would do . . . what? Oh, God damn bloody hell, *what*?

"Have you finished, Mr. Shaw?"

"What?" He looked up. The others had gone through everything they had. The colonel was pulling on his jacket again. "Yes, I've finished."

"Well, that's it, then," Matt said.

Erryn spoke without thinking, the idea already in words before it took proper shape in his brain. "No, it isn't. We switch piles."

They stared at him as though he were completely insane. Quite possibly they were right.

"Maybe one of us will notice something the other didn't. We switch piles."

"Erryn—"

"Another hour, that's all I'm asking. I've been following this son of a bitch around for months. Just give me another bloody hour, all right?"

"You were taken in, Mr. Shaw. Admit it, and call it a day. That's an order."

"Don't do that, sir," Matt murmured.

"I beg your pardon?"

"Don't do it. Shaw's good at this work. If he wants us to stand on our heads here, we owe it to him. Once, anyway."

Thanks, Matt.

"I'm not going to argue about it. This operation is over."

"Well, there's the rub, sir," Matt said calmly. "It may be over for your department; I respect that. But then there's the Halifax constabulary, which at the moment is me, and that's another matter. Until I'm satisfied there's no crime intended here, this investigation damn well stays open. We'll do one more search, just the two of us. But I'm asking you to stick around, sir. If Erryn's right, and we find something, it would be best if you were here. And if he's wrong, well, he's buying us the best dinner in town, and all the good liquor we can drink."

There was a long silence. The colonel pulled out his watch, examined it, and replaced it wearily. "Very well. One hour. I'll wait for you outside."

———•◦•———

It was, if possible, worse than before. Erryn shoved the colonel's pile and Matt's together with a few kicks of his boot, folded one of the heavier blankets into a small cushion, and sat down. Began again.

You never know when to quit.

He could hear his father's voice as though the man were right here, sitting just across this pile of discarded belongings. A man who'd fought in imperialist scraps over half the known world, his hard body marked up like a chopping block, his bony face tired and cold. A father of the old school, a lord of the lordliest manor, an earl to the marrow of his bones. *You never know when to quit.*

Of course, it was what they taught him, all of them, right from the nursery. He was English, and the English were the lords of the earth, the builders of its greatest empire, God's finest handiwork of man. He was privileged, and in return for privilege it was his duty never to quit—to be stronger, smarter, braver than anyone else.

To win every time.

Nobody ever explained how one could win every time and still know when to quit, except by being omniscient, no longer God's finest handiwork but God almighty himself. When he walked away from contests he considered stupid, he was reminded of his rank, his place, his duty. When he remained in others—always the wrong ones, of course, always for the wrong reasons—he was a fool, a romantic, a man who never knew when to quit. Thus he ended in the colonies, living on a borrowed name and seventy pounds a year . . .

Well, he thought, nothing so drastic could happen to him now. At worst, the colonel would write to Governor Monck and suggest he be dismissed as a hare-brained idiot . . . and God knew the colonel might very well be right.

Slowly, more carefully even than before, he went through the items piece by piece. Different things, and yet maddeningly the same. He had no idea how much time was passing, but he did not hurry. He picked each item up gently, searched it, put it aside. A fine linen shirt with a monogram, *JLR*. A soiled, empty bag. A nightgown, ragged and worn, with a dark stain near the top and down the sleeve, as though someone had taken coffee lying in bed and spilt it. Sweat ran into his eyes. He wiped it away, aware that he was growing numb with frustration, with the mindless sameness of it; aware also of something else, of a growing sense of monstrous incongruity, something absurd, something that made no sense because the rules of ordinary rationality no longer held. The goods themselves made no sense—some items of the finest quality, almost new; others worn to shreds; all of them jumbled together, all half spoiled, as though they had been left in a mouldering warehouse for weeks. To what end?

A ruse. More and more he began to think Matt was right. It was a ruse. And somewhere the Confederates sat drinking mint juleps and laughing their heads off at this pack of dumb colonials hunkered down for hours over a pile of dirty underwear.

There was, however, nothing to be done about it except continue, item by dreary item, all the time thinking that perhaps it was a ruse, and thinking it was a damned expensive ruse, and thinking also of Maury Janes, Janes like an incubus beside him, grinning and brazen and yet always so vague around the edges, talking of the coming victory, of his early fortune—almost bursting with it sometimes—holding it secret only because he had to, because otherwise he would lose it. But sure of it. Always so sure.

Everything about this smelled of a ruse. Nothing about Maury Janes smelled of a ruse maker. Janes believed in it; this Erryn would have sworn to. He believed in it, and he wasn't crazy; therefore there was something here.

Eton logic, Erryn. Marvellous stuff on paper, but the world isn't logical. You learned that years ago; the world is quite insane.

It was all mechanical now; he would finish because he had begun; he was a man who did not know when to quit. He looked at everything, because everything was equally perilous or equally trifling. He picked up yet another bible, opened it where the satin marker was placed: *Yea, though I walk through the valley of the shadow of death, I will fear no evil* . . . He read the family history, the marriage of Albert James Connors and Mary Ann Bedard by Reverend Tobias Damler, May 17, 1834, the children, Albert James Jr., David, Robert, Edwin. He thought, *More cannon fodder for the empire,* and then he felt ashamed; those were someone's beloved children, after all. He picked up a book of Mrs. Browning's sonnets, battered and sorry-looking, as though it had passed through innumerable hands. He leafed through the pages, glanced at the inside cover: *To my dear aunt Frances, with all my love, Sylvie.*

He was so spent, he had already closed the book and was laying it aside when he realized what he had read. He opened it again, read it again, and a great chaos of things rolled across his mind at once, like tumbling cargo after a train wreck—Nassau and the Irish Stone and General Amherst and Maury Janes's impossible victory and what did the man want with three ordinary shopkeepers in three Northern cities, questions without answers and answers that no longer needed questions. The meaning of it swept through him unresisted; he was utterly beyond resistance.

"Oh, sweet Jesus!"

He stumbled to his feet, took two or three clumsy steps, and doubled over, rigid, fighting the nausea spilling up into his throat. He tried to speak, but could not. He was barely aware of Matt's reaching arm, Matt's voice, gutter harsh the way it got when he was really angry or really scared. "What is it, mate, what's wrong, damn bloody hell, talk to me, what's wrong?"

He tried to steady himself, groping for a handkerchief to press against his face.

"Outside." His voice was little more than a whisper, harsh and choked. "Leave everything. Come outside."

Matt did not argue. He opened the door. Outside, the sun had slid from sight beyond Citadel Hill. The colonel sat on a rock, quietly smoking. He saw them and got to his feet.

"Well, I take it you've finally had enough?"

Erryn stood a moment, drawing deep gulps of air. Then he held up the book. "This belonged to Frances Harris."

"Oh, shit," Matt said softly.

Erryn stared at him. Matt still did not see it. Or rather, he was seeing something quite peripheral—how sad for Erryn Shaw, to stumble over this memento of his beloved's grief. Matt's face was full of sympathy. Not fear, just sympathy.

"And who is Frances Harris?" the colonel demanded.

"A woman who died of yellow fever. In Nassau. Where these trunks came from."

"So what—"

Erryn overrode him as though he had not opened his mouth. "Trunks full of bedding and nightclothes—oh, and a few trifles, a rag doll, a couple of bibles—things people might cling to in their sickbeds. God almighty, don't you see? This stuff is from people who died! It's contaminated! Matt, you remember Amherst, you told me the story yourself, General Amherst and the Mi'kmaq? His easy, bloodless victory with a cartload of blankets? All those people dead just for taking a gift? That's what

Maury Janes is after, don't you see? That's what somebody in Nassau gathered up and sent him! These are . . . they're plague trunks, Matt!"

Very little could turn Matt Calverley pale. He was white as paper now.

"Erryn, don't jump me for this, friend, but aren't you . . . isn't that a little bit over the edge?"

"Is it? Think about it. Where did this stuff come from? If people were just emptying out their closets, where are the shoes, the frock coats, the hats? I never saw one."

Erryn was speaking fiercely, desperately, sorting it and linking it even as he spoke—all the absurdities, the questions that never quite took shape, the constant niggles of discontent, *something doesn't make sense,* all making sense at once now, ugly and horrible, hammered out like blows.

"Why just bedclothes, mostly? Bedclothes that stink, and not just from being used and stored away, but way worse—they stink like sickness. They're stained. People with yellow fever vomit bile. I'm told the odour is ungodly. And who was Janes sending it to, in the States? Not just anybody. Two merchants and an auctioneer, who would sell it all willy-nilly!"

"But those are just front men!" the colonel protested. "They're just bodies to claim the cargo at the other end!"

"And if they're not?" Erryn demanded. He heard Matt suck in his breath, and went on: "Maybe they're *exactly* who the stuff is intended for—then what? Consider the destinations: Philadelphia, the second-largest city in the United States. Baltimore, strategic port, to say nothing of being a Southern city that didn't turn Rebel. New Bern, headquarters and launch point of the Atlantic Blockading Squadron. If I were a Confederate, I'd be hard pressed to find a better place to start a plague myself."

There was a long, painful silence. After a time the colonel said, very quietly, "We've been handling that stuff ourselves. For hours."

"Yes." *Handling it with a vengeance. Rolling up our sleeves, pawing it, groping in it, breathing its stench. All of us. Me. The poor old colonel, who just wanted to call it a bad idea and go home. My dear, dear Matt . . .*

"I'm sorry," Erryn said wretchedly. "I didn't . . . I never dreamt . . ."

"Who the hell could?" Matt paced, kicked rubbish, paced some more. Finally he stopped. "Look, it's a good theory, and you mostly know what you're doing, so you're probably right. But the fact is, we have to find out for sure."

"We can't find out for sure. Except by dying."

"Easy, mate," Matt said gently. "Not everybody who gets the yellow jack dies of it. That's the first thing. And the second thing is, I damn well mean to find out. I'm going to haul that son of a bitch down here and set him to packing his trunks."

———◆———

It was dusk. A single lamp spilled a yellow glare through the ordnance shed. Janes took one step inside the door and stood frozen. From his hiding place in the adjoining room, Erryn could not read the expression on his face, but the shocked rigidity of the man's body confirmed all his fears. Janes looked from one man to the other, and back to the scattered clothing again.

Oh, my God! He did not say the words, but he might as well have done so. *Oh my god oh my god oh my god . . . !*

It took a long time for him to find his voice. By then he had managed a degree of calm, even of pretended arrogance.

"What the devil is going on here, constable?"

"Just a routine search," Matt said amiably. "When I thought you were robbing Mr. Shaw last night, I had a look in your pockets, and found your letter and stuff. And then when Mr. Shaw woke up and told us you really were attacked, well, those papers started to look real suspicious. I thought like as not the villains were after whatever you were smuggling in those trunks."

"That's ridiculous! I wasn't smuggling anything in those trunks!"

"So we've discovered." Matt straightened his jacket a bit, as if the discussion were over and he were about to leave. "Sorry for the trouble, mate. You're free to pack your things and go."

"I'm free to pack them? You throw my property all over this dungheap of a shed, and I'm supposed to pack it up again? This is outrageous!"

"This is customs and excise. Same all over. Don't tell me you've never been searched before."

Janes started to speak and then paused, as if changing direction. "Gentlemen, for God's sake, I was attacked last night and beaten. I was thrown in jail for no reason. The least you can do is give my property back in the same condition as you took it."

"I'm sorry, Janes," Matt said. "But it ain't our job, see."

"All right, I can pay you to do it. I'll pay you decent—more'n you're used to, I expect."

Hawkins turned on him sharply. "A man who packs another man's trunks is his servant, Mr. Janes. Is that what officers in Her Majesty's service look like to you?"

"I didn't mean—oh, Christ, never mind. I'll go find someone on the street—"

"You can't do that," Matt said.

"What the devil do you mean, I can't do that?"

"It's too late. I'm going off duty, and we have to get this shed all cleaned and locked up before we leave. It's Her Majesty's property, you know."

"God damn it, constable, I can get a man back here in twenty minutes!"

"Maybe you can. Then again, maybe you'll just climb on one of those fancy blockade-runners and leave your rubbish behind. I mean, it ain't exactly worth much—"

"I give you my word I'll be back! I'll give you a bond. Here!" Janes groped inside his jacket and pulled out a wad of money. "Fifty Yankee dollars says I'll be back here in twenty minutes!"

Matt shook his head. "I can't take that. You got to post your bond at the station, where they write it all down and everything. You just give me money, well, that's like me taking a bribe."

"Fine, then, let's go to the damn station—"

"You deaf or something, Janes? I told you I'm off duty. Just pack your trunks and get it over with, will you? The colonel and me want our dinner."

Janes stared at him for a long moment, torn, it seemed, between bewildered disbelief and the first real whispers of fear— fear not simply of his deadly cargo lying so unexpectedly close, but fear of Matt Calverley too. There really was something spider-like about Matt when he dealt with an enemy, something sudden and silent and impossible to predict. And Janes saw it, or sensed it. But he did not fear it quite enough. Not yet.

"Go to hell," he said. He turned on his heel and strode to the door. It would not open. He shoved at it savagely, several times, kicked at it . . . and finally must have realized that it was locked.

He turned back to face the room, leaning against the door. Little was left now of his earlier composure. "What the devil is this about, sir?"

"Tidiness," Matt said with an airy gesture toward the piles of clothing. "We're tidy folks, we Haligonians. We pick up after our-selves."

Janes said nothing. He stayed rigid by the door. Matt looked curiously at him, then at the piles of clothing on the floor, then at him again. "I say, there isn't something *wrong* with this stuff, is there?"

"No, of course not."

"Well, you're bloody acting like there is. What do you think, colonel? Do you get the impression this bugger is *scared* of his own property?"

"I do indeed, constable."

"What are you scared of, Janes?"

"Nothing. It's dirty, that's all. It stinks. I don't like stuff that stinks."

"Should've thought of that sooner, shouldn't you?" Calmly, as if he were buttoning his cuff, Matt drew his pistol from its holster. "You are under arrest, Mr. Janes. Turn around and put your hands behind your back."

"Under arrest? For what?"

"Littering. Like I told you, this is Crown property. You can't leave your rubbish here. Turn around."

For a brief moment Janes hesitated. Then, perhaps, he saw an advantage in it, and obeyed. "Fine," he said bitterly. "Put me back in your rotten little jail. When I get out, I swear to God I'll see you ruined!"

Matt closed both cuffs on the man's wrists before he answered. "Oh," he said, "I'm not taking you to jail." He pushed Janes into the centre of the shed. "I'm going to shackle you to this pillar here, and I'm going to pile all these old rags around you so you don't get cold, and then I'm going home. Come morning, I figure you'll be a lot more co-operative."

Finally, terror. Even through the thin crack in the wall Erryn could see it—pure, undiluted terror on Janes's face. He struggled desperately, trying to hold himself rigid, to be shoved no closer to his precious cargo.

"You can't do this! You got no right! Colonel, stop him, he's got no authority—"

It was a short, uneven battle, lasting only till the first stained blanket fell across his chest.

"Don't, for Christ's sake, don't! You're going to kill me!"

"Kill you? How? With this?" Matt reached for another piece and held it up, laughing. It was the bitterest laugh Erryn had ever heard in his life. "It's just a bloody nightgown, Janes. Don't be such a ninny."

Janes huddled down against the pillar. "Please," he said. "Please. It's full of yellow jack."

They had to know for sure, of course they did. And yet to hear it was shattering. Erryn heard Matt spit out a curse; he saw the colonel sag like a rag doll and turn away; he felt his own bones chill and shiver. He thought himself worldly, even hard in certain ways, yet he could not, at this moment, understand a man like Maury Janes, understand what moved him to a deed such as this. For who was likely to buy his rubbish? Not the soldiers, surely, who were mostly well supplied by their quartermasters. No, it would be the poor and the homeless, the runaway slaves, the refugees—many of them *Southern* refugees, no doubt, in places like New Bern and Baltimore. Even by the terms of warfare it was a devil's bargain, the losses cruel and immediate, the gains merely guesswork. No one knew what the Northern government or its people would do in the face of such an epidemic. And if word got out, as well it might, as to how the epidemic had begun?

Long ago in Surrey, Erryn's tutor used to smile at him sometimes and make small, pithy observations about life. *Of all the qualities one might find in a man,* he said once, *there are none more dangerous to find together than ruthlessness and stupidity.* The tutor had been old even then, and he was dead now. Had he been living, Erryn would have wished for nothing just now but to lay his head on the old man's shoulder and weep.

CHAPTER 33

——◆——

The Nature of the Game

Men could not part us with their worldly jars,
Nor the seas change us, nor the tempests bend;
Our hands would touch for all the mountain-bars:
And, heaven being rolled between us at the end,
We should but vow the faster for the stars.
—*Elizabeth Barrett Browning*

THE FIRST WORD of the fight on Grafton Street reached the Den with the Wednesday morning deliveries. Working alone, Sylvie heard none of it, but once or twice in the halls she noticed small clusters of boarders whispering among themselves, and she supposed there had been news from the war. It was close to lunchtime when Aggie Breault, with a small wag of her head, signalled Sylvie to join her in the cellar. She spoke quickly, before Sylvie could begin to frame a question.

"Look," she said, "I don't know if any of this is true. I've heard three stories already, and they're all different. But I wanted to tell you before Dobbs got going on it in the kitchen. It seems there was a fight late last night, over by the soap factory. They're saying Erryn Shaw's been hurt, and Maury Janes is in jail for it."

"Erryn's hurt?"

460

"That's what I've heard. But don't go thinking the worst now, Sylvie. Mr. Winters just come a few minutes ago with the chickens, and he told me he talked to a fellow who was right there. This fellow didn't see the fight, but he saw most everything that happened after. And he said if Mr. Shaw was hurt bad they'd have taken him into the tavern and sent for a doctor, but instead they just took him off in a carriage. He said like as not they drove him home."

Sylvie forced herself to be calm. Fights were hardly rare in the mill towns, and many a man was carried off senseless by his friends and was back at his job the next day, laughing about it. But even as this bit of comfort came to her, a darker thought came hard on its heels.

"It were Mr. Janes who attacked him?"

"The police arrested him for it. But apparently he was yelling his head off that some ruffians jumped them and then ran away. So far, nobody seems to know for sure."

If it was Janes, she wondered, had she been the cause of it?

"It's your half day today. Will you change with me? Please, oh, please, Aggie! I have to know if he's all right!"

"I can't. I have to— I'm sorry, Sylvie, I just can't. Look, I'm sure he's all right—probably in his own bed right now, with a wet towel wrapped around his head. I might be able to find something out. I'll do what I can. All right?"

"You'll try really hard? Please?"

"I will."

She watched Aggie disappear up the stairwell and considered what to do. There was no point in asking Miss Susan for a bit of time off; such things simply were not done. She could, of course, just take off her bonnet and her apron and walk out the door. Erryn lived on Morris Street; she could be there in twenty minutes. But the act would be irrevocable. She would lose her place here. Worse, she would never get a reference, and no one else would hire her without one. Miss Susan would look down at her with scorn and dismay: *After all we've done for you, Bowen, really, I am appalled . . .* And if it was as Aggie said, just a street fight, and all Erryn had to grieve him was a headache? No, she thought, she had to wait until she knew more.

But it was hard waiting, and guilty waiting too, listening to Harry's mindless rant at lunchtime. *They say the poor man's head was split open like a melon . . . The constable probably did it himself, just so he could hang it on Mr. Janes. He's a real low-life, that Calverley, his mother was the worst whore on Barrack Street.*

"That will be enough, Dobbs!" Sanders said grimly.

This silenced him for all of a minute or so, then he was off again. For once Sylvie was thankful to go back to cleaning rooms. Aggie returned late from her half day and had little to report. No one she spoke to really knew what had happened. But two things were all but certain, she said: Mr. Shaw was not dead and he was not in the hospital.

"So he's all right, Sylvie. He must be all right."

The day ended, and another rose. The newspapers reached the Den, and finally she had a few scraps of information, spare and dry as old bones. There had been an altercation Tuesday night on Grafton Street, the papers said. A Halifax resident, Erryn Shaw, and a certain Mr. Janes, from North Carolina, had been attacked. Their unknown assailants had escaped, but both men were now in custody pending further investigation into a possible smuggling operation.

That was all. When Miss Susan summoned Sylvie to the parlour shortly after lunch, she rushed in, expecting news of Erryn, or perhaps even Erryn himself. Instead, she found an aging policeman with her mistress. For a brief moment she went icy with fear.

"Bowen, this is Constable Dufours. He is here to collect Mr. Janes's belongings. It seems Mr. Janes will not be returning to the Den. Will you please go with the constable and assist him?"

"Yes, m'um."

Dufours nodded to her faintly but said nothing until they were inside the boarder's room and the door was closed. Then he turned to her at once, speaking with a faint French Acadian accent. "Your name is Bowen? Sylvie Bowen?"

She stood very still. "Yes, sir."

"Then I have a letter for you. I was asked to pass it on by . . . by someone trustworthy. He said I should place it into no hands but yours." The constable held out a small, sealed letter.

"Oh, thank you so much, sir." She tucked it into her pocket, and helped him with his simple duty; heaven knew there was little enough to collect in Maury Janes's room. When she had seen him out and returned to prepare the room for its new tenant, she sat in the cane chair and carefully opened her letter. It was, to her surprise, in an unfamiliar hand, and very brief.

My dearest Sylvie,

You have no doubt heard by now that I was attacked on the street on Tuesday night, and that Mr. Janes and I were both arrested after. I am not much hurt, but I have injured my hand and so I must ask a friend to write this letter. The police are no longer holding me, but another matter of importance has come up and I must deal with it immediately. I will be gone for several weeks.

I am sorry for this, my heart, sorrier than I can ever say. I will come back as soon as I can, and then I shall do what I promised: I shall take you to dinner, and tempt you with bonbons and fine wines, and ask you again to marry me. And perhaps this time you will say yes. When all of this is over, I never want to be away from you again.

Leaving my heart with you, and all my hopes,

I remain,
Your Erryn

She reread the letter twice, cherishing its tenderness, surprised that he would send so deeply personal a message through the medium of another. Then, reading it yet again, she began to suspect why. Under all the careful crafting of his words, under all the love and sweetness, there lay a quiet, pervasive fear. He was going away, and he was afraid he might not come back. *I am sorry for this, my heart, sorrier than I can ever say.*

He had warned her once, the first time they walked out together after he'd told her of his work, "I can't always predict what I'm going to do, or where I'm going to be. One day I might just have to go, without a word of explanation. If you don't hear from me, you mustn't ever think it's because I want it so. It's just . . . it's just the nature of the game."

Only none of it was a game, and she had known as much right from the beginning. Now she knew it differently. Now she knew it as if she stood before an abyss.

She folded the letter carefully and put it back in her pocket, and went on with her work, trying not to be afraid, trying not to notice how the bright summer day seemed wrapped in shadows. *He'll make it back,* she promised herself over and over. *He's strong, he is, and real smart. He knows what he's doing. He'll make it back!*

Each day she made the same promise, every morning, every night. He would make it back. She would walk out of the Den on a Friday afternoon and he would be there, waiting. Laughing. And if he asked her once more to marry him, only once, she would say yes.

There was no surprise in the thought. There was not even a flicker of uncertainty. She did not know if her doubts had slipped away over time without her noticing or if this sudden threat of loss had burnt them up like dry leaves. They were simply gone. She would marry him, and give him what was left to her of life and time. And if he failed her as she once feared—she did not think he would, but if he did—well, that was a risk too, a risk like any other. It was the price one paid for love, for hope, for anything that mattered. It was, as he might have called it, the nature of the game.

EPILOGUE

---◆---

September 27, 1864

We have had great doings here, the last week, in honour of the
delegates who came here from the lower provinces to consider
the question of a Union of all these provinces.

—Lord Monck, 1864

ERRYN HAD NEVER seen a small room sparkle quite so brightly.
There were candles everywhere, and bouquets of brilliant
autumn flowers. Better still, there was comradeship and laughter,
and a place of safety in which to enjoy it. The estate of Colonel
Hawkins was tucked into a cove along the Northwest Arm, modest by the standards of his neighbours but even more discreetly
sheltered. The house itself lay well back from the water's edge,
and near it, half hidden among the trees, was a fine guest cottage.
He had built it for visiting relatives, he said, but after the American
war began it proved to have other, more interesting uses.

The old warhorse had been terribly matter-of-fact when he
asked Erryn to come by. Things were changing in the war, he said;
there were some matters they needed to discuss. "I'll send my
coachman for you. He's absolutely trustworthy, so you won't

need to bother with a disguise. Oh, and bring your new bride, I should like to meet her."

Erryn went, not knowing what to expect; he half wondered if he was going to be subjected to a grilling, or even dismissed, for having revealed his activities to Sylvie and Madame Mallette. He certainly had not expected bunting, and presents, and a table laid out for princes. Least of all had he expected to see Matt Calverley, dressed in a velvet waistcoat and grinning like a boy with stolen apples.

"Well," Matt said, "you didn't really think I'd let my best mate go and get himself married and not give me a chance to kiss the bride?"

They laughed and embraced. Erryn turned and took Sylvie's hand. "My heart, I would like you to meet my dear, dear friend, Matt Calverley."

She curtsied and let him kiss her cheeks in turn, affectionately. "You aren't, by chance, the one who keeps the spiders?"

"He is," Hawkins said. "And do you want to know the strangest thing about it? The man is sane. His room is crawling with those horrid, scrabbly, long-legged things. He likes them. He *feeds* them. And he's actually quite right in his head. The world, Mrs. Shaw, is filled with marvels."

It was an evening Erryn would remember for the rest of his life—just the four of them, not even a servant. They drank toast after toast, and ate plates of rich food, and laughed at everything. He could not judge for the others, but he knew that for himself the previous months were still raw in his mind, and gave his happiness a particularly fierce and burning edge. The ugliness of Maury Janes's plot, the long weeks of quarantine, his fear for himself and the others, for Sylvie if she were left all alone again—everything lay like a black swamp at his back, traversed but still too close to bear contemplation. So he gave himself over completely to the moment, to the joy of Sylvie laughing by his side, to the pleasure of his companions' open affection.

From time to time they spoke about the world, about the war in the States that was still dragging on, despite gains by the

Northern armies. Mostly they spoke about the delegates who had come back from Charlottetown just two days ago, and what they had accomplished there. It was Hawkins who had gone to the celebration dinner at the Halifax Hotel. The others listened, fascinated, to his account.

"You know, before they left, I thought they might accomplish something, but not a whole lot. I mean, Brown and Macdonald have hated each other for twenty-five years. French and English aren't the best of friends either, much of the time. The West is a thousand miles away. We need to make a nation here. I don't think anybody understands that better than Lord Monck. But I told him it would take those men years to get it done, maybe decades. Last night I changed my mind. They'll do it, and they'll do it quickly."

"Because of the war," Matt suggested.

"Not really. Oh, the war was a spur, no queston. But listening to those chaps last night, Brown especially, talking about what we could become—not just what we want to leave behind, but where we want to go. Something happened to them in Charlottetown, a kind of . . . I'd almost say a kind of vision, a discovery."

"I've heard they spent most of their time there enjoying themselves," Erryn said, "to the point where the puritans in town got all offended and wrote surly editorials about it."

"Trust a theatre man to mention that," Matt said cheerfully.

"Oh, I think it's quite wonderful. I'll wager it helped to make them friends—more than anything else could have, perhaps."

Hawkins cocked an eyebrow at him, but he did not disagree.

"What will they do now?" Sylvie asked.

"Travel around, talk about it. Get the public behind them as much as they can. They're meeting again in Quebec, in October."

"Well," Erryn said, "I think this calls for another toast." He got to his feet. He was quite sure they were expecting him to toast the delegates, or the union of the provinces, or something else formal and grand. Instead, he said quietly:

"To all of us being . . . and staying . . . friends."

It was very late. Party candles still danced in the cottage's curtained windows, but the big house was dark. The yard lay so quiet that a small, half-hearted bark from one of the colonel's watchdogs sounded as loud as a gunshot. Matt and Erryn strolled down to the pier and stood for a time together, saying nothing, just watching the moonlight bob in small slivers on the water.

"She seems an extraordinary young woman," Matt said at last. "I'd say you've done very well for yourself."

"You have no idea, my friend."

"Oh, I have some idea. I know you pretty well, and you're riding clouds tonight. Which is bloody good to see, by the way. Especially now." He paused for a long moment. "Christ, we were so lucky."

"Yes." They had handled all those garments of death, and none of them had died; they had not even fallen sick. It still felt like a miracle. It always would. "It's been a grand evening, Matt. It was the best gift you could possibly have given us. Either of you."

"The Hawk's a good man. I wasn't expecting this, you know, when I said we should have a little celebration for you since we couldn't go to your wedding. I thought . . . I wasn't sure, really—maybe a private club room somewhere. Not his home. He's a gentleman of the old school, after all, as I suppose you would put it. But he's an officer of the old school too."

"He is indeed."

"How are the Grey Tories taking your new status, do you know?"

"You mean my fall from social grace?"

"I wouldn't call it that."

"They would. Some of them, anyway." Erryn looked up at the stars. He was, he knew, rather drunk. It was a good feeling, one he had not allowed himself for a long time. "Jack Murray is taking it well. He actually came to the wedding and wished us happiness with all his heart. Orton feels sorry for me. He thinks I've fallen prey to a scheming hussy. MacNab—so I've heard on the grapevine—MacNab thinks it's all hilariously funny." He turned to his friend, although he could barely see Matt's face in the darkness. "I'm tired of them, Matt. I'm bloody God damn tired of them all."

"I know. But Hawkins figures most of the Reb shenanigans will be moving west. What with those so-called commissioners based in Toronto now, and all the Southern ports closed except Wilmington, he says Halifax won't be nearly as important to them anymore."

"You mean I might become an unnecessary expense? The GG might pat me on the head and tell me to run along now and find myself a nice theatre to play with?"

"Oh, I don't think you'll get off quite so easy, mate. But things are likely to get quieter."

This had been Erryn's own assessment of the situation, but it was comforting to have the others confirm it. Maybe this time the war really was winding down. The news of late had been good. Just days ago the Union had won a substantial victory in the Shenandoah Valley. Closer to home, on Lake Erie, a second attempt to capture the U.S. gunboat *Michigan* and free the prisoners at Johnson's Island had come to grief, the leader cheerfully sharing his plans with a prostitute on the Union payroll; and his men, at the critical moment, telling him they loved him dearly but they weren't going any farther with him, thank you very much. Clearly, Thompson and Clay were not having any better success operating out of Canada than their predecessors had had.

Most important of all, the diplomatic situation had changed. By now it was surely clear to Washington that, however many enemies they might have in London, they had none in Spencer Hall. Likewise, it was clear to Lord Monck that Mr. Lincoln's army of farm boys and factory workers was not going anywhere when this war was over except home. Barring the most extraordinary bad luck, the high tide for intervention was past.

"You know, mate," Erryn said, "we might all have a future yet."

"I think we do."

"Well then." Erryn wrapped his arm warmly around his friend's shoulder. "Let's go back inside and drink it a toast."

AFTERWORD

ALTHOUGH THE TIMING of events in *The Halifax Connection*
does not, in every case, match that of the historical record, many
of these events are based on fact. A number of prominent
Canadians aided the Confederacy in activities ranging from the
commercial and political to the clandestine and illegal. Others,
though less directly involved, were outspoken supporters of the
Confederate cause. Since it was my intention to re-create the
public roles of these men, and not their personalities or private
lives, I chose to create fictional characters in their place.
Alexander MacNab, Edmund Morrison, the Ortons, and their
circle are not historically real, but most of their activities on
behalf of the South are based directly on similar activities by
well-known citizens of the day.

Unlike those who served the Confederacy, the Canadians who
worked in counter-intelligence operations remain obscure; indeed,
there is no official reference to such operations prior to 1864.
However, given the high risk to Canadian security posed by the
American Civil War, and given Lord Monck's dedication and obvious preference for quiet, non-provocative solutions, I think he
might well have put a few agents in place as quickly as he could—in
other words, long before the second attempted raid on Johnson's
Island (the *Philo Parsons* affair), when, in order to reassure the

Americans, the placing of special "detectives" along the border was acknowledged openly.

In accounts of the day, references to such "detectives" and "informers" are common; names are hard to come by. They undoubtedly included everyone from professional police officers to the occasional amateur snoop. Here, Erryn Shaw, Sylvie Bowen, Matt Calverley, and Colonel Hawkins are all fictional persons, but I have involved them in real events. Captain Wilkinson's intended raid on the Federal prison camp at Johnson's Island was planned, and came to grief, very much as I have described it; I have merely added one link to the Canadian chain. Like my *Moravia*, the historic blockade-runner *Princess Royal* fell into the hands of the Union navy after details of its vital military cargo, departure date, and destination were published in a Halifax newspaper. Its capture was subsequently considered the most important blockade-runner seizure of the war. The *Chesapeake* affair is perhaps the best-known event of the Civil War in Canada.

The yellow fever plot is also documented, although the manner of its discovery is my own invention. In Hamilton, on April 12, 1865, Godfrey J. Hyams (the historic counterpart of Maury Janes) testified to Union authorities that trunks of clothing and bedding from yellow fever victims had been assembled in Nassau by Dr. Luke P. Blackburn for shipment to Halifax, where Hyams collected them. The materials were forwarded by Hyams to three American cities and sold by public auction.

After an epidemic in Bermuda, Blackburn assembled a second batch of contaminated materials there. This collection came to the attention of the authorities in St. George, perhaps as a result of Hyams's disclosures. They raided the house in question and found three trunks of blankets, sheets, underwear, etc., stained with "black vomit," as well as poultices from diseased victims. The trunks were labelled for shipment to Canada. Blackburn himself had already fled. He was later arrested and tried in Canada, but was acquitted on the grounds of insufficient evidence. Given that all of the relevant events took place in other countries, that persons who could have given eyewitness testimony were scattered around the world, and that no forensic science existed to prove that the materials in the trunks were systematically contaminated, no other verdict was likely in a court of law. Nonetheless, the body of circumstantial evidence for the plot is, in my opinion, convincing. Besides Hyams's testimony and the discoveries in St. George, there is the account of blockade-runner Thomas Taylor, who records in his memoirs that

> [an] eminent Confederate military doctor proposed to me during the prevalence of the yellow fever epidemic that he should ship by our boats to Nassau and Bermuda sundry cases of infected clothing, which were to be sent to the North with the idea of spreading the disease there. This was too much, and I shouted to him, not in the choicest language, to leave the office.

Also, according to historian Terry Tucker, after Blackburn's death his own widow admitted his involvement.

Decades later, researchers would prove that yellow fever was transmitted by mosquitoes, not by personal contact. Blackburn's plans failed, and would have gone on failing, from a lack of medical knowledge. This in no way lessens the ugliness of his intentions.

There is no documentary proof that these intentions were known to the Confederate authorities. However, Hyams had a close working relationship with Confederate agents in Montreal, who financed his trip to Halifax; with prominent "Grey Tories" in Toronto and Halifax; and subsequently with the Confederate commissioners to Canada. This suggests to me that he and Blackburn were not acting alone, but rather that they were engaged in an operation with significant official backing.

ACKNOWLEDGEMENTS

I WOULD LIKE TO THANK the many people in Halifax who helped me to carry out my research, especially Daniel Conlin for a much-appreciated tip, and the staff at the Nova Scotia Archives and at the library of Dalhousie University. I would also like to thank the wonderful students looking after O'Brien Hall, who took such good care of me there. Special thank yous for valuable information are due to Sarah Murphy, Alison Sinclair, Doug Hemmings, and a most helpful gentleman from Calgary STARS, whose name I carefully recorded and stored away, only to have it eaten by a filing cabinet gremlin. To him and to all mentioned above, a huge and heartfelt thank you.

The Halifax Connection was completed with financial assistance from the Alberta Foundation for the Arts, for which I am deeply grateful.

ABOUT THE AUTHOR

MARIE JAKOBER is the author of seven novels. She has won the Michael Shaara Award for Excellence in Civil War Fiction, and has twice won the Georges Bugnet Award for Novel at the Alberta Book Awards, most recently for *Sons of Liberty*. She grew up on a small farm in northern Alberta and currently resides in Calgary.